DEPTH CHARGE

DEPTH CHARGE

Edited by
Hank Davis &
Jamie Ibson

DEPTH CHARGE

Copyright © 2024 by Hank Davis and Jamie Ibson

A Baen Books Original

Baen Publishing Enterprises
P.O. Box 1403
Riverdale, NY 10471
www.baen.com

ISBN: 978-1-9821-9382-9

Cover art by Alan Pollack

First printing, December 2024

Distributed by Simon & Schuster
1230 Avenue of the Americas
New York, NY 10020

Library of Congress Cataloging-in-Publication Data:

Names: Davis, Hank, 1944- editor. | Ibson, Jamie, editor.
Title: Depth charge / edited by Hank Davis & Jamie Ibson.
Description: Riverdale, NY : Baen Publishing Enterprises, 2024.
Identifiers: LCCN 2024026773 (print) | LCCN 2024026774 (ebook) | ISBN
    9781982193829 (trade paperback) | ISBN 9781625799944 (ebook)
Subjects: LCSH: Science fiction, American. | Science fiction, English |
    Undersea colonies--Fiction. | Human-alien encounters--Fiction. | BISAC:
    FICTION / Science Fiction / Collections & Anthologies | FICTION /
    Science Fiction / Hard Science Fiction | LCGFT: Science fiction. | Sea
    fiction.
Classification: LCC PS648.S3 D46 2024 (print) | LCC PS648.S3 (ebook) |
    DDC 813/.0876208--dc23/eng/20240620
LC record available at https://lccn.loc.gov/2024026773
LC ebook record available at https://lccn.loc.gov/2024026774

Printed in the United States of America

10 9 8 7 6 5 4 3 2 1

Dedication

Hank has kindly left the dedication to me, and so I dedicate *Depth Charge* to Brandy Bolgeo Hendren and the late, dearly departed Uncle Timmy Bolgeo, in appreciation of their ongoing hard work to build and maintain the amazing time that is LibertyCon. There is a clear, direct sequence of events that started at LibertyCon 30—my first literary convention of any type—that quite literally changed the course of my life. That course correction brought me here, and for that I am ever grateful.

—Jamie Ibson

ACKNOWLEDGMENTS

Our thanks to those authors who permitted the use of their stories, and to the estates and their representatives who intervened for those authors unreachable without time travel (we raise a glass to absent friends).

Among the very helpful agents deserving thanks are the Scovil Galen Ghosh Literary Agency, Inc.; the Virginia Kidd Literary Agency; the Don Congdon Associates, Inc.; Spatterlight Press; and Barry N. Malzberg. Our thanks also to Mary Rosenblum's sons, Nathan and Jake, who kindly granted permission to reprint their late mother's work. Special thanks to Sean C.W. Korsgaard, who conceived the underwater theme and nifty title of the book, and recommended several of the stories which you are about to read.

And thanks to the Internet Speculative Fiction Database (ISFDB.org) for existing and being a handy source of raw data, and to the devoted volunteers who maintain that very useful site.

CONTENTS

CONTENTS

INTRODUCTION
Water, Water, Everywhere . . .
Hank Davis

In one of the hour-long episodes of that fondly remembered sixties TV show, *Secret Agent* (known as *Danger Man* until it crossed the Atlantic to the colonies), John Drake, superbly played by Patrick McGoohan, is talking with a woman in a room, wherein there is a globe of the Earth. She spins it and wishes she could put her finger on it and be instantly transported there. "I'd be careful," Drake says. "It's three-quarters water."

That's not just a twist on the adage "Be careful what you wish for," but also a witty reminder that the Earth is a water planet, with scarcely any company in that category in the solar system. Mercury, closest to the sun, is much too hot. Next out is Venus, whose clouds hiding its surface once gave the literary imagination of twentieth-century sf writers free rein to imagine a planet even wetter than Earth, maybe like our planet in its Carboniferous period, possibly even with homegrown dinosaur analogs lumbering through forests of giant ferns (oh, joy!), or even much wetter than Earth, with planetwide oceans covering Venus from pole to pole. Alas, radio telescopes in the mid 1950s were turned on the planet, and detected radio waves indicating the planet's clouds were at least as hot as boiling water. Further observations indicated that those clouds were composed of hydrocarbons rather than water vapor. After a Russian space probe landed on the planet's surface and confirmed that Venus is a plausible stand-in for Hell, if without brimstone, Brian Aldiss edited an anthology of stories set in the Venus we wanted but didn't get, titled *Farewell Fantastic Venus* (when that Brit book was reprinted across the pond, it was given the rather lame title of *All About Venus*, and

1

several stories were dropped). More recently George R.R. Martin and Gardner Dozois edited an all-original anthology, *Old Venus*, with more stories of the Venus that never was.

Mars, orbiting farther out than Earth, also stirred the imaginations of fiction writers even before H.G. Wells and his *War of the Worlds*, particularly after the Italian astronomer Giovanni Schiaparelli reported seeing channels on the planet's surface. Others, particularly the American astronomer Percival Lowell, postulated a dying civilization on Mars, sustained by a planetwide system of canals which collect water from the icecap at the pole and carry it out to the parched planet's surface. Observers watching Mars through telescopes during times of closest approach to Earth drew maps of the surface which we now know to be the product of the observers' imaginations.

Going outward to the gas giants, Jupiter may have plenty of water, but it also has a lot of methane and ammonia. One of its moons, Europa, is covered with ice, as in water ice, and may have an ocean underneath, and maybe even life. We'll have to await word from future space explorers.

Getting back to the oceans we have on the home world, while they cover most of the surface, they really are only a thin film, with an average depth of less than two and a half miles. Of course, the part of the atmosphere we humans inhabit is also only a thin film with the layer where the weather happens, the troposphere, only seven miles deep. (Other nations have different names for the different layers of the atmosphere, but troposphere, stratosphere, ionosphere, and exosphere are what I grew up with.) And puny humans, as the Hulk might put it, need supplemental oxygen above twenty thousand feet. But time and evolution have filled both those thin films with myriad inhabitants of all shapes and sizes, though the sizes of ocean dwellers dwarf those on land, thanks to water's buoyancy countering the pull of gravity.

And while the blue whale is the biggest animal on Earth that we know about, bigger critters may be lurking in the ocean deeps. If the long-suffering reader will bear with me, I'll resurrect a bit of the introductory material I wrote for my 2014 Baen anthology, *The Baen Big Book of Monsters*:

In Astounding Days, *his memoir-like salute to the magazine* Astounding Science-Fiction, *Arthur C. Clarke discusses the possibility of very large creatures of the deeps which are still unknown to us. After noting that the few specimens of the celebrated giant squid that have washed ashore may not represent full-grown adults, who might be up to one hundred and fifty feet in length according to one expert, he cited evidence that even bigger creatures might be hiding below the waves. In 1896 a badly decayed sea dweller washed ashore, weighing in at six or seven tons. It was thought to be a dead whale, and samples were taken and preserved. When one of the fragments was examined in 1971, the creature turned out to be an octopus, possibly two hundred feet in size. Incidentally (or perhaps not), shortly before I wrote this introduction, [that is, in 2014] news came out about a Great White, the superstar of sharks since Jaws, that had been tagged with a tracking device and was suddenly pulled down into really deep water, as if grabbed by a more formidable predator. The tracking device, without the shark attached, later washed up on a beach.*

Then there's the famed sea serpent, mostly thought to be legend, but then the giant squid, romantically known as the kraken, was also thought to be legend, until dead specimens turned up. The rocketry pioneer and distinguished science writer, Willy Ley, who has a crater on the Moon named after him, scoffed at flying saucers and ESP, but took reports of sea serpents seriously. Since none of the stories in this anthology involve sea serpents, I'll leave the question of their existence in the "interesting if true" category, though if a two-hundred-foot octopus can hide in the very big oceans, a mere fifty-or-so-foot-long serpentlike creature could certainly keep out of sight. Willy Ley also took seriously the legend of Atlantis, the continent which sank beneath the sea, though he suspected that Plato was passing on tales of warriors from an island which had the bad luck to have its volcano become active. Atlantis lore has expanded since Plato, with mystics claiming that it was a superscience realm with flying machines called vimanas, and other cool science fictional goodies. So advanced, in fact, that one wonders how a mere sinking continent could have wiped them out. Other mystics, wanting equal time for the Pacific, claim that there was yet another sunken continent, named Mu, hiding beneath that ocean, also loaded with gee-whiz advanced tech and mystic powers. But as P. Schuyler Miller, sf writer, indefatigable book reviewer, and amateur archaeologist, once commented, the proponents of Atlantis at least have Plato on their side, while the advocates for Mu have nothing but psychic revelations and other such mystic wordage as "proof." Take that, James Churchward.

Of course, legends about the sea must be as old as the primitive tribes who lived by its shores. They had no idea that the planets were anything but stars with odd paths in the sky, and the Moon, showing only one side, might be a flat plate. But the sea was right there, familiar yet mysterious, stretching far out beyond where the eye could see. Was there even another side to it? From things washing up on the shore, it was obvious it had odd inhabitants. Later civilizations had legends, too. I dimly recall that some eminent person (Mohammed?) was shown a fish by the Almighty which was so large that it took a day and a night to swim past him. Then there's the folly of sailors making camp on an island which turns out to be a very large fish or whale.

As others have noted, a technological society has its legends, too, such as science fiction, and sf heroes have been getting their feet wet for a long time. Jules Verne's *20,000 Leagues Under the Sea* is a well-known example, though it should be noted that submarines did exist prior to Captain Nemo's fictional *Nautilus*, and one was even used, if with mixed success, in the American Civil War. And, contrary to the Disney movie version, the *Nautilus* was not powered by atomic energy, but rather by electricity, which itself was advanced for the time. And the novel was part of Verne's series of Voyages Extraordinaire, which include *Five Weeks in a Balloon* and *Around the World in Eighty Days*, and the "20,000 leagues" of the title refers to the distance traveled while submerged, not the depth reached. A league is approximately three land miles, and even though the Mariana Trench, a sort of underwater Grand Canyon, holds the depth record, its floor is only a bit less than seven miles beneath the surface. Nonetheless, two monster movies of the 1950s may have been titled so as to sound Vernian: *The Beast from 20,000 Fathoms* and *The Phantom from 10,000 Leagues*. (If you didn't know, a fathom is six feet, which I hope helps the long-suffering reader to fathom what's wrong with the title.) At least *The Beast* was based on a Ray Bradbury story, "The Foghorn" (more accurately, about five minutes of it was), and boasted special effects by legendary master Ray Harryhausen, while *The Phantom* just had a big guy in a rubber suit which looked nothing like the more interesting critter on the movie's poster.

Arthur Conan Doyle had taken time off from Sherlock Holmes to write *The Lost World*, which stayed on dry land, and later wrote a short novel, *The Maracot Deep*, which started out well, but came up with an absurd explanation for the undersea explorers not being crushed by water pressure and ended with a flurry of the mysticism which absorbed Doyle in his later years. As far as I've been able to find out, the Maracot Deep is a part of the ocean existing only in Doyle's imagination, though in the late 1950s, Henry Slesar wrote a forgettable novelette, *The Secret of Maracot Deep*, recycling the name in the title.

Not forgettable at all was John Wyndham's novel *The Kraken Wakes*, the title recalling Tennyson's poem, which was retitled *Out of the Deeps* once it got to these less poetic shores, in which unfriendly aliens invade Earth by landing in the oceans, out of sight and out of reach, and put a stop to ocean travel, then proceed to melt the icecaps and flood the continents. Oddly, it has never been given a film treatment, though there was a good BBC radio adaptation which is worth hearing. Returning to Arthur C. Clarke, he wrote a short story, "The Deep Range," later adapted into a full-length novel. You can read the original short version here, just a few pages away, which may whet your appetite for the longer tale. Sf masters Frederik Pohl and Jack Williamson collaborated on a series of three novels for young adults, *Undersea Quest*, *Undersea Fleet*, and *Undersea City*, later combined in one volume as *The Undersea Trilogy* (Baen, 1992), beginning with a young trainee in Subsea Academy, a future sort of undersea West Point. Not quite up to Heinlein or Andre Norton's YA novels, but good fun for older folk who haven't become terminally grown-up. And a towering classic of the field, Olaf Stapledon's *Last and First Men* charts the story of the human race from the 1930s to the end of the species, as the aging sun is on the verge of becoming a nova. In one episode, set on a watery Venus (as I've said, nonexistent, alas), humans colonize the planet after being adapted to live underwater, an alteration that has had many later literary echoes, as in Kenneth Bulmer's *City Under the Sea*, and Gordon R. Dickson's connected novels *Home from the Shore* and *The Space Swimmers*. And in short stories such as Mary Rosenblum's "Selkies," included in these pages.

Movies and TV shows have gone underwater in search of scientifictional thrills. I've mentioned the Disney version of *20,000*

Leagues Under the Sea, but there was an earlier silent movie version, available on video, which is impressive for its time of shooting. In between those two epics, there was the movie serial *Undersea Kingdom*, starring Ray "Crash" Corrigan and Lon Chaney, Jr., in which an experimental rocket-powered sub discovers the undersea city of Atlantis, whose evil ruler, of course, plots to conquer the surface world.

NBC TV in 1953 offered *Operation Neptune* with another underwater civilization, named Nadiria this time, with another tyrannical ruler with an itch to conquer the surface world, but hampered by having to work his sinister plans on live TV with a skimpy special-effects budget, though I thought the jet-propelled submarines looked cool. The last episode of the show ended with the announcer telling the audience to watch for the return of *Operation Neptune* in the fall. It didn't return that fall, but then, they didn't say *which* fall.

An early sixties entry was the Irwin Allen production of *Voyage to the Bottom of the Sea*, which boasted an impressive cast and a fruitcake of a script, whose motivating gimmick is that the Van Allen radiation belts have caught on fire and are baking the planet below them. Probably the best thing about the movie was that Theodore Sturgeon was picked to write a novelization, which was much better than the movie script, and also made the flaming radiation belts more believable, though I later learned that Sturgeon had picked Isaac Asimov's brain on the subject. The movie gave rise to the TV show, which inexplicably stayed on ABC for several years, one of a handful of sf TV shows of dubious quality from Irwin Allen, such as *Time Tunnel*, *Land of the Giants*, and so on. I can't resist giving the title of the parody that *Mad* magazine published in the show's first year: "Voyage to See What's on the Bottom."

The year 1989 brought James Cameron's *The Abyss*, which suffered from being originally released in a cut version, but had a standout cast, and an intelligent script. At the time I wasn't sure if the nonhuman water dwellers were natives of Earth or visiting extraterrestrials, though the Orson Scott Card novelization of the movie assumes the latter. Critics complained that it was a watery *Close Encounters of the Third Kind*, but I liked it, and I liked the expanded rerelease even more, particularly since the extra footage made it clear why the head Navy SEAL was going bonkers, while the short version seemed to be recycling the standard Tinseltown limousine-liberal notion that all military personnel are psychotic killers at heart. Director Cameron later hit the oceanic jackpot with a cinematic retelling of the *Titanic*'s ill-fated maiden voyage.

I have by no means exhausted the subject of underwater sf, and I haven't gotten to Karel Čapek's brilliant satire, *War with the Newts*, or the better-than-it-sounds fifties monster flick, Roger Corman's *Attack of the Crab Monsters*, or another fondly remembered book from long ago, *Tom Swift and His Jetmarine* (I think I was ten or eleven by that time), but if the reader is still patiently slogging through this introduction, I'm keeping her or him from some nifty stories, so as usual, I'll close by lamenting the absence of several stories which I would have liked to include, but whose reprinting was not in the cards, such as Poul Anderson's "The Horn of Time the Hunter" (originally published in *Amazing Stories* as "Homo Aquaticus"), "Driftglass" by Samuel R. Delany, "The Doors of His Face, The Lamps of His Mouth" by Roger Zelazny, "Trouble Tide" by James H. Schmitz, "Waterclap" by Isaac Asimov, "The Selchey Kids" by Laurence Yep (his first published story back in 1968, which I nominated for the Nebula at the time), and H.G. Wells's "In the Abyss." I recommend all of these stories, and at least in the case of the Wells tale, anyone can read it online at Project Gutenberg.

I also want to give a grateful nod to two books which I was dazzled by when my age was barely in double digits: *Half Mile Down* by William Beebe, with a great deal about underwater facts and conjectures, culminating in the author's descent in the bathysphere which he and Otis Barton had constructed. And *The Silent World* by Jacques Cousteau, who became a hero of mine nearly a decade before he became a TV star on a series of programs narrated by no less than Rod Serling. I no longer have the paperback of the Cousteau book, but I think I recall it closing with something like, "As time passes, humanity can expect to get its feet wet." Which sounds good to me. And now I'll step aside and let expert writers get the readers' literary feet wet.

—Hank Davis
May 2024

THE DEEP RANGE
Arthur C. Clarke

Famed for his literary explorations of deep space and the far future, Sir Arthur C. Clarke was also an enthusiastic scuba diver, so this story was probably inevitable, though there also seems to be some influence from American Westerns.

There was a killer loose on the range. A copter patrol, five hundred miles off Greenland, had seen the great corpse staining the sea crimson as it wallowed in the waves. Within seconds, the intricate warning system had been alerted: men were plotting circles and moving counters on the North Atlantic chart—and Don Burley was still rubbing the sleep from his eyes as he dropped silently down to the twenty-fathom line.

The pattern of green lights on the tell-tale was a glowing symbol of security. As long as that pattern was unchanged, as long as none of those emerald stars winked to red, all was well with Don and his tiny craft. Air—fuel—power—this was the triumvirate which ruled his life. If any of them failed, he would be sinking in a steel coffin down toward the pelagic ooze, as Johnnie Tyndall had done the season before last. But there was no reason why they should fail; the accidents one foresaw, Don told himself reassuringly, were never the ones that happened.

He leaned across the tiny control board and spoke into the mike. Sub 5 was still close enough to the mother ship for radio to work, but before long he'd have to switch to the sonics.

"Setting course 255, speed 50 knots, depth 20 fathoms, full sonar coverage . . . Estimated time to target area, 70 minutes . . . Will report at 10-minute intervals. That is all . . . Out."

The acknowledgement, already weakening with range, came back at once from the *Herman Melville*.

"Message received and understood. Good hunting. What about the hounds?"

Don chewed his lower lip thoughtfully. This might be a job he'd have to handle alone. He had no idea, to within fifty miles either way, where Benj and Susan were at the moment.

They'd certainly follow if he signaled for them, but they couldn't maintain his speed and would soon have to drop behind. Besides, he might be heading for a pack of killers, and the last thing he wanted to do was to lead his carefully trained porpoises into trouble. That was common sense and good business. He was also very fond of Susan and Benj.

"It's too far, and I don't know what I'm running into," he replied. "If they're in the interception area when I get there, I may whistle them up."

The acknowledgment from the mother ship was barely audible, and Don switched off the set. It was time to look around.

He dimmed the cabin lights so that he could see the scanner screen more clearly, pulled the polaroid glasses down over his eyes, and peered into the depths. This was the moment when Don felt like a god, able to hold within his hands a circle of the Atlantic twenty miles across, and to see clear down to the still-unexplored deeps, three thousand fathoms below. The slowly rotating beam of inaudible sound was searching the world in which he floated, seeking out friend and foe in the eternal darkness where light could never penetrate. The pattern of soundless shrieks, too shrill even for the hearing of the bats who had invented sonar a million years before man, pulsed out into the watery night: the faint echoes came tingling back as floating, blue-green flecks on the screen.

Through long practice, Don could read their message with effortless ease. A thousand feet below, stretching out to his submerged horizon, was the scattering layer—the blanket of life that covered half the world. The sunken meadow of the sea, it rose and fell with the passage of the sun, hovering always at the edge of darkness. But the ultimate depths were no concern of his. The flocks he guarded, and the enemies who ravaged them, belonged to the upper levels of the sea.

Don flicked the switch of the depth-selector, and his sonar beam concentrated itself into the horizontal plane.

The glimmering echoes from the abyss vanished, but he could see more clearly what lay around him here in the ocean's stratospheric heights. That glowing cloud two miles ahead was a school of fish; he wondered if Base knew about it, and made an entry in his log. There were some larger, isolated blips at the edge of the school—the carnivores pursuing the cattle, insuring that the endlessly turning wheel of life and death would never lose momentum. But this conflict was no affair of Don's; he was after bigger game.

Sub 5 drove on toward the west, a steel needle swifter and more deadly than any other creature that roamed the seas.

The tiny cabin, lit only by the flicker of lights from the instrument board, pulsed with power as the spinning turbines thrust the water aside. Don glanced at the chart and wondered how the enemy had broken through this time. There were still many weak points, for fencing the oceans of the world had been a gigantic task. The tenuous electric fields, fanning out between generators many miles apart, could not always hold at bay the starving monsters of the deep. They were learning, too. When the fences were opened, they would sometimes slip through with the whales and wreak havoc before they were discovered.

The long-range receiver bleeped plaintively, and Don switched over to TRANSCRIBE. It wasn't practical to send speech any distance over an ultrasonic beam, and code had come back into its own. Don had never learned to read it by ear, but the ribbon of paper emerging from the slot saved him the trouble.

COPTER REPORTS SCHOOL 50–100 WHALES HEADING 95 DEGREES GRID REF X186475 Y438034 STOP. MOVING AT SPEED STOP. MELVILLE. OUT.

Don started to set the coordinates on the plotting grid, then saw that it was no longer necessary. At the extreme edge of his screen, a flotilla of faint stars had appeared. He altered course slightly, and drove head-on toward the approaching herd.

The copter was right: they were moving fast. Don felt a mounting excitement, for this could mean that they were on the run and luring the killers toward him. At the rate at which they were traveling he would be among them in five minutes. He cut the motors and felt the backward tug of water bringing him swiftly to rest.

Don Burley, a knight in armor, sat in his tiny dim-lit room fifty feet below the bright Atlantic waves, testing his weapons for the conflict that lay ahead. In these moments of poised suspense, before action began, his racing brain often explored such fantasies. He felt a kinship with all shepherds who had guarded their flocks back to the dawn of time. He was David, among ancient Palestinian hills, alert for the mountain lions that would prey upon his father's sheep. But far nearer in time, and far closer in spirit, were the men who had marshaled the great herds of cattle on the American plains, only a few lifetimes ago. They would have understood his work, though his implements would have been magic to them. The pattern was the same; only the scale had altered. It made no fundamental difference that the beasts Don herded weighed almost a hundred tons, and browsed on the endless savannahs of the sea.

The school was now less than two miles away, and Don checked his scanner's continuous circling to concentrate on the sector ahead. The picture on the screen altered to a fan-shaped wedge as the sonar beam started to flick from side to side; now he could count every whale in the school, and even make a good estimate of its size. With a practiced eye, he began to look for stragglers.

Don could never have explained what drew him at once toward those four echoes at the southern fringe of the school. It was true that they were a little apart from the rest, but others had fallen as far behind. There is some sixth sense that a man acquires when he has stared long enough into a sonar screen—some hunch which enables him to extract more from the moving flecks than he has any right to do. Without conscious thought, Don reached for the control which would start the turbines whirling into life. Sub 5 was just getting under way when three leaden thuds reverberated through the hull, as if someone was knocking on the front door and wanted to come in.

"Well I'm damned," said Don. "How did you get here?" He did not bother to switch on the TV; he'd know Benj's signal anywhere. The porpoises must have been in the neighborhood and had spotted him before he'd even switched on the hunting call. For the thousandth time, he marveled at their intelligence and loyalty. It was strange that Nature had played the same trick twice—on land with the dog, in the ocean with the porpoise. Why were these graceful sea-beasts so fond of man, to whom they owed so little? It made one feel that the human race was worth something after all, if it could inspire such unselfish devotion.

It had been known for centuries that the porpoise was at least as intelligent as the dog, and could obey quite complex verbal commands. The experiment was still in progress, but if it succeeded then the ancient partnership between shepherd and sheepdog would have a new lease on life.

Don switched on the speakers recessed into the sub's hull and began to talk to his escorts. Most of the sounds he uttered would have been meaningless to other human ears; they were the product of long research by the animal psychologists of the World Food Administration. He gave his orders twice to make sure that they were understood, then checked with the sonar screen to see that Benj and Susan were following astern as he had told them to.

The four echoes that had attracted his attention were clearer and closer now, and the main body of the whale pack had swept past him to the east. He had no fear of a collision; the great animals, even in their panic, could sense his presence as easily as he could detect theirs, and by similar means. Don wondered if he should switch on his beacon. They might recognize its sound pattern, and it would reassure them. But the still unknown enemy might recognize it too.

He closed for an interception, and hunched low over the screen as if to drag from it by sheer will power every scrap of information the scanner could give. There were two large echoes, some distance apart, and one was accompanied by a pair of smaller satellites. Don wondered if he was already too late. In his mind's eye, he could picture the death struggle taking place in the water less than a mile ahead.

Those two fainter blips would be the enemy—either shark or grampus—worrying a whale while one of its companions stood by in helpless terror, with no weapons of defense except its mighty flukes.

Now he was almost close enough for vision. The TV camera in Sub 5's prow strained through the gloom, but at first could show nothing but the fog of plankton. Then a vast shadowy shape began to form in the center of the screen, with two smaller companions below it. Don was seeing, with the greater precision but hopelessly limited range of ordinary light, what the sonar scanners had already told him.

Almost at once he saw his mistake. The two satellites were calves, not sharks. It was the first time he had ever met a whale with twins; although multiple births were not unknown, a cow could suckle only two young at once and usually only the stronger would survive. He choked down his disappointment; this error had cost him many minutes and he must begin the search again.

Then came the frantic tattoo on the hull that meant danger. It wasn't easy to scare Benj, and Don shouted his reassurance as he swung Sub 5 'round so that the camera could search the turgid waters. Automatically, he had turned toward the fourth blip on the sonar screen—the echo he had assumed, from its size, to be another adult whale.

And he saw that, after all, he had come to the right place.

"Jesus!" he said softly. "I didn't know they came that big." He'd seen larger sharks before, but they had all been harmless vegetarians. This, he could tell at a glance, was a Greenland shark, the killer of the northern seas. It was supposed to grow up to thirty feet long, but this specimen was bigger than Sub 5. It was every inch of forty feet from snout to tail, and when he spotted it, it was already turning in toward the kill. Like the coward it was, it had launched its attack at one of the calves.

Don yelled to Benj and Susan, and saw them racing ahead into his field of vision. He wondered fleetingly why porpoises had such an overwhelming hatred of sharks; then he loosed his hands from the controls as the autopilot locked on to the target. Twisting and turning as agilely as any other sea-creature of its size, Sub 5 began to close in upon the shark, leaving Don free to concentrate on his armament.

The killer had been so intent upon his prey that Benj caught him completely unawares, ramming him just behind the left eye. It must have been a painful blow: an iron-hard snout, backed by a quarter-ton of muscle moving at fifty miles an hour is something not to be laughed at even by the largest fish. The shark jerked round in an impossibly tight curve, and Don was almost jolted out of his seat as the sub snapped on to a new course. If this kept up, he'd find it hard to use his Sting. But at least the killer was too busy now to bother about his intended victims.

Benj and Susan were worrying the giant like dogs snapping at the heels of an angry bear. They were too agile to be caught in those ferocious jaws, and Don marveled at the coordination with which they worked. When either had to surface for air, the other would hold off for a minute until the attack could be resumed in strength.

There was no evidence that the shark realized that a far more dangerous adversary was closing in upon it, and that the porpoises were merely a distraction. That suited Don very nicely; the next operation was going to be difficult unless he could hold a steady course for at least fifteen seconds. At a pinch he could use the tiny rocket torps to make a kill. If he'd been alone, and faced with a pack of sharks he would certainly have done so. But it was messy, and there was a better way. He preferred the technique of the rapier to that of the hand-grenade.

Now he was only fifty feet away, and closing rapidly.

There might never be a better chance. He punched the launching stud.

From beneath the belly of the sub, something that looked like a sting-ray hurtled forward. Don had checked the speed of his own craft; there was no need to come any closer now. The tiny, arrow-shaped hydrofoil, only a couple of feet across, could move far faster than his vessel and would close the gap in seconds. As it raced forward, it spun out the thin line of the control wire, like some underwater spider laying its thread. Along that wire passed the energy that powered the Sting, and the signals that steered it to its goal.

Don had completely ignored his own larger craft in the effort of guiding this underwater missile. It responded to his touch so swiftly that he felt he was controlling some sensitive high-spirited steed.

The shark saw the danger less than a second before impact. The resemblance of the Sting to an ordinary ray confused it, as the designers had intended. Before the tiny brain could realize that no ray behaved like this, the missile had struck. The steel hypodermic, rammed forward by an exploding cartridge, drove through the shark's horny skin, and the great fish erupted in a frenzy of terror. Don backed rapidly away, for a blow from that tail would rattle him around like a pea in a can and might even cause damage to the sub. There was nothing more for him to do, except to speak into the microphone and call off his hounds.

The doomed killer was trying to arch its body so that it could snap at the poisoned dart. Don had now reeled the Sting back into its hiding place, pleased that he had been able to retrieve the missile undamaged. He watched without pity as the great fish succumbed to its paralysis.

Its struggles were weakening. It was swimming aimlessly back and forth, and once Don had to sidestep smartly to avoid a collision. As it lost control of buoyancy, the dying shark drifted up to the surface. Don did not bother to follow; that could wait until he had attended to more important business.

He found the cow and her two calves less than a mile away, and inspected them carefully. They were uninjured, so there was no need to call the vet in his highly specialized two-man sub which could handle any cetological crisis from a stomach-ache to a caesarian. Don made a note of the mother's number, stenciled just behind the flippers. The calves, as was obvious from their size, were this season's and had not yet been branded.

Don watched for a little while. They were no longer in the least alarmed, and a check on the sonar had shown that the whole school had ceased its panicky flight. He wondered how they knew what had happened; much had been learned about communication among whales, but much was still a mystery.

"I hope you appreciate what I've done for you, old lady," he muttered. Then, reflecting that fifty tons of mother love was a slightly awe-inspiring sight, he blew his tanks and surfaced.

It was calm, so he cracked the airlock and popped his head out of the tiny conning tower. The water was only inches below his chin, and from time to time a wave made a determined effort to swamp him. There was little danger of this happening, for he fitted the hatch so closely that he was quite an effective plug.

Fifty feet away, a long slate-colored mound, like an overturned boat, was rolling on the surface. Don looked at it thoughtfully and did some mental calculations. A brute this size should be valuable; with any luck there was a chance of a double bonus. In a few minutes he'd radio his report, but for the moment it was pleasant to drink the fresh Atlantic air and to feel the open sky above his head.

A gray thunderbolt shot up out of the depths and smashed back onto the surface of the water, smothering Don with spray. It was just Benj's modest way of drawing attention to himself; a moment later the porpoise had swum up to the conning tower, so that Don could reach down and tickle its head. The great, intelligent eyes stared back into his; was it pure imagination, or did an almost human sense of fun also lurk in their depths?

Susan, as usual, circled shyly at a distance until jealousy overpowered her and she butted Benj out of the way. Don distributed caresses impartially and apologized because he had nothing to give them. He undertook to make up for the omission as soon as he returned to the *Herman Melville*.

"I'll go for another swim with you, too," he promised, "as long as you behave yourselves next time." He rubbed thoughtfully at a large bruise caused by Benj's playfulness, and wondered if he was not getting a little too old for rough games like this.

"Time to go home," Don said firmly, sliding down into the cabin and slamming the hatch. He suddenly realized that he was very hungry, and had better do something about the breakfast he had missed. There were not many men on earth who had earned a better right to eat their morning meal. He had saved for humanity more tons of meat, oil and milk than could easily be estimated.

Don Burley was the happy warrior, coming home from one battle that man would always have to fight. He was holding at bay the specter of famine which had confronted all earlier ages, but which would never threaten the world again while the great plankton farms harvested their millions of tons of protein, and the whale herds obeyed their new masters. Man had come back to the sea after aeons of exile; until the oceans froze, he would never be hungry again . . .

Don glanced at the scanner as he set his course. He smiled as he saw the two echoes keeping pace with the central splash of light that marked his vessel. "Hang around," he said. "We mammals must stick together." Then, as the autopilot took over, he lay back in his chair.

And presently Benj and Susan heard a most peculiar noise, rising and falling against the drone of the turbines. It had filtered faintly through the thick walls of Sub 5, and only the sensitive ears of the porpoises could have detected it. But intelligent beasts though they were, they could hardly be expected to understand why Don Burley was announcing, in a highly unmusical voice, that he was heading for the Last Round-up . . .

SELKIES
Mary Rosenblum

A recurring sf theme, pioneered by Olaf Stapledon's monumental Last
and First Men, *is the concept of altering humans so that they can live,
and even thrive, in hostile environments, whether on other planets, or in
Earth's oceans. But how would an amphibious human feel about the
scientist who had made her that way?*

"Lights!" Jessamin covered her throat patch to block out the wind-
noise. Yellow light flooded the deck, and she clung to the satellite
antenna as a wave crashed across the twin-hulled boat. A welter of
foam surged across the deck, dirty white in the floodlights' glare. She
should have checked the sat-link for storms, this afternoon. She had
been careless. The wind screamed, plastering her wet bangs to her face,
flapping loose folds of her storm suit. Another wave slammed into the
boat, skidding the VTOL closer to the edge of the deck. Jessamin
grabbed for the loose guy line as the wind whipped it past her. The
little jet should have been tied down properly in the first place. Her
mistake. She let go of the antenna mount. You were responsible for
your mistakes, even if you were Jessamin Chen, head of Tanaka-
Pacific's Aquaculture Division.

Got it! The cable stung her palms as she clutched it, and she bared
her teeth to the stinging blast of wind-driven spray. You can't sink me,
you can't drown me. Go ahead and try—a lot of people have tried to
sink me over the last three decades, and they couldn't do it.

Of course, she was cheating. Jessamin touched her storm harness
and laughed. The line tethering her wasn't going to break, and you

19

couldn't sink this boat if you tried. No unnecessary risks—not if you want to get to the top and stay there.

The bow rode up a towering swell, foam streaming down its cambered sides. With a crash, it dropped into the deep trough beyond. Water boiled across the deck, and the VTOL slid again. Damn. She stretched for the tie-down ring, couldn't reach it. Carla would find out, if Jessamin ordered a new VTOL. She'd spend the time and money to discover why. It would be another point scored, a small private victory—that Jessamin had been careless.

You think I don't know how closely you watch me? Jessamin searched for a handy cleat. That's all right. I watch *you*, too. It's not time yet, daughter. Jessamin threw her head back, letting the wind rake the wet hair from her face. "You get the Aquaculture Division when *I* decide you're ready," she yelled into the storm. "*If* I decide you're ready." She whipped the VTOL's cable around a deck cleat, and hauled it tight. No, Carla was good, but not good enough. Not yet. Time to study patience, daughter. Jessamin headed forward to secure the rest of the VTOL's tie-downs, bent against the slashing rain. And don't sic your lover on me in public.

Paul had been so *transparent* in Zurich, trying to undercut her during their negotiations with the World Resource Council. Trying to make her look incompetent. *Her*. That bumbling puppy. Did he really think that Carla could save him if he seriously challenged her? Jessamin could swat him like a fly.

Well, maybe. Jessamin grimaced and hung onto the craft's forward tiedown as the next wave surged across the deck. She'd had her hands full with the Council, never mind Paul. They weren't going to rubber-stamp the renewal of Tanaka's monopoly contract on the Pacific Fishery this time around. The East European Coalition had thrown a serious challenge in their way, and the East block had a lot of votes on the Council. If Tanaka lost the Pacific Fishery, the Coalition would rape it. She yanked the cable tight, secured it.

Light turned the oncoming swells to mountains of green glass, capped with wind-shredded foam. Gray curtains of rain swept across the bow as the boat ploughed through the next swell. There was so much *life* down there. Food for humanity forever. If humanity didn't get too greedy.

The Coalition was greedy.

Jessamin licked her lips, tasting salt from the windblown spume, cold inside her storm suit. A few years ago, she could have brought the Council to heel in one session. *Maybe you are getting old.* Carla's voice in the wind?

No, daughter. Not yet. Jessamin squinted aft, checking the deck for anything else that might be coming loose in the storm. All secure. Go below, make yourself a toddy, and go to bed. As she started to head back to the companionway, a dark shape caught her eye out in the floodlit chaos. Driftwood? She leaned on the rail, metal cold beneath her bare palms. A dead seal? The dark shape slid down the side of a swell, and pale skin gleamed through ragged curtains of rain. Jessamin's stomach contracted. A body? Out here, so far from shore? Some fool of a sports fisherman who hadn't checked the sat-link for weather before he went out? Too late for him. He'd paid for his stupidity. He belonged to the sea, now.

Her hands were freezing and water had leaked in around her suit's hood, cold on her neck. Jessamin started to turn away. For an instant, the rain thinned. Light snagged a flicker of motion, dragged it into her peripheral vision; shoulders bunching, an arm lifting from white foam. Jessamin grabbed the rail, squinting down as the rain closed in once again. Yes, *movement.*

He was alive.

The boat slid up the next swell, and the weakly struggling swimmer slid aft, bumping against the hull now, sucked along toward the big intake port. "Engines, stop!" she yelled. "Bow thrusters only. Maintain stern into the wind." She ran aft, wind shoving her as the boat slowed and maneuvered. Her safety line snagged. She yanked at it, nearly fell over backward as it came suddenly loose. Where was he? Gone under? She grabbed the mounted buoy-launcher, swiveled it around, scanning the rainswept swells. There! He floundered to the surface, arms moving weakly. He wasn't trying for the boat, didn't even seem to be aware that it was there. If he was that far gone, he might not come back up next time. Bitter irony, to fight so hard and die so close to rescue. She respected a fighter.

Jessamin sighted just short of him, fired. The life-buoy launched, trailing its line, splashed down less than a meter from him. Bright orange nets popped out from the basketball-sized buoy, forming a floating skirt. The swimmer grabbed, hooked a pale arm through the mesh. Jessamin staggered as a wave slammed into the boat. Swearing, she braced herself against the rail. Come on, man. Her arms ached with strain. *Help me!*

He tried. A wave lifted him as he got closer, and he grabbed for the diving deck, beaching like a stranded orca as the wave broke across the waterline platform. Dark hair in a strange cut came to a point down between his shoulder blades. Like fur, one corner of her mind noticed. "Can you climb the ladder?" she yelled down. Not likely, and she couldn't open the deck-level hatch in this storm. Shit. The boat groaned as the next swell slammed it. The diving deck dipped into the green wall of water and the exhausted swimmer vanished.

Jessamin swung out onto the ladder, shaking her safety line loose from snags. Tie him to the ladder and worry about getting him up here later. Her foot slipped, and she gasped, hands coming loose from the rung. She fell a breathless meter, landed *whump* on the slippery deck as the next wave surged over it. Eyes squeezed shut, she grabbed for the ladder. Her feet lifted and she felt Patrick's touch in the water, like cold fingers stroking her skin. He was down there. Somewhere. *I'll see you,* he'd said on that last morning, kissing her so gently before he went down to the beach for his morning swim. *I'll see you.* As if he'd meant to come back.

He hadn't. It had been suicide, and it was *water* she felt, not ghostly fingers. The surge receded, and she got her feet under her. Sucking in a quick breath, Jessamin grabbed for the swimmer. Her hand closed on his shoulder, fingers digging into his armpit. Cold flesh, cold as Patrick's. Major hypothermia? "Can you hold onto the ladder?"

Amazingly, he struggled to his feet. Yes, this guy was a fighter. Another wave coming... Jessamin shoved him against the ladder. "Hang on!" Jessamin leaned against his corpse-cold body, struggling to loop her safety line around him. To her surprise, he started climbing, pulling himself upward one rung at a time. She shoved him higher, her hands sliding on naked flesh, snagging in a pair of swim trunks. What had this idiot been doing? Taking a quick dip in the storm? He faltered at the top, and she shoved him roughly onboard, scrambling after him, safe. "Main engines *on*." She clamped a hand over her throat patch. "Storm speed, hull down."

Jessamin staggered as the nav system kicked in the big props. The boat shied like a startled horse, and she fell hard to her knees beside the sprawled swimmer, shivering now, teeth chattering with cold and the aftermath of adrenaline. The man had curled fetal-wise on the wet deck, not shivering, which was a bad sign. Jessamin grabbed his shoulder and recoiled as he flinched away. *She*, not he, and young. She stared as the girl struggled to sit up. Light from the deck floods gleamed on small breasts set way too far apart, and highlighted the obscene bulge of flesh between them. That bulge ran like a wide flaccid tube from collarbone to hips, each end puckered into a purplish slash, like a badly healed surgical scar.

A gill tunnel. In the water, those puckered mouths would open, letting water flow through the delicate folded membranes that allowed this girl to breathe beneath the sea. Jessamin swallowed. Patrick had called them selkies, after some sea-dwellers of his childhood fairytales. She had refused to make it Tanaka's official name for them, had told him that Aquatic Specialist was better, more scientific, more acceptable. They'd fought about it one night, and he had stomped out in a rage. Later, he had brought her a dirt-grown white rose as a peace offering, and they had made love in front of the fireplace. The heat from the fire had washed his fair skin with ruddy light...

Jessamin shook her head, dizzy in this wave-rush of unexpected memory. In the end, names had made no difference at all. Ah, Patrick. You cared too much, and in the end it killed you.

"Are you... finished staring?" The girl gave Jessamin a glazed scowl and tried to get to her feet.

"Just take it easy." Teeth chattering, wet beneath her storm suit, Jessamin reached for the girl's arm, staggered with her weight. "Are you hurt?"

"No." The girl leaned on Jessamin, heavier than she looked. "Just hungry, I think. We get like this..."

Yes, they did. Because it took energy to keep a mammal warm in the cold sea, never mind how much body fat you coat them with. And it took energy to make the uric acid that balanced salt and water in their body fluids so that they could live in their saline environment. The details came back to her, each one like the stab of a small knife. Patrick had worked them all out with her, cross-legged on their rumpled bed, awake until the early morning hours as he grappled with the traits he needed to create *Homo aquaticus*. It wasn't his voice that had kept her from sleep. It had been his face that had held her—transformed with vision, eyes glowing in the soft light of her bedside lamp.

A faulty vision. Patrick was long dead, and she was cold. "Come on." Jessamin started for the main companionway, staggering with the wave motion and the added burden of the girl's weight. Vaguely, she noticed that the storm was finally easing. The girl was unsteady, but at least she was walking. The wind snatched the door from her hands and slammed it back on its hinges. With a grunt, Jessamin wrestled it closed. The sudden quiet made her ears ring. The girl broke away from her with a wrench and collapsed into the nearest chair.

It was always a shock to go from the raw reality of sea and sky to the warmth of wood, woven fabrics, and soft light. An intentional contrast. Jessamin grimaced at the water spotting the wooden floor and a corner of the carpet. The girl's presence made the room seem crowded, in spite of its spacious dimensions. She rarely invited anyone out to the boat. This was her refuge. Her space. "So, what are you doing out here?" Jessamin stepped back into the tiled entry, stripped out of her storm suit, and hung it on its hook. "You came from Briard?"

Jessamin glanced at her terminal desk. She hadn't programmed a course to Briard, had simply set a random-select autopilot to keep her moving and secure from anyone who might want to know where one of the most powerful women on the planet hid her vulnerable flesh.

They *were* close to Briard Research Station. Not very close, but within a possible swimming distance. Jessamin shivered. Coincidence. Of course she passed near Briard occasionally as she roved up and down the Pacific coast. Once upon a time, she had spent a lot of time there. When it had been Patrick's home and lab. Enough ghosts already. "We're a long swim from the station."

"Are we?" The girl's eyes flashed at Jessamin's sharp tone. "I don't know." She hunched in the chair, arms crossed protectively over her chest.

"You *should* know. You swam it." Jessamin walked past her, pissed at her ungrateful attitude. "What's your name? And how did you get permission to leave the station, anyway?" It had been closed to any access for years now, walled off by court injunctions against trespass. She stopped in front of her kitchen-wall, touched up the inventory on the little flatscreen. This kid was AWOL, and it was Carla's responsibility. She ran Research. If she really planned to inherit all of

Aquaculture, she'd damn well better know that one of Tanaka's expensive and dangerous genens was missing. Scowling, she touched in her choice.

"Who are you anyway?" The girl twisted around to face her, feet tucked up onto the chair. Pale folds of webbing stuck up between her long toes. "How do you know about Briard, anyway? You've got to work for Tanaka."

That surly tone wasn't anger. Jessamin gave her a quick sideways glance, and scooped up the drink packets that had dropped into the receiver tray. The kid was scared. "I'm Jess. I've worked for Tanaka." The past-tense came so automatically. Why? Automatic caution? Jessamin stabbed a straw into one of the plastic packets. "Drink all of these."

"What is it?" She took the packets warily, fingers spreading to reveal the translucent folds of webbing that joined them.

"A juice-protein drink. High fat, lots of calories." She kept it for after dives, hated it. "Strawberry. And you haven't told me your name."

"Shira." The girl took a swallow, grimaced. "Yuck. I'm Shira Doyle." She lifted her chin, her eyes dark and defiant.

Doyle.

Jessamin leaned against the kitchen-wall, needing all her skill to hide her expression. *I want a child, Jess,* Patrick had said so many years ago. And she had laughed, because she had just been named head of Aquaculture, and the world was hers, waiting for her to carve her name on it. And later, when there had been time and reason, it had been too late.

Patrick had begun with undifferentiated human gametes, had added and subtracted DNA segments as he sculpted them into his selkies. The original DNA had come from anonymous donors, selected for specific traits and filed by number. No names. No parentage issues. Transplanted into volunteer wombs, the engineered ova had grown, divided, had ultimately been born, the cutting edge of human genentech. Tanaka's new wonders. Children of genius Patrick, who had wanted to play God, even though Tanaka didn't really need a God. Costly mistakes. Jessamin closed her eyes briefly.

Patrick Doyle.

He'd used his *own* DNA to create this girl—oh yeah, you could see it in her face. That frown was his. *I want a child, Jess.* "I'm cold."

Jessamin straightened, joints aching, feeling *old* suddenly. "Drink those. I'm going to put on some dry clothes." She took the small circular stairway down to her bedroom without waiting for an answer.

The twin hulls were transparent, molded from prestressed polyglass. She'd had her main-deck living area painted to keep out the space of sea and sky. For that, you had to go outside, take weather with your view. Down here, there was only sea. She stepped off the stairway without turning on the lights. It was never completely dark. A school of squid jetted by, ghostly streaks of green light. Constellations of living stars twirled in the dark water, and something large veered away from the hull, its sides spotted with bright yellow light. The storm must be easing off if her nav system had slowed them down to slow cruise speed again. A pale oval appeared briefly on the far side of the thick glass, like a ghostly face pressed longingly against a window. She imagined Patrick peering in at her, face set into hard lines of reproach. "You're angry at me, aren't you?" Jessamin walked over to the hull, stopped just short of the smooth polyglass. "You wouldn't let me explain, you wouldn't *listen*." The luminescent shimmer of light seemed to coalesce into the girl's face, young and wary, looking at her with Patrick's eyes.

Jessamin clenched a fist, slammed it against the hull. The glowing blob of light skittered away, a fish or ray, nothing more. "Lights," she snapped, and blinked in the soft glow.

With the lights on, it became a bedroom with mirrored walls. No ghosts in here. Jessamin stripped quickly, tossing her damp clothes into a heap on the floor. Skinny, youthful body, dark hair, Chinese phenotype. She could pass for forty instead of sixty. A thick shirt and dry pants finally ended the shivering, and she sat down on the side of the big bed facing the entertainment-sized holo stage in the center of the room. "House, access Carla Chen." Carla would accept the access. She'd know all about Zurich by now. Jessamin stared at the empty stage, wondering which would come first; gloating over Jessamin's setback, or anger?

"Mother." Carla began to speak even before her image had fully focused onstage. "Paul just accessed me from Zurich. He said you didn't present your resignation at the meeting."

Anger. "Don't whine." Jessamin swallowed a surge of bitterness. She had chosen Carla's father from their stock of nameless donors, picked out a fine-boned, dark-haired Caucasian with the intelligence and creative quotients to complement her own genotype. Had this tendency to whine been embedded in there, too, between the genes for hazel eyes and the genes for a high IQ?

"I'm not whining." Carla flushed, the projector shading too heavily for red again, turning her face lobster-colored. "You said this was your last year. You were going to *retire*."

"I changed my mind." Jessamin shrugged. "If the Coalition gets the fishery, it'll take us a decade to get it back and a century to undo the damage. East Euro doesn't care if they strip the whole ocean bare, just so long as they pull out their maximum tonnage." She closed her eyes briefly, remembering the huge nets winched dripping from the sea, spewing flopping silvery life into the holds of the factory ships. So much wastage. Cleaning fish on the line, she had held the sea's raped guts in her numb, bloody hands, had listened to the old-timers bitch about the reduced catch, and, deep inside, in a hidden place . . . she had wept. I was so *young*. Jessamin opened her eyes, gave her daughter a thin smile. So idealistic and immature. "I am going to see this crisis through," she said.

"*This* crisis?" Carla's face went carefully smooth. "There's always a crisis! Someone is *always* after something. Don't give me *crisis*, Mother. Tanaka won't fail if we lose the monopoly. This is just another excuse to leave me stuck with Research. You're *never* going to retire," she said softly. "The damn doctors will keep you alive forever, and you'll never believe that anyone but Jessamin Chen could do an adequate job of running Aquaculture."

"When I'm no longer the best choice for the job, I'll resign."

"Who's going to decide, Mother?" Carla's voice was cold. "*You?*"

"Yes." Jessamin met her daughter's eyes. "And what was your reason for putting Paul up against me? Do you really think he has the finesse to *do* anything? He might be good in bed, dear, but he's a klutz in negotiations. Keep him where he belongs." She waited for her daughter to flush and react, but Carla's smile never faltered.

"I'm sorry you don't get along," Carla said in a carefully regretful tone. "I'm sorry you feel that he's a threat to you."

"He's not good enough to be a *threat*." But Jessamin felt a twinge of unease. This was not the reaction she'd expected from her volatile daughter. Was Carla finally learning self-control? This entire conversation was being recorded by both herself and her daughter. What was going on here? "Are you missing any aquatics?" she asked sourly. "Or do you know?"

This time Carla *did* flush. "You never quit, do you?" Her voice quivered just a hair. "You'll never stop looking over my shoulder!"

Aha. "I want your side of it," Jessamin snapped. "Right now."

"Don't use that tone on *me*." But Carla looked away. "In case you haven't noticed, I'm thirty-five. The aquatic involved claimed it was an accident, as your informant undoubtedly told you." Her mouth twitched. "My God, we've had the pickets and the protesters out there forever! By now, they're practically part of the landscape. The staff and the aquatics have all had extensive counseling on dealing with that kind of thing. *I* don't know what happened. It's her word against a half dozen witnesses, but considering that the witnesses are all anti-genen fanatics, what does *that* mean?"

Good question. Jessamin pressed her lips together. "So where is she?"

"If I knew, I'm sure you would, too." Carla didn't try to hide the sarcasm in her tone. "If the man hadn't died, it wouldn't be such a big deal. I'm going to find out who's reporting to you, you know."

If the man hadn't died. A lifetime of control kept Jessamin's expression neutral. "Why didn't you *tell* me? My *God* child . . ."

"*I am not a child.*" Carla's shoulders hunched, as if she had clenched her fists out of sight beneath her desk. "Why *should* I have told you? *You* stuck me with Research—the most marginal operation in Tanaka. *You* told me not to bother you with details, that you wanted me to do it on my own. So that you could judge my performance, right? So, then, *judge*." Her lips twisted. "I kept a lid on this, and it took work and money, let me tell you. I know what it could do to the Council vote on our Pacific contract if the media plays hacky sack with that story. *Rogue Tanaka Genen Kills Peaceful Protester.* It won't happen," she said bitterly. "So you can skip the lecture. No cops. Tanaka Security finds her, and we turn her over to the DA. They've got a court order to hold her until the World Court decides on the genens' legal status. The media's out of it. It's a done deal."

The girl upstairs, Shira, had killed a man. A prickle of ice touched Jessamin's neck, and she opened her mouth to tell Carla to get Briard security out here and fast.

She didn't say it. "All right. You've been handling it." She gave Carla a curt nod. "Keep me informed about this."

She snapped her fingers to break the connection, but not before Carla's look of wary surprise had registered. What? Jessamin made a face. Had Carla thought she was going to step in and take over? She probably *should.* Jessamin pressed her lips together. Kazi Itano had bowed to her, when she had taken Aquaculture from him so many, many years ago. She wasn't ready to bow to Carla yet.

"You didn't tell her."

Jessamin turned slowly. Shira sat on the bottom step, raised knees hiding her gill tunnel, folded webbing sticking out from her clenched fists. "She was talking about me and you knew it. Why didn't you tell her I was here?"

She had Patrick's transparent face, and she was scared beneath that surly anger. Terrified. "I want to hear your side," Jessamin said slowly. Why *hadn't* she told Carla? Just because this kid wore Patrick's face? "I want to hear your side of it before they lock you up in some jail cell for the umpteen years that the Court will manage to evade this damn issue."

"Prison." Shira spread her long fingers, staring at the pale stretch of skin between them. "What would I do in prison?" She shuddered, and balled her hand into a fist again.

What indeed. *Aquatic,* Carla had said. They were Aquatic Specialists on Tanaka's inventory, listed like alvins or factory seiners. They had been *Homo aquaticus* to Patrick, a new race.

Selkies.

The girl stood up suddenly, crossed the room to sit on the edge of the bed. She moved awkwardly. Her too-long toes snagged on the carpet, and the webbing between them stuck up in thick folds. Her thick, heavily muscled legs were too long for her short, broad torso. She looked *wrong* in this lighted, ordinary space. Jessamin felt a twinge of revulsion. It was the kind of revulsion you might feel for someone with a terrible deformity. You overlaid and disguised it with civilized compassion, but underneath, you were revolted—a primitive, gut-level xenophobia. *Alien. Different. Not-tribe.*

The sea is most of our world, Patrick had said in bed one night. *But we're aliens there, so we don't love it. We can't love it, and we need to love it, or we'll kill it.* His eyes had shone in the dark room like a wild animal's, or a prophet's. He had believed in what he was doing, and she had funded him because of that faith, and not because he was her lover. It had still been a mistake.

That was why she hadn't told Carla. Because this was Patrick's daughter. It would have hurt Patrick, that his daughter was a killer.

Bad reason—as bad a reason as faith. Or love. It reeked of nostalgia, and, once, she had known nostalgia for the dangerous thing it was. Maybe she was getting old. Maybe she *should* step aside for Carla.

Who decides, Mother?

Me, and I'm not losing it yet. Jessamin sat down on the bed across from Shira, noticed the girl's small flinch. "Tell me about this man you killed."

"Why?" Shira looked past her at her reflection in the glass wall. "The media's got to be full of it, by now. Check it out there." Her voice trembled the tiniest bit. "Will you . . . turn out the light again, please?"

"Lights off." Sea-darkness filled the room, lighted by the bioluminescent galaxies orbiting slowly past. Shira fit in this scene. "The media's out of it. For now." Jessamin stared out into that dark, life-filled water. "The why is because Patrick Doyle was my friend."

Shira looked up. "Doyle? The guy who . . . made us? They say he was a genius. You knew him, huh?" She looked away. "He was a bastard! I hate his guts!"

"No!" The word came out too loud, too fast.

Shira's face tightened, but she didn't look at Jessamin.

She didn't know, Jessamin realized suddenly. The gene stocks were numbered, but not cross-referenced to donor names. Last names had been a whimsical thing. "How old are you?"

"Sixteen." Shira watched a school of small fish hover beyond the hull, then arrow away in precise unison.

Her face had relaxed in the sea-lit darkness. Jessamin had to turn away. Patrick had looked like that some nights. "I want some tea. You?"

"Thanks."

Jessamin got up suddenly, went over to the dispenser on the wall. No, Shira didn't know. Patrick had died the year before she had been born. "Patrick loved you." You, personally, child, you as a new race. "He . . . sacrificed everything to create you." And now I'm defending him, *I*, who have every reason to accuse him. Jessamin picked up a porcelain mug from the dresser, held it under the spout. Amber tea swirled into her cup, and she filled a second one for Shira. "Why do you hate him?" She turned around to find Shira staring at her, her eyes dark as the nighttime sea in the dim light.

"So he loved us, huh?" Shira took the cup carefully, folding her webbing between her long fingers. "I have gills like a fish. That's what the people on shore call us, isn't it? Fish? That's all right." Her laugh was as harsh and dry as the sound of tearing paper. "We call you 'grubs.' My hair comes from fur-seal genes." She brushed one webbed hand over her head. "My metabolism comes from sharks and kangaroo rats and Weddell seals. I don't like your room upstairs. My gill gets squashed when I try to sleep in a bed, and it hurts. My toes catch on things, and you grubs don't make shoes to fit us." She raised her head slowly. "What am I, lady? Animal or human? You want to tell me? I guess the World Court is going to make up its mind one of these days. I can't wait." She stared down at the silk bedspread. "I spilled tea on your bed. I can't even hold a bloody cup."

"You can hold it just fine. Patrick made you as dexterous as any primate." Jessamin looked over the girl's bowed head, bitterness clogging her throat. Tanaka's marketing specialists had warned about a potential backlash against the proliferating genetic manipulation of the human genome. She hadn't listened. Because it had mattered so much to Patrick... and she had loved him.

Her mistake. You are responsible for your mistakes, even if you're Jessamin Chen.

But who had paid for this one? Patrick? This child and her siblings?

"We got sold out, you know." Shira stared into her cup. "Everybody knows it—that Tanaka nudged the media under the table. *Tanaka* really got the anti-fish riots going, just so they could shut down the program. Why?" Her voice quivered. "Because we cost too much? Why didn't they just *do* it—end the program? Why did they turn those crazies loose on us? They're out there all the time with their signs and their crosses and their slogans. Some of 'em have been around so long, they're almost... familiar." Her laugh had jagged edges, sharp as glass. "Like old friends."

"Tanaka didn't start the riots." The bitter, ugly truth of what Shira had just said dragged at her words, slowing them down. Tanaka hadn't *started* the riots, but neither had they tried very hard to defend their genen program. "The riots were directed against all human modification, not just you."

"But we were the only ones who weren't *people* anymore. We're *fish*. Because of *Doyle*." Shira flung her cup at the wall. It shattered, tea splashing everywhere, running down the glass wall like dirty tears. She faced Jessamin, her eyes wide and dark in her pale face, breathing hard. "Let me tell you about Aaron. We were the last two . . . to be born. So we were always close. We were the youngest, you know? I . . . loved him." Her voice trembled. "And it really bugged him that we didn't matter. We *should* have. We can take care of the fish schools, do the exploring and the mining, work on undersea construction so much better than divers, or alvins, or remotes. But no one'll let us. And every day, the protesters hang around just outside the markers that the court's injunction set up. Close enough so we can see them. Close enough to hear them. It's like the judge wanted us to hear what they yell." She closed her eyes briefly. "You get used to it," she said in a flat, dead tone. "You tell yourself that you don't really hear it anymore when they call us Satan's children, or fish, or Frankensteins. Only you *do*, you know. You hear every fucking word. And one day this guy in this little grungy boat started calling us names. So what else is new, but this time Aaron . . . lost it."

She drew a shuddering breath. "He just took off—past the markers that're supposed to keep those creeps away from us. I was yelling at him, but he didn't hear me. It was like he was deaf. He came up out of the water like an orca and knocked the guy back into his boat. The grub gets up bleeding, screaming at Aaron, really out of control. And he revs up his boat." She looked away, face working, fighting tears. "He . . . ran Aaron down. The propeller blades . . ." She swallowed, struggling. "There were three other boats out there. Some of the people . . . cheered. Aaron was alive but . . . it's a long way back, and he was bleeding so bad. He . . . died on the way in."

Selkies could cry. Patrick hadn't taken that human trait away from them. Jessamin put a hand on Shira's shoulder, withdrew it as she tensed. "I'm sorry." Inadequate words, overused and meaningless. Words had so little power to touch human pain. Jessamin sighed, anger smoldering inside her, as useless as the words. "What happened to the protester?"

"He . . . said that it was an accident. An *accident*." She straightened, brushing the heels of her hands across her eyes like a blow. "He got fined and he didn't even lose the damned boat. Because . . . everybody *else* out there said it was an accident, too." Bitterness razored her voice. "Except me, and I don't count. Because the courts haven't decided if I'm human or a *fish.*"

Jessamin looked beyond her, out into the depths of the sea. Black was softening to royal blue. Morning already? "So you went back and killed him?" she asked softly. "The one who ran Aaron down?"

"No." Shira looked away. "That's the really stupid part." Her voice cracked. "There were these guys—an old man and his kid—who ran tourists out in their boat. To look, you know? I think they gawked at the assholes with their silly signs more than at us." Her shoulders drooped. "I kind of knew them . . . I mean, they were always around. It was like . . . a job to them. They didn't hate us or anything. They'd come in real close to the markers, but the people on their boat never yelled anything at us, like they wouldn't let them." Her voice had faded to a whisper. "We were out working the fish pens, moving some young snapper into a new space. It's just a game." Her voice grew bitter again. "Not a real fishery. Tanaka doesn't want us to do anything *real*, but I guess they've got to give us something to do. Aaron used to say that it was so they could write us off on their taxes. Anyway, the tourist boat was in real close, and this woman on their boat started *yelling* at me." She picked at the folded webbing between her thumb and forefinger.

"All of a sudden it was . . . too much. I guess that's what happened to Aaron." Her voice faltered. "Anyway, I started for the boat. I don't know what I meant to do, but the old man picked up a boat hook when I got close. He hit me with it. It *hurt*, and I grabbed it. He was so *weak*." Her gill tunnel rippled and the puckered mouths opened, revealing a brief flash of blood-red membrane. "I pulled him overboard." She pressed both hands against her shuddering gill. "His head hit the side of the boat. It was such a wooden sound. And then he went down. I dove and grabbed him, but when I came up, everyone was screaming at me, and the kid was getting this *rifle* out from under the seat." She took her hands away from her gill, stared down at the faintly pulsing bulge. "I . . . I let go of him and took off."

Silence filled the room, thick as feathers.

"He drowned?"

Shira nodded, her eyes as bleak as a winter sky. "I didn't want to kill *him*."

Patrick's face, Patrick's eyes. Jessamin looked away from her, glaring into the blue depths of the dawn sea. You are a cold goddess, she thought bleakly. You demand blood, and we keep on providing blood for you. Patrick had looked at her with those same bleak eyes on that long-ago morning when she had told him that they were cutting the genen program, that they weren't going to fight the World Court's injunction. He hadn't gotten angry, hadn't said anything.

Instead, he had walked out; down to the beach for his morning swim. *You* walked out on her, Patrick. Bitterness filled Jessamin's throat, stinging her eyes. You walked out on your daughter, on all your children. You walked out on me, and you wouldn't even try to understand. You wouldn't *hear* me, damn it! *You let this happen.*

Beyond the hull, the water was fading from royal blue to turquoise. Morning, yes. Jessamin sighed, hearing the creak of years in her bones. You could buy the appearance of youth, but you aged behind that mask of youthful flesh.

"Who are you?" Shira's voice was dull as a wave-worn stone. "You got to be somebody big in Tanaka, to know all about this stuff, right? What's it to you, *grub*? You worried about bad PR?"

"Of course. Bad PR matters." Jessamin stared at the smooth, muscular curve of Shira's shoulders, at the fat-layered skin that kept out the cold. Patrick had spent so many *years* pregnant with this child. He had given her all his energy. There had been so little left for Jessamin, or anyone else. Jessamin leaned her forehead against the cool slick polyglass.

And once again, the fishery was up for grabs. Something moved in the turquoise distance beyond the hull—a small shark, perhaps, out cruising for breakfast. "Let me tell you a story," Jessamin said softly. "Once upon a time there was a man who loved the sea. He loved her so much that he got pregnant by her, and had a child who could live in the sea. And he was very proud of her, but one day, some fishermen threatened to kill the sea. The only thing that could save the sea was to sacrifice their daughter. The man who loved the sea couldn't do it."

The shark had vanished. Silvery bubbles trailed past the hull, and a jellyfish caught in the turbulence, as the boat moved slowly through the calming sea. What color had his towel been that morning? She'd found it with his shoes and his shorts, folded neatly above the high-tide line. They had never recovered his body. His lover had kept it. "I'm Jessamin Chen." She turned away from the window, feeling old, no matter how young science kept her flesh, feeling *ancient.*

"Jessamin Chen?" Shira's face went blank with surprise. "*The* Jessamin Chen? The one who runs the whole show?" She looked down at the silk comforter beneath her, lifted her head to stare around at the glass-walled room. "You really *are,* aren't you?" Webbing bulged whitely between her long fingers as she slowly clenched her fists. "You did it," she whispered. "*You're* the one who shut down our program. *You* stuck us in that cage and forgot about us! You *abandoned* us!"

Jessamin stepped back, suddenly aware of the strength in this child's body, aware of her own fragility. "I didn't forget you." Anger flooded her and she straightened, throwing her shoulders back. "I didn't finish my story. The man who loved the sea wouldn't sacrifice their daughter to save her. He loved her too much. So *I* did it," she said softly. "Hunger is very immediate. It blinds you to the future, and the world is very hungry. I threw you to them—to the hungry people—and while they squabbled over whether you were fish or human, I fenced the sea with bars that they couldn't get through. Not Tanaka. *Me. I* did it." Jessamin caught her breath, held out her hands, palm up, empty. "Patrick Doyle abandoned you when he committed suicide." And you abandoned me, too, Patrick. She closed her hands slowly, lowered them. Didn't you know how much you *meant* to me? "I didn't abandon you. *I* knew exactly what I was doing."

"Sacrificing us?" Shira lunged to her feet. "For your own damn good? *You, Tanaka,* the *grubs.* You won't let us *do* anything." She was shaking. "Aaron died because he didn't have any reason to *live.* Because you won't let us *matter. You* killed him!" She flung herself at Jessamin.

Jessamin slapped her. The backhand blow caught Shira full on the cheek, sent her reeling onto the bed. She caught herself with a cry, and crouched, eyes wide and wild, gill tunnel fluttering.

"Yes," Jessamin said harshly. "Sometimes you have to choose. Sometimes the right answer feels like shit, but it's *right,* so you choose it anyway. No matter who gets hurt. I had to choose between you and the sea. I chose the sea, because *none* of us can live without her." She rubbed her knuckles, eyeing the darkening bruise on Shira's face. "If you have to blame someone, blame Patrick for sticking me with the choice," she said bitterly. "Blame your *father*."

"No." Shira's body jerked as if Jessamin had slapped her again. "Not *my* father." Her eyes blazed. "I was *grown*, remember? I don't have any parents, I came from a petri dish."

"Oh, you're his, all right." Jessamin flung the words, hard as stones, wanting to hurt, because this was Patrick's daughter and the child of his lover, the sea. "Do you think your last name's an accident? Call up his picture from the files and then go look in the damn *mirror!*"

From beyond the hull, an engine muttered, growing louder. Not possible. Security would have warned her, identified the plane. Jessamin looked up the stair, suddenly uneasy. It sounded like a VTOL. Why would it be out here? Only one or two people in Tanaka knew how to find her. In the no-privacy world of the Net, safety came from invisibility in the physical world. This hard-to-find boat was her safety. "Security?" she said sharply. "Status report."

All secure.

Yeah, sure. The *clunk* of a landing shivered through the hull.

Security hadn't reported it—which wasn't possible, but Jessamin didn't waste any time on that one. Turning her back on Shira, she darted over to the terminal and touched it to life. Shifting curtains of light and color danced above the terminal stage. "System!" She snapped her fingers in a twisting skein of opalescent blue. "Security report."

Nothing happened.

No one could subvert her System. "Access Carla Chen, private, emergency interrupt."

Crimson spiraled through the shimmering light, spiked by bursts of lemon yellow. No face appeared. Someone had subverted her entire system. That couldn't happen. Someone had landed on her boat, when her Security system should have known instantly if any plane, boat, or sub for a hundred miles in any direction was even headed in her direction. Cold fear was gathering in her chest like a coastal fog. Jessamin walked over to the nightstand beside the bed and yanked open the drawer.

The licensed gun she kept there was gone.

Another impossibility. Add it to the list. Jessamin touched the smooth wood of the empty drawer. No one had been on this boat while she was in Zurich. Security would have logged it, right? Yeah, *right*. She laughed a single, dry note.

"What's wrong with you?" Shira was on her feet, back against the hull, as if she expected Jessamin to attack her.

"I have a visitor." She had never hidden in her life; not from truth, not from choices. Jessamin grabbed the handrail and started up the stairway. Halfway up, she paused, looked back. "I have no answers for you," she said softly. "I wish I did." Then she turned and marched up the stairs to the main deck.

Her intruder was waiting for her, lounging casually in her recliner.

Paul. He leaned back, his posture relaxed, the thick, fashionable tail of blond hair falling carefully over one shoulder. A pose, but his familiar perfect smile hit her harder than the sound of the landing plane, the crash of her System, or her missing gun. "What . . . are you doing here?" She clung to the railing, groping for anger, finding only the echoes of age and mortality. "You're still in Europe."

"Did I scare you, Jessamin?" He smiled. "I'm sorry. A lot of people think I'm in Europe, but I'm not. I got back before you did. You hired me because I was good with the Net, remember? That's why your security doorbell didn't ring."

That pleased smirk cut through Jessamin's fear. Prick. Damned if she was scared of *him*. She stomped up the stairs and stood in front of him. "Spill it, Paul." Brave words, riding on a fragile shell of precious anger. She had no control over this situation and she had *always* had control. Over Tanaka. Over Carla. Her control had begun to erode when she had dragged Patrick's daughter on board. With an effort, Jessamin didn't look back at the stair. He didn't seem to realize that Shira was down there. Her unknown presence increased Jessamin's confidence slightly. The situation wasn't as stable as Paul thought, and she'd had a lot of practice turning unstable situations into successes. "So you've been playing your skillful little games with my Network Security. You're better than I thought. I'm impressed." She eyed him as if he was a regional manager who'd fucked up. "What's your game, Paul?" Fearless words, but she heard the quiver in her voice, saw his eyes flicker as he heard it, too. "Tell me fast, because I'm busy, and you only have ten minutes before Tanaka Security shows up from Briard."

"We both know better than that, Jess." He held out his hand to her. "So let's stop playing games. It's time for you to retire. You were planning to do it in Zurich, remember? You promised Carla, and then you didn't come through."

"Carla." Jessamin took a step backward, lightheaded with sudden comprehension. Carla could give Paul the access he needed to get into her System. Carla knew about the gun in the bedside drawer. . . . "She can't wait?" The words caught like fishbones in her throat. "She was always too damned impatient."

"No!" Paul's eyes flashed. "This is *my* doing, not hers. She's been *too* patient. You're never going to give her a chance, never going to let anyone else run the show, because you'll never believe that anyone is as *good* as you!"

"She's *not* as good as me. Not yet." Jessamin lifted her chin, met his cold eyes—and saw belief there. The same faith she'd seen once in Patrick's eyes. It jarred her badly. Who did he have such faith in? Carla? "She's my daughter, Paul." Her voice shook, in spite of herself. "Do you think she'll let you run the show when she takes over?" Anger seized her in its fist, and suddenly she didn't *care*. "Do you think it matters to her that you're her lover? Are you that *stupid*?"

With an inarticulate growl, he lunged at her, hands reaching, face twisted with sudden rage.

Jessamin spun away from him, but her foot slipped on the water she and Shira had dripped all over the floor. Paul's hand closed on her arm, and he spun her against him, in a dark parody of a lover's embrace. Death and love, were they so far apart? Jessamin struggled for breath as his arms tightened around her. You opened your legs and your soul, you gave up a part of yourself that you never regained. Patrick had walked into the sea with his arms open, into the arms of his lover. He had chosen the sea over her, and he'd taken a part of her with him. "Let go of me," she gasped. "Will you stop and *think*, you fool?"

"Oh, I have. Accidental drowning," Paul panted in her ear. "Easy when you insist on going out on deck during a storm. Your Security videos show you out there, just before the system goes down. The waves are very unpredictable, and you're so sure you're immortal. You must have released your safety line while you were tying down the VTOL. People will believe it." His tone mocked her. "You're so *macho*." The door opened for them automatically, and Paul dragged her outside.

It shocked her, how strong he was. Because it showed her how weak *she* was? I am not weak, she wanted to scream. I have manipulated the world's use of the sea for three decades. I have controlled it. *I am not weak.* Crushed in his embrace, his harsh breath hot on her neck, she couldn't even struggle.

Carla knew about this, whether Paul admitted it or not. Carla wanted her dead. The wind had shredded the storm clouds, and bright sun shone in a blue sky, glittering up from a puddle on the wet deck. Paul dragged her closer to the railing, and, for a moment, her muscles went slack, accepting the verdict, accepting Death as a lover, as Patrick had done.

Yes, and they'd find Shira Doyle's traces all over the boat. One killing, two—it would be easier to believe the second time around. Carla was competent. She would feed Shira to the media as extra insurance against discovery. She, Jessamin, would have done the same in her place. The rail banged her hip. Jessamin closed her teeth against a cry as Paul levered her over, damned if she'd give him the satisfaction of her fear. Shira hadn't chosen to help her—Jessamin Chen, the enemy. Why should she? She didn't know Carla—didn't know that she would simply become another sacrifice, like Aaron. The rail banged her knee, and Jessamin felt one piercing moment of terror.

Falling... Rush of air... Crash of shock and spray, cold closing over her head, closing her throat. Cold arms... Patrick's arms? You played God, Patrick, she cried silently. You created your children from DNA's raw clay. But you weren't enough of a God to stay and love them. To stay and fight to protect them. Her head broke the surface and she gasped blessed air, choking as a wavelet slapped her face. *Cold.* She ignored it, ducked under the surface again, half afraid that Paul might mean to shoot her from the deck. But no, that would spoil the accidental drowning scenario if they recovered her body. She yanked her sweats down around her ankles, dragged her feet free. Better. Now the shirt. She broke the surface again, stripping her arms out of the sleeves, releasing the heavy waterlogged fabric to sink slowly into the depths.

Struggling to get her breath, to relax, Jessamin slid up the glassy hillside of an oncoming swell, enclosed by blue sky and green sea, her breasts lifting in the water as she swam slowly over the wave's crest.

The boat was so far *away*.

Paul had gauged the current accurately, had put her over where she would have to swim against it to catch up to the boat. That way, there would be no need to alter the nav system. Yes, it would look like an accident. Or murder by a distraught, angry child. Jessamin swam after the boat with slow, dogged strokes. She licked her lips. Salt. Patrick always tasted of salt when they made love, he always tasted of the sea. Once, she had been a strong swimmer. Once she had been young, and so sure of herself. Would Paul stay on the boat, waiting to make sure that she drowned? If he had crashed Security, he would have no way to see her except through binoculars. She slid down into another trough and the boat vanished, leaving her alone with endless sky and water. Fear squeezed her slowly, like a vise closing around her heart. She wasn't so strong anymore. Already her leg muscles ached.

Nothing to do but swim. She had never been a quitter. Not like you, Patrick. You quit. You wouldn't let yourself understand what I was doing. Instead you just walked away, into your damn lover's arms. Jessamin paused briefly, treading water. The cold was sucking energy from her body. Soon, she'd lose the struggle to keep swimming, would go down, her flesh fighting desperately for life in those last agonizing seconds. Patrick had died like that. I didn't betray you, she cried silently. Why wouldn't you *listen*? The boat seemed so distant now— another universe, one that had no real meaning. This was a world of water, and, out here, *she* was the alien. Patrick was right.

Only the sea can save us, someone said softly. *But only if we save the sea first* . . .

"Patrick?" Jessamin kicked, rising chest high out of the water. "Patrick, is that you?" Her strength failed and she sank, water stinging her nose, closing briefly over her head.

We're aliens here. His voice sounded close in her ear, intimate and relaxed, as if he was lying beside her in bed. *We don't belong and we know it, and because we know it, we don't really care* . . .

How could he sound so relaxed when she was dying? Jessamin broke the surface and gasped for breath. "I care! Damn it . . . I care . . . and I made sure Tanaka cares. Does it matter that we care for profit? Couldn't you *understand*? You were such a . . . damned *idealist*." He was there, down in the blue-green water, looking up at her. His dark hair drifted like weeds in the swell, and tiny, brilliant fish wove intricate patterns around him. He looked so *sad*.

"Patrick..." She swallowed, her throat tight with tears. I never cried, she thought dully. I never cried for you. "I saved the sea. *I* did, Patrick. I gave it to Tanaka and Tanaka takes care of it. Because I love it, too. I told you that, but you wouldn't listen, you wouldn't see beyond your own love, you couldn't let me *share*. Patrick?" Longing seized her suddenly, a compilation of all those nights alone, those days of struggle, walled in with silence. "I miss you."

He reached for her, his long fingers greenish white like the belly of a fish, trailing a strand of brown weed. Jessamin stretched to take his hand, tired suddenly, wanting so much to touch him again, to have him pull her close and hold her...

And his daughter would be blamed for two murders. And Jessamin would never know if her own daughter had asked Paul to kill her or not.

"No," she cried, and her mouth filled with water.

Patrick vanished. The sea clutched her, holding her with cold arms, lover Death. Jessamin kicked, summoning the last of her strength, struggling for the surface. Or was it the surface? And did it matter, if the boat was a mile away? Confused, blood roaring in her ears, Jessamin floundered. I don't want to die, she thought, and the *clarity* of that desire made her want to cry.

It was darker, as if she was sinking deeper, down to where Patrick waited for her. Too late, she thought bitterly. Just a little bit too late.

Something was hurting her. She almost ignored it, but there was more pain. With an effort, she focused on it; fingers digging into her flesh, pulling on her. That touch cleared the darkness from her vision, as if life itself was soaking through her rescuer's skin, seeping like oxygenated blood into her veins. Jessamin kicked, kicked again, lungs on fire suddenly, aching with the need to breathe *now. Now!*

Water exploded against her face and she gasped, choking as a wave slapped her, choking, coughing so hard that red agony squeezed her chest. How could it hurt so much to breathe? She was nothing but a pair of lungs. Everything else had dissolved into a distant gray mist beyond the immediacy of breathing. She panted, sucking air in tortured partial lungfuls, as if water had filled her up after all, as if she had drowned and been raised from the dead.

Almost.

"Lie *still*. You grubs can't swim for shit, and you're going to stick your elbow in my gill again. *I'll* do it."

"Shira?" The word came out as an incomprehensible croak. Jessamin twisted in the water, the kaleidoscope world refocusing slowly, solidifying into green sea, incredibly blue sky, and a view of Shira's pale cheek not too far from her own.

"You'll have to hang onto my shoulders," Shira panted. "Think you can do that much?"

She was swimming on her side, one shoulder rammed between Jessamin's shoulder blades, supporting her awkwardly, so that Jessamin didn't squash her gill tunnel closed. Jessamin rolled slowly over, terrified suddenly that Shira would let go, that she'd sink and the sea would claim her after all. Her hands closed on Shira's thick, cold shoulders.

"Ouch! Easy, okay?" Shira put her head down and began to swim.

Water would be flowing through that marvelous tunnel, loaded with oxygen. Fish-girl. Oh yes, I need you. Jessamin wanted to laugh, swallowed it because it was hysteria and once she started, she'd never stop. A swell lifted them, and Jessamin saw the distant hull of the boat, like a white swan, like salvation. "Paul," she whispered.

Shira paused, lifting her head out of the water. "If you mean the grub, he took off in his little plane. He didn't even *look* to see if anyone else was on board. Stupid grub!"

He *wouldn't* look. Security had showed Jessamin to him alone, before he crashed it. He wouldn't expect a selkie to show up, and he'd be afraid of leaving traces that a forensic team might pick up. You're *careless*, Paul! Jessamin stifled another clutch of laughter as they slid up and over the next well. That's why you're second-rate.

Slowly, slowly, the white swan enlarged to boat size. When they finally reached the dive-deck, Shira had to boost Jessamin out onto the mesh platform. Exhausted, shivering, Jessamin sprawled on the decking, basking in air that felt warm as July. Shira scrambled up beside her, awkward as a seal on land. Water clear as tears ran from her deflating gill. A tiny orange crab slid out through the puckering lips of the tunnel and scrabbled down across the blue fabric of her swim trunks. Jessamin shuddered in spite of herself. Slowly, she reached out to stroke the cold flaccid skin. Shira flinched and looked at her with bitter eyes.

"Fish," Jessamin said softly. "We're right to call you that, we grubs. You don't belong on land. Patrick Doyle didn't *want* you to belong. He wanted you to be as alien on land as we are in the sea. He didn't want you to give a damn about us." She drew an aching wonderful breath. "Why did you come help me?"

Shira looked out at the endless horizon of sky and sea. "Because you didn't...apologize." She pressed her lips together. "And because...I wanted to ask if you were...telling me the truth. About Patrick Doyle being...my father."

"Genetically, yes." Jessamin sat up. "You were right, though. You were made—by a man who played God and loved you. But not enough." Jessamin sighed, aware of the years graven in her flesh. Was the soul an endless quantity, or was it a finite thing? Could you run out of soul before your body died? We could have done it together, she thought and smothered a pang of sorrow. "I have to go talk to my daughter." She staggered to her feet, still shivering. "Right now."

"I'm out of here." Shira stood, her eyes narrowing, wariness descending over her face like a mask.

She was seeing Jessamin Chen, again. Enemy. Jailor with the keys to a prison cell. "Not yet." Jessamin held out a hand, unsteady on her feet. "Will you wait until I talk to Carla? I owe you, and I might be able to...do something." She tried to meet Shira's eyes, failed. "After that, I won't try to stop you if you want to run."

Shira hesitated, her face full of youth and suspicion, maybe regretting her impulsive rescue.

"For Aaron," Jessamin said and caught the girl's tiny twitch of reaction. "Please?"

"You can't do anything for Aaron." Shira's lips thinned. "But I'll stick around for a few minutes just to make sure you're okay."

Carla crossed her arms on her desktop, her expression impatient. "What is it now, Mother?"

Cold in spite of her dry clothes, Jessamin searched her daughter's face. Guilt? Surprise? Or was her resigned resentment of another interruption genuine? She couldn't tell. Carla was her mother's daughter, Jessamin thought bitterly. She drew a slow, careful breath. "I created you, Carla. I engineered you as surely as Patrick engineered his selkies." She swallowed, tears knotting her throat, because she had wanted Carla to be good, and she *was*. "I created you to run Tanaka as well as I do, and then I wouldn't let you do it. Paul was right about that much."

"What are you talking about?" Carla sat up straight.

"Did you try to kill me, Carla?"

She had wanted to see the mask drop for just an instant, to read hate perhaps on her daughter's face. What is hate, but the reverse of love, with as much power and as much intimacy? But Carla merely stared from the holo stage, her eyes as hard and unreadable as polished stones, her face still. "No," she said coolly. "Of course I didn't. Although I have considered it."

Jessamin bent her head, surprised by the strength of her disappointment. She had wanted to see . . . *some*thing on her daughter's face. "I thought about killing Kazi," she said softly. "It wasn't necessary, because he was never as good as I am. I crafted you. I made you in my image. Sometimes you have to choose between love and truth," she said softly. "It can be a hell of a choice. So I took the pain of that choice away from you. I made you better than me." Not "as good." Better. Not yet, but soon. Jessamin looked away from her daughter's cold face. "Paul tried to drown me, to make it look like an accident. There was a witness. Do you understand me, Carla?"

"The stupid little boy." Her tone gave nothing away. "I can believe he'd try something insane like that. The jerk."

No, Carla would never have to choose between love and duty. Love would never tip the scale for her. Jessamin wondered if Paul had truly thought he was doing this on his own, without Carla's knowledge. He would have been easy to manipulate. Perhaps it hadn't taken much of a hint at all. Or perhaps Carla hadn't even had to hint. Perhaps Paul *had* done this out of love. Poor fool. Jessamin straightened her shoulders, meeting her daughter's cold eyes. "This . . . affair was handled clumsily. If I choose, I can use it to take Aquaculture away from you forever. Do you understand me?"

"Yes." Carla's voice was steady, but twin spots of color glowed on her cheeks. "I made a mistake."

I made a mistake. The words settled like stones around Jessamin's neck; a necklace that she would wear forever. Jessamin straightened beneath its weight, and managed a cold smile. Next time, Carla wouldn't trust someone else. Next time, she would handle the job herself. You're responsible for your own mistakes, even if you're a Chen. Always. "You'll be good for Tanaka." Jessamin nodded. "You'll take care of the sea to keep Tanaka profitable. God help the Coalition, or anyone else who gets in your way."

"What is the price, Mother?"

Jessamin looked through the hull of the boat, out into the blue murk of the sea. A small school of squid jetted by like a flight of missiles. Alien world. She turned back to the holo stage and bowed; deeply, formally, like Kazuyuki Itano had bowed to her on that long ago afternoon when she had broken his power. "I am resigning." Jessamin suppressed a bitter smile at Carla's carefully neutral expression. Oh yes, she *was* good. "There's a price, of course. First, I want the selkies. I'm going to set up a private firm; a contract labor operation, most likely. I have enough to buy out their contracts without hurting Tanaka. They're a red-ink drain, anyway. We're both recording. I, Jessamin Chen, acknowledge that my resignation is effective as soon as the aforementioned transfer of the Aquatic Specialist contracts is complete."

Carla had gone still. She hadn't expected this. An upfront and open Jessamin Chen must be an unknown quantity to her. And to me, Jessamin thought and smiled. Carla was looking for the trap.

"It's a PR risk to Tanaka," she said at last.

"We'll negotiate it. Our media whiz-kids can work out the details of diverting world attention." It's not a trap, she wanted to say. I can't make up for you, or for Patrick, but maybe I can give his children a chance to grow up. She didn't say it. Carla wouldn't understand.

Carla was nodding, her expression wary, reassured perhaps by the recording. "What about . . . Paul?"

Will you ever put anyone ahead of Tanaka? Jessamin looked into her daughter's cold eyes, looked away. No, she wouldn't. "I'm not going to prosecute." Not with contract negotiations coming up. "I'm going to destroy him personally." Because word got around in the worldweb, and you were either strong or weak, predator or prey. She would never be prey. Jessamin let her breath out in a slow sigh, more tired than she had ever been. Perhaps she was running out of soul.

"Good-bye, Carla, and congratulations on your assumption of Aquaculture. You're going to have one hell of a fight with the Coalition, but you'll win. House? Endit." She turned away as Carla's wary face vanished.

Shira sat on the stairs, out of range of the video pickups, her face as wary and unbelieving as Carla's.

"I just bought your contract." She met Shira's angry young eyes.

"I'm going to form a new firm. Contract labor. Very specialized. We might even get some jobs from Tanaka."

"She tried to kill you." Shira's eyes didn't soften. "You're going to let her go."

"She's good." Jessamin met her stare. "The sea needs her."

"The sea." Shira's voice was low and rough. "That's what matters. Not *us*. The sea."

"That's right," Jessamin said softly. "That's what matters." I wanted you to understand, Patrick. That it mattered to me, too. I thought you did. She closed her eyes briefly.

"What about me?" Shira looked away, her shoulders drooping. "What about the man I killed?"

Too late for him and for Aaron. Almost too late for her. Jessamin sighed for the scared kid behind the angry eyes. "Life isn't fair, and it never will be. You can't just go back to your siblings."

"Another sacrifice?" Shira hunched her shoulders.

"Yes."

"Why shouldn't I just *leave*?" Shira's mouth twisted. "I could live in the sea. I don't need you, or your promises, or any of this shit."

"Aaron needed it," Jessamin said softly. "That's why he died, remember?"

Shira's head drooped. "What difference does it make?" she whispered. "We're *made*. Even if Tanaka wanted to make more of us, there's a moratorium on creating new genens, remember? We get to go extinct in a single generation."

"What?" Jessamin realized her mouth was hanging open, closed it abruptly. "If nobody's pregnant, then someone has used contraceptive implants on you. Don't you *know*?" So. Even within Tanaka, you could find a conspiracy of silence and prejudice. She laughed softly. "Patrick was a perfectionist, and he shared everything with me." Except his love for the sea. She wanted to laugh again, but it would have turned into a sob. "He was creating a new race, Shira, not some refined SCUBA system for Tanaka's workforce. He was playing God. Oh yes, you can get pregnant. You can have a dozen kids, and they'll be just like you. Patrick was good. He was the best." Her voice cracked and she reached out, touched Shira's too-cold cheek. "And I'm the best, too," she said sadly. She touched her fingertips to her lips, tasting salt, like the sea, like the taste of Patrick's skin when they made love. "Carla will take care of the sea," she said softly. "The rest is up to us."

"Us," Shira said slowly. "All right, *us*, then." She hunched her shoulders, then let them drop. "What about me?" she whispered. "The sacrifice."

"It's not hard to add a name and history to a personnel database. Not if you have the access and the talent, and I own better Net operators than Paul. So we'll add a new member to Briard's genen population. A female—assigned as personal caretaker of my so-private boat." She smiled crookedly. "All fish look alike to us grubs, right?" Jessamin stared into the soft turquoise of her alien world. Maybe . . . it hadn't been suicide after all. Maybe his lover had finally claimed him. "You're not just altered humans," she said softly. "You're something new. *Homo aquaticus*. One day, you'll take on Tanaka. And you'll win, because I will have taught you how to win." Sorry, Carla, but I'm better than you. For the moment. Jessamin held out her hand to Shira, palm cringing just a little at the soft alien feel of her folded webbing. *Selkies*. *Homo aquaticus*. "Your children will take the sea away from us," she said sadly. "You won't give them any choice."

THE FOUR
Robert Silverberg

*Humanity huddled in domed undersea cities, exiled from the surface
land, which war had turned into a radioactive hell. The masses were
content with their sealed environment, but four young people wanted to
return to the world above, even if that return could doom their city.*

*More than a mile of dark sea-water roofed the city. It lay off the
Atlantic coast of North America, nestling beneath the waves, cradled by
hundreds of atmospheres of pressure. In the official records, the city's
designation was Undersea Refuge PL-12. But the official records, like the
rest of the landside world, lay blasted and shattered, and the people of
Undersea Refuge PL-12 called their city New Baltimore. Eleven thousand
was New Baltimore's population, a figure set by long-dead landside
authorities and maintained by rigorous policies of control.*

*The history of New Baltimore stretched back for one hundred thirteen
years. Not one of its eleven thousand inhabitants had not been born in
the deep, under the laminated dome that was the city's shield. In the
ninetieth year of New Baltimore a child had been allotted to the Foyle
family, and Mary Foyle was born. And in the hundred thirteenth year of
the city—*

Mary Foyle lay coiled like a fetal snake in her room at the New
Baltimore Social Hall. She lay with feet drawn up, arms locked over
her bosom, eyes closed, mouth slightly open. She was twenty-three,
blonde, terrible in her wrath. She was not asleep.

At the ninth hour of the day and the second of her three-hour Free
Period, she sensed the approach of a visitor, and hatred gathered in

her cold mind. Bitterly, she disengaged herself from what she had been doing, and extended a tendril of thought as far as the door. The mind she encountered was weak, pliable, amiable.

Yes, she thought, Roger Carroll, the silly goose.

Roger's mind formed the thought, Mary, may I come in? and he verbalized as far as "Mary, may—" when she darted a hissing prong of thought at him, and he reddened, cut short his sentence and opened the door.

Lazily Mary Foyle tidied her wrappings and looked up at Roger. He was thin, like all men of New Baltimore, but well muscled and strong. He was a year her junior; gifted like her, with the Powers, but weak of will and flabby of purpose.

"You'll destroy your Powers if you don't give them free play," she thought coldly at him.

"I'm sorry. It was a slip."

She glared bleakly. "Suppose I slipped and blasted your silly mind?"

"Mary, I've never denied that you're more powerful than I am—than all three of us put together—"

"Quiet," she ordered. "The others are coming. Try not to look so much like a blithering fool."

Her mind had detected the arrival of the other two members of their little group. Moments later Roger's slower mind had received the signal, and he added his friendly welcome to Mary's cold one.

Michael Sharp entered first; after him, Tom Devers. They were in their late twenties. In them the Powers had ripened slowly, and Mary had found them out only two years before. Roger had been under her sway for nine years. She herself had first sensed the Powers stirring in her mind fifteen years earlier.

There was a moment of blending as the four minds met—Mary's as always, harshly dominant, never yielding for a moment the superiority that gave her the leadership of the group. The greeting was done with; the Four were as one, and the confines of the room seemed to shrink until it cradled their blended minds as securely as the Dome held back the sea from the buildings of New Baltimore.

"Well?" Mary demanded. The challenge rang out and she sensed Roger's involuntary flinch. "Well?" she asked again, deliberately more strident.

Slowly, sadly, came the response: affirmative from Michael,

affirmative from Tom, weakly affirmative from Roger. A slow smile spread over Mary's face. Affirmative!

Roger's mind added hesitantly, "Of course, there's grave danger—"

"Danger adds spice."

"If we're caught, we're finished—"

Impetuously Mary extended her mind toward Roger's, entered it, made slight adjustments in Roger's endocrine balance. Currents of fear ceased to flow through his body. Trepidation died away.

"All right," Roger said, his mental voice a whisper now. "I agree to join you."

"All agreed, then," Mary said. Her mind enfolded those of the three lean, pale men who faced her. The borders of the small room grew smaller yet, shrank to the size of Mary's skull, then expanded outward.

Four minds linked as one leaped five thousand feet skyward, toward the crisped and blackened land above.

Mary alone could not have done it. She had tried, and much of her bitterness stemmed from the fact that she had failed. She had sent her mind questing out along the sea-bottom, rippling through the coraled ooze to New Chicago and New London and New Miami and the other domed cities that dotted the Atlantic floor. It was strictly illegal for a Sensitive to make contact with the mind of an inhabitant of another Dome, but Mary had never cared much for what the legal authorities said.

She had reached the other cities of the sea-bottom easily enough—though the effort of getting to New London had left her sweat-soaked and panting—but breaking through to the surface eluded her. Time and again she sent shafts skyward, launching beams of thought through the thick blanket of water above, striving to pierce the ocean and see the land, the ruined land deserted and bare, the land made desolate by radiation. She wanted to see the sky in its blueness, and the golden terror of the naked sun.

She failed. Less than a thousand feet from the surface the impulse sagged, the spear of thought blunted and fell back. In the privacy of her room she tried again, and yet again, until her thin clothes were pasted to her body by sweat.

That was when she realized she would need help.

It was a bitter realization. Slowly Mary had sought out those she needed, from the two hundred Sensitives of New Baltimore. Roger she had known for years, and he was as much under her domination as was her hand or her leg. But Roger was not enough. She found Michael and she found Tom, and when rapport had been established she showed them what she proposed to do.

Using them as boosters, as amplifiers, she intended to hurl a psionic signal through the sea to the surface. She could not do it alone; in series, the four of them might do almost anything.

They lay, the four of them, sprawled on couches in Mary's room. With cold fury she whipped them together into the unit she needed. Michael had objected; after all, the penalty for projecting one's mind beyond the borders of New Baltimore was death. But Mary had quashed that objection, welded the Four into One, cajoled and commanded and pleaded and manipulated.

Now, tenuously, the threaded strand of four-ply thought wove toward the surface.

Mary had seen the tridims projected on the arching screens in General Hall. She had an idea of what the surface was like, all blacks and browns and fused glass and gaunt frameworks that had been buildings. But she wanted to see it for herself. She wanted direct visual experience of this surface world, this dead skin of the planet, cauterized by man's evil. Mary had a lively appreciation of evil.

Upward they traveled. Mary sensed Michael and Tom and Roger clinging to her mind, helping her force the impulse upward. Eyes closed, body coiled, she hurled herself to the task.

And the blackness of the water lightened to dark green as the sun-warmed zone approached. She had not got this far on her earlier solo attempts. Now her mind rose with little effort into the upper regions of the sea, and without warning cleaved through the barrier of water into the open air.

Michael and Tom and Roger were still with her.

The sight of landside was dazzling.

The first perception was of the sun; smaller than she had expected, but still an awesome object, glowing high in the metal-blue sky. White clouds lay fleecily under the sun.

New Baltimore was some miles out at sea. Drifting lazily but yet with the near-instantaneous speed of thought, they moved landward, ready and eager to see the desolation and ruin.

The shock was overwhelming.

Together, the Four drifted in from the sea, searching for the radiation-blackened fields, the dead land. Instead they saw delicate greenness, carpets of untrodden grass, vaulting thick trees heavy with fruit. Animals grazed peacefully in the lush fields. In the distance, glimmering in the sun, low sloping mountains decked in green rose slowly from the horizon.

Birds sang. Wind whistled gently through the swaying trees. It was as if the hand of man had never approached this land.

Can the scars have healed so soon? Mary wondered. Hardly a century since the bombings destroyed the surface; could the wounds have been covered so rapidly? In wonder she guided the multiple mind down through the warm sky to the ground.

They came alight in a grassy field, sweet with the odor of springtime. Mary felt the tingle of awe. Beings were approaching, floating over the grass without crushing it—not the misshapen mutants some thought might have survived on the surface, but tall godlike beings, smiling their welcome.

A surge of joy rippled through Mary and through her into her three comrades. It would not be hard to teleport their bodies up from the depths. They could live here, in this pleasant land, quitting the confines of New Baltimore. She extended the range of her perception. In every direction lay beauty and peace, and never a sign of the destruction that had been.

Perhaps there was no war, she thought. The landside people sent our ancestors down into the depths and then hoaxed them.

And for a hundred years we thought the surface was deadly, radiation-seared, unlivable!

For the first time in her life Mary felt no rancor. Bitterness was impossible in this green world of landside. The sun warmed the fertile land, and all was well.

Sudden constricting impulses tugged at the thread of thought by which the four dreamers held contact with landside.

"Mary, wake up! Come out of it."

She struggled, but not even the combined strength of the Four could resist. Inexorably she found herself being dragged away, back down into the depths, into New Baltimore, into wakefulness.

She opened her eyes and sat up. On the other couches, Michael and Tom and Roger were groggily returning to awareness.

The room was crowded. Six members of the New Baltimore Control Force stood by the door, glaring grimly at her.

Mary tried to lash out, but she was outnumbered; they were six of the strongest Sensitives in New Baltimore, and the fierce grip they held on her mind was unbreakable.

"By what right do you come in here?" she asked, using her voice.

It was Norman Myrick of the Control Force who gave the reply: "Mary, we've been watching you for years. You're under arrest on a charge of projecting beyond the boundaries of New Baltimore."

The trial was a farce.

Henry Markell sat in judgment upon them, in the General Hall of the City of New Baltimore. Procedure was simple. Markell, a Sensitive, opened his mind to the accusing members of the Control Force long enough to receive the evidence against the Four.

Then he offered Mary and her three satellites the chance to assert their innocence by opening their minds to him. Sullenly, Mary refused on behalf of the Four. She knew the case was hopeless. If she allowed Markell to peer, their guilt was proven. If she refused, it was an equally tacit admission of guilt. Either way, the penalty loomed. But Mary hoped to retain the integrity of her mind. She had a plan, and a mind-probe would ruin it.

Decision was reached almost immediately after the trial had begun.

Markell said, "I have examined the evidence presented by the Control Force. They have shown that you, Mary, have repeatedly violated our security by making contact with other Domes, and now have inveigled three other Sensitives into joining you for a still bolder attempt. Will you speak now, Mary?"

"We have no defense."

Markell sighed. "You certainly must be aware that our position under the Dome is a vulnerable one. We can never know when the madness that destroyed landside"—Mary smiled knowingly, saying nothing—"will return. We must therefore discourage unofficial contact between Domes by the most severe measures possible. We must retain our position of isolation.

"You, Mary, and your three confederates, have broken this law. The penalty is inevitable. Our borders are rigid here, our population fixed by inexorable boundaries. We cannot tolerate criminals here. The air and food you have consumed up to now is forfeit; four new individuals can be brought into being to replace you. I sentence you to death, you four. This evening you shall be conveyed to the West Aperture and cast through it into the sea."

Mary glared in icy hatred as she heard the death sentence pronounced. Around her, members of the Control Force maintained constant check on her powers, keeping her from loosing a possibly fatal bolt of mental force at the judge or at anyone else. She was straitjacketed. She had no alternative but to submit.

But she had a plan.

They were taken to the West Aperture—a circular sphinctered opening in the framework of the Dome, used only for the purpose of execution. An airlock the size of a man served as the barrier between the pressing tons of the sea and the safety of New Baltimore.

The Four were placed in the airlock, one at a time.

The airlock opened—once, twice, thrice, a fourth time. Mary felt the coolness first, Michael next, then Roger, then Tom. Instantly her mind sought theirs.

"Listen to me! We can save ourselves yet!"

"How? The pressure—"

"Listen! We can link again; teleport ourselves to the surface. You've seen what it's like up there. We can live there. Hurry, join with me!"

"The surface," Roger said. "We can't—"

"We can live there. Hurry!"

Michael objected, "Teleportation takes enormous energy. The backwash will smash the Dome. A whole section of the city will be flooded!"

"What do we care?" Mary demanded. "They condemned us to death, didn't they? Well, I condemn them!"

There was no more time for arguing. Their interchange had taken but a microsecond. They were beginning to drift; in moments, the pressure would kill.

Mary made use of her superior Powers to gather the other three to her. Debating was impossible now. Ruthlessly she drew their minds into hers. She heard Roger's faint protest, but swept it away. For the second time, the Four became One. Mary gathered strength for the giant leap, not even knowing if she could make it but not bothering to consider the possibility of failure now.

Upward.

The passage was instantaneous, as the four minds, linked in an exponential series, ripped upward through the boiling sea toward the surface. Toward the green, warm, fertile surface.

Toward the blackened, seared, radiation-roasted surface.

Mary had only an instant for surprise. The surface was not at all as her mind had viewed it. Congealed rivers of rock wound through the dark fields of ash. The sky hummed with radioactive particles. No life was visible.

Mary dropped to her knees in the blistering ash still warm from the fires of a century before. The heavy particles lanced through her body. How can this be? she wondered. We saw green lands.

An impulse reached her from Roger, dying of radiation to her left:

...fooled you, Mary. Superior to you in one power, anyway. Imaginative projection. I blanked out real image, substituted phony one. You couldn't tell the difference, could you? Happy dying, Mary...

She hissed her hatred and tried to reach him, to rip out his eyes with her nails, but strength failed her. She toppled face-forward, down against the terrible deadly soil of Mother Earth, and waited for the radiation death to overtake her.

Hoaxed, she thought bitterly.

Five thousand feet below, the angry sea, swollen and enraged by the passage of four humans upward through it, crashed against the West Aperture of the New Baltimore Dome, crashed again, finally broke through and came raging in, an equal and opposite reaction. Above, Mary Foyle writhed in death-throes under a leaden sky.

RAY OF LIGHT
Brad R. Torgersen

Very advanced and very unfriendly aliens had completely shut off the light of the sun, freezing the entire Earth and covering its oceans with ice. Humanity survived only in underwater cities, where a younger generation who had never seen the surface world or the sun except in pictures and videos was growing restless...

My crew boss Jake was waiting for me at the sealock door. I'd been eight hours outside, checking for microfractures in the metal hull. Tedious work, that. I'd turned my helmet communicator off so as not to be distracted. The look on Jake's face spooked me.

"What's happened?" I asked him, seawater dripping from the hair of my beard.

"Jenna," was all I got in reply. Which was enough.

I closed my eyes and tried to remain calm, fists balled around the ends of a threadbare terrycloth towel wrapped around my neck.

For a brief instant the hum-and-clank activity of the sub garage went away, and there was only my mental picture of my daughter sitting in her mother's lap. Two, maybe three years old. A delightful nest of unruly ringlets sprouting at odd angles from her scalp. She'd been a mischief-maker from day one—hell on wheels in a confined space like Deepwater 12.

Jenna was much older now, but that particular memory was burned into my brain because it was the last time I remember seeing my wife smile.

"Tell me," I said to my boss.

Jake ran a hand over his own beard. All of us had given up shaving years ago, when the gel, cream, and disposable razors ran out.

"It seems she went for a joyride with another teenager."

"How the hell did they get a sub without someone saying something?"

"The Evans boy, Bart, he's old enough to drive. I've had him on rotation with the other men for a few weeks, to see if he'd take to it. We need all the help we can get."

"Yeah, yeah, skip it, where are they now?"

Jake coughed and momentarily wouldn't meet my gaze.

"We don't know," he said. "I tasked Bart with a trip to Deepwater 4, the usual swap-and-trade run. He's now—they're now—two hours overdue."

"The acoustic transponder on the sub?" I said.

"It's either broken, or they turned it off."

"Good hell, even idiots know not to do that."

Jake just looked at me.

I pivoted on a heel and headed back the way I'd come. With my wet suit still on I didn't have to change. I'd grab the first sub I could muscle out of its cradle. Over my shoulder I said, "Whoever is on the next sortie, tell 'em I'm giving 'em the day off."

"Where are you going to look?" Jake said. "It's thousands of miles of dark water in every direction."

"I know a place," I said. "Jenna told me about it once."

My daughter was four when she first began asking the inevitable questions.

"How come we don't live where it's dry and sunny?"

All three of us were perched at the tiny family table in our little compartment. Lucille didn't even look up from her plate. As if she hadn't heard Jenna at all. Too much of that lately, for my taste. But I opted to not call my wife out on it. Lucille had become hot and cold—either she was screaming mad, or stone quiet. And I'd gotten tired of the screaming, so I settled for the quiet.

Folding my hands thoughtfully in front of me, I considered Jenna's inquiry.

"There isn't anywhere that's dry and sunny. Not anymore."

"But Chloe and Joey are always going to the park to play," Jenna said. "I want to go to the park too."

I grimaced. Chloe and Joey was a kids' show from before...from before everything. Lucille had been loath to let Jenna watch it, but had caved when it became obvious that Chloe and Joey were the only two people—well, animated talking teddy bears actually—capable of getting our daughter to sit still and be silent for any length of time. We'd done what every parent swears they won't do, and the LCD had become our babysitter. Now it was biting us in the butt.

My wife stabbed at the dark green leaves on her plate, the tines on her fork making pronounced *tack!* noises on the scarred plastic.

"There used to be parks," I said. "But everything is covered in ice now. And it's dark, not sunny. You can't even see the sun anymore."

"But why?" Jenna said, her utensils abandoned on the table.

The room lost focus and I briefly remembered my NASA days. Those had been happy times. Washington was pumping money back into the program because the Chinese were threatening to land on the moon.

I'd been on the International Space Station when the aliens abruptly came. It was a gas. I got to pretend I was a celebrity, being interviewed remotely by the news, along with my crewmates.

The mammoth alien ship parked next to us in orbit, for three whole days—a smoothed sphere of nickel-iron, miles and miles in circumference. No obvious drive systems nor apertures for egress. No sign nor sound from them which might have indicated their intentions.

Then the big ship promptly broke orbit and headed inward, toward Venus.

Six months later, the sun began to dim...

"It's hard to explain," I said to Jenna, noting that my wife's fork hovered over her last bit of hydroponic cabbage. "Some people came from another place—another star far away. We thought they would be our friends, but they wouldn't talk to us. They made the sunshine go away, and everything started getting cold really fast."

"They turned off the sun?" Jenna said, incredulous.

"Nothing can turn off the sun," I said. "But they did put something in the way—it blocks the sun's light from reaching Earth, so the surface is too cold for us to live there anymore."

I remembered being ordered down in July. We landed in Florida. It was snowing heavily. NASA had already converted over—by Presidential order—to devising emergency alternatives. The sun had become a shadow of itself, even at high noon. We cobbled together a launch: NASA's final planetary probe, to follow the path of the gargantuan alien ship and find out what was going on.

The probe discovered a mammoth cloud orbiting just inside of Earth's orbit: countless little mirrors, each impossibly thin and impossibly rigid. No alien ship in sight, but the cloud of mirrors was enormous, and growing every day. By themselves, they were nothing. But together they were screening out most of the sun's light. A little bit more gone, every week.

"So now we have to live at the bottom of the ocean?" Jenna asked.

"Yes," I said. "It's the only place warm enough for anything to survive."

Which may or may not have been true. In Iceland they'd put their money on surface habitats constructed near their volcanoes. Chancy gamble. Irregular eruptions made it dangerous, which is why the United States had abandoned the Big Island plan in Hawaii. Besides, assuming enough light was blocked, cryogenic precipitation would be a problem. First the oxygen would rain out, and then, eventually, the nitrogen too. Which is why the United States had also abandoned the Yellowstone plan.

People were dying all over the world when NASA and the Navy began deploying the Deepwater stations. The Russians and Chinese, the Indians, all began doing the same. There was heat at the boundaries between tectonic plates. Life had learned to live without the sun near hydrothermal vents. Humans would have to learn to live there too.

And we did, after a fashion.

I explained this as best as I could to my daughter.

She grew very sad. A tiny, perplexed frown on her face.

"I don't want to watch Chloe and Joey anymore," she said softly.

Lucille's fork clattered onto the floor and she fled the compartment, sobbing.

Number 6's electronics, air circulator, and propulsion motor blended into a single, complaining whine as I pushed the old sub through the eternal darkness along the bottom of the Pacific Ocean. Occasionally I passed one of the black smokers—chimneys made of minerals deposited by the expulsion of superheated water from along the tectonic ridge. The water flowed like ink from the tops of the smokers. Tube worms, white crabs and other life shied away from my lights.

I was watching for the tell-tale smoker formation that Jenna had told me about. It was a gargantuan one, multiple chimneys sprouting into something the kids had dubbed the Gak's Antlers. Dan McDermott had joined the search and was 200 yards behind me, his own lights arrayed in a wide pattern, looking.

We both spotted our target at the same time.

I could see why the kids might have liked the spot. In addition to the bizarre beauty of the Antlers, there was a shallow series of depressions surrounding the base—each just big enough to settle a sub down into. Cozy. Private.

I saw the top of a single sub, just barely poking up over the rock and sand.

I asked Dan to hang back while I pinged them with the short-range sonar. When I got no answer I motored right up to the edge of the depression, turned my exterior lights on extra-bright and aimed them down through the half-sphere pilot's canopy.

I blushed and looked away.

Then I flashed my lights repeatedly until the two occupants inside got the hint and scrambled to get their clothes on. One of them—a girl, I think, though not Jenna—dropped into the driver's seat and flipped a few switches until my short-range radio scratched and coughed at me.

"Hate to ruin your make-out," I said.

"Who are you?" came the girl's tense voice. Too young, I thought.

"Not your father, if it makes any difference," I said.

"How did you get here?"

"Same as you."

A boy's head poked into view. He took the radio mic from the girl.

"Get out of here, this is our place," he said, his young voice cracking with annoyance. I was tempted to tell him to shove his blue balls up his ass, then remembered myself when I'd been that young, coughed quietly into my arm while I steadied my temper, and tried diplomacy.

"I swear," I said. "I won't tell a soul about this little nookie nook. I just want to get my daughter back alive. Jenna Leighton is her name. She's about your age."

"Jenna?" said the girl.

"You know her?"

"I know her name. She's part of the Glimmer Club."

The boy tried to shush her, and take the mic away. "That's a secret!"

"Who cares now?" the girl said. "We're busted anyway."

"What's the Glimmer Club?" I said.

The girl chewed her lip for a moment.

"Please," I said. "It could be life or death."

"It's probably easiest if I just show you," she said. "Give me a few minutes to warm up our blades. I'll tell you what I can once we're under way."

Jenna was six when Lucille went to live on Deepwater 8. At the time, it had seemed reasonable. A chance for my wife to get away from her routine at home, be around some people neither of us had seen in a while, and get the wind back into her sails. It certainly wouldn't be any worse than it had been, with all the bickering and chronic insomnia. The doc had said it would do Lucille some good, so we packed her off and waved goodbye.

On Jenna's bunk wall there was an LCD picture frame that cycled through images, as a night light. I originally loaded it with cartoon characters, but once she swore off Chloe and Joey I let her choose her own photos from the station's substantial digital library.

I was surprised to see her assemble a collection of sunrises, sunsets, and other images of the sun—a thing she'd never seen. At night, I sometimes stood in the hatchway to the absurdly small family lavatory and watched Jenna lying in her blankets, eyes glazed and staring at the images as they gently shuffled past.

"What are you thinking about?" I once asked.

"How come it didn't burn you up?" she said.

"What?"

"Teacher told us the sun is a big giant ball of fire."

"That's true."

"Then why didn't it burn everyone up?"

"It's too far away for that."

"How far?"

"Millions of miles."

"Oh."

A few more images blended from one to the next, in silence.

"Daddy?"

"Yes?" I said, stroking Jenna's forehead.

"Am I ever going to get to see the sun? For real?"

I stopped stroking. It was a hell of a good question. One I wasn't sure I was qualified to know the answer to. Differences between the orbital speed of the mirror cloud and Earth's orbital velocity, combined with dispersion from the light pressure of the solar wind, would get Earth out from behind the death shadow eventually. How long this would take, or if it could happen before the last of us gave out—a few thousand remaining, from a population of over ten billion—was a matter of debate.

"Maybe," I said. "The surface is a giant glacier now. We can't even go up to look at the sky anymore because the ice has closed over the equator and it's too thick for our submarines to get through. If the sun comes back, things will melt. But it will probably take a long, long time."

Jenna turned in her bunk and stared at me, her eyes piercing as they always were when she was thinking.

"Why did the aliens do it?"

I sighed. That was the best question of all.

"Nobody knows," I said. "Some people think the aliens live a long, long time, and that they came to Earth and did this once or twice before."

"But why block out the sunshine? Especially since it killed people?"

"Maybe the aliens didn't know it would kill people. Last time the Earth froze over like it's frozen now, there were no people on the Earth, so the aliens might not have known better."

"But you tried to say hello," she said. "When you were on the space station. You told them you were there. You tried to make friends. They must be really mean, to take the sun away after all you did. The aliens . . . are bullies."

I couldn't argue with that. I'd thought the same thing more than once.

"Maybe they are," I said. "But there's not much we could do about it when they came, and there's not much we can do about it now, other than what we are doing. We've figured out how to live on the sea floor where it's still warm, and where the aliens can't get to us. We'll keep on finding a way to live here—as long as it takes."

I was a bit surprised by the emotion I put into the last few words. Jenna watched me.

I leaned in and kissed her cheek.

"Come on, it's time to sleep. We both have to be up early tomorrow."

"Okay Daddy," she said, smiling slightly. "I wish Mama could give me a kiss goodnight too."

"You and me both," I said.

"Daddy?"

"Yes?"

"Is Mama going to be alright?"

I paused, letting my breath out slowly.

"I sure hope so," I said, settling into the lower bunk beneath my daughter's—a bunk originally built for two, which felt conspicuously empty.

The clubhouse was actually a restored segment of Deepwater 3, long abandoned since the early days of the freeze-up.

Each of the Deepwater stations were built as sectional rings—large titanium cylinders joined at their ends to form spoked hexagons and octagons. Deepwater 3 had been stripped and sat derelict since a decompression accident killed half her crew. We'd taken what could be taken, and left the hulk to the elements.

The kids had really busted their butts getting it livable again.

I admired their chutzpah as I motored alongside the revived segment, its portholes gleaming softly with light. They'd re-rigged a smaller, cobbled-together heat engine to take advantage of the exhaust from the nearby hydrothermal vents, and I was able to mate the docking collar on my sub with the collar on the section as easy as you please.

The girl and boy from the other station didn't stick around to watch. They took me and Dan just far enough for us to see the distant light from the once-dead station, then fled. I didn't ask their names, but I didn't have to. I'd promised them anonymity in exchange for their help, and was eager to get onboard and find out what might have happened to my daughter. So far as I knew, I was the first adult to even hear about this place.

Only, nobody was home.

Dan hung around outside, giving Deepwater 3 a once-over with his lights and sonar, while I slowly went through the reactivated section.

It was a scene from a fantasy world.

They'd used cutting torches to rip out all the bulkheads, leaving only a few, thick support spars intact. The deck had been buried in soft, white, dry sand and the concave ceiling had been painted an almost surreal sky blue. Indirect lights made the ceiling glow, while a huge heat lamp had been welded into the ceiling at one end, glaring down across the "beach" with a mild humming sound. Makeshift beach chairs, beach blankets, and other furniture were positioned here and there, as the kids had seen fit.

Several stand-alone LCD screens had been wired into the walls, with horseshoes of disturbed sand surrounding them. I carefully approached one of the LCDs—my moist suit picking up sand on my feet and legs. Cycling through the LCD's drive I discovered many dozens of movies and television programs. Informational relics from before the aliens came. Videos about flying, and surfing, hiking, camping, and lots and lots of nature shows.

I went to two more LCD screens, and found similar content.

I walked to the middle of the section—realizing that I hadn't stood in a space that unconfined and open since before we'd all gone below—and used my mobile radio to call for Dan.

He hooked up at the docking collar on the opposite end of the section, and came in under the "sun," stopping short and whistling softly.

"Can you believe this?" I said.

Like me, Dan was an oldster from the astronaut days. Though he'd never had any children, nor even a girlfriend, since his wife had died in the mad rush to get to sea when the mirror cloud made life impossible on the surface.

"They've been busy," Dan said. "Is there anyone else here?"

"Not a soul," I said. "Though it looks like they left in a hurry."

"How can you figure?"

"Lights were left on."

I looked around the room again, noting how many teenagers might fit into the space, and the countless prints in the sand, the somewhat disheveled nature of the blankets.

"Frankie and Annette, eat your hearts out," I said.

Dan grunted and smiled. "I was at party or two like that, back in flight school."

"Me too," I admitted. "But something tells me they didn't just come here to get laid. Look at what they've been watching."

"Porn?" Dan said.

"No . . . yes. But not the kind you think."

I flipped on the LCDs and started them up playing whatever video was queued in memory. Instantly, the space was filled with the sound of crashing waves, rock music, images of people sky-diving and hang-gliding, aerial sweeps of the Klondike, the Sahara, all shot on clear days. Very few clouds in the sky. It was nonstop sunshine from screen to screen to screen.

Dan wasn't smiling anymore. He stared at the heat lamp in the ceiling, and the false sky, and then back at the sand.

"You ever go to church when you were a kid?" Dan asked me.

"Not really. Dad was an atheist, and Mom a lapsed Catholic."

"I went to church when I was a kid. Baptist, then Episcopal, then Lutheran. My dad was a spiritual shopper. Anyway, wherever we went, certain things were always the same. The pulpit, the huge bible open to a given scripture, the wooden pews. But more than that, they all felt a certain way. They had a vibe. You didn't have to get the doctrine to understand what the building was meant for."

"What does this have to do with anything, Dan?" I said, getting exasperated.

"Look around, man," Dan said, holding his arms wide. "This is a house of worship."

I stared at everything, not comprehending. Then, suddenly, it hit me.

"The club isn't a club."

"What?"

"The Glimmer Club. That's what she called it. She said many of the younger teens and a few of the older ones had started it up a couple of years ago. Not every kid was a member, but most of the other kids heard rumors. To be a member, you had to swear total secrecy."

My father had tended to consider all religions nuts, but he'd reserved special ire for the ones he called cults: the cracked-up fringe groups with the truly dangerous beliefs. He'd pointed to Jonestown as a textbook example of what could go wrong when people let belief get out of hand.

I experienced a quick chill down my spine.

"They're not coming back," I said.

"Where would they go?" Dan asked.

But I was already running across the sand to the hatch for my sub.

Jenna was ten years old when her mother committed suicide.

Neither of us was there when it happened of course. Lucille had moved around from station to station for her last several months, until the separate crew bosses on each of the stations got fed up with her behavior. Ultimately she put herself into a sea lock without a suit on, and flooded the lock before anyone could stop her. By the time they got the lock dry and could bring her out, she was gone. And I was left trying to explain all of this to Jenna, who cried for 48 hours straight, then slept an additional day in complete physical and emotional exhaustion.

For me, it was painful—but in a detached kind of way. Lucille and I had been coming apart for years. The docs mutually agreed that sunlight deprivation may have been part of the problem. It had happened with several others, all of whom had had to seek light therapy to try to compensate for their depression. In Lucille's case, the light therapy hadn't worked. In fact, nothing had seemed to brake her long, gradual decline into despair. I'd kept hoping Jenna—a mother's instinctive selflessness for the sake of her child—would pull Lucille through. But in hindsight it was clear Jenna had actually made things worse.

These thoughts I kept strictly to myself in the weeks and months that followed Lucille's departure from the living world. I poured myself into my role as Daddy and held Jenna through many a sad night when the bad dreams and missing Mommy got her and there was nobody for Jenna to turn to but me. Eventually the nightmares stopped and Jenna started to get back to her old self—something I was so pleased about I had a difficult time expressing it in words.

For Jenna's 12th birthday I gave her a computer pad I'd squirreled away before committing to the deep. My daughter had been going nuts decorating half the station with chalk drawings—our supply of paper having long since been exhausted. The pad was an artist's model, with several different styli and programs for Jenna to use. It liberated her from the limited medium of diatoms-on-metal, and fairly soon all of the LCDs in our little family compartment were alive with her digital paintings.

It was impressive stuff. She threw herself into it unlike anything I'd ever seen before. Vistas and landscapes, stars and planets, and people. Lots of people. Lots of filtered representations of Lucille, usually sad. I dutifully recorded it all onto the family portable drive where I hoped, perhaps one day, if humanity made it out of this hole alive, Jenna's work might find a wider audience. She'd certainly won over many of the other people on Deepwater 12, and was even getting some nice feedback from some of the other stations as well.

In retrospect, I probably should have seen the obvious.

All of Jenna's art—with rare exception—had one thematic element in common.

It all featured the sun. In one form or another. Sometimes as the focus of the work, but more often as merely an element.

All kids do it, right? The ubiquitous yellow ball in the crayon sky, with yellow lines sprouting out of it? Only, Jenna's suns were warmer, more varied in hue and color. They became characters in their own right. When she discovered how to use the animation software on the pad, she went whole-hog building breathtaking sequences of the sun rising, the sun setting; people and families frolicking beneath our benevolent yellow dwarf star called Sol.

If ever the aliens who'd taken our star from us entered Jenna's mind, it didn't show up in her work. But then, few of us thought of the aliens in any real sense anymore. They'd come, and so far as we knew, they'd gone. Dealing with the repercussions of their single, apocalyptic action had become far, far more important to all of us than dealing with the aliens themselves.

I remembered this as Number 6 creaked and groaned around me, the pressure warning lights letting me know that I was coming up too quickly—risking structural damage if I didn't bleed off pressure differences between the inside and the outside of the sub.

Dan wasn't with me. I'd convinced him to go back and let the others know about the Glimmer Club, and what the kids had done with Deepwater 3 behind our backs. He'd also been tasked with explaining why I'd disobeyed direct orders from a crew boss, risking my life and the old sub to chase a wild hair through the vast, dark ocean.

I couldn't be sure I was right. All I had to go on was a short conversation I'd had with Jenna on her 15th birthday, just a few months earlier.

At that age she spent most of her time with the other teens on the station, as teenagers throughout history have always been prone to do. Old me had stopped being the focus of her attention right about the time she'd hit puberty.

Which was why that particular conversation stood out.

"Dad," she said, "does anyone ever go check anymore?"

"On what?"

"On the surface. Up top."

"We used to send people all the time, but the thicker the ice got—especially when the equator closed over—the less point there seemed to be in it. So I don't think anyone has tried in several years."

"Why not? We can't just give up, can we? I mean, why are we doing any of this if people aren't going to ever go back to the surface?"

She had a good point. I am afraid I hemmed and hawed my way through that one, leaving her with a perplexed and somewhat unhappy expression on her face. If any of her friends had gotten better answers from their parents, I never found out. Though I now suspected that our big failure as adults had been our inability to imagine that our children wouldn't be satisfied to just scratch out a living on the ocean floor.

We who'd been through the freeze-out from the surface, we'd seen the destruction and the death brought by the forever night. We felt fortunate to be where we were. Alive.

But our kids? For them, the ice layer on the surface had become a thing of myth. An impenetrable but invisible bogey monster, forever warned about, but never seen nor experienced. For the Glimmer Club, I suspect, it got to the point where they wondered if all of the adults weren't crazy, or conspiring in a plot. How did anyone really know that the surface was frozen over? That aliens had blocked the sun?

To blindly accept a fundamental social truth upon which everyone agrees, is just part of what makes us human.

But in every era, however dark or desperate, there have also always been hopeful questioners.

I'd not slept for almost two days, and knew it when I caught myself slumped at the controls, chin in my chest; the sub's primitive autopilot beeping plaintively at me.

Sonar pings still didn't show me any subs.

But they hadn't shown me the underside of the ice sheet yet, either.

I used the sub's computer to run some calculations—based on the last known measurements to have been taken on the ice sheet's thickness. I used these to double check where I thought I was, versus what the instruments were telling me, and sat back to ponder.

Assuming the Glimmer Club had ascended as a group, without significant deviation—because the subs only have so much air and battery life to go around—I'd expected to spot them by now. Or at least hear them. Several quick pauses to capture and analyze ambient water noise had yielded depressing silence. Not even the cry of whales filled the sea anymore, because the whales and other sea mammals had all died out together.

If the aliens had had no regard for human sapience, what about the other intelligent creatures who had once called the Earth home?

If ever the oceans re-opened and humans reclaimed the planet, we'd find it an awfully empty place.

Exhausted, I kept going up.

Sonar pingbacks brought me awake the second time. There. A single object, roughly about the size of a sub. It was drifting ever so lazily back toward the bottom.

I spent a few minutes echo-locating, and when I did, my blood ran cold. There was a big crack in the pilot's canopy and the top hatch was hanging open. Dreading what I might find, I pointed my lights into the canopy and examined the interior of the little sub, down its entire length. If I'd expected to see bodies, I was relieved to see only emptiness. Trained from birth to salvage, they'd stripped the sub and continued on.

Wherever that happened to be.

Additional sonar pings sent back nothing. The ocean was silent in all directions, as black and lonely as space had ever been. On instinct alone, I resumed the long voyage to the ice.

The gentle rocking of the sub wasn't what woke me.

It was the occasional thumping against the hull.

I sat straight up, almost ripping my headset off in the process. My neck and back hurt, and my hands were unsteady as I grasped the controls.

No telling how long I'd been out that time. I scanned the control board and the autopilot seemed satisfied. When I saw that the depth gauge read zero, I had to tap the screen a few times. Something had to be wrong. The knocking on the hull suggested I'd found the lower boundary of the ice sheet, where the sea water grudgingly turned to sludge. I'd never actually been up this high since the oceans closed over, so maybe the equipment was wonky this close to the frozen crust?

I hit my lights, but just a few of them because I didn't have all the battery life left in the world.

It took me at least a minute to figure out what I was seeing.

A lapping line of water sloshed halfway up the canopy.

Had I drifted into an air pocket on the underside of the ice?

Scanning upward with the lights revealed nothing but blackness.

But wait, not black blackness. There was a distinct hint of color in the void.

I slowly reached a hand down and flicked the lights off, letting the gentle rocking of the boat and the knocking of the hull fill my ears. The blackness was pinpricked with white dots, and there was a gloaming light in the very far distance. Only, gloaming wasn't the right word. The light slowly but perceptibly began to grow in strength, and the blackness overhead began to graduate from obsidian, to purple, and finally flared into dark blue at the far, far horizon.

No!

My hands were shaking badly. I almost couldn't hit the switch to extend the sub's single, disused radio aerial. A tiny motor whined somewhere behind me, and I waited until the motor stopped before I gently rested my headset back onto my scalp, a gentle hiss of static filling my ears.

I depressed the SEND button on the sub's control stick.

"This is Thomas Leighton speaking for Deepwater 12, the United States. If anyone can hear and understand this broadcast, please respond."

The static crackled lifelessly.

It was a vain hope. My signal couldn't go too far. But I had to try.

"I say again, this is Thomas Leighton speaking—"

"Daddy?"

My breath caught in my throat. It had been a single word, broken by crackling interference. But it was probably the most beautiful word I'd ever heard spoken in my entire life.

"Jenna," I said softly into my mic. "Please tell me that's you?"

"You're just in time," her voice said. If I was relieved beyond words, she sounded excited to the point of bursting. But not because of me.

"Just in time for what?" I said.

"The sun!" she said. "We got here just as it was going down and had to spend the night on the surface. We opened the top hatches and the air is breathable! Very cold, but breathable. Oh Daddy, we knew it. We all knew it. I'm so glad you're here with us."

"Where the hell is here, Jenna, I can't see another soul."

"Go out on top and take a look," was all she said.

It took me a minute to get the interior hatch to Number 6's stubby sail open, then I climbed up the short ladder, banging side to side in the tight tunnel as the sub kept rocking. At the top hatch I paused, hands on the locking wheel. Nobody had breathed fresh air in almost two decades. Had I merely imagined my daughter's voice? It certainly was true I'd been in better mental states. Sleep deprivation will do that to you.

But I'd certainly come too far to stop. So, what the hell?

The wheel complained, then spun, and there was a hiss as the last bit of pressure difference bled off from the inside of the sub to the outside. If I'd done it right when I came up, I'd not get the bends—no deadly nitrogen bubbles in the blood. If I'd done it wrong...too late now.

Jenna had been right. The air was brutally frigid, and moving fast. Almost a wind. But also so invigorating that I pulled myself up all the way out of the sail and rested my butt on the edge of the hatch. I looked out across the rolling sea of slushy ice—which appeared to extend for many, many miles in all directions.

I also saw the sails of the other subs. Four of them. The kids on those boats waved to me, and I waved back with both arms. If I'd been promising myself at the start of this trip that I'd skin Jenna alive when I found her, that anger had long since melted into a bewildering feeling of astonished wonderment.

Because Jenna was right. The sun certainly was coming up.

And not an apparitional, atrophied sun; as we'd all seen in the last days before going to sea.

This was the real deal.

It crested the horizon like a phoenix, a blast of yellow-orange rays shooting across the sky and into the belly of a bank of clouds to our west. The clouds lit up brilliantly, and there was a raucous cheer from the other subs—all the kids out on deck to see the miracle.

I suddenly found myself cheering too. No, howling. I was on my feet, dangerously close to toppling off the sail and into the slush below, but I couldn't make it stop. I yelled until my voice was hoarse.

I looked around and saw all the kids standing, hips and knees rocking in time to the rhythm of their bobbing craft, eyes closed and arms stretching out to the sky, waiting... waiting...

I suddenly knew what they were waiting for. I did the same.

When the rays hit my skin—old, dark, and wrinkled—my nerves exploded with warmth. Stupendous, almost orgasmic warmth. No electric heater was capable of creating such a feeling.

I came back to myself and thought I saw my daughter waving to me from the sails of one of the other subs.

I jumped into the icy sea, and swam in great strokes.

Pulling myself out onto the back of Jenna's sub, I ignored the smiling but reserved faces of the other teenagers and used handrails on the sail to pull myself up to Jenna's level.

I didn't ask if it was okay for a hug, as I'd been doing since she'd turned 13.

She had to politely tap my shoulders to get me to release her.

"Sorry," I said, noting that water from my beard had gotten her face wet.

"It's okay," she said, wiping it with her palms.

"I found the clubhouse," I said. "I was afraid that you—all of you—had gone off and done something really stupid."

Jenna looked down.

"Are you mad that I didn't tell you?"

"At first," I said. "But it doesn't matter now. This is ... this is just ... incredible."

The sun had gained in the sky. The old, dark neoprene of my wet suit was growing hot and uncomfortable. I unzipped and pulled my arms and head out of the top, letting it drape around my waist. Delicious rays of light bathed my exposed, gray-haired chest. An unreasoning, almost explosive feeling of giddiness had seized me, and

I had to fight to maintain my bearing as the kids on the sub—all the kids on all the subs—began laughing and shoving each other into the water, paddling about and crooning like seals.

"Have you been in contact with anyone else?" I asked.

"We kept trying the radio," Jenna said, never moving away from my arm which had found its way protectively around her shoulders. "But you were the first person we heard."

"I wonder how many of the satellites still work," I said, looking up into the fantastically, outrageously blue sky. "We could rig a dish, one of the old VSAT units. I think we still have some down below..."

"We aren't going back," Jenna said suddenly, detaching herself.

I looked at my daughter.

"Where else can you possibly go?"

"We don't care, Dad. We're just not going back there. We swore it amongst the group. All of us."

"And what if the ice had still been solid? What would you have done then?" I said, a burst of sea wind suddenly giving me goosebumps.

"We don't know."

"You're goddamned lucky there was a gap to get through. Air to breathe. I am not sure any of us have enough oxygen or battery power to get all the way back down. Jenna, for all I knew, you and the others were going to get yourselves killed."

Jenna didn't meet my gaze.

"Somebody had to do something," she said. "We had to know if there was a chance the sun had returned. We hoped. We hoped so much. You and Jake and the others—everybody from before the freeze-up—it was like you'd all given up. Everyone determined not to die, but also determined not to live, either."

I nodded my head, slowly.

"So what's the plan now?" I asked.

She looked up at me, smiling again.

"Baja."

"What?"

"The Baja Peninsula is supposed to be a couple hundred miles northeast of here. We'll sail until we hit the shore."

"And if you simply hit the pack ice?"

"We'll leave the subs, and keep going."

"Do you have any idea what you're saying? Where's your food, where's your water, what kind of clothes do any of you have? What—"

"We're not going back, Daddy!"

She'd shouted it at me, her fists balled on my chest.

"Okay, okay," I said, thinking. "But consider this. You all stand a much better chance if you have help. Now that we know the ice is clearing and the air is breathable—and that the sun is back out again, by God—we can bring the others up. All of the Deepwater crews, and the stations too. It will take time, but if we do it in an organized, methodical fashion, we'll all stand a better chance of making land. Though I am not quite sure what we can expect to find when we get there."

Some of the other kids had pulled themselves out of the water to come listen to me talk. A few of them were nodding their heads in agreement.

"If you want," I said to them, looking around, "I'll be the one to go back down. But I'll need to get some air and electric power off these other subs first. I sure hope you all brought enough food to last a week or two. It's going to be at least that long, or longer, before anyone else comes up from below."

I went back down with what few reserves the kids could give me, about nine hundred digital pictures of the open water, the marvelously full sun, and the blue, blue sky—and a hell of a lot of hope in my heart.

It wouldn't be easy. Not all of the adults would want to believe me, at first. And raising the stations after so long at depth was liable to be even more dangerous than sinking them had been in the first place.

But I suspected Jenna was right. We couldn't go back. Not after what I'd just seen.

So I slowly dropped back down, gently, gently. Like a feather. The old sub wouldn't last a fast trip to the bottom, just as it wouldn't have lasted a fast trip to the top.

And though the darkness had resumed its hold, I felt light as a bird on the breeze.

Three days later, I stood in Deepwater 12's sub garage.

Dan had dutifully spread the word ahead of me, and he was in a crowd of adults as I slowly climbed down off Number 6's sail.

"You didn't find them," Jake said sternly. I could sense his extreme piss-off as I walked across the deck towards the group. Discipline was vital on the Deepwater crews, and I'd violated that discipline so extremely, I'd be lucky if Jake didn't bust my nose for me.

"Oh, I found 'em all right," I said.

"Dead?" Dan said, voice raised slightly.

"No," I said. "Take a look."

I tossed Dan the camera I'd used on the surface.

He looked at me questioningly, and I just looked back.

Dan turned the camera over, its little LCD screen exposed, and flipped the switch to slide show.

Adults crowded around Dan, including Jake.

They gasped in unison.

"It can't be," Dan said, voice caught in his throat.

"It is," I said. "And if you all don't mind, my daughter is waiting for us to join her up top. We've got a land expedition that needs support. I promised her I'd get her and the other kids the help they'd need to make it successful."

Dan cycled through the pictures and began playing one of the video files I'd also shot. The camera's little speaker blared loudly laughing, shouting teens and the sloshing of water against the hull of the sub I'd been standing on when I took the footage.

I noted tears falling down the faces of many of my compatriots. And for a tiny instant, I wished that Lucille had lived long enough to see this.

No matter. Lucille was a memory, but it was apparent I'd given the living something they'd desperately needed, without even knowing it. Just as much as I'd desperately needed it when I first opened Number 6's top hatch and smelled the tangy, frigid salt air whipping through my hair.

Jake, the crew boss, was shouting orders—with a wide smile on his face—while the camera made its way reverently from hand to hand.

I looked up at the ceiling, my eyes glazing and my spirit going up through the black deep to the top where Jenna waited. Hang on, little one. Dad'll be back soon.

THE GIFT OF GAB
Jack Vance

The planet's aquatic inhabitants seemed to have no language, so were considered only animals of low intelligence. It would be a pity, but perfectly legal, if an unscrupulous company drove them into extinction—unless a team of scientists could communicate with the endangered aliens.

Middle afternoon had come to the Shallows. The wind had died; the sea was listless and spread with silken gloss. In the south a black broom of rain hung under the clouds; elsewhere the air was thick with pink murk. Thick crusts of seaweed floated over the Shallows; one of these supported the Bio-Minerals raft, a metal rectangle two hundred feet long, a hundred feet wide.

At four o'clock an air horn high on the mast announced the change of shift. Sam Fletcher, assistant superintendent, came out of the mess hall, crossed the deck to the office, slid back the door, and looked in. The chair in which Carl Raight usually sat, filling out his production report, was empty. Fletcher looked back over his shoulder, down the deck toward the processing house, but Raight was nowhere in sight. Strange. Fletcher crossed the office, checked the day's tonnage:

Rhodium trichloride	4.01
Tantalum sulfide	0.87
Tripyridyl rhenichloride	0.43

The gross tonnage, by Fletcher's calculations, came to 5.31—an average shift. He still led Raight in the Pinch Bottle Sweepstakes.

Tomorrow was the end of the month; Fletcher could hardly fail to make off with Raight's Haig and Haig. Anticipating Raight's protests and complaints, Fletcher smiled and whistled through his teeth. He felt cheerful and confident. Another month would bring to an end his six-month contract; then it was back to Starholme with six months' pay to his credit.

Where in thunder was Raight? Fletcher looked out the window. In his range of vision was the helicopter—guyed to the deck against the Sabrian line-squalls—the mast, the black hump of the generator, the water tank, and at the far end of the raft, the pulverizers, the leaching vats, the Tswett columns, and the storage bins.

A dark shape filled the door. Fletcher turned, but it was Agostino, the day-shift operator, who had just now been relieved by Blue Murphy, Fletcher's operator.

"Where's Raight?" asked Fletcher.

Agostino looked around the office. "I thought he was in here."

"I thought he was over in the works."

"No, I just came from there."

Fletcher crossed the room and looked into the washroom. "Wrong again."

Agostino turned away. "I'm going up for a shower." He looked back from the door. "We're low on barnacles."

"I'll send out the barge." Fletcher followed Agostino out on deck and headed for the processing house.

He passed the dock where the barges were tied up and entered the pulverizing room. The No. 1 Rotary was grinding barnacles for tantalum; the No. 2 was pulverizing rhenium-rich sea slugs. The ball mill waited for a load of coral, orange-pink with nodules of rhodium salts.

Blue Murphy, who had a red face and a meager fringe of red hair, was making a routine check of bearings, shafts, chains, journals, valves, and gauges. Fletcher called in his ear to be heard over the noise of the crushers. "Has Raight come through?"

Murphy shook his head.

Fletcher went on, into the leaching chamber where the first separation of salts from pulp was effected, through the forest of Tswett tubes, and once more out onto the deck. No Raight. He must have gone on ahead to the office.

But the office was empty.

Fletcher continued around to the mess hall. Agostino was busy with a bowl of chili. Dave Jones, the hatchet-faced steward, stood in the doorway to the galley.

"Raight been here?" asked Fletcher.

Jones, who never used two words when one would do, gave his head a morose shake.

Agostino looked around. "Did you check the barnacle barge? He might have gone out to the shelves." Fletcher looked puzzled.

"What's wrong with Mahlberg?"

"He's putting new teeth on the drag-line bucket."

Fletcher tried to recall the line-up of barges along the dock. If Mahlberg the barge tender had been busy with repairs, Raight might well have gone out himself. Fletcher drew himself a cup of coffee. "That's where he must be." He sat down. "It's not like Raight to put in free overtime." Mahlberg came into the mess hall. "Where's Carl? I want to order some more teeth for the bucket."

Mahlberg laughed at the joke. "Catch himself a nice wire eel maybe. Or a dekabrach."

Dave Jones grunted. "He'll cook it himself."

"Seems like a dekabrach should make good eatin'," said Mahlberg, "close as they are to a seal."

"Who likes seal?" growled Jones.

"I'd say they're more like mermaids," Agostino remarked, "with ten-armed starfish for heads."

Fletcher put down his cup. "I wonder what time Raight left?"

Mahlberg shrugged; Agostino looked blank.

"It's only an hour out to the shelves. He ought to be back by now."

"He might have had a breakdown," said Mahlberg.

"Though the barge has been running good."

Fletcher rose to his feet. "I'll give him a call." He left the mess hall and returned to the office, where he dialed T3 on the intercom screen—the signal for the barnacle barge.

The screen remained blank.

Fletcher waited. The neon bulb pulsed off and on, indicating the call of the alarm on the barge.

No reply.

Fletcher felt a vague disturbance. He left the office, went to the mast, and rode up the man-lift to the cupola. From here he could overlook the half-acre of raft, the five-acre crust of seaweed, and a great circle of ocean.

In the far northeast distance, up near the edge of the Shallows, the new Pelagic Recoveries raft showed as a small dark spot, almost smeared from sight by the haze. To the south, where the Equatorial Current raced through a gap in the Shallows, the barnacle shelves were strung out in a long loose line. To the north, where the Macpherson Ridge, rising from the Deeps, came within thirty feet of breaking the surface, aluminum piles supported the sea-slug traps. Here and there floated masses of seaweed, sometimes anchored to the bottom, sometimes maintained in place by the action of the currents.

Fletcher turned his binoculars along the line of barnacle shelves and spotted the barge immediately. He steadied his arms, screwed up the magnification, and focused on the control cabin. He saw no one, although he could not hold the binoculars steady enough to make sure.

Fletcher scrutinized the rest of the barge.

Where was Carl Raight? Possibly in the control cabin, out of sight?

Fletcher descended to the deck, went around to the processing house, and looked in. "Hey, Blue!"

Murphy appeared, wiping his big red hands on a rag.

"I'm taking the launch out to the shelves," said Fletcher. "The barge is out there, but Raight doesn't answer the screen."

Murphy shook his big bald head in puzzlement. He accompanied Fletcher to the dock, where the launch floated at moorings. Fletcher heaved at the painter, swung in the stern of the launch, and jumped down on the deck.

Murphy called down to him, "Want me to come along? I'll get Hans to watch the works." Hans Heinz was the engineer-mechanic.

Fletcher hesitated. "I don't think so. If anything's happened to Raight—well, I can manage. Just keep an eye on the screen. I might call back in."

He stepped into the cockpit, seated himself, closed the dome over his head, and started the pump.

The launch rolled and bounced, picked up speed, shoved its blunt nose under the surface, then submerged till only the dome was clear.

Fletcher disengaged the pump; water rammed in through the nose and was converted to steam, then spat aft.

Bio-Minerals became a gray blot in the pink haze, while the

outlines of the barge and the shelves became hard and distinct, and gradually grew large. Fletcher de-staged the power; the launch surfaced and coasted up to the dark hull, where it grappled with magnetic balls that allowed barge and launch to surge independently on the slow swells.

Fletcher slid back the dome and jumped up to the deck of the barge. "Raight! Hey, Carl!"

There was no answer.

Fletcher looked up and down the deck. Raight was a big man, strong and active but there might have been an accident. Fletcher walked down the deck toward the control cabin. He passed the No. 1 hold, heaped with black-green barnacles. At the No. 2 hold the boom was winged out, with the grab engaged on a shelf, ready to hoist it clear of the water.

The No. 3 hold was still unladen. The control cabin was empty.

Carl Raight was nowhere aboard the barge.

He might have been taken off by helicopter or launch, or he might have fallen over the side. Fletcher made a slow check of the dark water in all directions. He suddenly leaned over the side, trying to see through the surface reflections. But the pale shape under the water was a dekabrach, long as a man, sleek as satin, moving quietly about its business.

Fletcher looked thoughtfully to the northeast, where the Pelagic Recoveries raft floated behind a curtain of pink murk. It was a new venture, only three months old, owned and operated by Ted Chrystal, former biochemist on the Bio-Minerals raft. The Sabrian Ocean was inexhaustible; the market for metal was insatiable; the two rafts were in no sense competitors. By no stretch of imagination could Fletcher conceive Chrystal or his men attacking Carl Raight.

He must have fallen overboard.

Fletcher returned to the control cabin and climbed the ladder to the flying bridge on top. He made a last check of the water around the barge, although he knew it to be a useless gesture—the current, moving through the gap at a steady two knots, would have swept Raight's body out over the Deeps. Fletcher scanned the horizon. The line of shelves dwindled away into the pink gloom. The mast on the Bio-Minerals raft marked the sky to the northwest. The Pelagic Recoveries raft could not be seen. There was no living creature in sight.

The screen signal sounded from the cabin. Fletcher went inside. Blue Murphy was calling from the raft. "What's the news?"

"None whatever," said Fletcher.

"What do you mean?"

"Raight's not out here."

The big red face creased. "Just who is out there?"

"Nobody. It looks like Raight fell over the side."

Murphy whistled. There seemed nothing to say. Finally he asked, "Any idea how it happened?"

Fletcher shook his head. "I can't figure it out."

Murphy licked his lips. "Maybe we ought to close down."

"Why?" asked Fletcher.

"Well—reverence to the dead, you might say."

Fletcher grinned humorlessly. "We might as well keep running."

"Just as you like. But we're low on the barnacles."

"Carl loaded a hold and a half." Fletcher hesitated, heaved a deep sigh. "I might as well shake in a few more shelves."

Murphy winced. "It's a squeamish business, Sam. You haven't a nerve in your body."

"It doesn't make any difference to Carl now," said Fletcher. "We've got to scrape barnacles some time. There's nothing to be gained by moping."

"I suppose you're right," said Murphy dubiously.

"I'll be back in a couple hours."

"Don't go overboard like Raight, now."

The screen went blank. Fletcher reflected that he was in charge, superintendent of the raft, until the arrival of the new crew, a month away. Responsibility, which he did not particularly want, was his.

He went slowly back out on deck and climbed into the winch pulpit. For an hour he pulled sections of shelves from the sea, suspending them over the hold while scraper arms wiped off the black-green clusters, then slid the shelves back into the ocean. Here was where Raight had been working just before his disappearance. How could he have fallen overboard from the winch pulpit?

Uneasiness inched along Fletcher's nerves, up into his brain. He shut down the winch and climbed down from the pulpit. He stopped short, staring at the rope on the deck.

It was a strange rope, glistening, translucent, an inch thick. It lay in a loose loop on the deck, and one end led over the side. Fletcher started down, then hesitated. Rope?

Certainly none of the barge's equipment.

Careful, thought Fletcher.

A hand scraper hung on the king post, a tool like a small adz. It was used for manual scraping of the shelves, if for some reason the automatic scrapers failed. It was two steps distant, across the rope. Fletcher stepped down to the deck. The rope quivered; the loop contracted, snapped around Fletcher's ankles.

Fletcher lunged and caught hold of the scraper. The rope gave a cruel jerk; Fletcher sprawled flat on his face, and the scraper jarred out of his hands. He kicked, struggled, but the rope drew him easily toward the gunwale. Fletcher made a convulsive grab for the scraper, barely reaching it. The rope was lifting his ankles to pull him over the rail.

Fletcher strained forward, hacking at it again and again.

The rope sagged, fell apart, and snaked over the side.

Fletcher gained his feet and staggered to the rail. Down into the water slid the rope, out of sight among the oily reflections of the sky. Then, for half a second, a wavefront held itself perpendicular to Fletcher's line of vision.

Three feet under the surface swam a dekabrach. Fletcher saw the pink-golden cluster of arms, radiating like the arms of a starfish, the black patch at their core which might be an eye.

Fletcher drew back from the gunwale, puzzled, frightened, oppressed by the nearness of death. He cursed his stupidity, his reckless carelessness; how could he have been so undiscerning as to remain out here loading the barge? It was clear from the first that Raight could never have died by accident.

Something had killed Raight, and Fletcher had invited it to kill him, too. He limped to the control cabin and started the pumps. Water was sucked in through the bow orifice and thrust out through the vents. The barge moved out away from the shelves. Fletcher set the course to northwest, toward Bio-Minerals, then went out on deck.

Day was almost at an end; the sky was darkening to maroon; the gloom grew thick as bloody water. Gideon, a dull red giant, largest of Sabria's two suns, dropped out of the sky.

For a few minutes only the light from blue-green Atreus played on the clouds. The gloom changed its quality to pale green, which by some illusion seemed brighter than the previous pink. Atreus sank and the sky went dark.

Ahead shone the Bio-Minerals masthead light, climbing into the sky as the barge approached. Fletcher saw the black shapes of men outlined against the glow. The entire crew was waiting for him: the two operators, Agostino and Murphy; Mahlberg the barge tender, Damon the bio-chemist, Dave Jones the steward, Manners the technician, Hans Heinz the engineer.

Fletcher docked the barge, climbed the soft stairs hacked from the wadded seaweed, and stopped in front of the silent men. He looked from face to face. Waiting on the raft they had felt the strangeness of Raight's death more vividly than he had: so much showed in their expressions.

Fletcher, answering the unspoken question, said, "It wasn't an accident. I know what happened."

"What?" someone asked.

"There's a thing like a white rope," said Fletcher. "It slides up out of the sea. If a man comes near it, it snakes around his leg and pulls him overboard."

Murphy asked in a hushed voice, "You're sure?"

"It just about got me."

Damon the biochemist asked in a skeptical voice, "A live rope?"

"I suppose it might have been alive."

"What else could it have been?"

Fletcher hesitated. "I looked over the side. I saw dekabrachs. One for sure, maybe two or three others."

There was silence. The men looked out over the water.

Murphy asked in a wondering voice, "Then the dekabrachs are the ones?"

"I don't know," said Fletcher in a strained sharp voice.

"A white rope, or fiber, nearly snared me. I cut it apart. When I looked over the side I saw dekabrachs."

The men made hushed noises of wonder and awe.

Fletcher turned away and started toward the mess hall. The men lingered on the dock, examining the ocean, talking in subdued voices. The lights of the raft shone past them, out into the darkness. There was nothing to be seen.

Later in the evening Fletcher climbed the stairs to the laboratory over the office, to find Eugene Damon busy at the microfilm viewer.

Damon had a thin, long-jawed face, lank blond hair, a fanatic's eyes. He was industrious and thorough, but he worked in the shadow of Ted Chrystal, who had quit Bio-Minerals to bring his own raft to Sabria. Chrystal was a man of great ability. He had adapted the vanadium-sequestering sea slug of Earth to Sabrian waters; he had developed the tantalum barnacle from a rare and sickly species into the hardy, high-yield producer that it was. Damon worked twice the hours that Chrystal had put in, and while he performed his routine duties efficiently, he lacked the flair and imaginative resource which Chrystal used to leap from problem to solution without apparent steps in between.

He looked up when Fletcher came into the lab, then turned back to the microscreen.

Fletcher watched a moment. "What are you looking for?" he asked presently.

Damon responded in the ponderous, slightly pedantic manner that sometimes amused, sometimes irritated Fletcher.

"I've been searching the index to identify the long white rope which attacked you."

Fletcher made a noncommittal sound and went to look at the settings on the microfile throw-out. Damon had coded for "long," "thin," "white." On these instructions, the selector, scanning the entire roster of Sabrian life forms, had pulled the cards of seven organisms.

"Find anything?" Fletcher asked.

"Not so far." Damon slid another card into the viewer. *Sabrian Annelid*, RRS-4924, read the title, and on the screen appeared a schematic outline of a long segmented worm. The scale showed it to be about two and a half meters long.

Fletcher shook his head. "The thing that got me was four or five times that long. And I don't think it was segmented."

"That's the most likely of the lot so far," said Damon. He turned a quizzical glance up at Fletcher. "I imagine you're pretty sure about this—long white marine rope?"

Fletcher, ignoring him, scooped up the seven cards, dropped them back into the file, then looked in the code book and reset the selector.

Damon had the codes memorized and was able to read directly off the dials. "'Appendages'—long—dimensions D, E, F, G.'"

The selector kicked three cards into the viewer.

The first was a pale saucer which swam like a skate, trailing four long whiskers. "That's not it," said Fletcher.

The second was a black, bullet-shaped water beetle, with a posterior flagellum.

"Not that one."

The third was a kind of mollusk, with a plasm based on selenium, silicon, fluorine, and carbon. The shell was a hemisphere of silicon carbide with a hump from which protruded a thin prehensile tendril.

The creature bore the name "Stryzkal's Monitor," after Esteban Stryzkal, the famous pioneer taxonomist of Sabria.

"That might be the guilty party," said Fletcher.

"It's not mobile," objected Damon. "Stryzkal finds it anchored to the North Shallows pegmatite dikes, in conjunction with the dekabrach colonies."

Fletcher was reading the descriptive material. "'The feeler is elastic without observable limit, and apparently functions as a food-gathering, spore-disseminating, exploratory organ. The monitor typically is found near the dekabrach colonies. Symbiosis between the two life forms is not impossible.'"

Damon looked at him questioningly. "Well?"

"I saw some dekabrachs out along the shelves."

"You can't be sure you were attacked by a monitor," Damon said dubiously. "After all, they don't swim."

"So they don't," said Fletcher, "according to Stryzkal."

Damon started to speak, then, noticing Fletcher's expression, said in a subdued voice, "Of course there's room for error. Not even Stryzkal could work out much more than a summary of planetary life."

Fletcher had been reading the screen. "Here's Chrystal's analysis of the one he brought up."

They studied the elements and primary compounds of a Stryzkal Monitor's constitution.

"Nothing of commercial interest," said Fletcher.

Damon was absorbed in a personal chain of thought. "Did Chrystal actually go down and trap a monitor?"

"That's right. In the water bug. He spent lots of time underwater."

"Everybody to their own methods," said Damon shortly.

Fletcher dropped the cards back in the file. "Whether you like him or not, he's a good field man. Give the devil his due."

"It seems to me that the field phase is over and done with," muttered Damon. "We've got the production line set up; it's a full-time job trying to increase the yield. Of course I may be wrong."

Fletcher laughed, slapped Damon on his skinny shoulder.

"I'm not finding fault, Gene. The plain fact is that there're too many avenues for one man to explore. We could keep four men busy."

"Four men?" said Damon. "A dozen is more like it. Three different protoplasmic phases on Sabria, to the single carbon group on Earth! Even Stryzkal only scratched the surface!" He watched Fletcher for a while, then asked curiously:

"What are you after now?"

Fletcher was once more running through the index. "What I came in here to check. The dekabrachs."

Damon leaned back in his chair. "Dekabrachs? Why?"

"There're lots of things about Sabria we don't know," said Fletcher mildly. "Have you ever been down to look at a dekabrach colony?"

Damon compressed his mouth. "No. I certainly haven't."

Fletcher dialed for the dekabrach card.

It snapped out of the file into the viewer. The screen showed Stryzkal's original photo-drawing, which in many ways conveyed more information than the color stereos. The specimen depicted was something over six feet long, with a pale, seal-like body terminating in three propulsive vanes.

At the head radiated the ten arms from which the creature derived its name—flexible members eighteen inches long, surrounding the black disk which Stryzkal had assumed to be an eye.

Fletcher skimmed through the rather sketchy account of the creature's habitat, diet, reproductive methods, and protoplasmic classification. He frowned in dissatisfaction. "There's not much information here considering that they're one of the more important species. Let's look at the anatomy." The dekabrach's skeleton was based on an anterior dome of bone with three flexible cartilaginous vertebrae, each terminating in a propulsive vane.

The information on the card came to an end. "I thought you said Chrystal made observations on the dekabrachs," growled Damon.

"So he did."

"If he's such a howling good field man, where's his data?"

Fletcher grinned. "Don't blame me, I just work here." He put the card through the screen again.

Under General Comments, Stryzkal had noted, "Dekabrachs appear to belong in the Sabrian Class A group, the silico-carbo-nitride phase, although they deviate in important respects." He had added a few lines of speculation regarding relationships of dekabrachs to other Sabrian species.

Chrystal had merely made the notation, "Checked for commercial application; no specific recommendation."

Fletcher made no comment.

"How closely did he check?" asked Damon.

"In his usual spectacular way. He went down in the water bug, harpooned one of them, and dragged it to the laboratory. Spent three days dissecting it."

"Precious little he's noted here," grumbled Damon. "If I worked three days on a new species like the dekabrachs, I could write a book."

They watched the information repeat itself.

Damon stabbed at the screen with his long bony finger.

"Look! That's been blanked over. See those black triangles in the margin? Cancellation marks!"

Fletcher rubbed his chin. "Stranger and stranger."

"It's downright mischievous," Damon cried indignantly, "erasing material without indicating motive or correction."

Fletcher nodded slowly. "It looks like somebody's going to have to consult Chrystal." He considered. "Well—why not now?" He descended to the office, where he called the Pelagic Recoveries raft.

Chrystal himself appeared on the screen. He was a large blond man with blooming pink skin and an affable innocence that camouflaged the directness of his mind; his plumpness similarly disguised a powerful musculature. He greeted Fletcher with cautious heartiness. "How's it going on Bio-Minerals? Sometimes I wish I was back with you fellows—this working on your own isn't all it's cracked up to be."

"We've had an accident over here," said Fletcher. "I thought I'd better pass on a warning."

"Accident?" Chrystal looked anxious. "What's happened?"

"Carl Raight took the barge out—and never came back."

Chrystal was shocked. "That's terrible! How . . . why—"

"Apparently something pulled him in. I think it was a monitor mollusk—Stryzkal's Monitor."

Chrystal's pink face wrinkled in puzzlement. "A monitor? Was the barge over shallow water? But there wouldn't be water that shallow. I don't get it."

"I don't either."

Chrystal twisted a cube of white metal between his fingers.

"That's certainly strange. Raight must be dead?"

Fletcher nodded somberly. "That's the presumption. I've warned everybody here not to go out alone; I thought I'd better do the same for you."

"That's decent of you, Sam." Chrystal frowned, looked at the cube of metal, and put it down. "There's never been trouble on Sabria before."

"I saw dekabrachs under the barge. They might be involved somehow."

Chrystal looked blank. "Dekabrachs? They're harmless enough."

Fletcher nodded noncommittally. "Incidentally, I tried to check on dekabrachs in the microlibrary. There wasn't much information. Quite a bit of material has been canceled out."

Chrystal raised his pale eyebrows. "Why tell me?"

"Because you might have done the canceling."

Chrystal looked aggrieved. "Now, why should I do something like that? I worked hard for Bio-Minerals, Sam—you know that as well as I do. Now I'm trying to make money for myself. It's no bed of roses, I'll tell you." He touched the cube of white metal, then noticing Fletcher's eyes on it, pushed it to the side of his desk, against Cosey's *Universal Handbook of Constants and Physical Relationships.*

After a pause Fletcher asked, "Well, did you or didn't you blank out part of the dekabrach story?"

Chrystal frowned in deep thought. "I might have canceled one or two ideas that turned out bad—nothing very important. I have a hazy idea that I pulled them out of the bank."

"Just what were those ideas?" Fletcher asked in a sardonic voice.

"I don't remember offhand. Something about feeding habits, probably. I suspected that the deks ingested plankton, but that doesn't seem to be the case."

"No?"

"They browse on underwater fungus that grows on the coral banks. That's my best guess."

"Is that all you cut out?"

"I can't think of anything more."

Fletcher's eyes went back to the cube of metal. He noticed that it covered the *Handbook* title from the angle of the *v* in *Universal* to the center of the *o* in *of*. "What's that you've got on your desk, Chrystal? Interesting yourself in metallurgy?"

"No, no," said Chrystal. He picked up the cube and looked at it critically. "Just a bit of alloy. Well, thanks for calling, Sam."

"You don't have any personal ideas on how Raight got it?"

Chrystal looked surprised. "Why on earth do you ask me?"

"You know more about the dekabrachs than anyone else on Sabria."

"I'm afraid I can't help you, Sam."

Fletcher nodded. "Good night."

"Good night, Sam."

Fletcher sat looking at the blank screen. Monitor mollusks, dekabrachs—the blanked microfilm. There was a drift here whose direction he could not identify. The dekabrachs seemed to be involved, and, by association, Chrystal.

Fletcher put no credence in Chrystal's protestations; he suspected that Chrystal lied as a matter of policy, on almost any subject. Fletcher's mind went to the cube of metal.

Chrystal had seemed rather too casual, too quick to brush the matter aside. Fletcher brought out his own *Handbook*. He measured the distance between the fork of the *v* and the center of the *o*: 4.9 centimeters. Now, if the block represented a kilogram mass, as was likely with such sample blocks—Fletcher calculated. In a cube, 4.9 centimeters on a side, were 119 cc. Hypothesizing a mass of 1,000 grams, the density worked out to 8.4 grams per cc.

Fletcher looked at the figure. In itself it was not particularly suggestive. It might be one of a hundred alloys. There was no point in going too far on a string of hypotheses—still, he looked in the *Handbook*. Nickel, 8.6 grams per cc. Cobalt, 8.7 grams per cc. Niobium, 8.4 grams per cc.

Fletcher sat back and considered. Niobium? An element costly and tedious to synthesize, with limited natural sources and an unsatisfied market. The idea was stimulating. Had Chrystal developed a biological source of niobium? If so, his fortune was made.

Fletcher relaxed in his chair. He felt done in—mentally and physically. His mind went to Carl Raight. He pictured the body drifting loose and haphazard through the night, sinking through miles of water into places where light would never reach. Why had Carl Raight been plundered of his life?

Fletcher began to ache with anger and frustration at the futility, the indignity of Raight's passing. Carl Raight was too good a man to be dragged to his death into the dark ocean of Sabria.

Fletcher jerked himself upright and marched out of the office, up the steps to the laboratory.

Damon was still busy with his routine work. He had three projects under way: two involving the sequestering of platinum by species of Sabrian algae; the third was an attempt to increase the rhenium absorption of an Alphard-Alpha flat-sponge. In each case his basic technique was the same: subjecting succeeding generations to an increasing concentration of metallic salt, under conditions favoring mutation. Certain of the organisms would presently begin to make functional use of the metal; they would be isolated: and transferred to Sabrian brine. A few might survive the shock; some might adapt to the new conditions and begin to absorb the now necessary element.

By selective breeding the desirable qualities of these latter organisms would be intensified; they would then be cultivated on a large-scale basis, and the inexhaustible Sabrian waters would presently be made to yield another product.

Coming into the lab, Fletcher found Damon arranging trays of algae cultures in geometrically exact lines. He looked rather sourly over his shoulder at Fletcher.

"I talked to Chrystal," said Fletcher.

Damon became interested. "What did he say?"

"He says he might have wiped a few bad guesses off the film."

"Ridiculous," snapped Damon.

Fletcher went to the table, looking thoughtfully along the row of algae cultures. "Have you run into any niobium on Sabria, Gene?"

"Niobium? No. Not in any appreciable concentration. There are traces in the ocean, naturally. I believe one of the corals shows a set of niobium lines." He cocked his head with birdlike inquisitiveness. "Why do you ask?"

"Just an idea, wild and random."

"I don't suppose Chrystal gave you any satisfaction."

"None at all."

"Then what's the next move?"

Fletcher hitched himself up on the table. "I'm not sure. There's not much I can do. Unless—" He hesitated.

"Unless what?"

"Unless I make an underwater survey myself."

Damon was appalled. "What do you hope to gain by that?"

Fletcher smiled. "If I knew, I wouldn't need to go. Remember, Chrystal went down, then he came back up and stripped the microfile."

"I realize that," said Damon. "Still, I think it's rather... well, foolhardy, after what's happened."

"Perhaps, perhaps not." Fletcher slid off the table to the deck. "I'll let it ride till tomorrow, anyway."

He left Damon making out his daily check sheet and descended to the main deck.

Blue Murphy was waiting at the foot of the stairs. Fletcher said, "Well, Murphy?"

The round red face displayed a puzzled frown. "Agostino up there with you?"

Fletcher stopped short. "No."

"He should have relieved me half an hour ago. He's not in the dormitory. He's not in the mess hall."

"Good God," said Fletcher. "Another one?"

Murphy looked over his shoulder at the ocean. "They saw him about an hour ago in the mess hall."

"Come on," said Fletcher. "Let's search the raft."

They looked everywhere—processing house, the cupola on the mast, all the nooks and crannies a man might take it into his head to explore. The barges were all at dock; the launch and catamaran swung at their moorings; the helicopter hulked on the deck with drooping blades.

Agostino was nowhere aboard the raft. No one knew where Agostino had gone; no one knew exactly when he had left.

The crew of the raft collected in the mess hall, making small nervous motions, looking out the portholes over the ocean.

Fletcher could think of very little to say. "Whatever is after us— and we don't know what it is—it can surprise us and it's watching. We've got to be careful—more than careful!"

Murphy pounded his fist softly on the table. "But what can we do? We can't just stand around like silly cows!"

"Sabria is theoretically a safe planet," said Damon. "According to Stryzkal and the Galactic Index, there are no hostile life forms here."

Murphy snorted, "I wish old Stryzkal was here now to tell me."

"He might be able to theorize back Raight and Agostino."

Dave Jones looked at the calendar. "A month to go."

"We'll only run one shift," said Fletcher, "until we get replacements."

"Call them reinforcements," muttered Mahlberg.

"Tomorrow," said Fletcher, "I'm going to take the water bug down, look around, and get an idea what's going on. In the meantime, everybody better carry hatchets or cleavers."

There was soft sound on the windows and on the deck outside. "Rain," said Mahlberg. He looked at the clock on the wall. "Midnight."

The rain hissed through the air, drummed on the walls; the decks ran with water and the masthead lights glared through the slanting streaks.

Fletcher went to the streaming windows and looked toward the process house. "I guess we better button up for the night. There's no reason to—" He squinted through the window, then ran to the door and out into the rain.

Water pelted into his face. He could see very little but the glare of the lights in the rain. And a hint of white along the shining gray-black of the deck, like an old white plastic hose.

A snatch at his ankles: his feet were yanked from under him. He fell flat upon the streaming metal.

Behind him came the thud of feet; there were excited curses, a clang and scrape; the grip on Fletcher's ankles loosened.

Fletcher jumped up, staggering back against the mast.

"Something's in the process house," he yelled.

The men pounded off through the rain. Fletcher came after.

But there was nothing in the process house. The doors were wide; the rooms were bright. The squat pulverizers stood on either hand;

behind were the pressure tanks, the vats, the pipes of six different colors.

Fletcher pulled the master switch; the hum and grind of the machinery died. "Let's lock up and get back to the dormitory."

Morning was the reverse of evening; first the green gloom of Atreus, warming to pink as Gideon rose behind the clouds.

It was a blustery day, with squalls trailing dark curtains all around the compass.

Fletcher ate breakfast, dressed in a skin-tight coverall threaded with heating filaments, then a waterproof garment with a plastic head-dome.

The water bug hung on davits at the east edge of the raft, a shell of transparent plastic with the pumps sealed in a metal cell amidships. Submerging, the hull filled with water through valves, which then closed; the bug could submerge to four hundred feet, the hull resisting about half the pressure, the enclosed water the rest.

Fletcher lowered himself into the cockpit; Murphy connected the hoses from the air tanks to Fletcher's helmet, then screwed the port shut. Mahlberg and Hans Heinz winged out the davits. Murphy went to stand by the hoist control; for a moment he hesitated, looking from the dark, pink-dappled water to Fletcher, and back at the water.

Fletcher waved his hand. "Lower away." His voice came from the loudspeaker on the bulkhead behind them.

Murphy swung the handle. The bug eased down. Water gushed in through the valves, up around Fletcher's body, over his head. Bubbles rose from the helmet exhaust valve.

Fletcher tested the pumps, then cast off the grapples. The bug slanted down into the water.

Murphy sighed. "He's got more nerve than I'm ever likely to have."

"He can get away from whatever's after him," said Damon.

"He might well be safer than we are here on the raft."

Murphy clapped him on the shoulder. "Damon, my lad you can climb. Up on top of the mast you'll be safe; it's unlikely that they'll come there to tug you into the water." Murphy raised his eyes to the cupola a hundred feet over the deck. "And I think that's where I'd take myself—if only someone would bring me my food."

Heinz pointed to the water. "There go the bubbles. He went under the raft. Now he's headed north."

The day became stormy. Spume blew over the raft, and it meant a drenching to venture out on deck. The clouds thinned enough to show the outlines of Gideon and Atreus, a blood orange and a lime. Suddenly the winds died; the ocean flattened into an uneasy calm. The crew sat in the mess hall drinking coffee, talking in staccato and uneasy voices.

Damon became restless and went up to his laboratory. He came running back down into the mess hall. "Dekabrachs—they're under the raft! I saw them from the observation deck!"

Murphy shrugged. "They're safe from me."

"I'd like to get hold of one," said Damon. "Alive."

"Don't we have enough trouble already?" growled Dave Jones.

Damon explained patiently. "We know nothing about dekabrachs. They're a highly developed species. Chrystal destroyed all the data we had, and I should have at least one specimen."

Murphy rose to his feet. "I suppose we can scoop one up in a net."

"Good," said Damon. "I'll set up the big tank to receive it." The crew went out on deck where the weather had turned sultry. The ocean was flat and oily; haze blurred sea and sky together in a smooth gradation of color, from dirty scarlet near the raft to pale pink overhead.

The boom was winged out; a parachute net was attached and lowered quietly into the water. Heinz stood by the winch; Murphy leaned over the rail, staring intently down into the water.

A pale shape drifted out from under the raft. "Lift!" bawled Murphy.

The line snapped taut; the net rose out of the water in a cascade of spray. In the center a six-foot dekabrach pulsed and thrashed, gill slits rasping for water.

The boom swung inboard; the net tripped; the dekabrach slid into the plastic tank.

It darted forward and backward; the plastic dented and bulged where it struck. Then it floated quiet in the center, head-tentacles folded back against the torso.

All hands crowded around the tank. The black eye-spot looked back through the transparent walls.

Murphy asked Damon, "Now what?"

"I'd like the tank lifted to the deck outside the laboratory where I can get at it."

"No sooner said than done."

The tank was hoisted and swung to the spot Damon had indicated. Damon went excitedly off to plan his research.

The crew watched the dekabrach for ten or fifteen minutes, then drifted back to the mess hall.

Time passed. Gusts of wind raked up the ocean into a sharp steep chop. At two o'clock the loudspeaker hissed; the crew stiffened and raised their heads.

Fletcher's voice came from the diaphragm. "Hello aboard the raft. I'm about two miles northwest. Stand by to haul me aboard."

"Ha!" cried Murphy, grinning. "He made it."

"I gave odds against him of four to one," Mahlberg said. "I'm lucky nobody took them."

"Get a move on. He'll be alongside before we're ready." The crew trooped out to the landing. The water bug came sliding over the ocean, its glistening back riding the dark disorder of the waters.

It slipped quietly up to the raft; grapples clamped to the plates fore and aft. The winch whined and the bug was lifted from the sea, draining its ballast of water.

Fletcher, in the cockpit, looked tense and tired. He climbed stiffly out of the bug, stretched, unzipped the waterproof suit, and pulled off the helmet.

"Well, I'm back." He looked around the group. "Surprised?"

"I'd have lost money on you," Mahlberg told him.

"What did you find out?" asked Damon. "Anything?"

Fletcher nodded. "Plenty. Let me get into clean clothes. I'm wringing wet—sweat." He stopped short, looking up at the tank on the laboratory deck. "When did that come aboard?"

"We netted it about noon," said Murphy. "Damon wanted to look one over."

Fletcher stood looking up at the tank with his shoulders drooping. "Something wrong?" asked Damon.

"No," said Fletcher. "We couldn't have it worse than it is already." He turned away toward the dormitory.

The crew waited for him in the mess hall; twenty minutes later he appeared. He drew himself a cup of coffee and sat down.

"Well," said Fletcher. "I can't be sure—but it looks as if we're in trouble."

"Dekabrachs?" asked Murphy.

Fletcher nodded.

"I knew it!" Murphy cried in triumph. "You can tell by looking at the blatherskites they're up to no good."

Damon frowned, disapproving of emotional judgments. "Just what is the situation?" he asked Fletcher. "At least, as it appears to you."

Fletcher chose his words carefully. "Things are going on that we've been unaware of. In the first place, the dekabrachs are socially organized."

"You mean to say—they're intelligent?"

Fletcher shook his head. "I don't know for sure. It's possible. It's equally possible that they live by instinct, like social insects."

"How in the world—" began Damon.

Fletcher held up a hand. "I'll tell you just what happened; you can ask all the questions you like afterwards." He drank his coffee.

"When I went down under, naturally I was on the alert and kept my eyes peeled. I felt safe enough in the water bug—but funny things have been happening, and I was a little nervous.

"As soon as I was in the water I saw the dekabrachs—five or six of them." Fletcher paused, sipped his coffee.

"What were they doing?" asked Damon.

"Nothing very much. Drifting near a big monitor which had attached itself to the seaweed. The arm was hanging down like a rope clear out of sight. I edged the bug in just to see what the deks would do; they began backing away. I didn't want to waste too much time under the raft, so I swung off north, toward the Deeps. Halfway there I saw an odd thing; in fact, I passed it, and swung around to take another look.

"There were about a dozen deks. They had a monitor—and this one was really big. A giant. It was hanging on a set of balloons or bubbles—some kind of pods that kept it floating, and the deks were easing it along. In this direction."

"In this direction, eh?" mused Murphy.

"What did you do?" asked Manners.

"Well, perhaps it was all an innocent outing—but I didn't want to take any chances. The arm of this monitor would be like a hawser. I turned the bug at the bubbles, burst some, scattered the rest. The monitor dropped like a stone. The deks took off in different directions.

I figured I'd won that round. I kept on going north, and pretty soon I came to where the slope starts down into the Deeps. I'd been traveling about twenty feet under; now I lowered to two hundred. I had to turn on the lights, of course this red twilight doesn't penetrate water too well." Fletcher took another gulp of coffee. "All the way across the Shallows I'd been passing over coral banks and dodging forests of kelp. Where the shelf slopes down to the Deeps the coral gets to be something fantastic—I suppose there's more water movement, more nourishment, more oxygen. It grows a hundred feet high, in spires and towers, umbrellas, platforms, arches white, pale blue, pale green.

"I came to the edge of a cliff. It was a shock—one minute my lights were on the coral, all these white towers and pinnacles then there was nothing. I was over the Deeps. I got a little nervous." Fletcher grinned. "Irrational, of course. I checked the fathometer—bottom was twelve thousand feet down. I still didn't like it, and I turned around and swung back. Then I noticed lights off to my right. I turned my own off and moved in to investigate. The lights spread out as if I was flying over a city—and that's just about what it was."

"Dekabrachs?" asked Damon.

Fletcher nodded. "Dekabrachs."

"You mean—-they built it themselves? Lights and all?"

Fletcher frowned. "That's what I can't be sure of. The coral had grown into shapes that gave them little cubicles to swim in and out of, and do whatever they'd want to do in a house. Certainly they don't need protection from the rain. They hadn't built these coral grottoes in the sense that we build a house—but it didn't look like natural coral either. It's as if they made the coral grow to suit them."

Murphy said doubtfully, "Then they're intelligent."

"No, not necessarily. After all, wasps build complicated nests with no more equipment than a set of instincts."

"What's your opinion?" asked Damon. "Just what impression does it give?"

Fletcher shook his head. "I can't be sure. I don't know what kind of standards to apply. 'Intelligence' is a word that means lots of different things, and the way we generally use it is artificial and specialized."

"I don't get you," said Murphy. "Do you mean these deks are intelligent or don't you?"

Fletcher laughed. "Are men intelligent?"

"Sure. So they say, at least."

"Well, what I'm trying to get across is that we can't use man's intelligence as a measure of the dekabrach's mind. We've got to judge him by a different set of values—dekabrach values. Men use tools of metal, ceramic, fiber: inorganic stuff—at least, dead. I can imagine a civilization dependent upon living tools—specialized creatures the master group uses for special purposes. Suppose the dekabrachs live on this basis? They force the coral to grow in the shape they want. They use the monitors for derricks, or hoists, or snares, or to grab at something in the upper air."

"Apparently, then," said Damon, "you believe that the dekabrachs are intelligent."

Fletcher shook his head. "Intelligence is just a word—a matter of definition. What the deks do may not be susceptible to human definition."

"It's beyond me," said Murphy, settling back in his chair.

Damon pressed the subject. "I am not a metaphysician or a semanticist. But it seems that we might apply, or try to apply, a crucial test."

"What difference does it make one way or the other?" asked Murphy.

Fletcher said, "It makes a big difference where the law is concerned."

"Ah," said Murphy, "the Doctrine of Responsibility."

Fletcher nodded. "We could be yanked off the planet for injuring or killing intelligent autochthons. It's been done."

"That's right," said Murphy. "I was on Alkaid Two when Graviton Corporation got in that kind of trouble."

"So if the deks are intelligent, we've got to watch our step. That's why I looked twice when I saw the dek in the tank."

"Well—are they or aren't they?" asked Mahlberg.

"There's one crucial test," Damon repeated.

The crew looked at him expectantly.

"Well?" asked Murphy. "Spill it."

"Communication."

Murphy nodded thoughtfully. "That seems to make sense." He looked at Fletcher. "Did you notice them communicating?"

Fletcher shook his head. "Tomorrow I'll take a camera out, and a sound recorder. Then we'll know for sure."

"Incidentally," said Damon, "why were you asking about niobium?"

Fletcher had almost forgotten. "Chrystal had a chunk of it on his desk. Or maybe he did—I'm not sure."

Damon nodded. "Well, it may be a coincidence, but the deks are loaded with it."

Fletcher stared.

"It's in their blood, and there's a strong concentration in the interior organs."

Fletcher sat with his cup halfway to his mouth. "Enough to make a profit on?"

Damon nodded. "Probably a hundred grams or more in the organism."

"Well, well," said Fletcher. "That's very interesting indeed."

Rain roared down during the night; a great wind came up, lifting and driving the rain and spume. Most of the crew had gone to bed: all except Dave Jones the steward and Manners the radio man, who sat up over a chess board.

A new sound rose over the wind and rain—a metallic groaning, a creaking discord that presently became too loud to ignore. Manners jumped to his feet and went to the window.

"The mast!"

Dimly it could be seen through the rain, swaying like a reed, the arc of oscillation increasing with each swing.

"What can we do?" cried Jones.

One set of guy lines snapped. "Nothing now."

"I'll call Fletcher." Jones ran for the passage to the dormitory.

The mast gave a sudden jerk, poised long seconds at an unlikely angle, then toppled across the process house.

Fletcher appeared and went over and stared out the window. With the masthead light no longer shining down, the raft was dark and ominous. Fletcher shrugged and turned away. "There's nothing we can do tonight. It's worth a man's life to go out on that deck."

In the morning, examination of the wreckage revealed that two of the guy lines had been sawed or clipped cleanly through. The mast, of lightweight construction, was quickly cut apart, and the twisted segments dragged to a corner of the deck. The raft seemed bald and flat.

"Someone or something," said Fletcher, "is anxious to give us as much trouble as possible." He looked across the leaden-pink ocean to where the Pelagic Recoveries raft floated beyond the range of vision.

"Apparently," said Damon, "you refer to Chrystal."

"I have suspicions."

Damon glanced out across the water. "I'm practically certain."

"Suspicion isn't proof," said Fletcher. "In the first place, what would Chrystal hope to gain by attacking us?"

"What would the dekabrachs gain?"

"I don't know," said Fletcher. "I'd like to find out." He went to dress himself in the submarine suit.

The water bug was made ready. Fletcher plugged a camera into the external mounting and connected a sound recorder to a sensitive diaphragm in the skin. He seated himself and pulled the blister over his head.

The water bug was lowered into the ocean. It filled with water, and its glistening back disappeared under the surface.

The crew patched the roof of the process house, then jury-rigged an antenna.

The day passed; twilight came, and plum-colored evening.

The loudspeaker hissed and sputtered; Fletcher's voice, tired and tense, said, "Stand by. I'm coming in."

The crew gathered by the rail, straining their eyes through the dusk.

One of the dully glistening wave-fronts held its shape, drew closer, and became the water bug.

The grapples were dropped; the water bug drained its ballast and was hoisted into the chocks.

Fletcher jumped down to the deck and leaned limply against one of the davits. "I've had enough submerging to last me a while."

"What did you find out?" Damon asked anxiously.

"I've got it all on film. I'll run it off as soon as my head stops ringing."

Fletcher took a hot shower, then came down to the mess hall and ate the bowl of stew Jones put in front of him, while Manners transferred the film Fletcher had shot from camera to projector.

"I've made up my mind about two things," said Fletcher.

"First—the deks are intelligent. Second, if they communicate with each other, it's by means imperceptible to human beings."

Damon blinked, surprised and dissatisfied. "That's almost a contradiction."

"Just watch," said Fletcher. "You can see for yourself." Manners started the projector; the screen went bright.

"The first few feet show nothing very much," said Fletcher.

"I drove directly out to the end of the shelf and cruised along the edge of the Deeps. It drops away like the end of the world—straight down. I found a big colony about ten miles west of the one I found yesterday—almost a city."

"'City' implies civilization," Damon asserted in a didactic voice.

Fletcher shrugged. "If civilization means manipulation of environment—somewhere I've heard that definition—they're civilized."

"But they don't communicate?"

"Check the film for yourself."

The screen was dark with the color of the ocean. "I made a circle out over the Deeps," said Fletcher, "turned off my lights, started the camera, and came in slow."

A pale constellation appeared in the center of the screen, separating into a swarm of sparks. They brightened and expanded; behind them appeared the outlines, tall and dim, of coral minarets, towers, spires, and spikes. They defined themselves as Fletcher moved closer. From the screen came Fletcher's recorded voice. "These formations vary in height from fifty to two hundred feet, along a front of about half a mile."

The picture expanded. Black holes showed on the face of the spires; pale dekabrach-shapes swam quietly in and out.

"Notice," said the voice, "the area in front of the colony. It seems to be a shelf, or a storage yard. From up here it's hard to see; I'll drop down a hundred feet or so." The picture changed; the screen darkened. "I'm dropping now—depth meter reads three hundred sixty feet . . . three eighty . . . I can't see too well; I hope the camera is getting it all."

Fletcher commented: "You're seeing it better now than I could; the luminous areas in the coral don't shine too strongly down there."

The screen showed the base of the coral structures and a nearly level bench fifty feet wide. The camera took a quick swing and peered down over the verge, into blackness.

"I was curious," said Fletcher. "The shelf didn't look natural. It isn't. Notice the outlines on down? They're just barely perceptible. The shelf is artificial—a terrace, a front porch."

The camera swung back to the bench, which now appeared to be marked off into areas vaguely differentiated in color.

Fletcher's voice said, "Those colored areas are like plots in a garden—there's a different kind of plant, or weed, or animal on each of them. I'll come in closer. Here are monitors." The screen showed two or three dozen heavy hemispheres, then passed on to what appeared to be eels with saw edges along their sides, attached to the bench by a sucker.

Next were float-bladders, then a great number of black cones with very long loose tails.

Damon said in a puzzled voice, "What keeps them there?"

"You'll have to ask the dekabrachs," said Fletcher.

"I would if I knew how."

"I still haven't seen them do anything intelligent," said Murphy.

"Watch," said Fletcher.

Into the field of vision swam a pair of dekabrachs, black eye-spots staring out of the screen at the men in the mess hall.

"Dekabrachs," came Fletcher's voice from the screen.

"Up to now, I don't think they noticed me," Fletcher himself commented. "I carried no lights and made no contrast against the background. Perhaps they felt the pump." The dekabrachs turned together and dropped sharply for the shelf.

"Notice," said Fletcher. "They saw a problem, and the same solution occurred to both, at the same time. There was no communication."

The dekabrachs had diminished to pale blurs against one of the dark areas along the shelf.

"I didn't know what was happening," said Fletcher, "but I decided to move. And then—the camera doesn't show this—I felt bumps on the hull, as if someone were throwing rocks. I couldn't see what was going on until something hit the dome right in front of my face. It was a little torpedo, with a long nose like a knitting needle. I took off fast, before the deks could try something else."

The screen went black. Fletcher's voice said, "I'm out over the

Deeps, running parallel with the edge of the Shallows." Indeterminate shapes swam across the screen, pale wisps blurred by watery distance. "I came back along the edge of the shelf," said Fletcher, "and found the colony I saw yesterday."

Once more the screen showed spires, tall structures, pale blue, pale green, ivory. "I'm going in close," came Fletcher's voice. "I'm going to look in one of those holes." The towers expanded; ahead was a dark hole.

"Right here I turned on the nose-light," said Fletcher. The black hole suddenly became a bright cylindrical chamber fifteen feet deep. The walls were lined with glistening colored globes, like Christmas tree ornaments. A dekabrach floated in the center of the chamber. Translucent tendrils ending in knobs extended from the chamber walls and seemed to be punching and kneading the creature's seal-smooth hide.

"The dek doesn't seem to like me looking in on him," said Fletcher.

The dekabrach backed to the rear of the chamber; the knobbed tendrils jerked away, into the walls.

"I looked into the next hole."

Another black hole became a bright chamber as the searchlight burnt in. A dekabrach floated quietly, holding a sphere of pink jelly before its eye. The wall-tendrils were not to be seen.

"This one didn't move," said Fletcher. "He was asleep or hypnotized or too scared. I started to take off and there was the most awful thump. I thought I was a goner." The image on the screen gave a great lurch. Something dark hurled past and on into the depths.

"I looked up," said Fletcher. "I couldn't see anything but about a dozen deks. Apparently they'd floated a big rock over me and dropped it. I started the pump and headed for home." The screen went blank.

Damon was impressed. "I agree that they show patterns of intelligent behavior. Did you detect any sounds?"

"Nothing. I had the recorder going all the time. Not a vibration other than the bumps on the hull."

Damon's face was wry with dissatisfaction. "They must communicate somehow—how could they get along otherwise?"

"Not unless they're telepathic," said Fletcher. "I watched carefully. They make no sounds or motions to each other—none at all."

Manners asked, "Could they possibly radiate radio waves? Or infrared?"

Damon said glumly, "The one in the tank doesn't."

"Oh, come now," said Murphy, "are there no intelligent races that don't communicate?"

"None," said Damon. "They use different methods—sounds, signals, radiation—but they all communicate."

"How about telepathy?" Heinz suggested.

"We've never come up against it; I don't believe we'll find it here," said Damon.

"My personal theory," said Fletcher, "is that they think alike and so don't need to communicate."

Damon shook his head dubiously.

"Assume that they work on a basis of communal empathy," Fletcher went on, "that this is the way they've evolved. Men are individualistic; they need speech. The deks are identical; they're aware of what's going on without words." He reflected a few seconds. "I suppose, in a certain sense, they do communicate. For instance, a dek wants to extend the garden in front of its tower. It possibly waits till another dek comes near, then carries out a rock—indicating what it wants to do."

"Communication by example," said Damon.

"That's right—if you can call it communication. It permits a measure of cooperation—but clearly no small talk, no planning for the future or traditions from the past."

"Perhaps not even awareness of time!" cried Damon.

"It's hard to estimate their native intelligence. It might be remarkably high or it might be low; the lack of communication must be a terrific handicap."

"Handicap or not," said Mahlberg, "they've certainly got us on the run."

"And why?" cried Murphy, pounding the table with his big red fist. "That's the question. We've never bothered them. And all of a sudden Raight's gone, and Agostino. Also our mast. Who knows what they'll think of tonight? Why? That's what I want to know."

"That," said Fletcher, "is a question I'm going to put to Ted Chrystal tomorrow."

Fletcher dressed himself in clean blue twill, ate a silent breakfast, and went out to the flight deck.

Murphy and Mahlberg had thrown the guy lines off the helicopter and wiped the dome clean of salt-film.

Fletcher climbed into the cabin and twisted the inspection knob. Green light—everything in order.

Murphy said, half-hopefully, "Maybe I better come with you, Sam—if there's any chance of trouble."

"Trouble? Why should there be trouble?"

"I wouldn't put much past Chrystal."

"I wouldn't either," said Fletcher. "But—there won't be any trouble."

He started the blades. The ram-tubes caught hold; the 'copter lifted and slanted up, away from the raft, and flew off to the northeast. Bio-Minerals became a bright tablet on the irregular wad of seaweed.

The day was dull, brooding, windless, apparently building up for one of the tremendous electrical storms that came every few weeks. Fletcher accelerated, hoping to get his errand over with as soon as possible.

Miles of ocean slid past; Pelagic Recoveries appeared ahead.

Twenty miles southwest of the raft, Fletcher overtook a small barge laden with raw material for Chrystal's macerators and leaching columns; he noticed that there were two men aboard, both huddled inside the plastic canopy. Pelagic Recoveries perhaps was having its troubles too, thought Fletcher.

Chrystal's raft was little different from Bio-Minerals, except that the mast still rose from the central deck, and there was activity in the process house. They had not shut down, whatever their troubles.

Fletcher landed the 'copter on the flight deck. As he stopped the blades, Chrystal came out of the office—a big blond man with a round, jocular face.

Fletcher jumped down to the deck. "Hello, Ted," he said in a guarded voice.

Chrystal approached with a cheerful smile. "Hello, Sam! Long time since we've seen you." He shook hands briskly. "What's new at Bio-Minerals? Certainly too bad about Carl."

"That's what I want to talk about." Fletcher looked around the deck. Two of the crew stood watching. "Can we go to your office?"

"Sure, by all means." Chrystal led the way to the office, slid back the door. "Here we are."

Fletcher entered the office. Chrystal walked behind his desk. "Have a seat." He sat down in his own chair. "Now—what's on your mind? But first, how about a drink? You like Scotch, as I recall."

"Not today, thanks." Fletcher shifted in his chair. "Ted, we're up against a serious problem here on Sabria, and we might as well talk plainly about it."

"Certainly," said Chrystal. "Go right ahead."

"Carl Raight's dead. And Agostino."

Chrystal's eyebrows rose in shock. "Agostino, too? How?"

"We don't know. He just disappeared."

Chrystal took a moment to digest the information. Then he shook his head in perplexity. "I can't understand it. We've never had trouble like this before."

"Nothing happening over here?"

Chrystal frowned. "Well—nothing to speak of. Your call put us on our guard."

"The dekabrachs seem to be responsible."

Chrystal blinked and pursed his lips, but said nothing.

"Have you been going out after dekabrachs, Ted?"

"Well now, Sam—" Chrystal hesitated, drumming his fingers on the desk. "That's hardly a fair question. Even if we were working with dekabrachs or polyps or club moss or wire eels—I don't think I'd want to say, one way or the other."

"I'm not interested in your business secrets," said Fletcher. "The point is this: the deks appear to be an intelligent species. I have reason to believe that you're processing them for their niobium content. Apparently they're doing their best to retaliate and don't care who they hurt. They've killed two of our men. I've got a right to know what's going on."

Chrystal nodded. "I can understand your viewpoint—but I don't follow your chain of reasoning. For instance, you told me that a monitor had done Raight in. Now you say dekabrach. Also, what leads you to believe I'm going for niobium?"

"Let's not try to kid each other, Ted." Chrystal looked shocked, then annoyed. "When you were still working for Bio-Minerals," Fletcher went on, "you discovered that the deks were full of niobium. You wiped all that information out of the files, got financial backing, and built this raft. Since then you've been hauling in dekabrachs."

Chrystal leaned back, surveying Fletcher coolly. "Aren't you jumping to conclusions?"

"If I am, all you've got to do is deny it."

"Your attitude isn't very pleasant, Sam."

"I didn't come here to be pleasant. We've lost two men, also our mast. We've had to shut down."

"I'm sorry to hear that—" began Chrystal.

Fletcher interrupted: "So far, Chrystal, I've given you the benefit of the doubt."

Chrystal was surprised. "How so?"

"I'm assuming you didn't know the deks were intelligent, that they're protected by the Responsibility Act."

"Well?"

"Now you know. You don't have the excuse of ignorance." Chrystal was silent for a few seconds. "Well, Sam—these are all rather astonishing statements."

"Do you deny them?"

"Of course I do!" said Chrystal, with a flash of spirit.

"And you're not processing dekabrachs?"

"Easy, now. After all, Sam, this is my raft. You can't come aboard and chase me back and forth. It's high time you understood it."

Fletcher drew himself back a little, as if Chrystal's mere proximity were unpleasant. "You're not giving me a plain answer."

Chrystal leaned back in his chair and put his fingers together, puffing out his cheeks. "I don't intend to."

The barge that Fletcher had passed on his way was edging close to the raft. Fletcher watched it work against the mooring stage, snap its grapples. He asked, "What's on that barge?"

"Frankly, it's none of your business."

Fletcher rose to his feet and went to the window. Chrystal made uneasy protesting noises. Fletcher ignored him. The two barge handlers had not emerged from the control cabin. They seemed to be waiting for a gangway, which was being swung into position by the cargo boom.

Fletcher watched in growing curiosity and puzzlement. The gangway was built like a trough, with high plywood walls.

He turned to Chrystal. "What's going on out there?"

Chrystal was chewing his lower lip, rather red in the face. "Sam, you come storming over here, making wild accusations, calling me dirty names—by implication—and I don't say a word. I try to allow for the strain you're under; I value the good will between our two outfits. I'll show you some documents that will prove once and for all—" He began to sort through a sheaf of miscellaneous pamphlets.

Fletcher stood by the window, with half an eye for Chrystal, half for what was occurring out on deck.

The gangway was dropped into position; the barge handlers were ready to disembark.

Fletcher decided to see what was going on. He started for the door.

Chrystal's face went stiff and cold. "Sam, I'm warning you, don't go out there!"

"Why not?"

"Because I say so."

Fletcher slid open the door. Chrystal made a motion to jump up from his chair, then he slowly sank back.

Fletcher walked out the door and crossed the deck, toward the barge.

A man in the process house saw him through the window and made urgent gestures.

Fletcher hesitated, then turned to look at the barge. A couple more steps and he could look into the hold. He stepped forward, craned his neck. From the corner of his eye, he saw the man's gestures becoming frantic, then the man disappeared from the window.

The hold was full of limp white dekabrachs.

"Get back, you fool!" came a yell from the process house.

Perhaps a faint sound warned Fletcher; instead of backing away, he threw himself to the deck. A small object flipped over his head from the direction of the ocean, with a peculiar fluttering buzz. It struck a bulkhead and dropped—a fishlike torpedo, with a long needlelike proboscis. It came flapping toward Fletcher, who rose to his feet and ran crouching and dodging back toward the office.

Two more of the fishlike darts missed him by inches; Fletcher hurled himself through the door into the office.

Chrystal had not moved from the desk. Fletcher went panting up to him. "Pity I didn't get stuck, isn't it?"

"I warned you not to go out there."

Fletcher turned to look across the deck. The barge handlers ran down the troughlike gangway to the process house. A glittering school of dart-fish flickered up out of the water, striking the plywood.

Fletcher turned back to Chrystal. "I saw dekabrachs in that barge. Hundreds of them."

Chrystal had regained whatever composure he had lost. "Well? What if there are?"

"You know they're intelligent as well as I do."

Chrystal smilingly shook his head.

Fletcher's temper was going raw. "You're ruining Sabria for all of us!"

Chrystal held up his hand. "Easy, Sam. Fish are fish."

"Not when they're intelligent and kill men in retaliation."

Chrystal wagged his head. "Are they intelligent?"

Fletcher waited until he could control his voice. "Yes. They are."

"How do you know they are? Have you talked with them?"

"Naturally I haven't talked with them."

"They display a few social patterns. So do seals."

Fletcher came up closer and glared down at Chrystal. "I'm not going to argue definitions with you. I want you to stop hunting dekabrach, because you're endangering lives aboard both our rafts."

Chrystal leaned back a trifle. "Now, Sam, you know you can't intimidate me."

"You've killed two men; I've escaped by inches three times now. I'm not running that kind of risk to put money in your pocket."

"You're jumping to conclusions," Chrystal protested. "In the first place, you've never proved—"

"I've proved enough! You've got to stop, that's all there is to it!"

Chrystal slowly shook his head. "I don't see how you're going to stop me, Sam." He brought his hand up from under the desk; it held a small gun. "Nobody's going to bulldoze me, not on my own raft."

Fletcher reacted instantly, taking Chrystal by surprise. He grabbed Chrystal's wrist and banged it against the angle of the desk. The gun flashed, seared a groove in the desk and fell from Chrystal's limp fingers to the floor. Chrystal hissed and cursed, bent to recover it, but Fletcher leaped over the desk and pushed the other man over backward in his chair. Chrystal kicked up at Fletcher's face, catching him a glancing blow on the cheek that sent Fletcher to his knees.

Both men dived for the gun. Fletcher reached it first, rose to his feet, and backed to the wall. "Now we know where we stand."

"Put down that gun!"

Fletcher shook his head. "I'm placing you under arrest—civilian arrest. You're coming to Bio-Minerals until the inspector arrives."

Chrystal seemed dumfounded. "What?"

"I said, I'm taking you to the Bio-Minerals raft. The inspector is due in three weeks, and I'll turn you over to him."

"You're crazy, Fletcher."

"Perhaps. But I'm taking no chances with you." Fletcher motioned with the gun. "Get going. Out to the 'copter." Chrystal coolly folded his arms. "I'm not going to move. You can't scare me by waving a gun."

Fletcher raised his arm, sighted, and pulled the trigger. The jet of fire grazed Chrystal's rump. Chrystal jumped, clapping his hand to the burn.

"Next shot will be somewhat closer," said Fletcher.

Chrystal glared like a boar from a thicket. "You realize I can bring kidnaping charges against you?"

"I'm not kidnaping you. I'm placing you under arrest."

"I'll sue Bio-Minerals for everything they've got."

"Unless Bio-Minerals sues you first. Get going!"

The entire crew met the returning helicopter: Damon, Blue Murphy, Manners, Hans Heinz, Mahlberg, and Dave Jones. Chrystal jumped haughtily to the deck and surveyed the men with whom he had once worked. "I've got something to say to you men."

The crew watched him silently.

Chrystal jerked his thumb at Fletcher. "Sam's got himself in a peck of trouble. I told him I'm going to throw the book at him, and that's what I'm going to do." He looked from face to face. "If you men help him, you'll be accessories. I advise you, take that gun away from him and fly me back to my raft."

He looked around the circle, but met only coolness and hostility. He shrugged angrily. "Very well, you'll be liable for the same penalties as Fletcher. Kidnaping is a serious crime."

Murphy asked Fletcher, "What shall we do with the varmint?"

"Put him in Carl's room—that's the best place for him. Come on, Chrystal."

Back in the mess hall, after locking the door on Chrystal, Fletcher told the crew, "I don't need to warn you—be careful of Chrystal. He's tricky. Don't talk to him. Don't run any errands of any kind. Call me if he wants anything. Everybody got that straight?"

Damon asked dubiously, "Aren't we getting in rather deep water?"

"Do you have an alternative suggestion?" asked Fletcher. "I'm certainly willing to listen."

Damon thought. "Wouldn't he agree to stop hunting dekabrach?"

"No. He refused point-blank."

"Well," said Damon reluctantly, "I guess we're doing the right thing. But we've got to prove a criminal charge. The inspector won't care whether or not Chrystal's cheated Bio-Minerals."

Fletcher said, "If there's any backfire on this, I'll take full responsibility."

"Nonsense," said Murphy. "We're all in this together. I say you did just right. In fact, we ought to hand the sculpin over to the deks, and see what they'd say to him."

After a few minutes Fletcher and Damon went up to the laboratory to look at the captive dekabrach. It floated quietly in the center of the tank, the ten arms at right angles to its body, the black eye-area staring through the glass.

"If it's intelligent," said Fletcher, "it must be as interested in us as we are in it."

"I'm not so sure it's intelligent," said Damon stubbornly.

"Why doesn't it try to communicate?"

"I hope the inspector doesn't think along the same lines," said Fletcher. "After all, we don't have an airtight case against Chrystal."

Damon looked worried. "Bevington isn't a very imaginative man. In fact, he's rather official in his outlook."

Fletcher and the dekabrach examined each other. "I know it's intelligent—but how can I prove it?"

"If it's intelligent," Damon insisted doggedly, "it can communicate."

"If it can't," said Fletcher, "then it's our move."

"What do you mean?"

"We'll have to teach it."

Damon's expression became so perplexed and worried that Fletcher broke into laughter.

"I don't see what's funny," Damon complained. "After all, what you propose is . . . well, it's unprecedented."

"I suppose it is," said Fletcher. "But it's got to be done, nevertheless. How's your linguistic background?"

"Very limited."

"Mine is even more so."

They stood looking at the dekabrach.

"Don't forget," said Damon, "we've got to keep it alive. That means, we've got to feed it." He gave Fletcher a caustic glance. "I suppose you'll admit it eats."

"I know for sure it doesn't live by photosynthesis," said Fletcher. "There's just not enough light. I believe Chrystal mentioned on the microfilm that it ate coral fungus. Just a minute." He started for the door.

"Where are you going?"

"To check with Chrystal. He's certainly noted their stomach contents."

"He won't tell you," Damon said to Fletcher's back.

Fletcher returned ten minutes later.

"Well?" asked Damon in a skeptical voice.

Fletcher looked rather pleased with himself. "Coral fungus, mostly. Bits of tender young kelp shoots, stylax worms, sea oranges."

"Chrystal told you all this?" asked Damon incredulously.

"That's right. I explained to him that he and the dekabrach were both our guests, that we planned to treat them exactly alike. If the dekabrach ate well, so would Chrystal. That was all he needed."

Later, Fletcher and Damon stood in the laboratory watching the dekabrach ingest black-green balls of fungus.

"Two days," said Damon sourly, "and what have we accomplished? Nothing."

Fletcher was less pessimistic. "We've made progress in a negative sense. We're pretty sure it has no auditory apparatus, that it doesn't react to sound, and that it apparently lacks means for making any sound. Therefore, we've got to use visual methods to make contact."

"I envy you your optimism," Damon declared. "The beast has given me no grounds to suspect either the capacity or the desire for communication."

"Patience," said Fletcher. "It still probably doesn't know what we're trying to do and it probably fears the worst."

"We not only have to teach it a language," grumbled Damon, "we've got to introduce it to the idea that communication is possible. And then invent a language."

Fletcher grinned. "Let's get to work."

They inspected the dekabrach, and the black eye-area stared back through the wall of the tank. "We've got to work out a set of visual conventions," said Fletcher. "The ten arms are its most sensitive organs, and they are presumably controlled by the most highly organized section of its brain. So—we work out a set of signals based on the dek's arm movements."

"Does that give us enough scope?"

"I should think so. The arms are flexible tubes of muscle. They can assume at least five distinct positions: straight forward, diagonal forward, perpendicular, diagonal back, and straight back. Since the beast has ten arms, evidently there are ten to the fifth power combinations—a hundred thousand."

"Certainly adequate."

"It's our job to work out the vocabulary and syntax—a little difficult for an engineer and a biochemist, but we'll have a go at it."

Damon was becoming interested in the project. "It's merely a matter of consistency and sound basic structure. If the dek's got any comprehension whatever, we'll put it across."

"If we don't," said Fletcher, "we're gone geese and Chrystal winds up taking over the Bio-Minerals raft."

They seated themselves at the laboratory table.

"We have to assume that the deks have no language," said Fletcher.

Damon grumbled uncertainly, and ran his fingers through his hair in annoyed confusion. "Not proven. Frankly, I don't think it's even likely. We can argue back and forth about whether they could get along on communal empathy, and such like but that's a couple of light-years from answering the question whether they do. They could be using telepathy, as we said; they could also be emitting modulated X-rays, establishing long and short code signals in some unknown-to-us subspace, or hyperspace, or interspace—they could be doing almost anything we never heard of.

"As I see it, our best bet—and best hope—is that they do have some form of encoding system by which they communicate between themselves. Obviously, as you know, they have to have an internal coding and communication system; that's what a neuromuscular structure, with feedback loops, is. Any complex organism has to have communication internally. The whole point of this requirement of language as a means of classifying alien life forms is to distinguish between true communities of individual thinking entities and the communal, insect type, with apparent intelligence.

"Now, if they've got something like an ant colony or beehive city over there, we're sunk, and Chrystal wins. You can't teach an ant to talk; the nest-group has intelligence, but the individual doesn't. So we've got to assume they do have a language—or, to be more general, a formalized encoding system for intercommunication. We can also assume it uses a pathway not available to our organisms. That sound sensible to you?"

Fletcher nodded. "Call it a working hypothesis, anyway. We know we haven't seen any indication that the dek has tried to signal to us."

"Which suggests the creature is not intelligent."

Fletcher ignored the comment. "If we knew more about their habits, emotions, attitudes, we'd have a better framework for this new language."

"It seems placid enough," Damon said.

The dekabrach moved its arms back and forth idly. The eye-area studied the two men.

"Well," said Fletcher with a sigh, "first, a system of notation." He brought forth a model of the dekabrach's head, which Manners had constructed. The arms were made of flexible conduit and could be bent into various positions.

"We number the arms zero to nine, around the clock, starting with this one here at the top. The five positions—forward, diagonal forward, erect, diagonal back, and back—we call A, B, K, X, Y. K is normal position, and when an arm is at K, it won't be noted."

Damon nodded his agreement. "That's sound enough."

"The logical first step would seem to be numbers."

Together they worked out a system of numeration and constructed a chart:

The colon (:) indicates a composite signal: i.e., two or more separate signals.

Number	0	1	2	et cetera
Signal	0Y	1Y	2Y	et cetera
	10	11	12	et cetera
	0Y, 1Y	0Y, 1Y:1Y	0Y, 1Y:2Y	et cetera
	20	21	22	et cetera

0Y, 2Y	0Y,2Y:1Y	0Y,2Y:2Y	et cetera
100	101	102	et cetera
0X, 1Y	0X,1Y:1Y	0X,1Y:0Y,1Y:2Y	et cetera
110	111	112	et cetera
0X,1Y:0Y,1Y	0X,1Y:0Y,1Y:1Y	0X,1Y:0Y,1Y:2Y	et cetera
120	121	122	et cetera
0X,1Y:0Y,2Y	0X,1Y:0Y,2Y:1Y	0X,1Y:0Y,2Y:2Y	et cetera
200	201	202	et cetera
0X,2Y			et cetera
1,000			et cetera
0B, 1Y			et cetera
2,000			et cetera
0B,2Y			et cetera

Damon said, "It's consistent—but cumbersome. For instance, to indicate five thousand, seven hundred sixty-six, it's necessary to make the signal...let's see: 0B, 5Y, then 0X, 7Y, then 0Y, 6Y, then 6Y."

"Don't forget that these are signals, not vocalizations," said Fletcher. "Even so, it's no more cumbersome than 'five thousand, seven hundred and sixty-six.'"

"I suppose you're right."

"Now—words."

Damon leaned back in his chair. "We can't just build a vocabulary and call it a language."

"I wish I knew more linguistic theory," said Fletcher. "Naturally, we won't go into any abstractions."

"Our basic English structure might be a good idea," Damon mused, "with English parts of speech. That is: nouns are things, adjectives are attributes of things, verbs are the displacements which things undergo or the absence of displacement."

Fletcher reflected. "We could simplify even further, to nouns, verbs, and verbal modifiers."

"Is that feasible? How, for instance, would you say, 'the large raft'?"

"We'd use a verb meaning 'to grow big.'" Raft expanded. "Something like that."

"Humph," grumbled Damon. "You don't envisage a very expressive language."

"I don't see why it shouldn't be. Presumably the deks will modify whatever we give them to suit their own needs. If we get across just a basic set of ideas, they'll take it from there. Or by that time someone'll be out here who knows what he's doing."

"O.K.," said Damon, "get on with your Basic Dekabrach."

"First, let's list the ideas a dek would find useful and familiar."

"I'll take the nouns," said Damon. "You take the verbs. You can also have your modifiers." He wrote, No. 1: water.

After considerable discussion and modification, a sparse list of basic nouns and verbs was agreed upon, with assigned signals.

The simulated dekabrach head was arranged before the tank, with a series of lights on a board nearby to represent numbers.

"With a coding machine we could simply type out our message," said Damon. "The machine would dictate the pulses to the arms of the model."

Fletcher nodded. "Fine, if we had the equipment and several weeks to tinker around with it. Too bad we don't. Now—let's start. The numbers first. You work the lights, I'll move the arms. Just one to nine for now."

Several hours passed. The dekabrach floated quietly, the black eye-spot observing.

Feeding time approached. Damon displayed the black-green fungus balls; Fletcher arranged the signal for "food" on the arms of the model. A few morsels were dropped into the tank.

The dekabrach quietly sucked them into its oral tube.

Damon went through the pantomime of offering food to the model. Fletcher moved the arms to the signal "food." Damon ostentatiously placed the fungus ball in the model's oral tube, then faced the tank and offered food to the dekabrach.

The dekabrach watched impassively.

✧ ✧ ✧

Two weeks passed. Fletcher went up to Raight's old room to talk to Chrystal, whom he found reading a book from the microfilm library.

Chrystal extinguished the image of the book, swung his legs over the side of the bed, and sat up.

Fletcher said, "In a very few days the inspector is due."

"So?"

"It's occurred to me that you might have made an honest mistake. At least I can see the possibility."

"Thanks," said Chrystal, "for nothing."

"I don't want to victimize you for what may be an honest mistake."

"Thanks again—but what do you want?"

"If you'll cooperate with me in having the dekabrachs recognized as an intelligent life form, I won't press charges against you."

Chrystal raised his eyebrows. "That's big of you. And I'm supposed to keep my complaints to myself?"

"If the deks are intelligent, you don't have any complaints."

Chrystal looked keenly at Fletcher. "You don't sound too happy. The dek won't talk, eh?"

Fletcher restrained his annoyance. "We're working on him."

"But you're beginning to suspect he's not so intelligent as you thought."

Fletcher turned to go. "This one only knows fourteen signals so far. But it's learning two or three a day."

"Hey!" called Chrystal. "Wait a minute!"

Fletcher stopped at the door. "What for?"

"I don't believe you."

"That's your privilege."

"Let me see this dek make signals."

Fletcher shook his head. "You're better off in here."

Chrystal glared. "Isn't that a rather unreasonable attitude?"

"I hope not." He looked around the room. "Anything you're lacking?"

"No." Chrystal turned the switch, and his book flashed once more on the ceiling screen.

Fletcher left the room. The door closed behind him; the bolts shot home. Chrystal sat up alertly and jumped to his feet with a peculiar lightness, went to the door, and listened.

Fletcher's footfalls diminished down the corridor. Chrystal

returned to the bed in two strides, reached under the pillow, and brought out a length of electric cord detached from a desk lamp. He had adapted two pencils as electrodes, making notches through the wood and binding a wire around the graphite core so exposed. For resistance in the circuit he included a lamp bulb.

He went to the window. He could see down the deck all the way to the eastern edge of the raft, and behind the office as far as the storage bins at the back of the process house. The deck was empty. The only movement was a white wisp of steam rising from the circulation flue, and behind it the hurrying pink and scarlet clouds.

Chrystal went to work, whistling soundlessly between intently pursed lips. He plugged the cord into the baseboard strip, held the two pencils to the window, struck an arc, and burnt at the groove which now ran nearly halfway around the window—it was the only means by which he could cut through the tempered beryl-silica glass.

It was slow work and very delicate. The arc was weak and fractious; fumes grated in Chrystal's throat. He persevered, blinking through watery eyes, twisting his head this way and that, until five-thirty, half an hour before his evening meal, when he put the equipment away. He dared not work after dark, for fear the flicker of light would arouse suspicion.

The days passed. Each morning Gideon and Atreus brought their respective flushes of scarlet and pale green to the dull sky; each evening they vanished in sad dark sunsets behind the western ocean.

A makeshift antenna had been jury-rigged from the top of the laboratory to a pole over the living quarters. Early one afternoon Manners blew the general alarm to short jubilant blasts, to announce a signal from the LG-19, now putting into Sabria on its regular semiannual call. Tomorrow evening lighters would swing down from orbit, bringing the inspector, supplies, and new crews for both Bio-Minerals and Pelagic Recoveries.

Bottles were broken out in the mess hall; there was loud talk, brave plans, laughter.

Exactly on schedule the lighters—four of them—burst through the clouds. Two settled into the ocean beside Bio-Minerals; two more dropped down to the Pelagic Recoveries raft.

Lines were carried out by the launch and the lighters were warped against the dock.

First aboard the raft was Inspector Bevington, a brisk little man, immaculate in his dark blue and white uniform. He represented the government, interpreting its multiplicity of rules, laws, and ordinances; he was empowered to adjudicate minor offences, take custody of criminals, investigate violations of galactic law, check living conditions and safety practices, collect imposts, bonds, and duties, and, in general, personify the government in all of its faces and phases.

The job might well have invited graft and petty tyranny, were not the inspectors themselves subject to minute inspection.

Bevington was considered the most conscientious and the most humorless man in the service. If he was not particularly liked, he was at least respected.

Fletcher met him at the edge of the raft. Bevington glanced at him sharply, wondering why Fletcher was grinning so broadly. Fletcher was thinking that now would be a dramatic moment for one of the dekabrach's monitors to reach up out of the sea and clutch Bevington's ankle. But there was no disturbance; Bevington leaped onto the raft without interference.

He shook hands with Fletcher, then looked around, up and down the deck. "Where's Mr. Raight?"

Fletcher was taken aback; he himself had become accustomed to Raight's absence. "Why—he's dead."

It was Bevington's turn to be startled. "Dead?"

"Come along to the office," said Fletcher, "and I'll tell you about it. This has been a wild month." He looked up to the window of Raight's old room, where he expected to see Chrystal looking down. But the window was empty. Fletcher halted. Empty! The window was vacant even of glass! He started down the deck.

"Here!" cried Bevington. "Where are you going?"

Fletcher paused long enough to call over his shoulder, "You'd better come with me!" He ran to the door leading into the mess hall, with Bevington hurrying after him, frowning in annoyance and surprise.

Fletcher looked into the mess hall, hesitated, then came back out on deck and looked up at the vacant window.

Where was Chrystal? Since he had not come along the deck at the front of the raft, he must have headed for the process house.

"This way," said Fletcher.

"Just a minute!" protested Bevington. "I want to know just what—"

But Fletcher was on his way down the eastern side of the raft toward the process house, where the lighter crew was already looking over the cases of precious metal to be trans-shipped. They glanced up as Fletcher and Bevington approached.

"Did anybody just come past?" asked Fletcher. "A big blond fellow?"

"He went in there." One of the lighter crewmen pointed toward the process house.

Fletcher whirled and ran through the doorway. Beside the leaching columns he found Hans Heinz, looking ruffled and angry.

"Chrystal come through here?" Fletcher asked, panting.

"Did he come through here! Like a hurricane. He gave me a push in the face."

"Where did he go?"

Heinz pointed. "Out on the front deck."

Fletcher and Bevington hurried off, Bevington demanding petulantly, "Exactly what's going on here?"

"I'll explain in a minute," yelled Fletcher. He ran out on deck, looked toward the barges and the launch.

No Ted Chrystal.

He could only have gone in one direction: back toward the living quarters, having led Fletcher and Bevington in a complete circle.

A sudden thought hit Fletcher. "The helicopter!"

But the helicopter stood undisturbed, with its guy lines taut.

Murphy came toward them, looking perplexedly over his shoulder.

"Seen Chrystal?" asked Fletcher.

Murphy pointed. "He just went up them steps."

"The laboratory!" cried Fletcher in sudden agony. Heart in his mouth, he pounded up the steps, with Murphy and Bevington at his heels. If only Damon were in the laboratory now, not down on deck, or in the mess hall!

The lab was empty—except for the tank containing the dekabrach.

The water was cloudy and bluish. The dekabrach was thrashing from end to end of the tank, its ten arms kinked and knotted.

Fletched jumped on a table, then vaulted directly into the tank. He wrapped his arms around the writhing body and lifted, but the supple shape squirmed out of his grasp.

Fletcher grabbed again, heaved in desperation, finally raised it out of the tank.

"Grab hold," he hissed to Murphy between clenched teeth. "Lay it on the table."

Damon came rushing in. "What's going on?"

"Poison," said Fletcher. "Give Murphy a hand."

Damon and Murphy managed to lay the dekabrach on the table. Fletcher barked, "Stand back—flood coming!" He slid the clamps from the side of the tank, and the flexible plastic collapsed. A thousand gallons of water gushed across the floor.

Fletcher's skin was beginning to burn, "Acid! Damon, get a bucket and wash off the dek. Keep him wet."

The circulatory system was still pumping brine into the tank.

Fletcher tore off his trousers, which held the acid against his skin, then gave himself a quick rinse and turned the brine pipe around the tank, flushing off the acid.

The dekabrach lay limp, its propulsion vanes twitching.

Fletcher felt sick and dull. "Try sodium carbonate," he told Damon. "Maybe we can neutralize some of the acid." On a sudden thought he turned to Murphy. "Go get Chrystal. Don't let him get away."

This was the moment that Chrystal chose to stroll into the laboratory. He looked around the room with an expression of mild surprise and hopped up on a chair to avoid the water.

"What's going on in here?"

Fletcher said grimly, "You'll find out." To Murphy: "Don't let him get away."

"Murderer!" cried Damon in a voice that broke with strain and grief.

Chrystal raised his eyebrows in shock. "Murderer?"

Bevington looked back and forth between Fletcher, Chrystal, and Damon. "Murderer? What is all this?"

"Just what the law specifies," said Fletcher. "Knowingly and willfully destroying one of an intelligent species. Murder." The tank was rinsed; he clamped up the sides. The fresh brine began to rise up the sides.

"Now," said Fletcher. "Hoist the dek back in."

Damon shook his head hopelessly. "He's done for. He's not moving."

"We'll put him back in anyway," said Fletcher.

"I'd like to put Chrystal in there with him," Damon said with passionate bitterness.

"Come now," Bevington reproved him, "let's have no more talk like that. I don't know what's going on, but I don't like anything of what I hear."

Chrystal, looking amused and aloof, said, "I don't know what's going on, either."

They lifted the dekabrach and lowered him into the tank.

The water was about six inches deep, the level rising too slowly to suit Fletcher.

"Oxygen," he called. Damon ran to the locker. Fletcher looked at Chrystal. "So you don't know what I'm talking about?"

"Your pet fish dies—-don't try to pin it on me."

Damon handed Fletcher a breather-tube from the oxygen tank; Fletcher thrust it into the water beside the dekabrach's gills. Oxygen bubbled up. Fletcher agitated the water, urged it into the gill openings. The water was nine inches deep.

"Sodium carbonate," Fletcher said over his shoulder. "Enough to neutralize what's left of the acid."

Bevington asked in an uncertain voice, "Is it going to live?"

"I don't know."

Bevington squinted sideways at Chrystal, who shook his head. "Don't blame me."

The water rose. The dekabrach's arms lay limp, floating in all directions like Medusa's locks.

Fletcher rubbed the sweat off his forehead. "If only I knew what to do! I can't give it a shot of brandy; I'd probably poison it."

The arms began to stiffen, extend. "Ah," breathed Fletcher, "that's better." He beckoned to Damon. "Gene, take over here—keep the oxygen going into the gills." He jumped to the floor where Murphy was flushing the area with buckets of water.

Chrystal was talking with great earnestness to Bevington. "I've gone in fear of my life these last three weeks! Fletcher is an absolute madman. You'd better send up for a doctor—or a psychiatrist." He caught Fletcher's eye and paused. Fletcher came slowly across the room. Chrystal turned back to the inspector, whose expression was harassed and uneasy.

"I'm registering an official complaint," said Chrystal. "Against Bio-Minerals in general and Sam Fletcher in particular. Since you're a representative of the law, I insist that you place Fletcher under arrest for criminal offenses against my person."

"Well," said Bevington, glancing cautiously at Fletcher. "I'll certainly make an investigation."

"He kidnaped me at the point of a gun!" cried Chrystal. "He's kept me locked up for three weeks!"

"To keep you from murdering the dekabrachs," said Fletcher.

"That's the second time you've said that," Chrystal remarked ominously. "Bevington is a witness. You're liable for slander."

"Truth isn't slander."

"I've netted dekabrach, so what? I also cut kelp and net coelacanths. You do the same."

"The deks are intelligent. That makes a difference." Fletcher turned to Bevington. "He knows it as well as I do. He'd process men for the calcium in their bones if he could make money at it!"

"You're a liar!" cried Chrystal.

Bevington held up his hands. "Let's have order here! I can't get to the bottom of this unless someone presents some facts."

"He doesn't have facts," Chrystal insisted. "He's trying to run my raft off of Sabria—can't stand the competition!"

Fletcher ignored him. He said to Bevington, "You want facts. That's why the dekabrach is in that tank, and that's why Chrystal poured acid in on him."

"Let's get something straight," said Bevington, giving Chrystal a hard stare. "Did you pour acid into that tank?"

Chrystal folded his arms. "The question is completely ridiculous."

"Did you? No evasions."

Chrystal hesitated, then said firmly, "No. And there's no vestige of proof that I did so."

Bevington nodded. "I see." He turned to Fletcher. "You spoke of facts. What facts?"

Fletcher went to the tank, where Damon was still swirling oxygenated water into the creature's gills. "How's he coming?"

Damon shook his head dubiously. "He's acting peculiar. I wonder if the acid got him internally?"

Fletcher watched the long pale shape for a few moments. "Well, let's try him. That's all we can do."

He crossed the room, then wheeled the model dekabrach forward. Chrystal laughed and turned away in disgust.

"What do you plan to demonstrate?" asked Bevington.

"I'm going to show you that the dekabrach is intelligent and is able to communicate."

"Well, well," said Bevington. "This is something new, is it not?"

"Correct." Fletcher arranged his notebook.

"How did you learn his language?"

"It isn't his—it's a code we worked out between us."

Bevington inspected the model, looked down at the notebook. "These are the signals?"

Fletcher explained the system. "He's got a vocabulary of fifty-eight words, not counting numbers up to nine."

"I see." Bevington took a seat. "Go ahead. It's your show."

Chrystal turned. "I don't have to watch this fakery."

Bevington said, "You'd better stay here and protect your interests—if you don't, no one else will."

Fletcher moved the arms of the model. "This is admittedly a crude setup; with time and money we'll work out something better. Now, I'll start with numbers."

Chrystal said contemptuously, "I could train a rabbit to count that way."

"After a minute," said Fletcher, "I'll try something harder. I'll ask who poisoned him."

"Just a minute!" bawled Chrystal. "You can't tie me up that way!"

Bevington reached for the notebook. "How will you ask? What signals do you use?"

Fletcher pointed them out. "First, interrogation. The idea of interrogation is an abstraction which the dek still doesn't completely understand. We've established a convention of choice, or alternation, like, 'Which do you want?' Maybe he'll catch on what I'm after."

"Very well—'interrogation.' Then what?"

"Dekabrach—receive—hot—water. 'Hot water' is for 'acid.' Interrogation: Man—give—hot—water?"

Bevington nodded. "That's fair enough. Go ahead."

Fletcher worked the signals. The black eye-area watched.

Damon said anxiously, "He's restless—very uneasy."

Fletcher completed the signals. The dekabrach's arms waved once or twice, then gave a puzzled jerk.

Fletcher repeated the set of signals, adding an extra "interrogation—man?"

The arms moved slowly.

"'Man,'" read Fletcher.

Bevington nodded. "Man. But which man?"

Fletcher said to Murphy, "Stand in front of the tank." And he signaled, "Man—give—hot—water—interrogation."

The dekabrach's arms moved.

"'Null-zero,'" read Fletcher. "No. Damon—step in front of the tank." He signaled the dekabrach. "'Man—give—hot—water—interrogation.'"

"'Null.'"

Fletcher turned to Bevington. "You stand in front of the tank." He signaled.

"'Null.'"

Everyone looked at Chrystal. "Your turn," said Fletcher. "Step forward, Chrystal."

Chrystal came slowly forward. "I'm not a chump, Fletcher. I can see through your gimmick."

The dekabrach was moving its arms. Fletcher read the signals, Bevington looking over his shoulder at the notebook.

"'Man—give—hot—water.'"

Chrystal started to protest.

Bevington quieted him. "Stand in front of the tank, Chrystal." To Fletcher: "Ask once again."

Fletcher signaled. The dekabrach responded. "'Man—give—hot—water. Yellow. Man. Sharp. Come. Give—hot—water—water. Go.'"

There was silence in the laboratory.

"Well," said Bevington flatly, "I think you've made your case, Fletcher."

"You're not going to get me that easy," said Chrystal.

"Quiet," rasped Bevington. "It's clear enough what's happened."

"It's clear what's going to happen," said Chrystal in a voice husky with rage. He was holding Fletcher's gun. "I secured this before I came up here, and it looks as if—" He raised the gun toward the tank, squinting, his big white hand tightened on the trigger. Fletcher's heart went dead and cold.

"Hey!" shouted Murphy.

Chrystal jerked. Murphy threw his bucket. Chrystal fired at Murphy, missed. Damon jumped at him, and Chrystal swung the gun around. The white-hot jet pierced Damon's shoulder. Damon, screaming like a hurt horse, wrapped his bony arms around Chrystal.

Fletcher and Murphy closed in, wrested away the gun, and locked Chrystal's arms behind him.

Bevington said grimly, "You're in trouble now, Chrystal, even if you weren't before."

Fletcher said, "He's killed hundreds and hundreds of deks. Indirectly he killed Carl Raight and John Agostino. He's got a lot to answer for."

The replacement crew had moved down to the raft from the LG-19. Fletcher, Damon, Murphy, and the rest of the old crew sat in the mess hall, six months of leisure ahead of them.

Damon's left arm hung in a sling; with his right he fiddled with his coffee cup. "I don't know quite what I'll be doing. I have no plans. The fact is, I'm rather up in the air." Fletcher went to the window, looked out across the dark scarlet ocean. "I'm staying on."

"What?" cried Murphy. "Did I hear you right?"

Fletcher came back to the table. "I can't understand it myself."

Murphy shook his head in total lack of comprehension.

"You can't be serious."

"I'm an engineer, a working man," said Fletcher. "I don't have a lust for power or any desire to change the universe—but it seems as if Damon and I set something into motion—something important—and I want to see it through."

"You mean, teaching the deks to communicate?"

"That's right. Chrystal attacked them, forced them to protect themselves. He revolutionized their lives. Damon and I revolutionized the life of this one dek in an entirely new way. But we've just started. Think of the potentialities! Imagine a population of men in a fertile land—men like ourselves, except that they never learned to talk. Then someone gives them contact with a new universe an intellectual stimulus like nothing they've ever experienced. Think of their reactions, their new attitude to life! The deks are in that same position—except that we've just started with them. It's anybody's guess what they'll achieve and somehow I want to be part of it. Even if I didn't, I couldn't leave with the job half done."

Damon said suddenly, "I think I'll stay on, too."

"You two have gone stir-crazy," said Jones. "I can't get away fast enough."

✦✦✦

The LG-19 had been gone three weeks; operations had become routine aboard the raft. Shift followed shift; the bins began to fill with new ingots, new blocks of precious metal.

Fletcher and Damon had worked long hours with the dekabrach; today would see the great experiment.

The tank was hoisted to the edge of the dock.

Fletcher signaled once again his final message. "Man show you signals. You bring many dekabrachs, man show signals. Interrogation."

The arms moved in assent. Fletcher backed away; the tank was hoisted and lowered over the side, then it submerged.

The dekabrach floated up, drifted a moment near the surface, and slid down into the dark water.

"There goes Prometheus," said Damon, "bearing the gift of the gods."

"Better call it the gift of gab," said Fletcher, grinning.

The pale shape had vanished from sight. "Ten gets you fifty he won't be back," Caldur, the new superintendent, offered them.

"I'm not betting," said Fletcher. "Just hoping."

"What will you do if he doesn't come back?"

Fletcher shrugged. "Perhaps net another, teach him. After a while it's bound to take hold."

Three hours went by. Mists began to close in; rain blurred the sky.

Damon, who had been peering over the side, looked up.

"I see a dek. But is it ours?"

A dekabrach came to the surface. It moved its arms.

"Many-dekabrachs. Show-signals."

"Professor Damon," said Fletcher. "Your first class."

FISH STORY
Fredric Brown

Legends of mermaids tell of their irresistible charm to sailors and other air-breathing men. But just how much are merfolk like the fish which they resemble?

Robert Palmer met his mermaid one midnight along the ocean front somewhere between Cape Cod and Miami. He was staying with friends but had not yet felt sleepy when they retired and had gone for a walk along the brightly moonlit beach. He rounded a curve in the shoreline and there she was, sitting on a log embedded in the sand, combing her beautiful, long black hair.

Robert knew, of course, that mermaids don't really exist—but, extant or not, there she was. He walked closer and when he was only a few steps away he cleared his throat.

With a startled movement she threw back her hair, which had been hiding her face and her breasts, and he saw that she was more beautiful than he had thought it possible for any creature to be.

She stared at him, her deep-blue eyes wide with fright at first. Then, "Are you a man?" she asked.

Robert didn't have any doubts on that point; he assured her that he was. The fear went out of her eyes and she smiled. "I've heard of men but never met one." She motioned for him to sit down beside her on the embedded log.

Robert didn't hesitate. He sat down and they talked and talked, and after a while his arm went around her and when at last she said that she must return to the sea, he kissed her good night and she promised to meet him again the next midnight.

He went back to his friends' house in a bright daze of happiness. He was in love.

For three nights in a row he saw her, and on the third night he told her that he loved her, that he would like to marry her—but that there was a problem—

"I love you too, Robert. And the problem you have in mind can be solved. I'll summon a Triton."

"Triton? I seem to know the word, but—"

"A sea demon. He has magical powers and can change things for us so we can marry, and then he'll marry us. Can you swim well? We'll have to swim out to meet him; Tritons never come quite to the shore."

He assured her that he was an excellent swimmer, and she promised to have the Triton there the next night.

He went back to his friends' house in a state of ecstasy. He didn't know whether the Triton would change his beloved into a human being or change him into a merman, but he didn't care. He was so mad about her that as long as they would both be the same, and able to marry, he didn't care in which form it would be.

She was waiting for him the next night, their wedding night. "Sit down," she told him. "The Triton will blow his conch shell trumpet when he arrives."

The sat with their arms around each other until they heard the sound of a conch shell trumpet blowing far out on the water. Robert quickly stripped off his clothes and carried her into the water; they swam until they reached the Triton. Robert treaded water while the Triton asked them, "Do you wish to be joined in marriage?" They each said a fervent "I do."

"Then," said the Triton, "I pronounce you merman and merwife." And Robert found himself no longer treading water; a few movements of a strong sinuous tail kept him at the surface easily. The Triton blew a note on his conch shell trumpet, deafening at so close a range, and swam away.

Robert swam to his wife's side, put his arms around her and kissed her. But something was wrong; the kiss was pleasant but there was no real thrill, no stirring in his loins as there had been when he had kissed her on shore. In fact, he suddenly realized, he *had* no loins that he could detect. But how—?

"But how—?" he asked her. "I mean, darling, how do we—?"

"Propagate? It's simple, dear, and nothing like the messy way land creatures do it. You see, mermaids are mammalian but oviparous. I lay an egg when the time comes and when it hatches I nurse our merchild. Your part—"

"Yes?" asked Robert anxiously.

"Like other fishes, dear. You simply swim over the egg and fertilize it. There's nothing to it."

Robert groaned, and suddenly deciding to drown himself, he let go of his bride and started swimming toward the bottom of the sea.

But of course he had gills and didn't drown.

SURFACE TENSION
James Blish

Size is relative, and the tiny inhabitants of a pond, or even a puddle might view it as an ocean. And if genetic engineering could reduce humans to microscopic size, they might want to explore beyond the limits of their micro-sea.

Dr. Chatvieux took a long time over the microscope, leaving la Ventura with nothing to do but look out at the dead landscape of Hydrot. Waterscape, he thought, would be a better word. The new world had shown only one small, triangular continent, set amid endless ocean; and even the continent was mostly swamp.

The wreck of the seed-ship lay broken squarely across the one real spur of rock Hydrot seemed to possess, which reared a magnificent twenty-one feet above sea level. From this eminence, la Ventura could see forty miles to the horizon across a flat bed of mud. The red light of the star Tau Ceti, glinting upon thousands of small lakes, pools, ponds, and puddles, made the watery plain look like a mosaic of onyx and ruby.

"If I were a religious man," the pilot said suddenly, "I'd call this a plain case of divine vengeance."

Chatvieux said: "Hmm?"

"It's as if we've been struck down for—is it hubris, arrogant pride?"

"Well, is it?" Chatvieux said, looking up at last. "I don't feel exactly swollen with pride at the moment. Do you?"

"I'm not exactly proud of my piloting," la Ventura admitted. "But that isn't quite what I meant. I was thinking about why we came here

133

in the first place. It takes arrogant pride to think that you can scatter men, or at least things like men, all over the face of the Galaxy. It takes even more pride to do the job—to pack up all the equipment and move from planet to planet and actually make men suitable for every place you touch."

"I suppose it does," Chatvieux said. "But we're only one of several hundred seed-ships in this limb of the Galaxy, so I doubt that the gods picked us out as special sinners." He smiled drily. "If they had, maybe they'd have left us our ultraphone, so the Colonization Council could hear about our cropper. Besides, Paul, we try to produce men adapted to Earthlike planets, nothing more. We've sense enough—humility enough, if you like—to know that we can't adapt men to Jupiter or to Tau Ceti."

"Anyhow, we're here," la Ventura said grimly. "And we aren't going to get off. Phil tells me that we don't even have our germ-cell bank any more, so we can't seed this place in the usual way. We've been thrown onto a dead world and dared to adapt to it. What are the panatropes going to do—provide built-in water-wings?"

"No," Chatvieux said calmly. "You and I and the rest of us are going to die, Paul. Panatropic techniques don't work on the body, only on the inheritance-carrying factors. We can't give you built-in water-wings, any more than we can give you a new set of brains. I think we'll be able to populate this world with men, but we won't live to see it."

The pilot thought about it, a lump of cold collecting gradually in his stomach.

"How long do you give us?" he said at last.

"Who knows? A month, perhaps."

The bulkhead leading to the wrecked section of the ship was pushed back, admitting salty, muggy air, heavy with carbon dioxide. Philip Strasvogel, the communications officer, came in, tracking mud. Like la Ventura, he was now a man without a function, but it did not appear to bother him. He unbuckled from around his waist a canvas belt into which plastic vials were stuffed like cartridges.

"More samples, Doc," he said. "All alike—water, very wet. 1 have some quicksand in one boot, too. Find anything?"

"A good deal, Phil. Thanks. Are the others around?"

Strasvogel poked his head out and hallooed. Other voices rang out over the mudflats. Minutes later, the rest of the survivors were crowding into the panatrope deck; Saltonstall, Chatvieux's senior assistant; Eunice Wagner, the only remaining ecologist; Eleftherios Venezuelos, the delegate from the Colonization Council; and Joan Heath, a midshipman whose duties, like la Ventura's and Strasvogel's, were now without meaning.

Five men and two women—to colonize a planet on which standing room meant treading water.

They came in quietly and found seats or resting places on the deck, on the edges of tables, in corners.

Venezuelos said: "What's the verdict, Dr. Chatvieux?"

"This place isn't dead," Chatvieux said. "There's life in the sea and in the fresh water, both. On the animal side of the ledger, evolution seems to have stopped with the crustacea; the most advanced form I've found is a tiny crayfish, from one of the local rivulets. The ponds and puddles are well-stocked with protozoa and small metazoans, right up to a wonderfully variegated rotifer population—including a castle-building rotifer like Earth's *Floscularidae*. The plants run from simple algae to the thallus-like species."

"The sea is about the same," Eunice said. "I've found some of the larger simple metazoans—jellyfish and so on—and some crayfish almost as big as lobsters. But it's normal to find salt-water species running larger than fresh-water."

"In short," Chatvieux said, "We'll survive here—if we fight."

"Wait a minute," la Ventura said. "You've just finished telling me that we wouldn't survive. And you were talking about us, not about the species, because we don't have our germ-cell banks any more. What's—"

"I'll get to that again in a moment," Chatvieux said. "Saltonstall, what would you think of taking to the sea? We came out of it once; maybe we could come out of it again."

"No good," Saltonstall said immediately. "*I* like the idea, but I don't think this planet ever heard of Swinburne, or Homer, either. Looking at it as a colonization problem, as if we weren't involved ourselves, I wouldn't give you a credit for *epi oinopa ponton*. The evolutionary pressure there is too high, the competition from other species is prohibitive; seeding the sea should be the last thing we attempt. The colonists wouldn't have a chance to learn a thing before they were destroyed."

"Why?" la Ventura said. The death in his stomach was becoming hard to placate.

"Eunice, do your sea-going Coelenterates include anything like the Portuguese man-of-war?" The ecologist nodded.

"There's your answer, Paul," Saltonstall said. "The sea is out. It's got to be fresh water, where the competing creatures are less formidable and there are more places to hide."

"We can't compete with a jellyfish?" la Ventura asked, swallowing.

"No, Paul," Chatvieux said. "The panatropes make adaptations, not gods. They take human germ-cells—in this case, our own, since our bank was wiped out in the crash—and modify them toward creatures who can live in any reasonable environment. The result will be manlike and intelligent. It usually shows the donor's personality pattern, too.

"But we can't transmit memory. The adapted man is worse than a child in his new environment. He has no history, no techniques, no precedents, not even a language. Ordinarily the seeding teams more or less take him through elementary school before they leave the planet, but we won't survive long enough for that. We'll have to design our colonists with plenty of built-in protections and locate them in the most favorable environment possible, so that at least some of them will survive the learning process." The pilot thought about it, but nothing occurred to him which did not make the disaster seem realer and more intimate with each passing second. "One of the new creatures can have my personality pattern, but it won't be able to remember being me. Is that right?"

"That's it. There may be just the faintest of residuums—panatropy's given us some data which seem to support the old Jungian notion of ancestral memory. But we're all going to die on Hydrot, Paul. There's no avoiding that. Somewhere we'll leave behind people who behave as we would, think and feel as we would, but who won't remember la Ventura, or Chatvieux, or Joan Heath—or Earth."

The pilot said nothing more. There was a gray taste in his mouth.

"Saltonstall, what do you recommend as a form?"

The panatropist pulled reflectively at his nose. "Webbed extremities, of course, with thumbs and big toes heavy and thornlike for defense until the creature has had a chance to learn. Book-lungs, like the arachnids, working out of intercostal spiracles—they are gradually adaptable to atmosphere-breathing, if it ever decides to come out of the water. Also I'd suggest sporulation. As an aquatic animal, our colonist is going to have an indefinite lifespan, but we'll have to give it a breeding cycle of about six weeks to keep its numbers up during the learning period; so there'll have to be a definite break of some duration in its active year. Otherwise it'll hit the population problem before it's learned enough to cope with it."

"Also, it'll be better if our colonists could winter inside a good hard shell," Eunice Wagner added in agreement. "So sporulation's the obvious answer. Most microscopic creatures have it."

"Microscopic?" Phil said incredulously.

"Certainly," Chatvieux said, amused. "We can't very well crowd a six-foot man into a two-foot puddle. But that raises a question. We'll have tough competition from the rotifers, and some of them aren't strictly microscopic. I don't think your average colonist should run under 25 microns, Saltonstall. Give them a chance to slug it out."

"I was thinking of making them twice that big."

"Then they'd be the biggest things in their environment," Eunice Wagner pointed out, "and won't ever develop any skills. Besides, if you make them about rotifer size, I'll give them an incentive for pushing out the castle-building rotifers. They'll be able to take over the castles as dwellings."

Chatvieux nodded. "All right, let's get started. While the panatropes are being calibrated, the rest of us can put our heads together on leaving a record for these people. We'll micro-engrave the record on a set of corrosion-proof metal leaves, of a size our colonists can handle conveniently. Some day they may puzzle it out."

"Question," Eunice Wagner said. "Are we going to tell them they're microscopic? I'm opposed to it. It'll saddle their entire early history with a gods-and-demons mythology they'd be better off without."

"Yes, we are," Chatvieux said; and la Ventura could tell by the change in the tone of his voice that he was speaking now as their senior. "These people will be of the race of men, Eunice. We want them to win their way back to the community of men. They are not toys, to be protected from the truth forever in a fresh-water womb."

"I'll make that official," Venezuelos said, and that was that.

And then, essentially, it was all over. They went through the motions. Already they were beginning to be hungry. After la Ventura had had his personality pattern recorded, he was out of it.

He sat by himself at the far end of the ledge, watching Tau Ceti go redly down, chucking pebbles into the nearest pond, wondering morosely which nameless puddle was to be his Lethe.

He never found out, of course. None of them did.

Old Shar set down the heavy metal plate at last, and gazed instead out the window of the castle, apparently resting his eyes on the glowing green-gold obscurity of the summer waters. In the soft fluorescence which played down upon him, from the Noc dozing impassively in the groined vault of the chamber, Lavon could see that he was in fact a young man. His face was so delicately formed as to suggest that it had not been many seasons since he had first emerged from his spore.

But of course there had been no real reason to expect an old man. All the Shars had been referred to traditionally as "old" Shar. The reason, like the reasons for everything else, had been forgotten, but the custom had persisted; the adjective at least gave weight and dignity to the office.

The present Shar belonged to the generation XVI, and hence would have to be at least two seasons younger than Lavon himself. If he was old, it was only in knowledge.

"Lavon, I'm going to have to be honest with you," Shar said at last, still looking out of the tall, irregular window. "You've come to me for the secrets on the metal plates, just as your predecessors did to mine. I can give some of them to you—-but for the most part, I don't know what they mean."

"After so many generations?" Lavon asked, surprised. "Wasn't it Shar III who first found out how to read them? That was a long time ago."

The young man turned and looked at Lavon with eyes made dark and wide by the depths into which they had been staring. "I can read what's on the plates, but most of it seems to make no sense. Worst of all, the plates are incomplete. You didn't know that? They are. One of them was lost in a battle during the final war with the Eaters, while these castles were still in their hands."

"What am I here for, then?" Lavon said. "Isn't there anything of value on the remaining plates? Do they really contain 'the wisdom of the Creators' or is that another myth?"

"No. No, that's true," Shar said slowly, "as far as it goes."

He paused and both men turned and gazed at the ghostly creature which had appeared suddenly outside the window. Then Shar said gravely, "Come in, Para."

The slipper-shaped organism, nearly transparent except for the thousands of black-and-silver granules and frothy bubbles which packed its interior, glided into the chamber and hovered, with a muted whirring of cilia. For a moment it remained silent, probably speaking telepathically to the Noc floating in the vault, after the ceremonious fashion of all the protos. No human had ever intercepted one of these colloquies, but there was no doubt about their reality: humans had used them for long-range communications for generations.

Then the Para's cilia buzzed once more. Each separate hairlike process vibrated at an independent, changing rate; the resulting sound waves spread through the water, intermodulating, reinforcing or canceling each other. The aggregate wave-front, by the time it reached human ears, was recognizable human speech.

"We are arrived, Shar and Lavon, according to the custom."

"And welcome," said Shar. "Lavon, let's leave this matter of the plates for a while, until you hear what Para has to say; that's a part of the knowledge Lavons must have as they come of age, and it comes with the plates. I can give you some hints of what we are. First Para has to tell you something about what we aren't."

Lavon nodded, willingly enough, and watched the proto as it settled gently to the surface of the hewn table at which Shar had been sitting. There was in the entity such a perfection and economy of organization, such a grace and surety of movement, that he could hardly believe in his own new-won maturity. Para, like all the protos, made him feel not, perhaps, poorly thought-out, but at least unfinished.

"We know that in this universe there is logically no place for man," the gleaming, now immobile cylinder upon the table droned abruptly. "Our memory is the common property to all our races. It reaches back to a time when there were no such creatures as men here. It remembers also that once upon a day there were men here, suddenly, and in some numbers. Their spores littered the bottom; we found the spores only a short time after our season's Awakening, and in them we saw the forms of men slumbering.

"Then men shattered their spores and emerged. They were intelligent, active. And they were gifted with a trait, a character,

possessed by no other creature in this world. Not even the savage
Eaters had it. Men organized us to exterminate the Eaters and therein
lay the difference. Men had initiative. We have the word *no*, which you
gave us, and we apply it, but we still do not know what the thing is that
it labels."

"You fought beside us," Lavon said.

"Gladly. We would never have thought of that war by ourselves, but
it was good and brought good. Yet we wondered. We saw that men
were poor swimmers, poor walkers, poor crawlers, poor climbers. We
saw that men were formed to make and use tools, a concept we still do
not understand, for so wonderful a gift is wasted in this universe, and
there is no other. What good are tool-useful members such as the
hands of men? We do not know. It seems plain that so radical a thing
should lead to a much greater rulership over the world than has, in
fact, proven to be possible for men."

Lavon's head was spinning. "Para, I had no notion that you people
were philosophers."

"The protos are old," Shar said. He had again turned to look out the
window, his hands locked behind his back. "They aren't philosophers,
Lavon, but they are remorseless logicians. Listen to Para."

"To this reasoning there could be but one outcome," the Para said.
"Our strange ally, Man, was like nothing else in this universe. He was
and is ill-fitted for it. He does not belong here; he has been—adopted.
This drives us to think that there are other universes besides this one,
but where these universes might lie, and what their properties might
be, it is impossible to imagine. We have no imagination, as men know."

Was the creature being ironic? Lavon could not tell. He said slowly:
"Other universes? How could that be true?"

"We do not know," the Para's uninflected voice hummed. Lavon
waited, but obviously the proto had nothing more to say.

Shar had resumed sitting on the window sill, clasping his knees,
watching the come and go of dim shapes in the lighted gulf. "It is quite
true," he said. "What is written on the remaining plates makes it plain.
Let me tell you now what they say.

"*We were made*, Lavon. We were made by men who are not as we
are, but men who were our ancestors all the same. They were caught
in some disaster, and they made us, and put us here in our universe—
so that, even though they had to die, the race of men would live."

Lavon surged up from the woven spirogyra mat upon which he had been sitting. "You must think I'm a fool!" he said sharply.

"No. You're our Lavon; you have a right to know the facts. Make what you like of them." Shar swung his webbed toes back into the chamber. "What I've told you may be hard to believe, but it seems to be so; what Para says backs it up. Our unfitness to live here is self-evident. I'll give you some examples:

"The past four Shars discovered that we won't get any further in our studies until we learn how to control heat. We've produced enough heat chemically to show that even the water around us changes when the temperature gets high enough. But there we're stopped."

"Why?"

"Because heat produced in open water is carried off as rapidly as it's produced. Once we tried to enclose that heat, and we blew up a whole tube of the castle and killed everything in range; the shock was terrible. We measured the pressures that were involved in that explosion, and we discovered that no substance we know could have resisted them. Theory suggests some stronger substances—*but we need heat to form them!*

"Take our chemistry. We live in water. Everything seems to dissolve in water, to some extent. How do we confine a chemical test to the crucible we put it in? How do we maintain a solution at one dilution? I don't know. Every avenue leads me to the same stone door. We're thinking creatures, Lavon, but there's something drastically wrong in the way we think about this universe we live in. It just doesn't seem to lead to results."

Lavon pushed back his floating hair futilely. "Maybe you're thinking about the wrong results. We've had no trouble with warfare, or crops, or practical things like that. If we can't create much heat, well, most of us won't miss it; we don't need any. What's the other universe supposed to be like, the one our ancestors lived in? Is it any better than this one?"

"I don't know," Shar admitted. "It was so different that it's hard to compare the two. The metal plates tell a story about men who were traveling from one place to another in a container that moved by itself. The only analogy I can think of is the shallops of diatom shells that our youngsters use to sled along the thermocline; but evidently what's meant is something much bigger.

"I picture a huge shallop, closed on all sides, big enough to hold many people—maybe twenty or thirty. It had to travel for generations through some kind of space where there wasn't any water to breathe, so that the people had to carry their own water and renew it constantly. There were no seasons; no yearly turnover; no ice forming on the sky, because there wasn't any sky in a closed shallop; no spore formation.

"Then the shallop was wrecked somehow. The people in it knew they were going to die. They made us, and put us here, as if we were their children. Because they had to die, they wrote their story on the plates, to tell us what had happened. I suppose we'd understand it better if we had the plate Shar III lost during the war, but we don't."

"The whole thing sounds like a parable," Lavon said, shrugging. "Or a song. I can see why you don't understand it. What I can't see is why you bother to try."

"Because of the plates," Shar said. "You've handled them yourself, so you know that we've nothing like them. We have crude, impure metals we've hammered out, metals that last for a while and then decay. But the plates shine on and on, generation after generation. They don't change; our hammers and graving tools break against them; the little heat we can generate leaves them unharmed. Those plates weren't formed in our universe—and that one fact makes every word on them important to me. Someone went to a great deal of trouble to make those plates indestructible to give them to us. Someone to whom the word 'stars' was important enough to be worth fourteen repetitions, despite the fact that the word doesn't seem to mean anything. I'm ready to think that if our makers repeated the word even twice on a record that seems likely to last forever, it's important for us to know what it means."

"All these extra universes and huge shallops and meaningless words—I can't say that they don't exist, but I don't see what difference it makes. The Shars of a few generations ago spent their whole lives breeding better algae crops for us, and showing us how to cultivate them instead of living haphazardly off bacteria. That was work worth doing. The Lavons of those days evidently got along without the metal plates, and saw to it that the Shars did, too: Well, as far as I'm concerned, you're welcome to the plates, if you like them better than crop improvement—but I think they ought to be thrown away."

"All right," Shar said, shrugging. "If you don't want them, that ends the traditional interview. We'll go our—"

There was a rising drone from the table-top. The Para was lifting itself, waves of motion passing over its cilia, like the waves which went across the fruiting stalks of the fields of delicate fungi with which the bottom was planted. It had been so silent that Lavon had forgotten it; he could tell from Shar's startlement that Shar had, too.

"This is a great decision," the waves of sound washing from the creature throbbed. "Every proto has heard it and agrees with it. We have been afraid of these metal plates for a long time, afraid that men would learn to understand them and to follow what they say to some secret place, leaving the protos behind. Now we are not afraid."

"There wasn't anything to be afraid of," Lavon said indulgently.

"No Lavon before you had said so," Para said. "We are glad. We will throw the plates away."

With that, the shining creature swooped toward the embrasure. With it, it bore away the remaining plates, which had been resting under it on the table-top, suspended delicately in the curved tips of its supple cilia. With a cry, Shar plunged through the water to the opening.

"Stop, Para!"

But Para was already gone, so swiftly that he had not even heard the call. Shar twisted his body and brought up on one shoulder against the tower wall. He said nothing. His face was enough. Lavon could not look at it for more than an instant.

The shadows of the two men moved slowly along the uneven cobbled floor. The Noc descended toward them from the vault, its single thick tentacle stirring the water, its internal light flaring and fading irregularly. It, too, drifted through the window after its cousin, and sank slowly away toward the bottom. Gently its living glow dimmed, flickered, winked out.

For many days, Lavon was able to avoid thinking much about the loss. There was always a great deal of work to be done. Maintenance of the castles, which had been built by the now-extinct Eaters rather than by human hands, was a never-ending task. The thousand dichotomously branching wings tended to crumble, especially at their bases where they sprouted from each other, and no Shar had yet come forward with a mortar as good as the rotifer-spittle which had once held them together. In addition, the breaking through of windows and the construction of chambers in the early days had been haphazard and often unsound. The instinctive architecture of the rotifers, after all, had not been meant to meet the needs of human occupants.

And then there were the crops. Men no longer fed precariously upon passing bacteria; now there were the drifting mats of specific water-fungi, rich and nourishing, which had been bred by five generations of Shars. These had to be tended constantly to keep the strains pure, and to keep the older and less intelligent species of the protos from grazing on them. In this latter task, to be sure, the more intricate, and far-seeing proto types cooperated, but men were needed to supervise.

There had been a time, after the war with the Eaters, when it had been customary to prey upon the slow-moving and stupid diatoms, whose exquisite and fragile glass shells were so easily burst, and who were unable to learn that a friendly voice did not necessarily mean a friend. There were still people who would crack open a diatom when no one else was looking, but they were regarded as barbarians, to the puzzlement of the protos. The blurred and simpleminded speech of the gorgeously engraved plants had brought them into the category of pets—a concept which the protos were utterly unable to grasp, especially since men admitted that diatoms on the half-frustule were delicious.

Lavon had had to agree, very early, that the distinction was tiny. After all, humans did eat the desmids, which differed from the diatoms only in three particulars: their shells were flexible, they could not move, and they did not speak. Yet to Lavon, as to most men, there did seem to be some kind of distinction, whether the protos could see it or not, and that was that. Under the circumstance he felt that it was a part of his duty, as a leader of men, to protect the diatoms from the occasional poachers who browsed upon them, in defiance of custom, in the high levels of the sunlit sky.

Yet Lavon found it impossible to keep himself busy enough to forget that moment when the last clues to Man's origin and destination had been seized and borne away into dim space.

It might be possible to ask Para for the return of the plates, explain that a mistake had been made. The protos were creatures of implacable logic, but they respected Man, were used to illogic in Man, and might reverse their decision if pressed—

We are sorry. The plates were carried over the bar and released in the gulf. We will have the bottom there searched, but...

With a sick feeling he could not repress, Lavon knew that when the protos decided something was worthless, they did not hide it in some chamber like old women. They threw it away—efficiently.

Yet despite the tormenting of his conscience, Lavon was convinced that the plates were well lost. What had they ever done for man, except to provide Shars with useless things to think about in the late seasons of their lives? What the Shars themselves had done to benefit Man, here, in the water, in the world, in the universe, had been done by direct experimentation. No bit of useful knowledge ever had come from the plates. There had never been anything in the plates but things best left unthought. The protos were right.

Lavon shifted his position on the plant frond, where he had been sitting in order to overlook the harvesting of an experimental crop of blue-green, oil-rich algae drifting in a clotted mass close to the top of the sky, and scratched his back gently against the coarse bole. The protos were seldom wrong, after all. Their lack of creativity, their inability to think an original thought, was a gift as well as a limitation. It allowed them to see and feel things at all times as they were—not as they hoped they might be, for they had no ability to hope, either.

"La-von! Laa-vah-on!"

The long halloo came floating up from the sleepy depths. Propping one hand against the top of the frond, Lavon bent and looked down. One of the harvesters was looking up at him, holding loosely the adze with which he had been splitting free the glutinous tetrads of the algae.

"Up here. What's the matter?"

"We have the ripened quadrant cut free. Shall we tow it away?"

"Tow it away," Lavon said, with a lazy gesture. He leaned back again. At the same instant, a brilliant reddish glory burst into being above him, and cast itself down toward the depths like mesh after mesh of the finest-drawn gold. The great light which lived above the sky during the day, brightening or dimming according to some pattern no Shar ever had fathomed, was blooming again.

Few men, caught in the warm glow of that light, could resist looking up at it—especially when the top of the sky itself wrinkled and smiled just a moment's climb or swim away. Yet, as always, Lavon's bemused upward look gave him back nothing but his own distorted, bobbling reflection, and a reflection of the plant on which he rested.

Here was the upper limit, the third of the three surfaces of the universe.

The first surface was the bottom, where the water ended.

The second surface was the thermocline, the invisible division between the colder waters of the bottom and the warm, light waters of the sky. During the height of the warm weather, the thermocline was so definite a division as to make for good sledding and for chilly passage. A real interface formed between the cold, denser bottom waters and the warm reaches above, and maintained itself almost for the whole of the warm season.

The third surface was the sky. One could no more pass through that surface than one could penetrate the bottom, nor was there any better reason to try. There the universe ended. The light which played over it daily, waxing and waning as it chose, seemed to be one of its properties.

Toward the end of the season, the water gradually grew colder and more difficult to breathe, while at the same time the light became duller and stayed for shorter periods between darknesses. Slow currents started to move. The high waters turned chill and began to fall. The bottom mud stirred and smoked away, carrying with it the spores of the fields of fungi. The thermocline tossed, became choppy, and melted away. The sky began to fog with particles of soft silt carried up from the bottom, the walls, the corners of the universe. Before very long, the whole world was cold, inhospitable, flocculent with yellowing, dying creatures.

Then the protos encysted; the bacteria, even most of the plants and, not long afterward, men, too, curled up in their oil-filled amber shells. The world died until the first tentative current of warm water broke the winter silence.

"La-von!"

Just after the long call, a shining bubble rose past Lavon. He reached out and poked it, but it bounced away from his sharp thumb. The gas-bubbles which rose from the bottom in late summer were almost invulnerable—and when some especially hard blow or edge did penetrate them, they broke into smaller bubbles which nothing could touch, and fled toward the sky, leaving behind a remarkably bad smell.

Gas. There was no water inside a bubble. A man who got inside a bubble would have nothing to breathe.

But, of course, it was impossible to penetrate a bubble. The surface tension was too strong. As strong as Shar's metal plates. As strong as the top of the sky.

As strong as the top of the sky. And above that—once the bubble was broken—a world of gas instead of water? Were all worlds bubbles of water drifting in gas?

If it were so, travel between them would be out of the question, since it would be impossible to pierce the sky to begin with. Nor did the infant cosmology include any provisions for bottoms for the worlds.

And yet some of the local creatures did burrow *into* the bottom, quite deeply, seeking something in those depths which was beyond the reach of Man. Even the surface of the ooze, in high summer, crawled with tiny creatures for which mud was a natural medium.

Man, too, passed freely between the two countries of water which were divided by the thermocline, though many of the creatures with which he lived could not pass that line at all, once it had established itself.

And if the new universe of which Shar had spoken existed at all, it had to exist beyond the sky, where the light was. Why could not the sky be passed, after all? The fact that bubbles could be broken showed that the surface skin that formed between water and gas wasn't completely invulnerable. Had it ever been tried?

Lavon did not suppose that one man could butt his way through the top of the sky, any more than he could burrow into the bottom, but there might be ways around the difficulty. Here at his back, for instance, was a plant which gave every appearance of continuing beyond the sky; its uppermost fronds broke off and were bent back only by a trick of reflection.

It had always been assumed that the plants died where they touched the sky. For the most part, they did, for frequently the dead extension could be seen, leached and yellow, the boxes of its component cells empty, floating imbedded in the perfect mirror.

But some were simply chopped off, like the one which sheltered him now. Perhaps that was only an illusion, and instead it soared indefinitely into some other place—some place where men might once have been born, and might still live...

The plates were gone. There was only one other way to find out.

Determinedly, Lavon began to climb toward the wavering mirror of the sky. His thorn-thumbed feet trampled obliviously upon the clustered sheaves of fragile stippled diatoms. The tulip-heads of Vortae, placid and murmurous cousins of Para, retracted startledly out of his way upon coiling stalks, to make silly gossip behind him.

Lavon did not hear them. He continued to climb doggedly toward the light, his fingers and toes gripping the plant-bole.

"Lavon! Where are you going? Lavon!"

He leaned out and looked down. The man with the adze, a doll-like figure, was beckoning to him from a patch of blue-green retreating over a violet abyss. Dizzily he looked away, clinging to the bole; he had never been so high before. Then he began to climb again.

After a while, he touched the sky with one hand. He stopped to breathe. Curious bacteria gathered about the base of his thumb where blood from a small cut was fogging away, scattered at his gesture, and wriggled mindlessly back toward the dull red lure.

He waited until he no longer felt winded, and resumed climbing. The sky pressed down against the top of his head, against the back of his neck, against his shoulders. It seemed to give slightly, with a tough, frictionless elasticity. The water here was intensely bright, and quite colorless. He climbed another step, driving his shoulders against that enormous weight.

It was fruitless. He might as well have tried to penetrate a cliff.

Again he had to rest. While he panted, he made a curious discovery. All around the bole of the water plant, the steel surface of the sky curved upward, making a kind of sheath. He found that he could insert his hand into it—there was almost enough space to admit his head as well. Clinging closely to the bole, he looked up into the inside of the sheath, probing with his injured hand. The glare was blinding.

There was a kind of soundless explosion. His whole wrist was suddenly encircled in an intense, impersonal grip, as if it were being cut in two. In blind astonishment, he lunged upward.

The ring of pain traveled smoothly down his upflung arm as he rose, was suddenly around his shoulders and chest. Another lunge and his knees were being squeezed in the circular vise. Another—

Something was horribly wrong. He clung to the bole and tried to gasp, but there was nothing to breathe.

The water came streaming out of his body, from his mouth, his nostrils, the spiracles in his sides, spurting in tangible jets. An intense and fiery itching crawled over the entire surface of his body. At each spasm, long knives ran into him, and from a great distance he heard more water being expelled from his book-lungs in an obscene, frothy sputtering.

Lavon was drowning.

With a final convulsion, he kicked himself away from the splintery bole, and fell. A hard impact shook him; and then the water, which had clung to him so tightly when he had first attempted to leave it, took him back with cold violence.

Sprawling and tumbling grotesquely, he drifted, down and down and down, toward the bottom.

For many days, Lavon lay curled insensibly in his spore, as if in the winter sleep. The shock of cold which he had felt on re-entering his native universe had been taken by his body as a sign of coming winter, as it had taken the oxygen starvation of his brief sojourn above the sky. The spore-forming glands had at once begun to function.

Had it not been for this, Lavon would surely have died. The danger of drowning disappeared even as he fell, as the air bubbled out of his lungs and readmitted the life-giving water. But for acute desiccation and third-degree sunburn, the sunken universe knew no remedy. The healing amnionic fluid generated by the spore-forming glands, after the transparent amber sphere had enclosed him, offered Lavon his only chance.

The brown sphere was spotted after some days by a prowling ameba, quiescent in the eternal winter of the bottom. Down there the temperature was always an even 4°, no matter what the season, but it was unheard of that a spore should be found there while the high epilimnion was still warm and rich in oxygen.

Within an hour, the spore was surrounded by scores of astonished protos, jostling each other to bump their blunt eyeless prows against the shell. Another hour later, a squad of worried men came plunging from the castles far above to press their own noses against the transparent wall. Then swift orders were given.

Four Paras grouped themselves about the amber sphere, and there was a subdued explosion as the trichocysts which lay embedded at the bases of their cilia, just under the pellicle, burst and cast fine lines of a quickly solidifying liquid into the water. The four Paras thrummed and lifted, tugging.

Lavon's spore swayed gently in the mud and then rose slowly, entangled in the web. Nearby, a Noc cast a cold pulsating glow over the operation—not for the Paras, who did not need the light, but for the balled knot of men. The sleeping figure of Lavon, head bowed, knees drawn up to its chest, revolved with an absurd solemnity inside the shell as it was moved.

"Take him to Shar, Para."

The young Shar justified, by minding his own business, the traditional wisdom with which his hereditary office had invested him. He observed at once that there was nothing he could do for the encysted Lavon which would not be classifiable as simple meddling.

He had the sphere deposited in a high tower room of his castle, where there was plenty of light and the water was warm, which should suggest to the hibernating form that spring was again on the way. Beyond that, he simply sat and watched, and kept his speculations to himself.

Inside the spore, Lavon's body seemed rapidly to be shedding its skin, in long strips and patches. Gradually, his curious shrunkenness disappeared. His withered arms and legs and sunken abdomen filled out again.

The days went by while Shar watched. Finally he could discern no more changes, and, on a hunch, had the spore taken up to the topmost battlements of the tower, into the direct daylight.

An hour later, Lavon moved in his amber prison.

He uncurled and stretched, turned blank eyes up toward the light. His expression was that of a man who had not yet awakened from a ferocious nightmare. His whole body shone with a strange pink newness.

Shar knocked gently on the wall of the spore. Lavon turned his blind face toward the sound, life coming into his eyes. He smiled tentatively and braced his hands and feet against the inner wall of the shell.

The whole sphere fell abruptly to pieces with a sharp crackling. The amnionic fluid dissipated around him and Shar, carrying away with it the suggestive odor of a bitter struggle against death.

Lavon stood among the bits of shell and looked at Shar silently. At last he said:

"Shar—I've been beyond the sky."

"I know," Shar said gently.

Again Lavon was silent. Shar said, "Don't be humble, Lavon. You've done an epoch-making thing. It nearly cost you your life. You must tell me the rest—all of it."

"The rest?"

"You taught me a lot while you slept. Or are you still opposed to useless knowledge?"

Lavon could say nothing. He no longer could tell what he knew from what he wanted to know. He had only one question left, but he could not utter it. He could only look dumbly into Shar's delicate face.

"You have answered me," Shar said, even more gently. "Come, my friend; join me at my table. We will plan our journey to the stars."

It was two winter sleeps after Lavon's disastrous climb beyond the sky that all work on the spaceship stopped. By then, Lavon knew that he had hardened and weathered into that temporarily ageless state a man enters after he has just reached his prime; and he knew also that there were wrinkles engraved upon his brow, to stay and to deepen.

"Old" Shar, too, had changed, his features losing some of their delicacy as he came into his maturity. Though the wedge-shaped bony structure of his face would give him a withdrawn and poetic look for as long as he lived, participation in the plan had given his expression a kind of executive overlay, which at best gave it a masklike rigidity, and at worst coarsened it somehow.

Yet despite the bleeding away of the years, the spaceship was still only a hulk. It lay upon a platform built above the tumbled boulders of the sandbar which stretched out from one wall of the world. It was an immense hull of pegged wood, broken by regularly spaced gaps through which the raw beams of the skeleton could be seen.

Work upon it had progressed fairly rapidly at first, for it was not hard to visualize what kind of vehicle would be needed to crawl through empty space without losing its water. It had been recognized that the sheer size of the machine would enforce a long period of construction, perhaps two full seasons; but neither Shar nor Lavon had anticipated any serious snag.

For that matter, part of the vehicle's apparent incompleteness was an illusion. About a third of its fittings were to consist of living creatures, which could not be expected to install themselves in the vessel much before the actual takeoff.

Yet time and time again, work on the ship had had to be halted for long periods. Several times whole sections needed to be ripped out, as it became more and more evident that hardly a single normal, understandable concept could be applied to the problem of space travel.

The lack of the history plates, which the Para steadfastly refused to deliver up, was a double handicap. Immediately upon their loss, Shar had set himself to reproduce them from memory; but unlike the more religious of his people, he had never regarded them as holy writ, and hence had never set himself to memorizing them word by word. Even before the theft, he had accumulated a set of variant translations of passages presenting specific experimental problems, which were stored in his library, carved in wood. But most of these translations tended to contradict each other, and none of them related to spaceship construction, upon which the original had been vague in any case.

No duplicates of the cryptic characters of the original had ever been made, for the simple reason that there was nothing in the sunken universe, capable of destroying the originals, nor of duplicating their apparently changeless permanence. Shar remarked too late that through simple caution they should have made a number of verbatim temporary records but after generations of green-gold peace, simple caution no longer covers preparation against catastrophe. (Nor, for that matter, did a culture which had to dig each letter of its simple alphabet into pulpy waterlogged wood with a flake of stonewort, encourage the keeping of records in triplicate.)

As a result, Shar's imperfect memory of the contents of the history plates, plus the constant and millennial doubt as to the accuracy of the various translations, proved finally to be the worst obstacle to progress on the spaceship itself.

"Men must paddle before they can swim," Lavon observed belatedly, and Shar was forced to agree with him.

Obviously, whatever the ancients had known about spaceship construction, very little of that knowledge was usable to a people still trying to build its first spaceship from scratch. In retrospect, it was not surprising that the great hulk still rested incomplete upon its platform above the sand boulders, exuding a musty odor of wood steadily losing its strength, two generations after its flat bottom had been laid down.

The fat-faced young man who headed the strike delegation was Phil XX, a man two generations younger than Lavon, four younger than Shar. There were crow's-feet at the corners of his eyes, which made him look both like a querulous old man and like an infant spoiled in the spore.

"We're calling a halt to this crazy project," he said bluntly. "We've slaved our youth away on it, but now that we're our own masters, it's over, that's all. Over."

"Nobody's compelled you," Lavon said angrily.

"Society does; our parents do," a gaunt member of the delegation said. "But now we're going to start living in the real world. Everybody these days knows that there's no other world but this one. You oldsters can hang on to your superstitions if you like. We don't intend to."

Baffled, Lavon looked over at Shar. The scientist smiled and said, "Let them go, Lavon. We have no use for the faint-hearted."

The fat-faced young man flushed. "You can't insult us into going back to work. We're through. Build your own ship to no place!"

"All right," Lavon said evenly. "Go on, beat it. Don't stand around here orating about it. You've made your decision and we're not interested in your self-justifications. Good-by."

The fat-faced young man evidently still had quite a bit of heroism to dramatize which Lavon's dismissal had short-circuited. An examination of Lavon's stony face, however, convinced him that he had to take his victory as he found it. He and the delegation trailed ingloriously out the archway.

"Now what?" Lavon asked when they had gone. "I must admit, Shar, that I would have tried to persuade them. We do need the workers, after all."

"Not as much as they need us," Shar said tranquilly. "How many volunteers have you got for the crew of the ship?"

"Hundreds. Every young man of the generation after Phil's wants to go along. Phil's wrong about that segment of the population, at least. The project catches the imagination of the very young."

"Did you give them any encouragement?"

"Sure," Lavon said. "I told them we'd call on them if they were chosen. But you can't take that seriously! We'd do badly to displace our picked group of specialists with youths who have enthusiasm and nothing else."

"That's not what I had in mind, Lavon. Didn't I see a Noc in your chambers somewhere? Oh, there he is, asleep in the dome. Noc!"

The creature stirred its tentacles lazily.

"Noc, I've a message," Shar called. "The protos are to tell all men that those who wish to go to the next world with the spaceship must come to the staging area right away. Say that we can't promise to take everyone, but that only those who help us build the ship will be considered at all."

The Noc curled its tentacles again and appeared to go back to sleep. Actually, of course, it was sending its message through the water in all directions.

Lavon turned from the arrangement of speaking-tube megaphones which was his control board and looked at the Para. "One last try," he said. "Will you give us back the plates?"

"No, Lavon. We have never denied you anything before, but this we must."

"You're going with us though, Para. Unless you give us the knowledge we need, you'll lose your life if we lose ours."

"What is one Para?" the creature said. "We are all alike. This cell will die; but the protos need to know how you fare on this journey. We believe you should make it without the plates."

"Why?"

The proto was silent. Lavon stared at it a moment, then turned deliberately back to the speaking tubes. "Everyone hang on," he said. He felt shaky. "We're about to start. Tol, is the ship sealed?"

"As far as I can tell, Lavon."

Lavon shifted to another megaphone. He took a deep breath.

Already the water seemed stifling, though the ship hadn't moved.

"Ready with one-quarter power. One, two, three, go."

The whole ship jerked and settled back into place again. The raphe diatoms along the under hull settled into their niches, their jelly treads turning against broad endless belts of crude leather.

Wooden gears creaked, stepping up the slow power of the creatures, transmitting it to the sixteen axles of the ship's wheels.

The ship rocked and began to roll slowly along the sandbar.

Lavon looked tensely through the mica port. The world flowed painfully past him. The ship canted and began to climb the slope. Behind him, he could feel the electric silence of Shar, Para, the two alternate pilots, as if their gaze were stabbing directly through his body and on out the port. The world looked different, now that he was leaving it. How had he missed all this beauty before?

The slapping of the endless belts and the squeaking and groaning of the gears and axles grew louder as the slope steepened. The ship continued to climb, lurching. Around it, squadrons of men and protos dipped and wheeled, escorting it toward the sky.

Gradually the sky lowered and pressed down toward the top of the ship.

"A little more work from your diatoms, Tanol," Lavon said. "Boulder ahead." The ship swung ponderously. "All right, slow them up again. Give us a shove from your side, Than—no, that's too much— there, that's it. Back to normal; you're still turning us! Tanol, give us one burst to line us up again. Good. All right, steady drive on all sides. Won't be long now."

"How can you think in webs like that?" the Para wondered behind him.

"I just do, that's all. It's the way men think. Overseers, a little more thrust now; the grade's getting steeper."

The gears groaned. The ship nosed up. The sky brightened in Lavon's face. Despite himself, he began to be frightened. His lungs seemed to burn, and in his mind he felt his long fall through nothingness toward the chill slap of water as if he were experiencing it for the first time. His skin itched and burned. Could he go up there again? Up there into the burning void, the great gasping agony where no life should go?

The sandbar began to level out and the going became a little easier. Up here, the sky was so close that the lumbering motion of the huge ship disturbed it. Shadows of wavelets ran across the sand. Silently, the thick-barreled bands of blue-green algae drank in the light and converted it to oxygen, writhing in their slow mindless dance just under the long mica skylight which ran along the spine of the ship. In the hold, beneath the latticed corridor and cabin floors, whirring Vortae kept the ship's water in motion, fueling themselves upon drifting organic particles.

One by one, the figures wheeling about the ship outside waved arms or cilia and fell back, coasting down the slope of the sandbar toward the familiar world, dwindling and disappearing. There was at last only one single Euglena, half-plant cousin of the protos, forging along beside the spaceship into the marches of the shallows. It loved the light, but finally it, too, was driven away into cooler, deeper waters, its single whiplike tentacle undulating placidly as it went. It was not very bright, but Lavon felt deserted when it left.

Where they were going, though, none could follow.

Now the sky was nothing but a thin, resistant skin of water coating the top of the ship. The vessel slowed, and when Lavon called for more power, it began to dig itself in among the sand grains.

"That's not going to work," Shar said tensely.

"I think we'd better step down the gear ratio, Lavon, so you can apply stress more slowly."

"All right," Lavon agreed. "Full stop, everybody, Shar, will you supervise gear-changing, please?"

Insane brilliance of empty space looked Lavon full in the face just beyond his big mica bull's eye. It was maddening to be forced to stop here upon the threshold of infinity; and it was dangerous, too. Lavon could feel building in him the old fear of the outside. A few moments more of inaction, he knew with a gathering coldness at the pit of his stomach, and he would be unable to go through with it.

Surely, he thought, there must be a better way to change gear-ratios than the traditional one, which involved dismantling almost the entire gear-box. Why couldn't a number of gears of different sizes be carried on the same shaft, not necessarily all in action all at once, but awaiting use simply by shoving the axle back and forth longitudinally in its sockets? It would still be clumsy, but it could be worked on orders from the bridge and would not involve shutting down the entire machine— and throwing the new pilot into a blue-green funk.

Shar came lunging up through the trap and swam himself to a stop.

"All set," he said. "The big reduction gears aren't taking the strain too well, though."

"Splintering?"

"Yes. I'd go it slow at first."

Lavon nodded mutely. Without allowing himself to stop, even for a moment, to consider the consequences of his words, he called: "Half power."

The ship hunched itself down again and began to move, very slowly indeed, but more smoothly than before. Overhead, the sky thinned to complete transparency. The great light came blasting in. Behind Lavon there was an uneasy stir. The whiteness grew at the front ports.

Again the ship slowed, straining against the blinding barrier.

Lavon swallowed and called for more power. The ship groaned like something about to die. It was now almost at a standstill.

"More power," Lavon ground out.

Once more, with infinite slowness, the ship began to move.

Gently, it tilted upward.

Then it lunged forward and every board and beam in it began to squall.

"Lavon! Lavon!"

Lavon started sharply at the shout. The voice was coming at him from one of the megaphones, the one marked for the port at the rear of the ship.

"Lavon!"

"What is it? Stop your damn yelling."

"I can see the top of the sky! From the other side, from the top side! It's like a big flat sheet of metal. We're going away from it.

"We're above the sky, Lavon, we're above the sky!"

Another violent start swung Lavon around toward the forward port. On the outside of the mica, the water was evaporating with shocking swiftness, taking with it strange distortions and patterns made of rainbows.

Lavon saw Space.

It was at first like a deserted and cruelly dry version of the bottom. There were enormous boulders, great cliffs, tumbled, split, riven, jagged rocks going up and away in all directions.

But it had a sky of its own—a deep blue dome so far away that he could not believe in, let alone compute, what its distance might be. And in this dome was a ball of white fire that seared his eyeballs.

The wilderness of rock was still a long way away from the ship, which now seemed to be resting upon a level, glistening plain. Beneath the surface-shine, the plain seemed to be made of sand, nothing but familiar sand, the same substance which had heaped up to form a bar in Lavon's own universe, the bar along which the ship had climbed. But the glassy, colorful skin over it—

Suddenly Lavon became conscious of another shout from the megaphone banks. He shook his head savagely and asked, "What is it now?"

"Lavon, this is Than. What have you gotten us into? The belts are locked. The diatoms can't move them. They aren't faking, either; we've rapped them hard enough to make them think we were trying to break their shell, but they still can't give us more power."

"Leave them alone," Lavon snapped. "They can't fake; they haven't enough intelligence. If they say they can't give you more power, they can't."

"Well, then, you get us out of it," Than's voice said frighteningly.

Shar came forward to Lavon's elbow. "We're on a space-water interface, where the surface tension is very high," he said softly. "This is why I insisted on our building the ship so that we could lift the wheels off the ground whenever necessary. For a long while I couldn't understand the reference of the history plates to 'retractable landing gear,' but it finally occurred to me that the tension along a space-water interface—or, to be more exact, a space-mud interface—would hold any large object pretty tightly. It you order the wheels pulled up now, I think we'll make better progress for a while on the belly treads."

"Good enough," Lavon said. "Hello below—up landing gear. Evidently the ancients knew their business after all, Shar."

Quite a few minutes later, for shifting power to the belly treads involved another setting of the gear-box, the ship was crawling along the shore toward the tumbled rock. Anxiously, Lavon scanned the jagged, threatening wall for a break. There was a sort of rivulet off toward the left which might offer a route, though a dubious one, to the next world. After some thought, Lavon ordered his ship turned toward it.

"Do you suppose that thing in the sky is a 'star'?" he asked.

"But there were supposed to be lots of them. Only one is up there—and one's plenty for my taste."

"I don't know," Shar admitted. "But I'm beginning to get a picture of the way the universe is made, I think. Evidently our world is a sort of cup in the bottom of this huge one. This one has a sky of its own;

perhaps it, too, is only a cup in the bottom of a still huger world, and so on and on without end. It's a hard concept to grasp, I'll admit. Maybe it would be more sensible to assume that all the worlds are cups in this one common surface, and that the great light shines on them all impartially."

"Then what makes it seem to go out every night, and dim even in the day during winter?" Lavon demanded.

"Perhaps it travels in circles, over first one world, then another. How could I know yet?"

"Well, if you're right, it means that all we have to do is crawl along here for a while, until we hit the top of the sky of another world," Lavon said. "Then we dive in. Somehow it seems too simple, after all our preparations."

Shar chuckled, but the sound did not suggest that he had discovered anything funny. "Simple? Have you noticed the temperature yet?"

Lavon had noticed it, just beneath the surface of awareness, but at Shar's remark he realized that he was gradually being stifled.

The oxygen content of the water, luckily, had not dropped, but the temperature suggested the shallows in the last and worst part of the autumn. It was like trying to breathe soup.

"Than, give us more action from the Vortae," Lavon called. "This is going to be unbearable unless we get more circulation."

It was all he could do now to keep his attention on the business of steering the ship.

The cut or defile in the scattered razor-edged rocks was a little closer, but there still seemed to be many miles of rough desert to cross. After a while, the ship settled into a steady, painfully slow crawling, with less pitching and jerking than before, but also with less progress. Under it, there was now a sliding, grinding sound, rasping against the hull of the ship itself, as if it were treadmilling over some coarse lubricant whose particles were each as big as a man's head.

Finally Shar said, "Lavon, we'll have to stop again. The sand this far up is dry, and we're wasting energy using the treads."

"Are you sure we can take it?" Lavon asked, gasping for breath. "At least we are moving. If we stop to lower the wheels and change gears again, we'll boil."

"We'll boil if we don't," Shar said calmly. "Some of our algae are already dead and the rest are withering. That's a pretty good sign that we can't take much more. I don't think we'll make it into the shadows, unless we do change over and put on some speed."

There was a gulping sound from one of the mechanics. "We ought to turn back," he said raggedly. "We were never meant to be out here in the first place. We were made for the water, not this hell."

"We'll stop," Lavon said, "but we're not turning back. That's final."

The words made a brave sound, but the man had upset Lavon more than he dared to admit, even to himself. "Shar," he said, "make it fast, will you?"

The scientist nodded and dived below.

The minutes stretched out. The great white globe in the sky blazed and blazed. It had moved down the sky, far down, so that the light was pouring into the ship directly in Lavon's face, illuminating every floating particle, its rays like long milky streamers. The currents of water passing Lavon's check were almost hot.

How could they dare go directly forward into that inferno? The land directly under the "star" must be even hotter than it was here!

"Lavon! Look at Para!"

Lavon forced himself to turn and look at his proto ally. The great slipper had settled to the deck, where it was lying with only a feeble pulsation of its cilia. Inside, its vacuoles were beginning to swell, to become bloated, pear-shaped bubbles, crowding the granulated protoplasm, pressing upon the dark nuclei.

"This cell is dying," Para said, as coldly as always. "But go on—go on. There is much to learn, and you may live, even though we do not. Go on."

"You're . . . for us now?" Lavon whispered.

"We have always been for you. Push your folly to its uttermost. We will benefit in the end, and so will Man."

The whisper died away. Lavon called the creature again, but it did not respond.

There was a wooden clashing from below, and then Shar's voice came tinnily from one of the megaphones. "Lavon, go ahead! The diatoms are dying, too, and then we'll be without power. Make it as quickly and directly as you can."

Grimly, Lavon leaned forward. "The 'star' is directly over the land we're approaching."

"It is? It may go lower still and the shadows will get longer. That's our only hope."

Lavon had not thought of that. He rasped into the banked megaphones. Once more, the ship began to move.

It got hotter.

Steadily, with a perceptible motion, the "star" sank in Lavon's face. Suddenly a new terror struck him. Suppose it should continue to go down until it was gone entirely? Blasting though it was now, it was the only source of heat. Would not space become bitter cold on the instant—and the ship an expanding, bursting block of ice?

The shadows lengthened menacingly, stretched across the desert toward the forward-rolling vessel. There was no talking in the cabin, just the sound of ragged breathing and the creaking of the machinery.

Then the jagged horizon seemed to rush upon them. Stony teeth cut into the lower rim of the ball of fire, devoured it swiftly. It was gone.

They were in the lee of the cliffs. Lavon ordered the ship turned to parallel the rock-line; it responded heavily, sluggishly. Far above, the sky deepened steadily, from blue to indigo.

Shar came silently up through the trap and stood beside Lavon, studying that deepening color and the lengthening of the shadows down the beach toward their world. He said nothing, but Lavon knew that the same chilling thought was in his mind.

"Lavon."

Lavon jumped. Shar's voice had iron in it. "Yes?"

"We'll have to keep moving. We must make the next world, wherever it is, very shortly."

"How can we dare move when we can't see where we're going? Why not sleep it over—if the cold will let us?"

"It will let us," Shar said. "It can't get dangerously cold up here. If it did, the sky—or what we used to think of as the sky—would have frozen over every night, even in summer. But what I'm thinking about is the water. The plants will go to sleep now. In our world that wouldn't matter; the supply of oxygen is enough to last through the night. But in this confined space, with so many creatures in it and no source of fresh water, we will probably smother."

Shar seemed hardly to be involved at all, but spoke rather with the voice of implacable physical laws.

"Furthermore," he said, staring unseeingly out at the raw landscape, "the diatoms are plants, too. In other words, we must stay on the move for as long as we have oxygen and power—and pray that we make it."

"Shar, we had quite a few protos on board this ship once. And Para there isn't quite dead yet. If he were, the cabin would be intolerable. The ship is nearly sterile of bacteria, because all the protos have been eating them as a matter of course and there's no outside supply of them, any more than there is for oxygen. But still and all there would have been some decay."

Shar bent and tested the pellicle of the motionless Para with a probing finger. "You're right, he's still alive. What does that prove?"

"The Vortae are also alive; I can feel the water circulating. Which proves it wasn't the heat that hurt Para. It was the light. Remember how badly my skin was affected after I climbed beyond the sky? Undiluted starlight is deadly. We should add that to the information on the plates."

"I still don't see the point."

"It's this. We've got three or four Noc down below. They were shielded from the light, and so must be alive. If we concentrate them in the diatom galleys, the dumb diatoms will think it's still daylight and will go on working. Or we can concentrate them up along the spine of the ship, and keep the algae putting out oxygen. So the question is: which do we need more, oxygen or power? Or can we split the difference?"

Shar actually grinned. "A brilliant piece of thinking. We'll make a Shar of you yet, Lavon. No, I'd say that we can't split the difference. There's something about daylight, some quality, that the light Noc emits doesn't have. You and I can't detect it, but the green plants can, and without it they don't make oxygen. So we'll have to settle for the diatoms for power."

Lavon brought the vessel away from the rocky lee of the cliff, out onto the smoother sand. All trace of direct light was gone now, although there was still a soft, general glow on the sky.

"Now, then," Shar said thoughtfully, "I would guess that there's water over there in the canyon, if we can reach it. I'll go below and arrange—"

Lavon gasped.

"What's the matter?"

Silently, Lavon pointed, his heart pounding.

The entire dome of indigo above them was spangled with tiny, incredibly brilliant lights. There were, hundreds of them, and more and more were becoming visible as the darkness deepened. And far away, over the ultimate edge of the rocks, was a dim red globe, crescented with ghostly silver. Near the zenith was another such body, much smaller, and silvered all over...

Under the two moons of Hydrot, and under the eternal stars, the two-inch wooden spaceship and its microscopic cargo toiled down the slope toward the drying little rivulet.

The ship rested on the bottom of the canyon for the rest of the night. The great square doors were thrown open to admit the raw, irradiated, life-giving water from outside—and the wriggling bacteria which were fresh food.

No other creatures approached them, either with curiosity or with predatory intent, while they slept, though Lavon had posted guards at the doors. Evidently, even up here on the very floor of space, highly organized creatures were quiescent at night.

But when the first flush of light filtered through the water, trouble threatened.

First of all, there was the bug-eyed monster. The thing was green and had two snapping claws, either one of which could have broken the ship in two like a spirogyra straw. Its eyes were black and globular, on the ends of short columns, and its long feelers were as thick as a plantbole. It passed in a kicking fury of motion, however, never noticing the ship at all.

"Is that—a sample of the kind of life we can expect in the next world?" Lavon whispered. Nobody answered, for the very good reason that nobody knew.

After a while, Lavon risked moving the ship forward against the current, which was slow but heavy. Enormous writhing worms whipped past them. One struck the hull a heavy blow, then thrashed on obliviously.

"They don't notice us," Shar said. "We're too small. Lavon, the ancients warned us of the immensity of space, but even when you see it, it's impossible to grasp. And all those stars—can they mean what I think they mean? It's beyond thought, beyond belief!"

"The bottom's sloping," Lavon said, looking ahead intently.

"The walls of the canyon are retreating, and the water's becoming rather silty. Let the stars wait, Shar; we're coming toward the entrance of our new world."

Shar subsided moodily. His vision of space had disturbed him, perhaps seriously. He took little notice of the great thing that was happening, but instead huddled worriedly over his own expanding speculations. Lavon felt the old gap between their two minds widening once more.

Now the bottom was tilting upward again. Lavon had no experience with delta-formation, for no rivulets left his own world, and the phenomenon worried him. But his worries were swept away in wonder as the ship topped the rise and nosed over.

Ahead, the bottom sloped away again, indefinitely, into glimmering depths. A proper sky was over them once more, and Lavon could see small rafts of plankton floating placidly beneath it.

Almost at once, too, he saw several of the smaller kinds of protos, a few of which were already approaching the ship—

Then the girl came darting out of the depths, her features distorted with terror. At first she did not see the ship at all. She came twisting and turning lithely through the water, obviously hoping only to throw herself over the ridge of the delta and into the savage streamlet beyond.

Lavon was stunned. Not that there were men here—he had hoped for that—but at the girl's single-minded flight toward suicide.

"What—"

Then a dim buzzing began to grow in his ears, and he understood.

"Shar! Than! Tanol!" he bawled. "Break out crossbows and spears! Knock out all the windows!" He lifted a foot and kicked through the big port in front of him. Someone thrust a crossbow into his hand.

"Eh? What's happening?" Shar blurted.

"*Rotifers!*"

The cry went through the ship like a galvanic shock. The rotifers back in Lavon's own world were virtually extinct, but everyone knew thoroughly the grim history of the long battle man and proto had waged against them.

The girl spotted the ship suddenly and paused, stricken by despair at the sight of the new monster. She drifted with her own momentum, her eyes alternately fixed hypnotically upon the ship and glancing back over her shoulder, toward where the buzzing snarled louder and louder in the dimness.

"Don't stop!" Lavon shouted. "This way, this way! We're friends! We'll help!"

Three great semi-transparent trumpets of smooth flesh bored over the rise, the many thick cilia of their coronas whirring greedily. Dicrans—the most predacious of the entire tribe of Eaters. They were quarreling thickly among themselves as they moved, with the few blurred, pre-symbolic noises which made up their "language."

Carefully, Lavon wound the crossbow, brought it to his shoulder, and fired. The bolt sang away through the water. It lost momentum rapidly, and was caught by a stray current which brought it closer to the girl than to the Eater at which Lavon had aimed.

He bit his lip, lowered the weapon, wound it up again. It did not pay to underestimate the range; he would have to wait until he could fire with effect. Another bolt, cutting through the water from a side port, made him issue orders to cease firing.

The sudden irruption of the rotifers decided the girl. The motionless wooden monster was strange to her and had not yet menaced her—but she must have known what it would be like to have three Dicrans over her, each trying to grab away from the other the biggest share. She threw herself toward the big port. The Eaters screamed with fury and greed and bored after her.

She probably would not have made it, had not the dull vision of the lead Dicran made out the wooden shape of the ship at the last instant. It backed off, buzzing, and the other two sheered away to avoid colliding with it. After that they had another argument, though they could hardly have formulated what it was that they were fighting about. They were incapable of saying anything much more complicated than the equivalent of "Yaah," "Drop dead," and "You're another."

While they were still snarling at each other, Lavon pierced the nearest one all the way through with an arbalest bolt. It disintegrated promptly—rotifers are delicately organized creatures despite their ferocity—and the remaining two were at once involved in a lethal battle over the remains.

"Than, take a party out and spear me those two Eaters while they're still fighting," Lavon ordered. "Don't forget to destroy their eggs, too.

I can see that this world needs a little taming." The girl shot through the port and brought up against the far wall of the cabin, flailing in terror. Lavon tried to approach her, but from somewhere she produced a flake of stonewort chipped to a nasty point. He sat down on the stool before his control board and waited while she took in the cabin, Lavon, Shar, the pilot, the senescent Para.

At last she said: "Are—you—the gods from beyond the sky?"

"We're from beyond the sky, all right," Lavon said. "But we're not gods. We're human beings, like yourself. Are there many humans here?"

The girl seemed to assess the situation very rapidly, savage though she was. Lavon had the odd and impossible impression that he should recognize her. She tucked the knife back into her matted hair—ah, Lavon thought, that's a trick I may need to remember—and shook her head.

"We are few. The Eaters are everywhere. Soon they will have the last of us."

Her fatalism was so complete that she actually did not seem to care.

"And you've never cooperated against them? Or asked the protos to help?"

"The protos?" She shrugged. "They are as helpless as we are against the Eaters. We have no weapons which kill at a distance, like yours. And it is too late now for such weapons to do any good. We are too few, the Eaters too many."

Lavon shook his head emphatically. "You've had one weapon that counts, all along. Against it, numbers mean nothing. We'll show you how we've used it. You may be able to use it even better than we did, once you've given it a try."

The girl shrugged again. "We have dreamed of such a weapon now and then, but never found it. I do not think that what you say is true. What is this weapon?"

"Brains," Lavon said. "Not just one brain, but brains. Working together. Cooperation."

"Lavon speaks the truth," a weak voice said from the deck.

The Para stirred feebly. The girl watched it with wide eyes.

The sound of the Para using human speech seemed to impress her more than the ship or anything else it contained.

"The Eaters can be conquered," the thin, buzzing voice said. "The protos will help, as they helped in the world from which we came. They fought this flight through space, and deprived Man of his records; but Man made the trip without the records. The protos will never oppose men again. I have already spoken to the protos of this world and have told them what Man can dream, Man can do, whether the protos wish it or not.

"Shar, your metal records are with you. They were hidden in the ship. My brothers will lead you to them.

"This organism dies now. It dies in confidence of knowledge, as an intelligent creature dies. Man has taught us this. There is nothing that knowledge...cannot do. With it, men...have crossed...have crossed space..."

The voice whispered away. The shining slipper did not change, but something about it was gone. Lavon looked at the girl; their eyes met.

"We have crossed space," Lavon repeated softly.

Shar's voice came to him across a great distance. The young-old man was whispering: "But have we?"

"As far as I'm concerned, yes," said Lavon.

LATER THAN YOU THINK
Fritz Leiber

But just how late is it—and who is doing the thinking?

Obviously the Archeologist's study belonged to an era vastly distant from today. Familiar similarities here and there only sharpened the feeling of alienage. The sunlight that filtered through the windows in the ceiling had a wan and greenish cast and was augmented by radiation from some luminous material impregnating the walls and floor. Even the wide desk and the commodious hassocks glowed with a restful light. Across the former were scattered metal-backed wax tablets, styluses, and a pair of large and oddly formed spectacles. The crammed bookcases were not particularly unusual, but the books were bound in metal and the script on their spines would have been utterly unfamiliar to the most erudite of modern linguists. One of the books, lying open on a hassock, showed leaves of a thin, flexible, rustless metal covered with luminous characters. Between the bookcases were phosphorescent oil paintings, mainly of sea bottoms, in somber greens and browns. Their style, neither wholly realistic nor abstract, would have baffled the historian of art.

A blackboard with large colored crayons hinted equally at the schoolroom and the studio.

In the center of the room, midway to the ceiling, hung a fish with iridescent scales of breathtaking beauty. So invisible was its means of support that—also taking into account the strange paintings and the greenish light—one would have sworn that the object was to create an underwater scene.

The Explorer made his entrance in a theatrical swirl of movement.

169

He embraced the Archeologist with a warmth calculated to startle that crusty old fellow. Then he settled himself on a hassock, looked up and asked a question in a speech and idiom so different from any we know that it must be called another means of communication rather than another language. The import was, "Well, what about it?"

If the Archeologist were taken aback, he concealed it. His expression showed only pleasure at being reunited with a long-absent friend.

"What about what?" he queried.

"About your discovery!"

"What discovery?" The Archeologist's incomprehension was playful.

The Explorer threw up his arms. "Why, what else but your discovery, here on Earth, of the remains of an intelligent species? It's the find of the age! Am I going to have to coax you? Out with it!"

"I didn't make the discovery," the other said tranquilly. "I only supervised the excavations and directed the correlation of material. *You* ought to be doing the talking. *You're* the one who's just returned from the stars."

"Forget that." The Explorer brushed the question aside. "As soon as our spaceship got within radio range of Earth, they started to send us a continuous newscast covering the period of our absence. One of the items, exasperatingly brief, mentioned your discovery. It captured my imagination. I couldn't wait to hear the details." He paused, then confessed, "You get so eager out there in space—a metal-filmed droplet of life lost in immensity. You rediscover your emotions..." He changed color, then finished rapidly, "As soon as I could decently get away, I came straight to you. I wanted to hear about it from the best authority—yourself."

The Archeologist regarded him quizzically. "I'm pleased that you should think of me and my work, and I'm very happy to see you again. But admit it now, isn't there something a bit odd about your getting so worked up over this thing? I can understand that after your long absence from Earth, any news of Earth would seem especially important. But isn't there an additional reason?"

The Explorer twisted impatiently. "Oh, I suppose there is. Disappointment, for one thing. We were hoping to get in touch with intelligent life out there. We were specially trained in techniques for establishing mental contact with alien intelligent life forms. Well, we found some planets with life upon them, all right. But it was primitive life, not worth bothering about."

Again he hesitated embarrassedly. "Out there you get to thinking of the preciousness of intelligence. There's so little of it, and it's so lonely. And we so greatly need intercourse with another intelligent species to give depth and balance to our thoughts. I suppose I set too much store by my hopes of establishing a contact." He paused. "At any rate, when I heard that what we were looking for, you had found here at home— even though dead and done for—I felt that at least it was something. I was suddenly very eager. It is odd, I know, to get so worked up about an extinct species—as if my interest could mean anything to them now—but that's the way it hit me."

Several small shadows crossed the windows overhead. They might have been birds, except they moved too slowly.

"I think I understand," the Archeologist said softly.

"So get on with it and tell me about your discovery!" the Explorer exploded.

"I've already told you that it wasn't my discovery," the Archeologist reminded him. "A few years after your expedition left, there was begun a detailed resurvey of Earth's mineral resources. In the course of some deep continental borings, one party discovered a cache—either a very large box or a rather small room—with metallic walls of great strength and toughness. Evidently its makers had intended it for the very purpose of carrying a message down through the ages. It proved to contain artifacts; models of buildings, vehicles, and machines, objects of art, pictures, and books—hundreds of books, along with elaborate pictorial dictionaries for interpreting them. So now we even understand their languages."

"Languages?" interrupted the Explorer. "That's queer. Somehow one thinks of an alien species as having just one language."

"Like our own, this species had several, though there were some words and symbols that were alike in all their languages. These words and symbols seem to have come down unchanged from their most distant prehistory."

The Explorer burst out, "I am not interested in all that dry stuff! Give me the wet! What were they like? How did they live? What did they create? What did they want?"

The Archeologist gently waved aside the questions. "All in good time. If I am to tell you everything you want to know, I must tell it my own way. Now that you are back on Earth, you will have to reacquire those orderly and composed habits of thought which you have partly lost in the course of your wild interstellar adventurings."

"Curse you, I think you're just trying to tantalize me."

The Archeologist's expression showed that this was not altogether untrue. He casually fondled an animal that had wriggled up onto his desk, and which looked rather more like an eel than a snake. "Cute little brute, isn't it?" he remarked. When it became apparent that the Explorer wasn't to be provoked into another outburst, he continued, "It became my task to interpret the contents of the cache, to reconstruct its makers' climb from animalism and savagery to civilization, their rather rapid spread across the world's surface, their first fumbling attempts to escape from the Earth."

"They had spaceships?"

"It's barely possible. I rather hope they did, since it would mean the chance of a survival elsewhere, though the negative results of your expedition rather lessen that." He went on, "The cache was laid down when they were first attempting space flight, just after their discovery of atomic power, in the first flush of their youth. It was probably created in a kind of exuberant fancifulness, with no serious belief that it would ever serve the purpose for which it was intended." He looked at the Explorer strangely. "If I am not mistaken, we have laid down similar caches."

After a moment the Archeologist continued, "My reconstruction of their history, subsequent to the laying down of the cache, has been largely hypothetical. I can only guess at the reasons for their decline and fall. Supplementary material has been very slow in coming in, though we are still making extensive excavations at widely separated points. Here are the last reports." He tossed the Explorer a small metal-leaf pamphlet. It flew with a curiously slow motion.

"That's what struck me so queer right from the start," the Explorer observed, putting the pamphlet aside after a glance. "If these creatures were relatively advanced, why haven't we learned about them before? They must have left so many things—buildings, machines, engineering projects, some of them on a large scale. You'd think we'd be turning up traces everywhere."

"I have four answers to that," the Archeologist replied. "The first is the most obvious. Time. Geologic ages of it. The second is more subtle. What if we should have been looking in the wrong place? I mean, what if the creatures occupied a very different portion of the Earth than our own? Third, it's possible that atomic energy, out of control, finished the race and destroyed its traces. The present distribution of radioactive compounds throughout the Earth's surface lends some support to this theory.

"Fourth," he went on, "it's my belief that when an intelligent species begins to retrogress, it tends to destroy, or, rather, debase all the things it has laboriously created. Large buildings are torn down to make smaller ones. Machines are broken up and worked into primitive tools and weapons. There is a kind of unraveling or erasing. A cultural Second Law of Thermodynamics begins to operate, whereby the intellect and all its works are gradually degraded to the lowest level of meaning and creativity."

"But why?" The Explorer sounded anguished. "Why should any intelligent species end like that? I grant the possibility of atomic power getting out of hand, though one would have thought they'd have taken the greatest precautions. Still, it could happen. But that fourth answer—it's morbid."

"Cultures and civilizations die," said the Archeologist evenly. "That has happened repeatedly in our own history. Why not species? An individual dies—and is there anything intrinsically more terrible in the death of a species than in the death of an individual?"

He paused. "With respect to the members of this one species, I think that a certain temperamental instability hastened their end. Their appetites and emotions were not sufficiently subordinated to their understanding and to their sense of drama—their enjoyment of the comedy and tragedy of existence. They were impatient and easily incapacitated by frustration. They seem to have been singularly guilty in their pleasures, behaving either like gloomy moralists or gluttons.

"Because of taboos and an overgrown possessiveness," he continued, "each individual tended to limit his affection to a tiny family; in many cases he focused his love on himself alone. They set great store by personal prestige, by the amassing of wealth and the exercise of power. Their notable capacity for thought and manipulative activity was expended on things rather than persons or feelings. Their technology outstripped their psychology. They skimped fatally when it came to hard thinking about the purpose of life and intellectual activity, and the means for preserving them."

Again the slow shadows drifted overhead.

"And finally," the Archeologist said, "they were a strangely haunted species. They seem to have been obsessed by the notion that others, greater than themselves, had prospered before them and then died, leaving them to rebuild a civilization from ruins. It was from those others that they thought they derived the few words and symbols common to all their languages."

"Gods?" mused the Explorer.

The Archeologist shrugged. "Who knows?"

The Explorer turned away. His excitement had visibly evaporated, leaving behind a cold and miserable residue of feeling. "I am not sure I want to hear much more about them," he said. "They sound too much like us. Perhaps it was a mistake, my coming here. Pardon me, old friend, but out there in space even *our* emotions become undisciplined. Everything becomes indescribably poignant. Moods are tempestuous. You shift in an instant from zenith to nadir—and remember, out there you can see both.

"I was very eager to hear about this lost species," he added in a sad voice. "I thought I would feel a kind of fellowship with them across the eons. Instead, I touch only corpses. It reminds me of when, out in space, there looms up before your prow, faint in the starlight, a dead sun. They were a young race. They thought they were getting somewhere. They promised themselves an eternity of effort. And all the while there was wriggling toward them out of that future for which they yearned . . . oh, it's so completely futile and unfair."

"I disagree," the Archeologist said spiritedly. "Really, your absence from Earth has unsettled you even more than I first surmised. Look at the matter squarely. Death comes to everything in the end. Our past is strewn with our dead. That species died, it's true. But what they achieved, they achieved. What happiness they had, they had. What they did in their short span is as significant as what they might have done had they lived a billion years. The present is always more important than the future. And no creature can have all the future—it must be shared, left to others."

"Maybe so," the Explorer said slowly. "Yes, I guess you're right. But

I still feel a horrible wistfulness about them, and I hug to myself the hope that a few of them escaped and set up a colony on some planet we haven't yet visited." There was a long silence. Then the Explorer turned back. "You old devil," he said in a manner that showed his gayer and more boisterous mood had returned, though diminished, "you still haven't told me anything definite about them."

"So I haven't," replied the Archeologist with guileful innocence. "Well, they were vertebrates."

"Oh?"

"Yes. What's more, they were mammals."

"Mammals? I was expecting something different."

"I thought you were."

The Explorer shifted. "All this matter of evolutionary categories is pretty cut-and-dried. Even a knowledge of how they looked doesn't mean much. I'd like to approach them in a more intimate way. How did they think of themselves? What did they call themselves? I know the word won't mean anything to me, but it will give me a feeling—of recognition."

"I can't say the word," the Archeologist told him, "because I haven't the proper vocal equipment. But I know enough of their script to be able to write it for you as they would have written it. Incidentally, it is one of those words common to all their languages, that they attributed to an earlier race of beings."

The Archeologist extended one of his eight tentacles toward the blackboard. The suckers at its tip firmly grasped a bit of orange crayon. Another of his tentacles took up the spectacles and adjusted them over his three-inch protruding pupils.

The eel-like glittering pet drifted back into the room and nosed curiously about the crayon as it traced:

RAT

THE SONG OF UULLIOLL
Gray Rinehart

Whales and porpoises have demonstrated high intelligence, nearly human level according to some researchers. It might be that they are as curious about us as we are about them. And youngsters are known for taking chances...

Uullioll cruised the dark deep, alone and brooding. He was full, yet he still filtered tasteless morsels from the salty-wet. He thought of diving down to the hard below where the wide crabs walked, but he had watched them so often that they no longer amused him. From below and behind him came the high-pitched, tuneless song of two youngsters chasing each other. Uullioll had been that carefree once, migrations gone by.

Their feeding time was almost over, but the pod wasn't ready to move yet. Osheeoroth would wait until this cycle of the puller above was complete before he sang them to head to the warm stills. And it would be the same as ever, their lives an endless migration.

Frustration rumbled through him, a note too low even for him to hear, and spurred him up and up and through the barrier into the cold dry-clear. The bright hot was unfortunately away, and Uullioll missed its clean warmth. The puller above was a cold, half-closed eye, its light reflecting off the salty-wet and the icy rocks floating in it. For an instant and an eon Uullioll hung there, savoring the dry-clear and releasing his tension with a blast. Then he splashed back through the barrier and into the salty-wet, where he let himself float, waiting, dutifully waiting.

✦ ✦ ✦

The bright hot was high in the dry-clear when Uullioll surfaced a fin's length away from the hard fish. Most of the pod was ahead, intent on their trek to the warm stills, but Uullioll often left the pod to investigate these hard fish—small ones and huge ones, noisy creatures that never dove, and big dark silent ones that dove and sometimes sang tuneless, one-note songs. This one was about twice as long as he was, and smacked the barrier with a hollow sound as it rode along on top.

Uullioll spouted into the dry-clear. A pod of upright crabs chirped from where they stood upon the hard fish's back.

The bright hot felt good on his back as he glided back into the salty-wet. Uullioll waved his tail flukes in the dry-clear, and dove deep. The chirps of the upright crabs became thumps that rang through the salty-wet from the skin of the hard fish and faded into the pulsing beat of its tail.

Uullioll had loved the bright hot as long as he could remember. Once, when he was very young and craved the bright hot's warmth, he had swum in its direction as it moved behind the edge of the salty-wet, but he tired quickly and failed to catch it. On the next migration, when he had grown stronger and faster, after he had eaten his fill he tried again—but the bright hot still outraced him.

Uullioll sang a brief song, a song of his joy at the feel of the bright hot on his back, as he swam into the dark below.

Aaheereeosh, older by two seasons but still small for his age, came alongside him and sang, "That song is madness, Uullioll."

Uullioll did a slow turn through the cool dark. He marked how far the hard fish had moved and his course back to it. "Why?"

"The bright hot will burn you."

"No, Aaheereeosh, it is pleasant. It brightens all, no matter where we are in our migrations. It brightens above the icy cold where we eat, where the big crabs crawl on the hard below. And it brightens above the warm stills where the girls become mothers. I like the bright hot. It floats above the dry-clear we breathe, how can you not like it?"

"I think the bright hot has already burned your brain, Uullioll."

"If so, then I hope it consumes me completely," Uullioll sang as he sped away toward the hard fish. It kept its uncommonly straight course, churning the salty-wet with its toothy tail, and Uullioll pushed himself faster until he breached the barrier and sailed into the dry-clear.

Out of his right eye he saw the upright crabs lining the side of the hard fish. As he cleared the salty-wet and breathed deep, they flapped their claws together and tried to sing out of their mouths, but their song was faint noise to him. He rolled a little and watched the bright hot as he hit the barrier and the salty-wet closed over him again.

The puller above began to brighten again, and the pod moved farther toward the warm stills. Uullioll and Aaheereeosh swam together about thirty lengths of an adult from the triple barrier where the hard below rose from the salty-wet into the dry-clear. A group of the upright crabs moved around on the hard below near the edge of the salty-wet; some scuttled about in the waves, and a few came in the wet and floated on thin reeds or tried to swim with awkward splashes of their claws.

"The bright hot above must favor them," Uullioll sang. "They get to live in its light all the time."

"Are you still swimming in that direction? You're feeding on hot wet, empty wet."

Uullioll did not care what Aaheereeosh thought. His friend had never understood Uullioll's lust for the bright hot's warmth, but he was still a good friend. After Uullioll's attempts to catch the bright hot failed, last migration he had tried another approach: he knew that when the bright hot fell below the edge of the world it always came back from the other direction, so he swam into a cut in the triple barrier, into wet that was no longer salty, looking for the route to the bright hot. The wet there tasted funny and Uullioll met many hard fish with the funny upright crabs on them, but he did not find the bright hot's home. Aaheereeosh had been waiting for him when he swam back into the salty-wet.

Now, Uullioll rolled enough to splash Aaheereeosh with his fin. "Have you forgotten the old stories? Our people used to live in the dry-clear, just like those upright crabs do, before we came into the salty-wet."

"My mother told me that one. It's just a story for long swims. So what?"

"But look at them. They live in the same dry-clear we breathe, but they come in the salty-wet."

"So what?"

"If they can come into the wet, why can't we go back into the dry?"

"Because we are where we belong," Aaheereeosh sang. "You're still young, Uullioll. When you're my age, you'll understand."

Uullioll sang a discordant note. "All you understand is how badly you want to get to the warm stills so you can mate."

Aaheereeosh did not deny it, he just dove under and left Uullioll on the surface to watch and wonder as he swam.

Uullioll cruised along the dark depths, swimming first above and then below the distinction between the warm wet and the colder wet. Osheeoroth's song sounded a little different above the distinction than below it, just as the salty-wet felt different above than below. Uullioll wondered about it, as he wondered about so many things.

Soon Uullioll tired of listening to Osheeoroth's song as it echoed and was repeated by other adults—so similar to last migration's song, always the same theme of moving and spawning. Uullioll had had enough of the pod, of Osheeoroth and his insistent goading, of Aaheereeosh and his derision. He swam upward to see the bright hot on the edge of the salty-wet, its color deep and its heat much less intense.

Uullioll still loved the bright hot and hungered for its warmth. But this migration he would not chase it. He would wait for it. And here, partway between the cold feeding wets and the warm mating wets, would be a fine place to wait. He would find a place where he could rest and let the bright hot come to him. The pod could go on without him.

The puller above felt especially potent as the bright hot deepened and dove. Uullioll turned toward the triple barrier and swam, hard, fast, faster. The salty-wet frothed around him, and when it lifted him a little he felt the weightless exhilaration he did when he breached. He pushed harder, riding the salty-wet until it deposited him on the hard below, above the triple barrier.

The hard below, was both. Uullioll settled into it; he wriggled a little, the way some of the burrowing fish did. It was rough on his skin, but not unpleasant.

The dry-clear was cool, and moved against his right side. It chilled him, and he closed his eye on that side. A shiver moved along his skin; deep inside he was warm enough, and the bright hot would come and warm him soon.

The salty-wet rose behind him and touched his tail, then receded again. He felt the pulses through the hard below, matched them to odd, moving sounds.

A monotone song bit his attention. It was an irritating noise, and Uullioll was grateful when one of the upright crabs moved quickly away to his left and took the sound with it.

He sighed, contented, and closed his other eye to await the coming of the bright hot.

The salty-wet receded behind Uullioll and left him on the rapidly drying hard below. He could still hear and feel the rhythmic pulsing below and behind him—less intense, but a constant reassurance like his mother's heartbeat from so many migrations ago.

Chittering noises overlaid the wet rhythm, and Uullioll opened his eyes. The puller above was still bright, though it had moved a little toward his tail. Several of the upright crabs were gathering around him, scuttling here and there and waving their claws. Some held cold little brights, and Uullioll blinked as one shone right in his eye. A small, different kind of crab, one on little low legs, jumped and scurried about with frequent, annoying shrieks. Not a singer, that one, but the way it moved fascinated him.

Uullioll tried to stand like the little low crab, but his fins were too weak. He wondered how long it would take to strengthen them. He sighed and settled back down to the hard below. It was difficult to breathe deep.

The noises from the upright crabs pulsated in crazy, rhythmless tones. Pitch and intensity rose and fell, more voices and fewer and more again. They kept a respectable distance, at least a head's length away, but more and more of them gathered as the puller above moved out of his field of vision. Uullioll wondered if they were dangerous and decided they weren't: their little claws and tiny mouths were no threat.

Gradually the upright crabs dispersed until only a few were left. These hunkered down to the hard below, alone or in groups of two or three, watching Uullioll with their forward-facing eyes. What did they expect him to do? At least they were quieter now, and once again he could hear and feel the rhythms of the salty-wet.

He lifted his tail and let it fall with the salty-wet rhythm. He closed his eyes again and thought of how to greet the bright hot.

✧ ✧ ✧

A shudder rippled through him and he came wide awake as one of the upright crabs touched his flank. There were more of them around him again, and closer than before, and for a moment Uullioll was afraid. But he had been right: their claws did no damage. Instead they flung wet skins across his back. They were heavy and smooth, not gritty like the hard below, and the upright crabs splashed Uullioll with the salty-wet. It felt good.

Other upright crabs burrowed into the hard below all around him. They built a reef around him and filled it with salty-wet.

It felt right somehow that these upright crabs should minister to him so. That they should welcome him up from the salty deeps and honor his pursuit of the bright hot. He was grateful that they would share the bright hot with him.

He marked the rhythms as the salty-wet crept closer again and above lightened with the coming of the bright hot. With a mighty convulsion, Uullioll twisted so he could see the bright hot's round eye crest over the hard below. He flicked his tail in the salty-wet and sang a hymn to the bright hot, of joy at its coming and thanks for its servants the upright crabs, a hymn that matched the rhythms of the salty-wet as it pounded against the hard below.

But Uullioll's voice didn't sound the same in the dry-clear. It sounded hollow. He could barely hear it, and knew it wouldn't carry to the bright hot. His joyful song of warmth and light and solidity below him turned into a mournful tune of disappointment, shame, and lonely grief.

And yet the bright hot still favored Uullioll with warmth. Uullioll closed his eyes against the growing brightness and concentrated on the warmth seeping into his skin. He sang again his song of joy, but only in his mind.

The upright crabs continued to splash salty-wet on him, and Uullioll wished Aaheereeosh were with him to see how they served him. Whose song is madness now?

As the bright hot coursed above him, Uullioll marked many changes in the noises around him. Upright crabs came and went, and big noisy snails that moved on round legs, and birds that hung motionless in the dry-clear above. The pulsings behind him could only be several hard fish, floating on the salty-wet.

The first tentacle around his flukes caught Uullioll by surprise.

He thrashed his tail, afraid of the danger he couldn't see. His mother had warned him about tentacle-bearers, some bigger than three of him, in the cold, dark deeps. Then a second tentacle, and a third, looped around his tail.

"Help me," Uullioll sang. His voice sounded empty as the dry-clear.

Some of the upright crabs must have heard, because they gathered around him and laid their claws on him. He relaxed, and sang silent thanks to the bright hot, until he felt the pull from behind—and the upright crabs began to push him backward.

Uullioll was stunned. What had he done wrong? Why would they not save him?

"No, help me," he sang again. "Don't take me away from the bright hot. I want to rest on the hard below, I want to feel the dry-clear on my skin." He thrashed against the tentacles' pull, but gained only an eye's width for every fin's length he lost.

The salty-wet came up around him, buoyed him, and the treacherous upright crabs screeched to each other. They pulled the wet skins from him and pushed at him, and Uullioll almost wished they would flay him with their tender claws. Selfish crabs, to keep the bright hot and the hard below to themselves and feed him to the tentacle-bearer.

Then the tentacles fell away from his tail and Uullioll turned to see three hard fish, trailing tentacles behind their churning tails. Tall crabs on the hard fish waved their claws and screeched, and the upright crabs standing near him in the salty-wet did likewise. One of the upright crabs scurried out of the wet and grabbed another with its claws, and the strange, short crab leapt around them and yelped.

Even though he could not understand it—even though it was discord to him—the crabs' song sounded triumphant.

They sing to one another, but not to me? They force me out of the bright hot's grace, back into the salty-wet, and they gloat?

Uullioll blasted his frustration and the upright crabs screeched even louder, mocking the depth of his rejection. He swam in a circle and approached the triple barrier, but a line of crabs blocked his way and one of the hard fish sped toward him. He turned again and sang his anger into the salty-wet.

And a voice answered him.

Uullioll stopped. He floated there, listening. It was hard to make out the voice in the cacophony around him.

Uullioll swam away from the triple barrier, away from the feckless upright crabs, and sang again his desperate rage. The voice answered again, and it was not one voice but a dozen. He heard Aaheereeosh, and even Osheeoroth, and it was not the song to pull the pod to the warm stills but a new, different song. A song to welcome Uullioll back into the salty-wet. To welcome him home.

Uullioll rolled and let the bright hot warm his side, his stomach, his other side, then floated again with the warmth seeping into his back.

The pod beckoned from the deeps. The bright hot beckoned from above. Uullioll dove below the barrier but stayed in the shadowy shallows. There was only one place he would be welcomed; did that mean there was only one place where he belonged?

Uullioll cruised the dark deep, alone and thinking.

He was full, yet still he filtered tasteless morsels from the salty-wet. Above him, above the barrier, the puller was an open eye again. It was almost time.

From below and behind him came the high-pitched, tuneless song of his spawn as it chased after its mother. Uullioll had been that carefree once, long before Osheeoroth died. So many migrations gone by, and now Aaheereeosh was also dead and the pod looked to him for guidance.

Uullioll swam up to the barrier but did not breach. The dry-clear was cold, and he floated on the surface under the pale glow of the puller above. A few lengths away, one of the big icy rocks floated; it shone in the puller's light. As Uullioll watched, a bit of it sheared off: unbalanced, the remainder spun and writhed in the salty-wet. It flung itself about, split off pieces that floated away in all directions.

One, then another of the small icy rocks touched Uullioll's side. What was left of the big cold rock slowed and settled until it floated very near to where it began. Uullioll heard himself in its thrashing: motion without progress, frantic action that only served to diminish it.

Uullioll spouted a sigh. There must be more to these migrations, somewhere, and he despaired that he had never found it. But now he had responsibilities; now it was time to head to the warm stills, to let the girls become mothers of new generations that might pursue and finally catch the bright hot.

Uullioll filled his lungs with dry-clear. And he sang.

THE OCEAN OF THE BLIND
James L. Cambias

The planet's inhabitants were intelligent, but without eyesight, perceiving their undersea realm by a sort of sonar. The visiting human had arrived with a special suit that absorbed all sound waves, rendering him invisible—or inaudible—and was going to study the natives up close. What could possibly go wrong?

By the end of his second month at Hitode Station, Rob Freeman had already come up with 85 ways to murder Henri Kerlerec. That put him third in the station's rankings—Josef Palashnik was first with 143, followed by Nadia Kyle with 97. In general, the number and sheer viciousness of the suggested methods was in proportion to the amount of time each one spent with Henri.

Josef, as the primary submarine pilot, had to spend hours and hours each week in close quarters with Henri, so his list concentrated on swift and brutal techniques suitable for a small cockpit. Nadia shared lab space with Henri—which in practice meant she did her dissections in the kitchen or on the floor of her bedroom—and her techniques were mostly obscure poisons and subtle death traps.

Rob's specialty was underwater photography and drone operation. All through training he had been led to expect he would be filming the exotic life forms of Ilmatar, exploring the unique environment of the remote icy world, and helping the science team understand the alien biology and ecology. Within a week of arrival he found himself somehow locked into the role of Henri Kerlerec's personal cameraman, gofer, and captive audience. His list of murder methods began with "strangling HK with that stupid ankh necklace" and progressed through cutting the air hose on Henri's dry suit, jamming him into a thermal vent, abandoning him in mid-ocean with no inertial compass, and feeding him to an *Aenocampus*. Some of the others on the station who routinely read the hidden "Death To HK" board had protested that last one as being too cruel to the *Aenocampus*.

Rob's first exposure to killing Henri came at a party given by Nadia and her husband Pierre Adler in their room, just after the support vehicle left orbit for the six-month voyage back to Earth. With four guests there was barely enough room, and to avoid overloading the ventilators they had to leave the door open. For refreshment they had melons from the hydroponic garden filled with some of Palashnik's home-brew potato vodka. One drank melon-flavored vodka until the hollow interior was empty, then cut vodka-flavored melon slices.

"I've got a new one," said Nadia after her third melon slice. "Put a piece of paper next to Le Nuke for a few months until it's radioactive, then write him a fan letter and slip it under his door. He'd keep the letter for his collection and die of gradual exposure."

"Too long," said Josef. "Even if he kept it in his pocket, it would take years to kill him."

"But you'd have the fun of watching him lose his hair," said Nadia.

"I would rather just lock him in the reactor shed and leave him there," said Josef.

"Who are they talking about?" Rob asked.

"Henri Kerlerec," whispered the person squeezed onto the bed next to him.

"Irradiate his hair gel," said Pierre. "That way he'd put more on every day and it would be right next to his brain."

"Ha! That part has been dead for years!"

"Replace the argon in his breathing unit with chlorine," said someone Rob couldn't see, and then the room went quiet.

Henri was standing in the doorway. As usual, he was grinning. "Planning to murder somebody? Our esteemed station director, I hope." He glanced behind him to make sure Dr. Sen wasn't in earshot. "I have thought of an infallible technique: I would strike him over the head with a large ham or gigot or something of that kind, and then when the police come, I would serve it to them to destroy the evidence. They would never suspect!"

"Roald Dahl," murmured Nadia. "And it was a *frozen* leg of lamb."

Henri didn't hear her. "You see the beauty of it? The police eat the murder weapon. Perhaps I shall write a detective novel about it when I get back to Earth. Well, goodnight everyone!" He gave a little wave and went off toward Hab Three.

This particular morning Rob was trying to think of an especially sadistic fate for Henri. Kerlerec had awakened him at 0500—three hours early!—and summoned him to the dive room with a great show of secrecy.

The dive room occupied the bottom of Hab One. It was a big circular room with suits and breathing gear stowed on the walls, benches for getting into one's gear, and a moon pool in the center where the Terran explorers could pass into Ilmatar's dark ocean. It was usually the coldest room in the entire station, chilled by the subzero seawater.

Henri was there, waiting at the base of the access ladder. As soon as Rob climbed down he slammed the hatch shut. "Now we can talk privately together. I have an important job for you."

"What?"

"Tonight at 0100 we are going out on a dive. Tell nobody. Do not write anything in the dive log."

"What? Why tonight? And why did you have to get me up at five in the goddamned morning to have this conversation?"

"It must be kept absolutely secret."

"Henri, I'm not doing anything until you tell me exactly what is going on. Enough cloak and dagger stuff."

"Come and see." Henri led him to the hatch into Hab Three, opened it a crack to peek through, then gestured for Rob to follow as he led the way to the lab space he shared with Nadia Kyle. It was a little room about twice the size of a sleeping cabin, littered with native artifacts, unlabeled data storage, and tanks holding live specimens. Standing in the middle was a large gray plastic container as tall as a man. It had stenciled markings in Cyrillic and a sky blue UNICA shipping label.

Henri touched his thumb to a lock pad and the door swung open to reveal a bulky diving suit. It was entirely black, even the faceplate, and had a sleek, seamless look.

"Nice suit. What's so secret about it?"

"This is not a common sort of diving suit," said Henri. "I arranged specially for it to be sent to me. Nobody else has anything like it. It is a Russian Navy stealth suit, for deactivating underwater smart mines or sonar pods. The surface is completely anechoic. Invisible to any kind of sonar imaging. Even the fins are low-noise."

"How does it work?" Rob's inner geek prompted him to ask.

Henri gave a shrug. "That is for technical people to worry about. All I care is that it does work. It must—it cost me six million euros to get it here."

"Okay, so you've got the coolest diving suit on Ilmatar. Why are you keeping it locked up? I'm sure the bio people would love to be able to get close to native life without being heard."

"Pah. When I am done they can watch all the shrimps and worms they wish to. But first, I am going to use this suit to observe the Ilmatarans up close. Imagine it, Robert! I can swim among their houses, perhaps even go right inside! Stand close enough to touch them! They will never notice I am there!"

"What about the contact rules?"

"Contact? What contact? Didn't you hear—the Ilmatarans will not notice me! I will stand among them, recording at close range, but with this suit I will be invisible to them!"

"Doctor Sen's going to shit a brick when he finds out."

"By the time he finds out it will be done. What can he do to me? Send me home? I will go back to Earth on the next ship in triumph!"

"The space agencies aren't going to like it either."

"Robert, before I left Earth I did some checking. Do you know how many people regularly access space agency sites or subscribe to their news feeds? About fifty million people, worldwide. Do you know how many people watched the video of my Titan expedition? Ninety-six million! I have twice as many viewers, and that makes me twice as important. The agencies all love me."

Rob suspected Henri's numbers were made up on the spur of the moment, the way most of his numbers were, but it was probably true enough that Henri Kerlerec, the famous scientist-explorer and shameless media whore, got more eyeballs than the rest of the entire interstellar program.

He could feel himself being sucked into the mighty whirlpool of Henri's ego, and tried to struggle against it. "I don't want to get in any trouble."

"You have nothing to worry about. Now, listen: here is what we will do. You come down here quietly at about 0030 and get everything ready. Bring the cameras, and a couple of the quiet impeller units. Also a drone or two. I will get this suit on myself in here, and then at 0100 we go out. With the impellers we can get as far as the Maury 3 vent. There is a little Ilmataran settlement there."

"That's a long way to go by impeller. Maury 3's what, sixty kilometers from here?"

"Three hours out, three hours back, and perhaps two hours at the site. We will get back at about 0900, while the others are still eating breakfast. They may not even notice we have gone."

"And if they do?"

"Then we just say we have been doing some shooting around the habitat outside." Henri began locking up the stealth suit's container. "I tell you, they will never suspect a thing. Leave all the talking to me. Now: not another word! We have too much to do! I am going to sleep this afternoon to be fresh for our dive tonight. You must do the same. And do not speak of this to anyone!"

Broadtail is nervous. He cannot pay attention to the speaker, and constantly checks the reel holding his text. He is to speak next, his first address to the Bitterwater Company of Scholars. It is an audition of sorts—Broadtail hopes the members find his work interesting enough to invite him to join them.

Smoothshell 24 Midden finishes her address on high-altitude creatures and takes a few questions from the audience. They aren't easy questions, either, and Broadtail worries about making a fool of himself before all these respected scholars. When she finishes, Longpincer 16 Bitterwater clacks his pincers for quiet.

"Welcome now to Broadtail 38 Sandyslope, who comes to us from a great distance to speak about ancient languages. Broadtail?"

Broadtail nearly drops his reel, but catches it before it can come unrolled and scuttles to the end of the room. It is a wonderful chamber for speaking, with a sloped floor so that everyone can hear directly, and walls of quiet pumice stone. He finds the end of his reel and begins, running it carefully between his feeding-tendrils as he speaks aloud. His tendrils feel the knots in the string as it passes by them. The patterns of knots indicate numbers, and the numbers match words.

He remembers being careful to space his knots and tie them tightly, as this copy is for the Bitterwater library. The reel is a single unbroken cord, expensive to buy and horribly complicated to work with—very different from the original draft, a tangle of short notes tied together all anyhow.

Once he begins, Broadtail's fear dissipates. His own fascination with his topic asserts itself, and he feels himself speeding up as his excitement grows. When he pauses, he can hear his audience rustling and scrabbling, and he supposes that is a good sign. At least they aren't all going torpid.

The anchor of his speech is the description of the echo-carvings from the ruined city near his home vent of Continuous Abundance. By correlating the images of the echo-carvings with the number markings below them, Broadtail believes he can create a lexicon for the ancient city builders. He reads the Company some of his translations of other markings in the ruins.

Upon finishing, he faces a torrent of questions. Huge old Roundhead 19 Downcurrent has several tough ones—he is generally recognized as the expert on ancient cities and their builders, and he means to make sure some provincial upstart doesn't encroach on his territory.

Roundhead and some others quickly home in on some of the weak parts of Broadtail's argument. A couple of them make reference to the writings of the dead scholar Thickfeelers 19 Swiftcurrent, and Broadtail feels a pang of jealousy because he can't afford to buy copies of such rare works. As the questions continue, Broadtail feels himself getting angry in defense of his work, and struggles to retain his temper. The presentation may be a disaster, but he must remain polite.

At last it is over, and he rolls up his reel and heads for a seat at the rear of the room. He'd like to just keep going, slink outside and swim for home, but it would be rude.

A scholar Broadtail doesn't recognize scuttles to the lectern and begins struggling with a tangled reel. Longpincer sits next to Broadtail and speaks privately with shell-taps. "That was very well done. I think you describe some extremely important discoveries."

"You do? I was just thinking of using the reel to mend nets."

"Because of all the questions? Don't worry. That's a good sign. If the hearers ask questions it means they're thinking, and that's the whole purpose of this Company. I don't know of any reason not to make you a member. I'm sure the others agree."

All kinds of emotions flood through Broadtail—relief, excitement, and sheer happiness. He can barely keep from speaking aloud. His shell-taps are rapid. "I'm very grateful. I plan to revise the reel to address some of Roundhead's questions."

"Of course. I imagine some of the others want copies, too. Ah, he's starting."

The scholar at the lectern begins to read a reel about a new system for measuring the heat of springs, but Broadtail is too happy to really pay attention.

At midnight, Rob was lying on his bunk trying to come up with some excuse not to go with Henri. Say he was sick, maybe? The trouble was that he was a rotten liar. He tried to make himself feel sick—maybe an upset stomach from ingesting seawater? His body unhelpfully continued to feel okay.

Maybe he just wouldn't go. Stay in bed and lock the door. Henri could hardly complain to Dr. Sen about him not going on an unauthorized dive. But of course Henri could and undoubtedly would make his life miserable with nagging and blustering until he finally gave in.

And of course the truth was that Rob did want to go. He really wanted to be the one in the stealth suit, getting within arm's reach of the Ilmatarans and filming them close up, instead of getting a few murky long-distance drone pictures. Probably everyone else at Hitode Station felt the same way. Putting them here, actually on the sea bottom of Ilmatar, yet forbidding them to get close to the natives, was like telling a pack of horny teenagers they could get naked in bed together, but not touch.

He checked his watch. It was 0020. He got up and slung his camera bag over his shoulder. Damn Henri anyway.

Rob made it to the dive room without encountering anyone. The station wasn't like a space vehicle with round-the-clock shifts. Everyone slept from about 2400 to 0800, and only one poor soul had to stay in the control room in case of emergency. Tonight it was Dickie Graves on duty, and Rob suspected that Henri had managed to square him somehow so that the exterior hydrophones wouldn't pick up their little jaunt.

He took one of the drones off the rack and ran a quick check. It was a flexible robot fish about a meter long, more Navy surplus—American, this time. It wasn't especially stealthy, but instead was designed to mimic a mackerel's sonar signature. Presumably the Ilmatarans would figure it was some native organism and ignore it. His computer linked up with the drone brain by laser. All powered up and ready to go. He told it to hold position and await further instructions, then dropped it into the water. Just to be on the safe side, Rob fired up a second drone and tossed it into the moon pool after the first.

Next the impellers. They were simple enough—a motor, a battery, and a pair of counter-rotating propellors. You controlled your speed with a thumb switch on the handle. They were supposedly quiet, though in Rob's experience they weren't any more stealthy than the ones you could rent at any dive shop back on Earth. Some contractor in Japan had made a bundle on them. Rob found two with full batteries and hooked them on the edge of the pool for easy access.

Now for the hard part: suiting himself up without any help. Rob took off his frayed and smelly insulated jumpsuit and stripped to the skin. First the diaper—he and Henri were going to be out for eight hours, and getting the inside of his suit wet would invite death from hypothermia. Then a set of thick fleece long johns, like a child's pajamas. The water outside was well below freezing; only the pressure and salinity kept it liquid. He'd need all the insulation he could get.

Then the dry suit, double-layered and also insulated. In the chilly air of the changing room he was getting red-faced and hot with all this protection on. The hood was next, a snug fleece balaclava with built-in earphones. Then the helmet, a plastic fishbowl more like a space helmet than most diving gear, which zipped onto the suit to make a watertight seal. The back of the helmet was packed with electronics—biomonitors, microphones, sonar unit, and an elaborate heads-up display which could project text and data on the inside of the faceplate. There was also a freshwater tube, which he sipped before going on to the next stage.

Panting with the exertion, Rob struggled into the heavy APOS backpack, carefully started it up *before* attaching the hoses to his helmet, and took a few breaths to make sure it was really working. The APOS gear made the whole Ilmatar expedition possible. It made oxygen out of seawater by electrolysis, supplying it at ambient pressure. Little sensors and a pretty sophisticated computer adjusted the supply to the wearer's demand. The oxygen mixed with a closed-loop argon supply; at the colossal pressures of Ilmatar's ocean bottom, the proper air mix was about 1,000 parts argon to 1 part oxygen. Hitode Station and the subs each had bigger versions, which was how humans could live under six kilometers of water and ice.

The price, of course, was that it took six days to go up to the surface. The pressure difference between the 300 atmospheres at the bottom of the sea and the half standard at the surface station meant a human wouldn't just get the bends if he went up quickly—he'd literally explode. There were other dangers, too. All the crew at Hitode took a regimen of drugs to ward off the scary side effects of high pressure.

With his APOS running (though for now its little computer was sensible enough to simply feed him air from the room outside), Rob pulled on his three layers of gloves, buckled on his fins, put on his weight belt, switched on his shoulder lamp, and then crouched on the edge of the moon pool to let himself tumble backwards into the water. It felt pleasantly cool, rather than lethally cold, and he bled a little extra gas into his suit to keep him afloat until Henri could join him.

He gave the drones instructions to follow at a distance of four meters, and created a little window on his faceplate to let him watch through their eyes. He checked over the camera clamped to his shoulder to make sure it was working. Everything nominal. It was 0120 now. Where was Henri?

Kerlerec lumbered into view ten minutes later. In the bulky stealth suit he looked like a big black toad. The foam cover of his faceplate was hanging down over his chest, and Rob could see that he was red and sweating. Henri waddled to the edge of the pool and fell back into the water with an enormous splash. After a moment he bobbed up next to Rob.

"God, it is hot in this thing. You would not believe how hot it is. For once I am glad to be in the water. Do you have everything?"

"Yep. So how are you going to use the camera in that thing? Won't it spoil the whole stealth effect?"

"I will not use the big camera. That is for you to take pictures of me at long range. I have a couple of little cameras inside my helmet. One points forward to see what I see, the other is for my face. Link up."

They got the laser link established and Rob opened two new windows at the bottom of his faceplate. One showed his own face as Henri saw him—a pale, stubbly face inside a bubble helmet—and the other showed Henri in extreme close-up from inside his helmet. The huge green-lit face beaded with sweat looked a bit like the Great and Powerful Oz after a three-day drunk.

"Now we will get away from the station and try out your sonar on my suit. You will not be able to detect me at all."

Personally Rob doubted it. Some Russian had made a cool couple of million Euros selling Henri and his sponsors at ScienceMonde a failed prototype or just a fake.

The two of them sank down until they were underneath Hab One, only a couple of meters above the seafloor. The light shining down from the moon pool made a pale cone in the silty water, with solid blackness beyond.

Henri led the way away from the station, swimming with his headlamp and his safety strobe on until they were a few hundred meters out. "This is good," he said. "Start recording."

Rob got the camera locked in on Henri's image. "You're on."

Henri's voice instantly became the calm, friendly but all-knowing voice of Henri Kerlerec, scientific media star. "I am here in the dark ocean of Ilmatar, preparing to test the high-tech stealth diving suit which will enable me to get close to the Ilmatarans without being detected. I am covering up the faceplate with the special stealth coating now. My cameraman will try to locate me by sonar. Because the Ilmatarans live in a completely dark environment, they are entirely blind to visible light, so I will leave my safety strobe and headlamp on."

Rob opened up a window to display sonar images and began recording. First on passive—his computer could build up a vague image of the surroundings just from ambient noise and interference patterns. No sign of Henri, even though Rob could see his bobbing headlamp as he swam back and forth ten meters away.

Not bad, Rob had to admit. Those Russians knew a few things about sonar baffling. He tried the active sonar. The seabottom and the rocks flickered into clear relief, an eerie false-color landscape where green meant soft and yellow meant hard surfaces. The ocean itself was completely black on active. Henri was a green-black shadow against a black background. Even with the computer synthesizing both the active and passive signals, he was almost impossible to see.

"Wonderful!" said Henri when Rob sent him the images. "I told you: completely invisible! We will edit this part down, of course—just the sonar images with me explaining it in voice-over. Now come along. We have a long trip ahead of us."

The Bitterwater Company are waking up. Longpincer's servants scuttle along the halls of his house, listening carefully at the entrance to each guest chamber and informing the ones already awake that a meal is ready in the main hall.

Broadtail savors the elegance of having someone to come wake him when the food is ready. At his own house, all would starve if he waited for his apprentices to prepare the meals. He wonders briefly how they are getting along without him. The three of them are reasonably competent, and can certainly tend his pipes and crops without him. Broadtail does worry about how well they can handle an emergency— what if a pipe breaks or one of his nets is snagged? He imagines returning home to find chaos and ruin.

But it is so very nice here at Longpincer's house. Mansion, really. The Bitterwater vent isn't nearly as large as Continuous Abundance or the other town vents, but Longpincer controls the entire flow. Everything for ten cables in any direction belongs to him. He has a staff of servants and hired workers. Even his apprentices scarcely need to lift a pincer themselves.

Broadtail doesn't want to miss the meal. Longpincer's larder is as opulent as everything else at Bitterwater. As he crawls to the main hall he marvels again at the thick growths on the walls and floor. Some of his own farm pipes don't support this much life. Is it just that Longpincer's large household generates enough waste to support lush indoor growth? Or is he rich enough to pipe some excess vent water through the house itself? Either way it's far more than Broadtail's chilly property and tepid flow rights can achieve.

As he approaches the main hall Broadtail can taste a tremendous and varied feast laid out. It sounds as if half a dozen of the Company are already there; it says much for Longpincer's kitchen that the only sounds Broadtail can hear are those of eating.

He finds a place between Smoothshell and a quiet individual whose name Broadtail can't recall. He runs his feelers over the food before him and feels more admiration mixed with jealousy for Longpincer. There are cakes of pressed sourleaf, whole towfin eggs, fresh jellyfronds, and some little bottom-crawling creatures Broadtail isn't familiar with, neatly impaled on thorns and still wiggling.

Broadtail can't recall having a feast like this since he inherited the Northslope property and gave the funeral banquet for old Flatbody. He is just reaching for a third jellyfrond when Longpincer clicks loudly for attention from the end of the hall.

"I suggest a small excursion for the Company," he says. "About ten cables beyond my boundary stones upcurrent is a small vent, too tepid and bitter to be worth piping. I forbid my workers to drag nets there, and I recall finding several interesting creatures feeding at the vent. I propose swimming there to look for specimens."

"May I suggest applying Sharpfrill's technique for temperature measurement to those waters?" says Smoothshell.

"Excellent idea!" cries Longpincer. Sharpfrill mutters something about not having his proper equipment, but the others bring him around. They all finish eating (Broadtail notices several of the company stowing delicacies in pouches, and grabs the last towfin egg to fill his own), and set out for the edge of Longpincer's property.

Swimming is quicker than walking, so the party of scholars cruise at just above net height. At that height Broadtail can only get a general impression of the land below, but it all seems neat and orderly—a well-planned network of stone pipes radiating out from the main vent, carrying the hot, nutrient-rich water to nourish thousands of plants and bacteria colonies. Leaks from the pipes and the waste from the crops and Longpincer's household feeds clouds of tiny swimmers, which in turn attract larger creatures from the cold waters around. Broadtail notes with approval the placement of Longpincer's nets, in staggered rows along the prevailing current. With a little envy he estimates that Longpincer's nets probably produce as much wealth as his own entire property.

Beyond the boundary stones the scholars instinctively gather into a more compact group. There is less conversation and more careful listening and pinging. Longpincer assures them that he allows no bandits or scavengers around his vent, but even he pings behind them once or twice, just to make sure. But all anyone can hear are a few wild children, who flee quickly at the approach of adults.

Henri and Rob didn't talk much on the way to the vent community. Both of them were paying close attention to the navigation displays inside their helmets. Getting around on Ilmatar was deceptively easy: take a bearing by inertial compass, point the impeller in the right direction, and off you go. But occasionally Rob found himself thinking about just how hard it would be to navigate without electronic help. The stars were hidden by a kilometer of ice overhead, and Ilmatar had no magnetic field worth speaking of. It was barely possible to tell up from down—if you had your searchlights on and could see the bottom and weren't enveloped in a cloud of silt—but maintaining a constant depth depended entirely on watching the sonar display and the pressure gauge. A human without navigation equipment on Ilmatar would be blind, deaf, and completely lost.

At 0500 they were nearing the site. "Passive sonar only," said Henri. "And we must be as quiet as possible. Can you film from a hundred meters away?"

"It'll need enhancement and cleaning up afterward, but yes."

"Good. You take up a position there—" Henri gestured vaguely into the darkness.

"Where?"

"That big clump of rocks at, let me see, bearing one hundred degrees, about fifty meters out."

"Okay."

"Stay there and do not make any noise. I will go on ahead toward the vent. Keep one of the drones with me."

"Right. What are you going to do?"

"I will walk right into the settlement."

Shaking his head, Rob found a relatively comfortable spot among the stones. While he waited for the silt to settle, he noticed that this wasn't a natural outcrop—these were cut stones, the remains of a structure of some kind. Some of the surfaces were even carved into patterns of lines. He made sure to take pictures of everything. The other xeno people back at Hitode would kill him if he didn't.

Henri went marching past in a cloud of silt. The big camera was going to be useless with him churning up the bottom like that, so Rob relied entirely on the drones. One followed Henri about ten meters back, the second was above him looking down. The laser link through the water was a little noisy from suspended particulates, but he didn't need a whole lot of detail. The drone cameras could store everything internally, so Rob was satisfied with just enough sight to steer them. Since he was comfortably seated and could use his hands, he called up a virtual joystick instead of relying on voice commands or the really irritating eye-tracking menu device.

"Look at that!" Henri called suddenly.

"What? Where?"

Henri's forward camera swung up to show eight Ilmatarans swimming along in formation, about ten meters up. They were all adults, wearing belts and harnesses stuffed with gear. A couple carried spears. Ever since the first drone pictures of Ilmatarans, they had been described as looking like giant lobsters, but watching them swim overhead, Rob had to disagree. They were more like beluga whales in armor, with their big flukes and blunt heads. Adults ranged from three to four meters long. Each had a dozen limbs folded neatly against the undersides of their shells: walking legs in back, four manipulators in front, and the big praying-mantis pincers on the front pair. They also had raspy feeding tendrils and long sensory feelers under the head. The head itself was a smooth featureless dome, flaring out over the neck like a coal-scuttle helmet—the origin of the Ilmatarans' scientific name *Salletocephalus structor*. Henri's passive microphones picked up the clicks and pops of the Ilmatarans' sonar, with an occasional loud ping like a harpsichord note.

The two humans watched as the group soared over Henri's head. "What do you think they're doing?" asked Rob when they had passed.

"I am not sure. Perhaps a hunting party. I will follow them."

Rob wanted to argue, but knew it was pointless. "Don't go too far."

Henri kicked up from the bottom and began to follow the Ilmatarans. It was hard for a human to keep up with them, even when wearing fins. Henri was sweaty and breathing hard after just a couple of minutes, but he struggled along. "They are stopping," he said after ten minutes, sounding relieved.

The Ilmatarans were dropping down to a small vent formation, which Rob's computer identified as Maury 3b. Through the drone cameras Rob watched as Henri crept closer to the Ilmatarans. At first he moved with clumsy stealth, then abandoned all pretense and simply waded in among them. Rob waited for a reaction, but the Ilmatarans seemed intent on their own business.

A rock is missing. Broadtail remembers a big chunk of old shells welded together by vent-water minerals and mud, just five armspans away across-current. But now it's gone. Is his memory faulty? He pings again. There it is, just where it should be. Odd. He goes back to gathering shells.

"—you hear me? Broadtail!" It is Longpincer. He appears out of nowhere just in front of Broadtail, sounding alarmed.

"I'm here. What's wrong?"

"Nothing," says Longpincer. "My own mistake."

"Wait. Tell me."

"It's very odd. I remember hearing you clattering over the rocks, then silence. I recall pinging and sensing nothing."

"I remember a similar experience—a rock seeming to vanish and then return."

Smoothshell comes up. "What's the problem?" After they explain she asks, "Could there be a reflective layer here? Cold water meeting hot does that."

"I don't feel any change in the water temperature," says Longpincer. "The current here is strong enough to keep everything mixed."

"Let's listen," says Broadtail. The three of them stand silently, tails together, heads outward. Broadtail relaxes, letting the sounds and interference patterns of his surroundings create a model in his mind. The vent is there, rumbling and hissing. Someone is scrabbling up the side—probably Sharpfrill with his jars of temperature-sensitive plants. Roundhead and the quiet person are talking together half a cable away, or rather Roundhead is talking and his companion is making occasional polite clicks. Two others are swishing nets through the water upcurrent.

But there is something else. Something is moving nearby. He can't quite hear it, but it blocks other sounds and changes the interference patterns. He reaches over to Smoothshell and taps on her leg. "There is a strange effect in the water in front of me, moving slowly from left to right."

She turns and listens that way while Broadtail taps the same message on Longpincer's shell. "I think I hear what you mean," she says. "It's like a big lump of very soft mud, or pumice stone."

"Yes," Broadtail agrees. "Except that it's moving. I'm going to ping it now." He tenses his resonator muscle and pings as hard as he can, loud enough to stun a few small swimmers near his head. All the other Company members about the vent stop what they are doing.

He hears the entire landscape in front of him—quiet mud, sharp echoes from rocks, muffled and chaotic patterns from patches of plants. And right in the center, only a few armspans in front of him, is a hole in the water. It's big, whatever it is: almost the size of a young adult, standing upright like a boundary marker.

Henri was completely gonzo. He was rattling off narration for the audience completely off the top of his head. Occasionally he would forget to use his media star voice and give way to an outburst of pure cackling glee. Rob was pretty excited, too, watching through the cameras as Henri got within arm's reach of the Ilmatarans.

"Here we see a group of Ilmatarans gathering food around one of the seabottom vents. Some are using handmade nets to catch fish, while these three close to me appear to be scraping algae off the rocks."

"Henri, you're using Earth life names again. Those aren't fish, or algae either."

"Never mind that now. I will dub in the proper words later if I must. The audience will understand better if I use words they understand. This is wonderful, don't you think? I can pat them on the backs if I want to!"

"Remember, no contact."

"Yes, yes." Back into his narrator voice. "The exact nature of Ilmataran social organization is still not well understood. We know they live in communities of up to a hundred individuals, sharing the work of food production, craftwork, and defense. The harvest these bring back to their community will be divided among all."

"Henri, you can't just make stuff up like that. Some of the audience are going to want links to more info about Ilmataran society. We don't know how they allocate resources."

"Then there is nothing to say that this is untrue. Robert, people do not want to hear that aliens are just like us. They want wise angels and noble savages. Besides, I am certain I am right. The Ilmatarans behave exactly like early human societies. Remember I am an archaeologist by training. I recognize the signs." He shifted back into media mode. "Life is difficult in these icy seas. The Ilmatarans must make use of every available source of food to ward off starvation. I am going to get closer to these individuals so that we can watch them at their work."

"Don't get too close. They might be able to smell you or something."

"I am being careful. How is the picture quality?"

"Well, the water's pretty cloudy. I've got the drone providing an overhead view of you, but the helmet camera's the only thing giving us any detail."

"I will bend down to get a better view, then. How is that?"

"Better. This is great stuff." Rob checked the drone image. "Uh, Henri, why are they all facing toward you?"

"We must capture it," says Longpincer. "I don't remember reading about anything like this."

"How to capture something we can barely make out?" asks Broadtail.

"Surround it," suggests Smoothshell. She calls to the others. "Here, quickly! Form a circle!"

With a lot of clicking questions the other members of the Bitterwater Company gather around—except for Sharpfrill, who is far too absorbed in placing his little colonies of temperature indicators on the vent.

"Keep pinging steadily," says Longpincer. "As hard as you can. Who has a net?"

"Here!" says Raggedclaw.

"Good. Can you make it out? Get the net on it!"

The thing starts to swim upward clumsily, churning up lots of sediment and making a faint but audible swishing noise with its tails. Under Longpincer's direction the Company form a box around it, like soldiers escorting a convoy. Raggedclaw gets above it with the net. There is a moment of struggling as the thing tries to dodge aside, then the scientists close in around it.

It cuts at the net with a sharp claw, and kicks with its limbs. Broadtail feels the claw grate along his shell. Longpincer and Roundhead move in with ropes, and soon the thing's limbs are pinned. It sinks to the bottom.

"I suggest we take it to my laboratory," says Longpincer. "I am sure we all wish to study this remarkable creature."

It continues to struggle, but the netting and ropes are strong enough to hold it. Whatever it is, it's too heavy to carry swimming, so the group must walk along the bottom with their catch while Longpincer swims ahead to fetch servants with a litter to help. They all ping about them constantly, fearful that more of the strange silent creatures are lurking about.

"Robert! In the name of God, help me!" The laser link was full of static and skips, what with all the interference from nets, Ilmatarans, and sediment. The video image of Henri degenerated into a series of still shots illustrating panic, terror, and desperation.

"Don't worry!" he called back, although he had no idea what to do. How could he rescue Henri without revealing himself and blowing all the contact protocols to hell? For that matter, even if he did reveal himself, how could he overcome half a dozen full-grown Ilmatarans?

"Ah, bon Dieu!" Henri started what sounded like praying in French. Rob muted the audio to give himself a chance to think, and because it didn't seem right to listen in.

He tried to list his options. Call for help? Too far from the station, and it would take an hour or more for a sub to arrive. Go charging in to the rescue? Rob really didn't want to do that, and not just because it was against the contact regs. On the other hand he didn't like to think of himself as a coward, either. Skip that one and come back to it.

Create a distraction? That might work. He could fire up the hydrophone and make a lot of noise, maybe use the drones as decoys. The Ilmatarans might drop Henri to go investigate, or run away in terror. Worth a shot, anyway.

He sent the two drones in at top speed, and searched through his computer's sound library for something suitable to broadcast. "Ride of the Valkyries"? Tarzan yells? "O Fortuna"? No time to be clever; he selected the first item in the playlist and started blasting Billie Holiday as loud as the drone speakers could go. Rob left his camera gear with Henri's impeller, and used his own to get a little closer to the group of Ilmatarans carrying Henri.

✧ ✧ ✧

Broadtail hears the weird sounds first, and alerts the others. The noise is coming from a pair of swimming creatures he doesn't recognize, approaching fast from the left. The sounds are unlike anything he remembers—a mix of low tones, whistles, rattles, and buzzes. There is an underlying rhythm, and Broadtail is sure this is some kind of animal call, not just noise.

The swimmers swoop past low overhead, then, amazingly, circle around together for another pass, like trained performing animals. "Do those creatures belong to Longpincer?" Broadtail asks the others.

"I don't think so," says Smoothshell. "I don't remember hearing them in his house."

"Does anyone have a net?"

"Don't be greedy," says Roundhead. "This is a valuable specimen. We shouldn't risk it to chase after others."

Broadtail starts to object, but he realizes Roundhead is right. This thing is obviously more important. Still—"I suggest we return here to search for them after sleeping."

"Agreed."

The swimmers continue diving at them and making noise until Longpincer's servants show up to help carry the specimen.

Rob had hoped the Ilmatarans would scatter in terror when he sent in the drones, but they barely even noticed them even with the speaker volume maxed out. He couldn't tell if they were too dumb to pay attention, or smart enough to focus on one thing at a time.

He gunned the impeller, closing in on the little group. Enough subtlety. He could see the lights on Henri's suit about fifty meters away, bobbing and wiggling as the Ilmatarans carried him. Rob slowed to a stop about ten meters from the Ilmatarans. The two big floodlights on the impeller showed them clearly.

Enough subtlety and sneaking around. He turned on his suit hydrophone. "Hey!" He had his dive knife in his right hand in case of trouble.

Broadtail is relieved to be rid of the strange beast. He is getting tired and hungry, and wants nothing more than to be back at Longpincer's house snacking on threadfin paste and heat-cured eggs.

Then he hears a new noise. A whine, accompanied by the burble of turbulent water. Off to the left about three lengths there is some large swimmer. It gives a loud call. The captive creature struggles harder.

Broadtail pings the new arrival. It is very odd indeed. It has a hard cylindrical body like a riftcruiser, but at the back it branches out into a bunch of jointed limbs covered with soft skin. The thing gives another cry and waves a couple of limbs.

Broadtail moves toward it, trying to figure out what it is. Two creatures, maybe? And what is it doing? Is this a territorial challenge? He keeps his own pincers folded so as not to alarm it.

"Be careful, Broadtail," Longpincer calls.

"Don't worry." He doesn't approach any closer, but evidently he's already too close. The thing cries out one more time, then charges him. Broadtail doesn't want the other Bitterwater scholars to hear him flee, so he splays his legs and braces himself, ready to grapple with this unknown monster.

But just before it hits him, the thing veers off and disappears into the silent distance. Listening carefully lest it return, Broadtail backs toward the rest of the group and they resume their journey to Longpincer's house.

Everyone agrees that this expedition is stranger than anything any of them remember. Longpincer seems pleased.

Rob stopped his impeller and let the drones catch up. He couldn't think of anything else to do. The Ilmatarans wouldn't be scared off, and there was no way Rob could attack them. Whatever happened to Henri, Rob did not want to be the first human to harm an alien.

The link with Henri was still open. The video showed him looking quite calm, almost serene.

"Henri?" he said. "I tried everything I could think of. I can't get you out. There are too many of them."

"It is all right, Robert," said Henri, sounding surprisingly cheerful. "I do not think they will harm me. Otherwise why go to all the trouble to capture me alive? Listen: I think they have realized I am an intelligent being like themselves. This is our first contact with the Ilmatarans. I will be humanity's ambassador."

"You think so?" For once Rob found himself hoping Henri was right.

"I am certain of it. Keep the link open. The video will show history being made."

Rob sent in one drone to act as a relay as the Ilmatarans carried Henri into a large rambling building near the Maury 3a vent. As he disappeared inside, Henri managed a grin for the camera.

Longpincer approaches the strange creature, laid out on the floor of his study. The others are all gathered around to help and watch. Broadtail has a fresh reel of cord and is making a record of the proceeding. Longpincer begins. "The hide is thick, but flexible, and is a nearly perfect sound absorber. The loudest of pings barely produce any image at all. There are four limbs. The forward pair appear to be for feeding, while the rear limbs apparently function as both walking legs and what one might call a double tail for swimming. Roundhead, do you know of any such creature recorded elsewhere?"

"I certainly do not recall reading of such a thing. It seems absolutely unique."

"Please note as much, Broadtail. My first incision is along the underside. Cutting the hide releases a great many bubbles. The hide peels away very easily; there is no connective tissue at all. I feel what seems to be another layer underneath. The creature's interior is remarkably warm, painful to touch."

"The poor thing," says Raggedclaw. "I do hate causing it pain."

"As do we all, I'm sure," says Longpincer. "I am cutting through the under-layer. It is extremely tough and fibrous. I hear more bubbles. The warmth is extraordinary—like pipe-water direct from the vent."

"How can it survive such heat?" asks Roundhead.

"Can you taste any blood, Longpincer?" adds Sharpfrill.

"No blood that I can taste. Some odd flavors in the water, but I judge that to be from the tissues and space between. I am peeling back the under-layer now. Amazing! Yet another layer beneath it. This one has a very different texture—fleshy rather than fibrous. It is even warmer. I can feel a trembling sensation and spasmodic movements."

"Does anyone remember hearing sounds like that before?" says Smoothshell. "It sounds like no creature I know of."

"I recall that other thing making similar sounds," says Broadtail.

"I now cut through this layer. Ah—now we come to viscera. The blood tastes very odd. Come, everyone, and feel how hot this thing is. And feel this! Some kind of rigid structures within the flesh."

"It is not moving," says Roundhead.

"Now let us examine the head. Someone help me pull off the shell here. Just pull. Good. Thank you, Raggedclaw. What a lot of bubbles! I wonder what this structure is?"

The trip back was awful. Rob couldn't keep from replaying Henri's death in his mind. He got back to the station hours late, exhausted and half out of his mind. As a small mercy Rob didn't have to tell anyone what had happened—they could watch the video.

There were consequences, of course. But because the next supply vehicle wasn't due for another twenty months, it all happened in slow motion. Rob knew he'd be going back to Earth, and guessed that he'd never make another interstellar trip again. He didn't go out on dives; instead he took over drone maintenance and general tech work from Sergei, and stayed inside the station.

Nobody blamed him, at least not exactly. At the end of his debriefing, Dr. Sen did look at Rob over his little Gandhi glasses and say "I do think it was rather irresponsible of you both to go off like that. But I am sure you know that already."

Sen also deleted the "Death to HK" list from the station's network, but someone must have saved a copy. The next day it was anonymously relayed to Rob's computer with a final method added: "Let a group of Ilmatarans catch him and slice him up."

Rob didn't think it was funny at all.

CLASH BY NIGHT
Henry Kuttner & C.L. Moore

Earth was lost, turned into a flaming star by atomic weapons, and humans survived only in domed cities beneath the oceans of Venus, where war still continued, though combat was now constrained by laws prohibiting the use of planet-killing weapons ever again. At least, that was the theory...

INTRODUCTION

A half-mile beneath the shallow Venusian sea, the black impervium dome that protects Montana Keep rests frowning the on the bottom. Within the Keep is carnival, for the Montanans celebrate the four-hundred-year anniversary of Earthman's landing on Venus. Under the great dome that houses the city all is light and colour and gaiety. Masked men and women, bright in celoflex and silks, wonder through the broad streets, laughing, drinking the strong native wines of Venus. The seabottom has been combed, like the hydroponic tanks, for rare delicacies to grace the tables of the nobles.

Through the festival grim shadows stalk, men whose faces mark them unmistakably as members of a Free Company. Their finery cannot disguise that stamp, hard-won through years of battle. Under the Domino masks their mouths are hard and harsh. Unlike the undersea dwellers, their skins are burned black with the ultraviolet rays that filter through the cloud layer of Venus. They are skeletons at the feast. They are respected, but resented. They are Free Companions—

We are on Venus, nine hundred years ago, beneath the sea of shoals, not much north of the equator. But there is a wide range in time and space. All over the cloud planet the underwater Keeps are dotted, and life will not change for many centuries. Looking back, as we do now, from the civilized days of the Thirty-fourth Century, it is too easy to regard the men of the Keeps as savages, groping, stupid and brutal. The Free Companies have long since vanished. The islands and continents of Venus have been tamed, and there is no war.

But in periods of transition, of desperate rivalry, there is always war. The Keeps fought among themselves, each striving to draw the fangs of the others by depriving them of their resources of korium, the power source of the day. Students of that era find pleasure in sifting the legends and winnowing out the basic social and geopolitical truths. It is fairly well known that only one factor saved the Keeps from annihilating one another—the gentlemen's agreement that left war to the warriors, and allowed the undersea cities to develop their science and social cultures. That particular compromise was, perhaps, inevitable. And it caused the organization of the Free Companies, the roving bands of mercenaries, highly trained for their duties, who hired themselves out to fight for whatever Keeps were attacked or wished to attack.

Ap Towrn, in his monumental "Cycle of Venus," tells the saga through symbolic legends. Many historians have recorded the sober truth, which, unfortunately, seems often Mars-dry. But it is not generally realized that the Free Companions were almost directly responsible for our present high culture. War, because of them, was not permitted to usurp the place of peacetime social and scientific work. Fighting was highly specialized, and, because of technical advances, manpower was no longer important. Each band of Free Companions numbered a few thousand, seldom more.

It was a strange, lonely life they must have led, shut out from the normal life of the Keeps. They were vestigian but necessary, like the fangs of the marsupians who eventually evolved into Homo sapiens. *But without those warriors, the Keeps would have been plunged completely into total war, with fatally destructive results.*

Harsh, gallant, indomitable, serving the god of battles so that it might be destroyed—working toward their own obliteration—the Free Companies roar down the pages of history, the banner of Mars streaming above them in the misty air of Venus. They were doomed as Tyrannosaurus rex *was doomed, and they fought on as he did, serving, in their strange way, the shape of Minerva that stood behind Mars.*

Now they are gone. We can learn much by studying the place they held in the Undersea Period. For, because of them, civilization rose again to the heights it had once reached on Earth, and far beyond.

> *"These lords shall light the mystery*
> *Of mastery or victory,*
> *And these ride high in history,*
> *But these shall not return."*

The Free Companions hold their place in interplanetary literature. They are a legend now, archaic and strange. For they were fighters, and war has gone with unification. But we can understand them a little more than could the people of the Keeps.

This story, built on legends and fact, is about a typical warrior of the period—Captain Brian Scott of Doone's Free Companions. He may never have existed—

1

O, it's Tommy this, an' Tommy that, an' "Tommy, go away";
But it's "Thank you, Mr. Atkins," when the band begins to play,
The band begins to play, my boys, the band begins to play—
O, it's "Thank you, Mr. Atkins," when the band begins to play.
　　　　　　　　　　　　　　　　　—R. Kipling, circa 1900

Scott drank stinging uisqueplus and glowered across the smoky tavern. He was a hard, stocky man, with thick gray-shot brown hair and the scar of an old wound crinkling his chin. He was thirty-odd, looking like the veteran he was, and he had sense enough to wear a plain suit of blue celoflex, rather than the garish silks and rainbow fabrics that were all around him.

Outside, through the transparent walls, a laughing throng was carried to and fro along the moveable ways. But in the tavern it was silent, except for the low voice of a harpman as he chanted some old ballad, accompanying himself on his complicated instrument. The song came to an end. There was scattered applause, and from the hot-box overhead the blaring music of an orchestra burst out. Instantly the restraint was gone. In the booths and at the bar men and women began to laugh and talk with casual unrestraint. Couples were dancing now.

The girl beside Scott, a slim, tan-skinned figure with glossy black ringlets cascading to her shoulders, turned inquiring eyes to him.

"Want to, Brian?"

Scott's mouth twisted in a wry grimace. "Suppose so, Jeana. Eh?" He rose, and she came gracefully into his arms. Brian did not dance too well, but what he lacked in practice he made up in integration. Jeana's heart-shaped face, with its high cheekbones and vividly crimson lips, lifted to him.

210

"Forget Bienne. He's just trying to ride you."

Scott glanced toward a distant booth, where two girls sat with a man—Commander Fredric Bienne of the Doones. He was a gaunt, tall, bitter-faced man, his regular features twisted into a perpetual sneer, his eyes somber under heavy dark brows. He was pointing, now, toward the couple on the floor.

"I know," Scott said. "He's doing it, too. Well, the hell with him. So I'm a captain now and he's still a commander. That's tough. Next time he'll obey orders and not send his ship out of the line, trying to ram."

"That was it, eh?" Jeana asked. "I wasn't sure. There's plenty of talk."

"There always is. Oh, Bienne's hated me for years. I reciprocate. We simply don't get on together. Never did. Every time I got a promotion, he chewed his nails. Figured he had a longer service record than I had, and deserved to move up faster. But he's too much of an individualist— at the wrong times."

"He's drinking a lot," Jeana said.

"Let him. Three months we've been in Montana Keep. The boys get tired of inaction—being treated like this." Scott nodded toward the door, where a Free Companion was arguing with the keeper. "No noncoms allowed in here. Well, the devil with it."

They could not hear the conversation above the hubbub, but its importance was evident. Presently the soldier shrugged, his mouth forming a curse, and departed. A fat man in scarlet silks shouted encouragement.

"—want any . . . Companions here!"

Scott saw Commander Bienne, his eyes half closed, get up and walk toward the fat man's booth. His shoulder moved in an imperceptible shrug. The hell with civilians, anyhow. Serve the lug right if Bienne smashed his greasy face. And that seemed the probable outcome. For the fat man was accompanied by a girl, and obviously wasn't going to back down, though Bienne, standing too close to him, was saying something insulting, apparently.

The auxiliary hot-box snapped some quick syllables, lost in the general tumult. But Scott's trained ear caught the words. He nodded to Jeana, made a significant clicking noise with his tongue, and said, "This is it."

She, too, had heard. She let Scott go. He headed toward the fat man's booth just in time to see the beginning of a brawl. The civilian, red as a turkey cock, had struck out suddenly, landing purely by accident on Bienne's gaunt cheek. The commander, grinning tightly, stepped back a pace, his fist clenching. Scott caught the other's arm.

"Hold it, Commander."

Bienne swung around, glaring. "What business is it of yours? Let—"

The fat man, seeing his opponent's attention distracted, acquired more courage and came in swinging. Scott reached past Bienne, planted his open hand in the civilian's face, and pushed hard. The fat man almost fell backward on his table.

As he rebounded, he saw a gun in Scott's hand. The captain said curtly, "Tend to your knitting, mister."

The civilian licked his lips, hesitated, and sat down. Under his breath he muttered something about too-damn-cocky Free Companions.

Bienne was trying to break free, ready to swing on the captain. Scott holstered his gun. "Orders," he told the other, jerking his head toward the hot-box. "Get it?"

"—mobilization. Doonemen report to headquarters. Captain Scott to Administration. Immediate mobilization—"

"Oh," Bienne said, though he still scowled. "O.K. I'll take over. There was time for me to take a crack at that louse, though."

"You know what instant mobilization means," Scott grunted. "We may have to leave at an instant's notice. Orders, Commander."

Bienne saluted halfheartedly and turned away. Scott went back to his own booth. Jeana had already gathered her purse and gloves and was applying lip juice.

She met his eyes calmly enough.

"I'll be at the apartment, Brian. Luck."

He kissed her briefly, conscious of a surging excitement at the prospect of a new venture. Jeana understood his emotion. She gave him a quick, wry smile, touched his hair lightly, and rose. They went out into the gay tumult of the ways.

Perfumed wind blew into Scott's face. He wrinkled his nose disgustedly. During carnival seasons the Keeps were less pleasant to the Free Companions than otherwise; they felt more keenly the gulf that lay between them and the undersea dwellers. Scott pushed his way through the crowd and took Jeana across the ways to the center fast-speed strip. They found seats.

At a clover-leaf intersection Scott left the girl, heading toward Administration, the cluster of taller buildings in the city's center. The technical and political headquarters were centered here, except for the laboratories, which were in the suburbs near the base of the Dome. There were a few small test-domes a mile or so distant from the city, but these were used only for more precarious experiments. Glancing up, Scott was reminded of the catastrophe that had unified science into something like a free-masonry. Above him, hanging without gravity over a central plaza, was the globe of the Earth, half shrouded by the folds of a black plastic pall. In every Keep on Venus there was a similar ever-present reminder of the lost mother planet.

Scott's gaze went up farther, to the Dome, as though he could penetrate the impervium and the mile-deep layer of water and the clouded atmosphere to the white star that hung in space, one quarter as brilliant as the Sun. A star—all that remained of Earth, since atomic power had been unleashed there two centuries ago. The scourge had spread like flame, melting continents and leveling mountains. In the libraries there were wire-tape pictorial records of the Holocaust. A religious cult—Men of the New Judgment—had sprung up, and advocated the complete destruction of science; followers of that dogma still existed here and there. But the cult's teeth had been drawn when technicians unified, outlawing experiments with atomic power forever, making use of that force punishable by death, and permitting no one to join their society without taking the Minervan Oath.

"—to work for the ultimate good of mankind...taking all precaution against harming humanity and science...requiring permission from those in authority before undertaking any experiment involving peril to the race...remembering always the extent of the trust placed in us and remembering forever the death of the mother planet through misuse of knowledge—"

The Earth. A strange sort of world it must have been, Scott thought. Sunlight, for one thing, unfiltered by a cloud layer. In the old days, there had been few unexplored areas left on Earth. But here on Venus, where the continents had not yet been conquered—there was no need, of course, since everything necessary to life could be produced under the Domes—here on Venus, there was still a frontier. In the Keeps, a highly specialized social culture. Above the surface, a primeval world, where only the Free Companions had their fortresses and navies—the navies for fighting, the forts to house the technicians who provided the latter-day sinews of war, science instead of money. The Keeps tolerated visits from the Free Companions, but would not offer them headquarters, so violent the feeling, so sharp the schism, in the public mind, between war and cultural progress.

Under Scott's feet the sliding way turned into an escalator, carrying him into the Administration Building. He stepped to another way which took him to a lift, and, a moment or two later, was facing the door-curtain bearing the face of President Dane Crosby of Montana Keep.

Crosby's voice said, "Come in, Captain," and Scott brushed through the curtain, finding himself in a medium-sized room with muraled walls and a great window overlooking the city. Crosby, a white-haired, thin figure in blue silks, was at his desk. He looked like a tired old clerk out of Dickens, Scott thought suddenly, entirely undistinguished and ordinary. Yet Crosby was one of the greatest socio-politicians on Venus.

Cinc Rhys, leader of Doone's Free Companions, was sitting in a relaxer, the apparent antithesis of Crosby. All the moisture in Rhys's body seemed to have been sucked out of him years ago by ultraviolet actinic, leaving a mummy of brown leather and whipcord sinew. There was no softness in the man. His smile was a grimace. Muscles lay like wire under the swarthy cheeks.

Scott saluted. Rhys waved him to a relaxer. The look of subdued eagerness in the cinc's eyes was significant—an eagle poising himself, smelling blood. Crosby sensed that, and a wry grin showed on his pale face.

"Every man to his trade," he remarked, semi-ironically. "I suppose I'd be bored stiff if I had too long a vacation. But you'll have quite a battle on your hands this time, Cinc Rhys."

Scott's stocky body tensed automatically. Rhys glanced at him.

"Virginia Keep is attacking, Captain. They've hired the Helldivers—Flynn's outfit."

There was a pause. Both Free Companions were anxious to discuss the angles, but unwilling to do so in the presence of a civilian, even the president of Montana Keep. Crosby rose.

"The money settlement's satisfactory, then?"

Rhys nodded. "Yes, that's all right. I expect the battle will take place in a couple of days. In the neighborhood of Venus Deep, at a rough guess."

"Good. I've a favor to ask, so if you'll excuse me for a few minutes, I'll—" He left the sentence unfinished and went out through the door-curtain. Rhys offered Scott a cigarette.

"You get the implications, Captain—the Helldivers?"

"Yes, sir. Thanks. We can't do it alone."

"Right. We're short on manpower and armament both. And the Helldivers recently merged with O'Brien's Legion, after O'Brien was killed in that polar scrap. They're a strong outfit, plenty strong. Then they've got their specialty—submarine attack. I'd say we'll have to use H-plan 7."

Scott closed his eyes, remembering the files. Each Free Company kept up-to-date plans of attack suited to the merits of every other Company of Venus. Frequently revised as new advances were made, as groups merged, and as the balance of power changed on each side, the plans were so detailed that they could be carried into action at literally a moment's notice. H-plan 7, Scott recalled, involving enlisting the aid of the Mob, a small but well-organized band of Free Companions led by Cinc Tom Mendez.

"Right," Scott said. "Can you get him?"

"I think so. We haven't agreed yet on the bonus. I've been telaudioing him on a tight beam, but he keeps putting me off—waiting till the last moment, when he can dictate his own terms."

"What's he asking, sir?"

"Fifty thousand cash and a fifty percent cut on the loot."

"I'd say thirty percent would be about right."

Rhys nodded. "I've offered him thirty-five. I may send you to his fort—carte blanche. We can get another Company, but Mendez has got beautiful sub-detectors—which would come in handy against the Helldivers. Maybe I can settle things by audio. If not, you'll have to fly over to Mendez and buy his services, at less than fifty per if you can."

Scott rubbed the old scar on his chin with a calloused forefinger. "Meantime Commander Bienne's in charge of mobilization. When—"

"I telaudioed our fort. Air transports are on the way now."

"It'll be quite a scrap," Scott said, and the eyes of the two men met in perfect understanding. Rhys chuckled dryly.

"And good profits. Virginia Keep has a big supply of korium ... dunno how much, but plenty."

"What started the fracas this time?"

"The usual thing, I suppose," Rhys said disinterestedly. "Imperialism. Somebody in Virginia Keep worked out a new plan for annexing the rest of the Keeps. Same as usual."

They stood up as the door-curtain swung back, admitting President Crosby, another man, and a girl. The man looked young, his boyish face not yet toughened under actinic burn. The girl was lovely in the manner of a plastic figurine, lit from within by vibrant life. Her blond hair was cropped in the prevalent mode, and her eyes, Scott saw, were an unusual shade of green. She was more than merely pretty—she was instantly exciting.

Crosby said, "My niece, Ilene Kane—and my nephew, Norman Kane." He performed introductions, and they found seats.

"What about drinks?" Ilene suggested. "This is rather revoltingly formal. The fight hasn't started yet, after all."

Crosby shook his head at her. "You weren't invited here anyway. Don't try to turn this into a party—there isn't too much time, under the circumstances."

"O.K.," Ilene murmured. "I can wait." She eyed Scott interestedly.

Norman Kane broke in. "I'd like to join Doone's Free Companions, sir. I've already applied, but now that there's a battle coming up, I hate to wait until my application's approved. So I thought—"

Crosby looked at Cinc Rhys. "A personal favor, but the decision's up to you. My nephew's a misfit—a romanticist. Never liked the life of a Keep. A year ago he went off and joined Starling's outfit."

Rhys raised an eyebrow. "That gang? It's not a recommendation, Kane. They're not even classed as Free Companions. More like a band of guerillas, and entirely without ethics. There've even been rumors they're messing around with atomic power."

Crosby looked startled. "I hadn't heard that."

"It's no more than a rumor. If it's ever proved, the Free Companions—all of them—will get together and smash Starling in a hurry."

Norman Kane looked slightly uncomfortable. "I suppose I was rather a fool. But I wanted to get in the fighting game, and Starling's group appealed to me—"

The cinc made a sound in his throat. "They would. Swashbuckling romantics, with no idea of what war means. They've not more than a dozen technicians. And they've no discipline—it's like a pirate outfit. War today, Kane, isn't won by romantic animals dashing at forlorn hopes. The modern soldier is a tactician who knows how to think, integrate, and obey. If you join our Company, you'll have to forget what you learned with Starling."

"Will you take me, sir?"

"I think it would be unwise. You need the training course."

"I've had experience—"

Crosby said, "It would be a favor, Cinc Rhys, if you'd skip the red tape. I'd appreciate it. Since my nephew wants to be a soldier, I'd much prefer to see him with the Doones."

Rhys shrugged. "Very well. Captain Scott will give you your orders, Kane. Remember that discipline is vitally important with us."

The boy tried to force back a delighted grin. "Thank you, sir."

"Captain—"

Scott rose and nodded to Kane. They went out together. In the anteroom was a telaudio set, and Scott called the Doone's local headquarters in Montana Keep. An integrator answered, his face looking inquiringly from the screen.

"Captain Scott calling, subject induction."

"Yes, sir. Ready to record."

Scott drew Kane forward. "Photosnap this man. He'll report to headquarters immediately. Name, Norman Kane. Enlist him without training course—special orders from Cinc Rhys."

"Acknowledged, sir."

Scott broke the connection. Kane couldn't quite repress his grin.

"All right," the captain grunted, a sympathetic gleam in his eyes. "That fixes it. They'll put you in my command. What's your specialty?"

"Flitterboats, sir."

"Good. One more thing. Don't forget what Cinc Rhys said, Kane. Discipline is damned important, and you may not have realized that yet. This isn't a cloak-and-sword war. There are no Charges of the Light Brigades. No grandstand plays—that stuff went out with the Crusades. Just obey orders, and you'll have no trouble. Good luck."

"Thank you, sir." Kane saluted and strode out with a perceptible swagger. Scott grinned. The kid would have *that* knocked out of him pretty soon.

A voice at his side made him turn quickly. Ilene Kane was standing there, slim and lovely in her celoflex gown.

"You seem pretty human after all, Captain," she said. "I heard what you told Norman."

Scott shrugged. "I did that for his own good—and the good of the Company. One man off the beam can cause plenty of trouble, Mistress Kane."

"I envy Norman," she said. "It must be a fascinating life you lead. I'd like it—for a while. Not for long. I'm one of the useless offshoots of this civilization, not much good for anything. So I've perfected one talent."

"What's that?"

"Oh, hedonism, I suppose you'd call it. I enjoy myself. It's not often too boring. But I'm a bit bored now. I'd like to talk to you, Captain."

"Well, I'm listening," Scott said.

Ilene Kane made a small grimace. "Wrong semantic term. I'd like to get inside of you psychologically. But painlessly. Dinner and dancing. Can do?"

"There's no time," Scott told her. "We may get our orders at any moment." He wasn't sure he wanted to go out with this girl of the Keeps, though there was definitely a subtle fascination for him, an appeal he could not analyze. She typified the most pleasurable part of a world he did not know. The other facets of that world could not impinge on him; geopolitics or nonmilitary science held no appeal, were too alien. But all worlds touch at one point—pleasure. Scott could understand the relaxations of the undersea groups, as he could not understand or feel sympathy for their work or their social impulses.

Cinc Rhys came through the door-curtain, his eyes narrowed. "I've some telaudioing to do, Captain," he said. Scott knew what implications the words held: the incipient bargain with Cinc Mendez. He nodded.

"Yes, sir. Shall I report to headquarters?"

Rhys's harsh face seemed to relax suddenly as he looked from Ilene to Scott. "You're free till dawn. I won't need you till then, but report to me at six a.m. No doubt you've a few details to clean up."

"Very well, sir." Scott watched Rhys go out. The cinc had meant Jeana, of course. But Ilene did not know that.

"So?" she asked. "Do I get a turn-down? You might buy me a drink, anyway."

There was plenty of time. Scott said, "It'll be a pleasure," and Ilene linked her arm with his. They took the dropper to ground-level.

As they came out on one of the ways, Ilene turned her head and caught Scott's glance. "I forgot something, Captain. You may have a previous engagement. I didn't realize—"

"There's nothing," he said. "Nothing important."

It was true; he felt a mild gratitude toward Jeana at the realization. His relationship with her was the peculiar one rendered advisable by his career. Free-marriage was the word for it; Jeana was neither his wife nor his mistress, but something midway between. The Free Companions had no firmly grounded foundation for social life; in the Keeps they were visitors, and in their coastal forts they were—well, soldiers. One would no more bring a woman to a fort than aboard a ship of the line. So the women of the Free Companions lived in the Keeps, moving from one to another as their men did; and because of the ever-present shadow of death, ties were purposely left loose. Jeana and Scott had been free-married for five years now. Neither made demands on the other. No one expected fidelity of a Free Companion. Soldiers lived under such iron disciplines that when they were released, during the brief peacetimes, the pendulum often swung far in the opposite direction.

To Scott, Ilene Kane was a key that might unlock the doors of the Keep—doors that opened to a world of which he was not a part, and which he could not quite understand.

2

I, a stranger and afraid
in a world I never made.
—Housman

There were nuances, Scott found, which he had never known existed. A hedonist like Ilene devoted her life to such nuances; they were her career. Such minor matters as making the powerful, insipid Moonflower Cocktails more palatable by filtering them through lime-soaked sugar held between the teeth. Scott was a uisqueplus man, having the average soldier's contempt for what he termed hydroponic drinks, but the cocktails Ilene suggested were quite as effective as acrid, burning amber uisqueplus. She taught him, that night, such tricks as pausing between glasses to sniff lightly at happy-gas, to mingle sensual excitement with mental by trying the amusement rides designed to give one the violent physical intoxication of breathless speed. Nuances all, which only a girl with Ilene's background could know. She was not representative of Keep life. As she had said, she was an offshoot, a casual and useless flower on the great vine that struck up inexorably to the skies, its strength in its tough, reaching tendrils—scientists and technicians and socio-politicians. She was doomed in her own way, as Scott was in his. The undersea folk served Minerva; Scott served Mars; and Ilene served Aphrodite—not purely the sexual goddess, but the patron of arts and pleasure. Between Scott and Ilene was the difference between Wagner and Strauss; the difference between crashing chords and tinkling arpeggios. In both was a muted bittersweet sadness, seldom realized by either. But that undertone was brought out by their contact. The sense of dim hopelessness in each responded to the other.

It was carnival, but neither Ilene nor Scott wore masks. Their faces were masks enough, and both had been trained to reserve, though in different ways. Scott's hard mouth kept its tight grimness even when he smiled. And Ilene's smiles came so often that they were meaningless.

Through her, Scott was able to understand more of the undersea life than he had ever done before. She was for him a catalyst. A tacit understanding grew between them, not needing words. Both realized that, in the course of progress, they would eventually die out. Mankind tolerated them because that was necessary for a little time. Each responded differently. Scott served Mars; he served actively; and the girl, who was passive, was attracted by the antithesis.

Scott's drunkenness struck psychically deep. He did not show it. His stiff silver-brown hair was not disarranged, and his hard, burned face was impassive as ever. But when his brown eyes met Ilene's green ones a spark of—something—met between them.

Color and light and sound. They began to form a pattern now, were not quite meaningless to Scott. They were, long past midnight, sitting in an Olympus, which was a private cosmos. The walls of the room in which they were seemed nonexistent. The gusty tides of gray, faintly luminous clouds seemed to drive chaotically past them, and, dimly, they could hear the muffled screaming of an artificial wind. They had the isolation of the gods.

And the Earth was without form, and void; and darkness was upon the face of the deep—That was, of course, the theory of the Olympus room. No one existed, no world existed, outside of the chamber; values automatically shifted, and inhibitions seemed absurd.

Scott relaxed on a translucent cushion like a cloud. Beside him, Ilene lifted the bit of a happy-gas tube to his nostrils. He shook his head.

"Not now, Ilene."

She let the tube slide back into its reel. "Nor I. Too much of anything is unsatisfactory, Brian. There should always be something untasted, some anticipation left. You have that, I haven't."

"How?"

"Pleasures—well, there's a limit. There's a limit to human endurance: And eventually I build up a resistance psychically, as I do physically, to everything. With you, there's always the last adventure.

You never know when death will come. You can't plan. Plans are dull; it's the unexpected that's important."

Scott shook his head slightly. "Death isn't important either. It's an automatic cancellation of values. Or, rather—" He hesitated, seeking words. "In this life you can plan, you can work out values, because they're all based on certain conditions. On—let's say—arithmetic. Death is a change to a different plane of conditions, quite unknown. Arithmetical rules don't apply as such to geometry."

"You think death has its rules?"

"It may be a lack of rules, Ilene. One lives realizing that life is subject to death; civilization is based on that. That's why civilization concentrates on the race instead of the individual. Social self-preservation."

She looked at him gravely. "I didn't think a Free Companion could theorize that way."

Scott closed his eyes, relaxing. "The Keeps know nothing about Free Companions. They don't want to. We're men. Intelligent men. Our technicians are as great as the scientists under the Domes."

"But they work for war."

"War's necessary," Scott said. "Now, anyway."

"How did you get into it? Should I ask?"

He laughed a little at that. "Oh, I've no dark secrets in my past. I'm not a runaway murderer. One—drifts. I was born in Australia Keep. My father was a tech, but my grandfather had been a soldier. I guess it was in my blood.

"I tried various trades and professions. Meaningless. I wanted something that . . . hell, I don't know. Something, maybe, that needs all of a man. Fighting does. It's like a religion. Those cultists—Men of the New Judgment—they're fanatics, but you can see that their religion is the only thing that matters to them."

"Bearded, dirty men with twisted minds, though."

"It happens to be a religion based on false premises. There are others, appealing to different types. But religion was too passive for me, in these days."

Ilene examined his harsh face. "You'd have preferred the church militant—the Knights of Malta, fighting Saracens."

"I suppose. I had no values. Anyhow, I'm a fighter."

"Just how important is it to you? The Free Companions?"

Scott opened his eyes and grinned at the girl. He looked unexpectedly boyish.

"Damn little, really. It has emotional appeal. Intellectually, I know that it's a huge fake. Always has been. As absurd as the Men of the New Judgment. Fighting's doomed. So we've no real purpose. I suppose most of us know there's no future for the Free Companions. In a few hundred years—well!"

"And still you go on. Why? It isn't money."

"No. There is a ... a drunkenness to it. The ancient Norsemen had their berserker madness. We have something similar. To a Dooneman, his group is father, mother, child, and God Almighty. He fights the other Free Companions when he's paid to do so, but he doesn't hate the others. They serve the same toppling idol. And it is toppling, Ilene. Each battle we win or lose brings us closer to the end. We fight to protect the culture that eventually will wipe us out. The Keeps—when they finally unify, will they need a military arm? I can see the trend. If war was an essential part of civilization, each Keep would maintain its own military. But they shut us out—a necessary evil. If they would end war now!" Scott's fist unconsciously clenched. "So many men would find happier places in Venus—undersea. But as long as the Free Companions exist, there'll be new recruits."

Ilene sipped her cocktail, watching the gray chaos of clouds flow like a tide around them. In the dimly luminous light Scott's face seemed like dark stone, flecks of brightness showing in his eyes. She touched his hand gently.

"You're a soldier, Brian. You wouldn't change."

His laugh was intensely bitter. "Like hell I wouldn't, Mistress Ilene Kane! Do you think fighting's just pulling a trigger? I'm a military strategist. That took ten years. Harder cramming than I'd have had in a Keep Tech-Institute. I have to know everything about war from trajectories to mass psychology. This is the greatest science the System has ever known, and the most useless. Because war will die in a few centuries at most. Ilene—you've never seen a Free Company's fort. It's science, marvelous science, aimed at military ends only. We have our psych-specialists. We have our engineers, who plan everything from ordnance to the frictional quotient on flitterboats. We have the foundries and mills. Each fortress is a city made for war, as the Keeps are made for social progress."

"As complicated as that?"

"Beautifully complicated and beautifully useless. There are so many of us who realize that. Oh, we fight—it's a poison. We worship the Company—that is an emotional poison. But we live only during wartime. It's an incomplete life. Men in the Keeps have full lives; they have their work, and their relaxations are geared to fit them. We don't fit."

"Not all the undersea races," Ilene said. "There's always the fringe that doesn't fit. At least you have a raison d'être. You're a soldier. I can't make a lifework out of pleasure. But there's nothing else for me."

Scott's fingers tightened on hers. "You're the product of a civilization, at least. I'm left out."

"With you, Brian, it might be better. For a while. I don't think it would last for long."

"It might."

"You think so now. It's quite a horrible thing, feeling yourself a shadow."

"I know."

"I want you, Brian," Ilene said, turning to face him. "I want you to come to Montana Keep and stay here. Until our experiment fails. I think it'll fail presently. But, perhaps, not for some time. I need your strength. I can show you how to get the most out of this sort of life— how to enter into it. True hedonism. You can give me—companionship perhaps. For me the companionship of hedonists who know nothing else isn't enough."

Scott was silent. Ilene watched him for a while.

"Is war so important?" she asked at last.

"No," he said, "it isn't at all. It's a balloon. And it's empty, I know that. Honor of the regiment!" Scott laughed. "I'm not hesitating, really. I've been shut out for a long time. A social unit shouldn't be founded on an obviously doomed fallacy. Men and women are important, nothing else, I suppose."

"Men and women—or the race?"

"Not the race," he said with abrupt violence. "Damn the race! It's done nothing for me. I can fit myself into a new life. Not necessarily hedonism. I'm an expert in several lines; I have to be. I can find work in Montana Keep."

"If you like. I've never tried. I'm more of a fatalist, I suppose. But... what about it, Brian?"

Her eyes were almost luminous, like shining emerald, in the ghostly light.

"Yes," Scott said. "I'll come back. To stay."

Ilene said, "Come back? Why not stay now?"

"Because I'm a complete fool, I guess. I'm a key man, and Cinc Rhys needs me just now."

"Is it Rhys or the Company?"

Scott smiled crookedly. "Not the Company. It's just a job I have to do. When I think how many years I've been slaving, pretending absurdities were important, knowing that I was bowing to a straw dummy—No! I want your life—the sort of life I didn't know could exist in the Keeps. I'll be back, Ilene. It's something more important than love. Separately we're halves. Together we may be a complete whole."

She didn't answer. Her eyes were steady on Scott's. He kissed her.

Before morning bell he was back in the apartment.

Jeana had already packed the necessary light equipment.

She was asleep, her dark hair cascading over the pillow, and Scott did not waken her. Quietly he shaved, showered, and dressed. A heavy, waiting silence seemed to fill the city like a cup brimmed with stillness.

As he emerged from the bathroom, buttoning his tunic, he saw the table had been let down and two places set at it. Jeana came in, wearing a cool morning frock. She set cups down and poured coffee.

"Morning, soldier," she said. "You've time for this, haven't you?"

"Uh-huh." Scott kissed her, a bit hesitantly. Up till this moment, the breaking with Jeana had seemed easy enough.

She would raise no objections. That was the chief reason for free-marriage. However—

She was sitting in the relaxer, sweeting the coffee, opening a fresh celo-pack of cigarettes. "Hung over?"

"No. I vitamized. Feel pretty good." Most bars had a vitamizing chamber to nullify the effects of too much stimulant. Scott was, in fact, feeling fresh and keenly alert. He was wondering how to broach the subject of Ilene to Jeana.

She saved him the trouble.

"If it's a girl, Brian, just take it easy. No use doing anything till this war's over. How long will it take?"

"Oh, not long. A week at most. One battle may settle it, you know. The girl—"

"She's not a Keep girl."

"Yes."

Jeana looked up, startled. "You're crazy."

"I started to tell you," Scott said impatiently. "It isn't just—her. I'm sick of the Doones. I'm going to quit."

"Hm-m-m. Like that?"

"Like that."

Jeana shook her head. "Keep women aren't tough."

"They don't need to be. Their men aren't soldiers."

"Have it your own way. I'll wait till you get back. Maybe I've got a hunch. You see, Brian, we've been together for five years. We fit. Not because of anything like philosophy or psychology—it's a lot more personal. It's just us. As man and woman, we get along comfortably. There's love, too. Those close emotional feelings are more important, really, than the long view. You can get excited about futures, but you can't live them."

Scott shrugged. "Could be I'm starting to forget about futures. Concentrating on Brian Scott."

"More coffee . . . there. Well, for five years now I've gone with you from Keep to Keep, waiting every time you went off to war, wondering if you'd come back, knowing that I was just a part of your life, but—I sometimes thought—the most important part. Soldiering's seventy-five percent. I'm the other quarter. I think you need that quarter—you need the whole thing, in that proportion, actually. You could find another woman, but she'd have to be willing to take twenty-five percent."

Scott didn't answer. Jeana blew smoke through her nostrils.

"O.K., Brian. I'll wait."

"It isn't the girl so much. She happens to fit into the pattern of what I want. You—"

"I'd never be able to fit that pattern," Jeana said softly. "The Free Companions need women who are willing to be soldiers' wives. Free-wives, if you like. Chiefly it's a matter of not being too demanding. But there are other things. No, Brian. Even if you wanted that, I couldn't make myself over into one of the Keep people. It wouldn't be me. I wouldn't respect myself, living a life that'd be false to me; and you wouldn't like me that way either. I couldn't and wouldn't change. I'll have to stay as I am. A soldier's wife. As long as you're a Dooneman, you'll need me. But if you change—" She didn't finish.

Scott lit a cigarette, scowling. "It's hard to know, exactly."

"I may not understand you, but I don't ask questions and I don't try to change you. As long as you want that, you can have it from me. I've nothing else to offer you. It's enough for a Free Companion. It's not enough—or too much—for a Keep-dweller."

"I'll miss you," he said.

"That'll depend, too. I'll miss you." Under the table her fingers writhed together, but her face did not change. "It's getting late. Here, let me check your chronometer." Jeana leaned across the table, lifted Scott's wrist, and compared his watch with the central-time clock on the wall. "O.K. On your way, soldier."

Scott stood up, tightening his belt. He bent to kiss Jeana, and, though she began to turn her face away, after a moment she raised her lips to his.

They didn't speak. Scott went out quickly, and the girl sat motionless, the cigarette smoldering out unheeded between her fingers. Somehow it did not matter so much now that Brian was leaving her for another woman and another life. As always, the one thing of real importance was that he was going into danger.

Guard him from harm, she thought, not knowing that she was praying. Guard him from harm!

And now there would be silence, and waiting. That, at least, had not changed. Her eyes turned to the clock.

Already the minutes were longer.

3

'E's a kind of a giddy harumfrodite
—Soldier an' Sailor too!
—Kipling

Commander Bienne was superintending the embarkation of the last Dooneman when Scott arrived at headquarters. He saluted the captain briskly, apparently untired by his night's work of handling the transportation routine.

"All checked, sir."

Scott nodded. "Good. Is Cinc Rhys here?"

"He just arrived." Bienne nodded toward a door-curtain. As Scott moved away, the other followed.

"What's up, Commander?"

Bienne pitched his voice low. "Bronson's laid up with endemic fever." He forgot to say "sir." "He was to handle the left wing of the fleet. I'd appreciate that job."

"I'll see if I can do it."

Bienne's lips tightened, but he said nothing more. He turned back to his men, and Scott went on into the cinc's office. Rhys was at the telaudio. He looked up, his eyes narrowed.

"Morning, Captain. I've just heard from Mendez."

"Yes, sir?"

"He's still holding out for a fifty-percent cut on the korium ransom from Virginia Keep. You'll have to see him. Try and get the Mob for less than fifty if you can. Telaudio me from Mendez's fort."

"Check, sir."

"Another thing. Bronson's in sick bay."

"I heard that. If I may suggest Commander Bienne to take his place at left-wing command—"

But Cinc Rhys raised his hand. "Not this time. We can't afford individualism. The commander tried to play a lone hand in the last war. You know we can't risk it till he's back in line—thinking of the Doones instead of Fredric Bienne."

"He's a good man, sir. A fine strategist."

"But not yet a good integrating factor. Perhaps next time. Put Commander Geer on the left wing. Keep Bienne with you. He needs discipline. And—take a flitterboat to Mendez."

"Not a plane?"

"One of the technicians just finished a new tight-beam camouflager for communications. I'm having it installed immediately on all our planes and gliders. Use the boat; it isn't far to the Mob's fort—that long peninsula on the coast of Southern Hell."

Even on the charts that continent was named Hell—for obvious reasons. Heat was only one of them. And, even with the best equipment, a party exploring the jungle there would soon find itself suffering the tortures of the damned. On the land of Venus, flora and fauna combined diabolically to make the place uninhabitable to Earthmen. Many of the plants even exhaled poisonous gases. Only the protected coastal forts of the Free Companies could exist—and that was because they *were* forts.

Cinc Rhys frowned at Scott. "We'll use H-plan 7 if we can get the Mob. Otherwise we'll have to fall back on another outfit, and I don't want to do that. The Helldivers have too many subs, and we haven't enough detectors. So do your damnedest."

Scott saluted. "I'll do that, sir." Rhys waved him away, and he went out into the next room, finding Commander Bienne alone. The officer turned an inquiring look toward him.

"Sorry," Scott said. "Geer gets the left-wing command this time."

Bienne's sour face turned dark red. "I'm sorry I didn't take a crack at you before mobilization," he said. "You hate competition, don't you?"

Scott's nostrils flared. "If it had been up to me, you'd have got that command, Bienne."

"Sure. I'll bet. All right, Captain. Where's my bunk? A flitterboat?"

"You'll be on right wing, with me. Control ship *Flintlock*."

"With you. Under you, you mean," Bienne said tightly. His eyes were blazing. "Yeah."

Scott's dark cheeks were flushed too. "Orders, Commander," he snapped. "Get me a flitterboat pilot. I'm going topside."

Without a word Bienne turned to the telaudio. Scott, a tight, furious knot in his stomach, stamped out of headquarters, trying to fight down his anger. Bienne was a jackass. A lot he cared about the Doones—

Scott caught himself and grinned sheepishly. Well, he cared little about the Doones himself. But while he was in the Company, discipline was important—integration with the smoothly running fighting machine. No place for individualism. One thing he and Bienne had in common; neither had any sentiment about the Company.

He took a lift to the ceiling of the Dome. Beneath him Montana Keep dropped away, shrinking to doll size. Somewhere down there, he thought, was Ilene. He'd be back.

Perhaps this war would be a short one—not that they were ever much longer than a week, except in unusual cases where a Company developed new strategies.

He was conducted through an air lock into a bubble, a tough, transparent sphere with a central vertical core through which the cable ran. Except for Scott, the bubble was empty. After a moment it started up with a slight jar.

Gradually the water outside the curving walls changed from black to deep green, and thence to translucent chartreuse. Sea creatures were visible, but they were nothing new to Scott; he scarcely saw them.

The bubble broke surface. Since air pressure had been constant, there was no possibility of the bends, and Scott opened the panel and stepped out on one of the buoyant floats that dotted the water above Montana Keep. A few sightseers crowded into the chamber he had left, and presently it was drawn down, out of sight.

In the distance Free Companions were embarking from a larger float to an air ferry. Scott glanced up with a weather eye. No storm, he saw, though the low ceiling was, as usual, torn and twisted into boiling currents by the winds. He remembered, suddenly, that the battle would probably take place over Venus Deep. That would make it somewhat harder for the gliders—there would be few of the thermals found, for instance, above the Sea of Shallows here.

A flitterboat, low, fast, and beautifully maneuverable, shot in toward the quay. The pilot flipped back the overhead shell and saluted Scott. It was Norman Kane, looking shipshape in his tight-fitting gray uniform, and apparently ready to grin at the slightest provocation.

Scott jumped lightly down into the craft and seated himself beside the pilot. Kane drew the transparent shell back over them. He looked at Scott.

"Orders, Captain?"

"Know where the Mob's fort is? Good. Head there. Fast."

Kane shot the flitterboat out from the float with a curtain of V-shaped spray rising from the bow. Drawing little water, maneuverable, incredibly fast, these tiny craft were invaluable in naval battle. It was difficult to hit one, they moved so fast. They had no armor to slow them down. They carried high-explosive bullets fired from small-caliber guns, and were, as a rule, two-man craft. They complemented the heavier ordnance of the battlewagons and destroyers.

Scott handed Kane a cigarette. The boy hesitated.

"We're not under fire," the captain chuckled. "Discipline clamps down during a battle, but it's O.K. for you to have a smoke with me. Here!" He lit the white tube for Kane.

"Thanks, sir. I guess I'm a bit—over-anxious?"

"Well, war has its rules. Not many, but they mustn't be broken." Both men were silent for a while, watching the blank gray surface of the ocean ahead. A transport plane passed them, flying low.

"Is Ilene Kane your sister?" Scott asked presently.

Kane nodded. "Yes, sir."

"Thought so. If she'd been a man, I imagine she'd have been a Free Companion."

The boy shrugged. "Oh, I don't know. She doesn't have the—I don't know. She'd consider it too much effort. She doesn't like discipline."

"Do you?"

"It's fighting that's important to me. Sir." That was an afterthought. "Winning, really."

"You can lose a battle even though you win it," Scott said rather somberly.

"Well, I'd rather be a Free Companion than do anything else I know of. Not that I've had much experience."

"You've had experience of war with Starling's outfit, but you probably learned some dangerous stuff at the same time. War isn't swashbuckling piracy these days. If the Doones tried to win battles by that sort of thing, there'd be no more Doones in a week or so."

"But—" Kane hesitated. "Isn't that sort of thing rather necessary? Taking blind chances, I mean—"

"There are desperate chances," Scott told him, "but there are no blind chances in war—not to a good soldier. When I was green in the service, I ran a cruiser out of the line to ram. I was demoted, for a very good reason. The enemy ship I rammed wasn't as important to the enemy as our cruiser was to us. If I'd stayed on course, I'd have helped sink three or four ships instead of disabling one and putting my cruiser out of action. It's the great god integration we worship, Kane. It's much more important now than it ever was on Earth, because the military has consolidated. Army, navy, air, undersea—they're all part of one organization now. I suppose the only important change was in the air."

"Gliders, you mean? I knew powered planes couldn't be used in battle."

"Not in the atmosphere of Venus," Scott agreed.

"Once powered planes get up in the cloud strata, they're fighting crosscurrents and pockets so much they've got no time to do accurate firing. If they're armored, they're slow. If they're light, detectors can spot them and antiaircraft can smash them. Unpowered gliders are valuable not for bombing but for directing attacks. They get into the clouds, stay hidden, and use infrared telecameras which are broadcast on a tight beam back to the control ships. They're the eyes of the fleet. They can tell us—White water ahead, Kane! Swerve!"

The pilot had already seen the ominous boiling froth foaming out in front of the bow. Instinctively he swung the flitterboat in a wrenching turn. The craft heeled sidewise, throwing its occupants almost out of their seats.

"Sea beast?" Scott asked, and answered his own question. "No, not with those spouts. It's volcanic. And it's spreading fast."

"I can circle it, sir," Kane suggested.

Scott shook his head. "Too dangerous. Backtrack."

Obediently the boy sent the flitterboat racing out of the area of danger. Scott had been right about the extent of the danger; the boiling turmoil was widening almost faster than the tiny ship could flee. Suddenly the line of white water caught up with them. The flitterboat jounced like a chip, the wheel being nearly torn from Kane's grip. Scott reached over and helped steady it. Even with two men handling the wheel, there was a possibility that it might wrench itself free. Steam rose in veils beyond the transparent shell. The water had turned a scummy brown under the froth.

Kane jammed on the power. The flitterboat sprang forward like a ricocheting bullet, dancing over the surface of the seething waves. Once they plunged head-on into a swell, and a screaming of outraged metal vibrated through the craft. Kane, tight-lipped, instantly slammed in the auxiliary, cutting out the smashed motor unit. Then, unexpectedly, they were in clear water, cutting back toward Montana Keep.

Scott grinned. "Nice handling. Lucky you didn't try to circle. We'd never have made it."

"Yes, sir." Kane took a deep breath. His eyes were bright with excitement.

"Circle now. Here." He thrust a lighted cigarette between the boy's lips. "You'll be a good Dooneman, Kane. Your reactions are good and fast."

"Thanks, sir."

Scott smoked silently for a while. He glanced toward the north, but, with the poor visibility, he could not make out the towering range of volcanic peaks that were the backbone of Southern Hell. Venus was a comparatively young planet, the internal fires still bursting forth unexpectedly.

Which was why no forts were ever built on islands—they had an unhappy habit of disappearing without warning!

The flitterboat rode hard, at this speed, despite the insulating system of springs and shock absorbers. After a ride in one of these "spankers"—the irreverent name the soldiers had for them—a man needed arnica if not a chiropractor. Scott shifted his weight on the soft air cushions under him, which felt like cement.

Under his breath he hummed:

"It ain't the 'eavy 'aulin' that 'urts the 'orses' 'oofs, It's the 'ammer, 'ammer, 'ammer on the 'ard 'ighway!"

The flitterboat scooted on, surrounded by monotonous sea and cloud, till finally the rampart of the coast grew before the bow, bursting suddenly from the fog-veiled horizon. Scott glanced at his chronometer and sighed with relief. They had made good time, in spite of the slight delay caused by the subsea volcano.

The fortress of the Mob was a huge metal and stone castle on the tip of the peninsula. The narrow strip that separated it from the mainland had been cleared, and the pockmarks of shell craters showed where guns had driven back onslaughts from the jungle—the reptilian, ferocious giants of Venus, partially intelligent but absolutely intractable because of the gulf that existed between their methods of thinking and the culture of mankind. Overtures had been made often enough; but it had been found that the reptile-folk were better left alone. They would not parley.

They were blindly bestial savages, with whom it was impossible to make truce. They stayed in the jungle, emerging only to hurl furious attacks at the forts—attacks doomed to failure, since tang and talon were matched against lead-jacketed bullet and high explosive.

As the flitterboat shot into a jetty, Scott kept his eyes straight ahead—it was not considered good form for a Free Companion to seem too curious when visiting the fort of another Company. Several men were on the quay, apparently waiting for him. They saluted as Scott stepped out of the boat.

He gave his name and rank. A corporal stepped forward.

"Cinc Mendez is expecting you, sir. Cinc Rhys telaudioed an hour or so back. If you'll come this way—"

"All right, Corporal. My pilot—"

"He'll be taken care of, sir. A rubdown and a drink, perhaps, after a spanker ride."

Scott nodded and followed the other into the bastion that thrust out from the overhanging wall of the fort. The sea gate was open, and he walked swiftly through the courtyard in the corporal's wake, passing a door-curtain, mounting an escalator, and finding himself, presently, before another curtain that bore the face of Cinc Mendez, plump, hoglike, and bald as a bullet.

Entering, he saw Mendez himself at the head of a long table, where nearly a dozen officers of the Mob were also seated. In person Mendez was somewhat more prepossessing than in effigy. He looked like a boar rather than a pig—a fighter, not a gourmand. His sharp black eyes seemed to drive into Scott with the impact of a physical blow.

He stood up, his officers following suit. "Sit down, Captain. There's a place at the foot of the table. No reflections on rank, but I prefer to be face to face with the man I'm dealing with. But first—you just arrived? If you'd like a quick rubdown, we'll be glad to wait."

Scott took his place. "Thank you, no, Cinc Mendez. I'd prefer not to lose time."

"Then we'll waste none on introductions. However, you can probably stand a drink." He spoke to the orderly at the door, and presently a filled glass stood at Scott's elbow.

His quick gaze ran along the rows of faces. Good soldiers, he thought—tough, well trained, and experienced.

They had been under fire. A small outfit, the Mob, but a powerful one.

Cinc Mendez sipped his own drink. "To business. The Doonemen wish to hire our help in fighting the Helldivers. Virginia Keep has bought the services of the Helldivers to attack Montana Keep." He enumerated on stubby fingers.

"You offer us fifty thousand cash and thirty-five percent of the korium ransom. So?"

"That's correct."

"We ask fifty percent."

"It's high. The Doones have superior manpower and equipment."

"To us, not to the Helldivers. Besides, the percentage is contingent. If we should lose, we get only the cash payment."

Scott nodded. "That's correct, but the only real danger from the Helldivers is their submarine corps. The Doones have plenty of surface and air equipment. We might lick the Helldivers without you."

"I don't think so." Mendez shook his bald head. "They have some new underwater torpedoes that make hash out of heavy armor plate. But we have new sub-detectors. We can blast the Helldivers' subs for you before they get within torpedo range."

Scott said bluntly, "You've been stalling, Cinc Mendez. We're not that bad off. If we can't get you, we'll find another outfit."

"With sub-detectors?"

"Yardley's Company is good at undersea work."

A major near the head of the table spoke up. "That's true, sir. They have suicide subs—not too dependable, but they have them."

Cinc Mendez wiped his bald head with his palms in a slow circular motion. "Hm-m-m. Well, Captain, I don't know. Yardley's Company isn't as good as ours for this job."

"All right," Scott said, "I've carte blanche. We don't know how much korium Virginia Keep has in her vaults. How would this proposition strike you: the Mob gets fifty percent of the korium ransom up to a quarter of a million; thirty-five percent above that."

"Forty-five."

"Forty, above a quarter of a million; forty-five below that sum."

"Gentlemen?" Cinc Mendez asked, looking down the table. "Your vote?"

There were several ayes, and a scattering of nays.

Mendez shrugged. "Then I have the deciding vote. Very well. We get forty-five percent of the Virginia Keep ransom up to a quarter of a million; forty percent on any amount above that. Agreed. We'll drink to it."

Orderlies served drinks. As Mendez rose, the others followed his example. The cinc nodded to Scott.

"Will you propose a toast, Captain?"

"With pleasure. Nelson's toast, then—a willing foe and sea room!"

They drank to that, as Free Companions had always drunk that toast on the eve of battle. As they seated themselves once more, Mendez said, "Major Matson, please telaudio Cinc Rhys and arrange details. We must know his plans."

"Yes, sir."

Mendez glanced at Scott. "Now how else may I serve you?"

"Nothing else. I'll get back to our fort. Details can be worked out on the telaudio, on tight beam."

"If you're going back in that flitterboat," Mendez said sardonically, "I strongly advise a rubdown. There's time to spare, now we've come to an agreement."

Scott hesitated. "Very well. I'm...uh...starting to ache." He stood up. "Oh, one thing I forgot. We've heard rumors that Starling's outfit is using atomic power." Mendez's mouth twisted into a grimace of distaste.

"Hadn't heard that. Know anything about it, gentlemen?" Heads were shaken. One officer said, "I've heard a little talk about it, but only talk, so far."

Mendez said, "After this war, we'll investigate further.

If there's truth in the story, we'll join you, of course, in mopping up the Starlings. No court-martial is necessary for that crime!"

"Thanks. I'll get in touch with other Companies and see what they've heard. Now, if you'll excuse me—" He saluted and went out, exultation flaming within him.

The bargain had been a good one—for the Doonemen badly needed the Mob's help against the Helldivers. Cinc Rhys would be satisfied with the arrangement.

An orderly took him to the baths, where a rubdown relaxed his aching muscles. Presently he was on the quay again, climbing into the flitterboat. A glance behind him showed that the gears of war were beginning to grind.

There was little he could see, but men were moving about through the courtyard with purposeful strides, to the shops, to administration, to the laboratories. The battlewagons were anchored down the coast, Scott knew, in a protected bay, but they would soon move out to their rendezvous with the Doones.

Kane, at the controls of the flitterboat, said, "They repaired the auxiliary unit for us, sir."

"Courtesies of the trade." Scott lifted a friendly hand to the men on the quay as the boat slid toward open water.

"The Doone fort, now. Know it?"

"Yes, sir. Are . . . are the Mob fighting with us, if I may ask?"

"They are. And they're a grand lot of fighters. You're going to see action, Kane. When you hear battle stations next, it's going to mean one of the sweetest scraps that happened on Venus. Push down that throttle—we're in a hurry!"

The flitterboat raced southwest at top speed, its course marked by the flying V of spray.

"One last fight," Scott thought to himself. "I'm glad it's going to be a good one."

4

We eat and drink our own damnation.
— *The Book of Common Prayer*

The motor failed when they were about eight miles from the Doone fort.

It was a catastrophe rather than merely a failure. The overstrained and overheated engine, running at top speed, blew back. The previous accident, at the subsea volcano, had brought out hidden flaws in the alloy which the Mob's repairmen had failed to detect when they replaced the smashed single unit. Sheer luck had the flitterboat poised on a swell when the crack-up happened. The engine blew out and down, ripping the bow to shreds. Had they been bow-deep, the blast would have been unfortunate for Scott and the pilot—more so than it was.

They were perhaps a half mile from the shore. Scott was deafened by the explosion and simultaneously saw the horizon swinging in a drunken swoop. The boat turned turtle, the shell smacking into water with a loud cracking sound.

But the plastic held. Both men were tangled together on what had been their ceiling, sliding forward as the flitterboat began to sink bow first. Steam sizzled from the ruined engine.

Kane managed to touch one of the emergency buttons.

The shell was, of course, jammed, but a few of the segments slid aside, admitting a gush of acrid sea water. For a moment they struggled there, fighting the cross-currents till the air had been displaced. Scott, peering through cloudy green gloom, saw Kane's dark shadow twist and kick out through a gap. He followed.

Beneath him the black bulk of the boat dropped slowly and was gone. His head broke surface, and he gasped for breath, shaking droplets from his lashes and glancing around. Where was Kane?

The boy appeared, his helmet gone, sleek hair plastered to his forehead. Scott caught his eye and pulled the trigger on his life vest, the inflatable undergarment which was always worn under the blouse on sea duty. As chemicals mixed, light gas rushed into the vest, lifting Scott higher in the water. He felt the collar cushion inflate against the back of his head—the skull-fitting pillow that allowed shipwrecked men to float and rest without danger of drowning in their sleep. But he had no need for this now.

Kane, he saw, had triggered his own life vest. Scott hurled himself up, searching for signs of life. There weren't any. The gray-green sea lay desolate to the misty horizon.

A half mile away was a mottled chartreuse wall that marked the jungle. Above and beyond that dim sulphurous red lit the clouds.

Scott got out his leaf-bladed smatchet, gesturing for Kane to do the same. The boy did not seem worried. No doubt this was merely an exciting adventure for him, Scott thought wryly. Oh, well.

Gripping the smatchet between his teeth, the captain began to swim shoreward. Kane kept at his side. Once Scott warned his companion to stillness and bent forward, burying his face in the water and peering down at a great dim shadow that coiled away and was gone—a sea snake, but, luckily, not hungry. The oceans of Venus were perilous with teeming, ferocious life. Precautions were fairly useless. When a man was once in the water, it was up to him to get out of it as rapidly as possible.

Scott touched a small cylinder attached to his belt and felt bubbles rushing against his palm. He was slightly relieved. When he had inflated the vest, this tube of compressed gas had automatically begun to release, sending out a foul-smelling vapor that permeated the water for some distance around. The principle was that of the skunk adjusted to the environment of the squid, and dangerous undersea life was supposed to be driven away by the Mellison tubes; but it didn't work with carrion eaters like the snakes. Scott averted his nose. The gadgets were named Mellison tubes, but the men called them Stinkers, a far more appropriate term.

Tides on Venus are unpredictable. The clouded planet has no moon, but it is closer to the Sun than Earth. As a rule the tides are mild, except during volcanic activity, when tidal waves sweep the shores. Scott, keeping a weather eye out for danger, rode the waves in toward the beach, searching the strip of dull blackness for signs of life.

Nothing.

He scrambled out at last, shaking himself like a dog, and instantly changed the clip in his automatic for high explosive. The weapon, of course, was watertight—a necessity on Venus. As Kane sat down with a grunt and deflated his vest, Scott stood eyeing the wall of jungle thirty feet away. It stopped there abruptly, for nothing could grow on black sand.

The rush and whisper of the waves made the only sound. Most of the trees were liana-like, eking out a precarious existence, as the saying went, by taking in each other's washing. The moment one of them showed signs of solidity, it was immediately assailed by parasitic vines flinging themselves madly upward to reach the filtered sunlight of Venus. The leaves did not begin for thirty feet above the ground; they made a regular roof up there, lying like crazy shingles, and would have shut out all light had they not been of light translucent green. Whitish tendrils crawled like reaching serpents from tree to tree, tentacles of vegetable octopi. There were two types of Venusian fauna: the giants who could crash through the forest, and the supple, small ground-dwellers—insects and reptiles mostly—who depended on poison sacs for self-protection. Neither kind was pleasant company.

There were flying creatures, too, but these lived in the upper strata, among the leaves. And there were ambiguous horrors that lived in the deep mud and the stagnant pools under the forest, but no one knew much about these.

"Well," Scott said, "that's that."

Kane nodded. "I guess I should have checked the motors."

"You wouldn't have found anything. Latent flaws—it would have taken black night to bring 'em out. Just one of those things. Keep your gas mask handy, now. If we get anywhere near poison flowers and the wind's blowing this way, we're apt to keel over like that." Scott opened a waterproof wallet and took out a strip of sensitized litmus, which he clipped to his wrist. "If this turns blue, that means gas, even if we don't smell it."

"Yes, sir. What now?"

"We-el—the boat's gone. We can't telaudio for help." Scott fingered the blade of his smatchet and slipped it into the belt sheath. "We head for the fort. Eight miles. Two hours, if we can stick to the beach and if we don't run into trouble. More than that if Signal Rock's ahead of us, because we'll have to detour inland in that case." He drew out a collapsible single-lenser telescope and looked southwest along the shore. "Uh-huh. We detour."

A breath of sickening sweetness gusted down from the jungle roof. From above, Scott knew, the forest looked surprisingly lovely. It always reminded him of an antique candlewick spread he had once bought Jeana—immense rainbow flowers scattered over a background of pale green.

Even among the flora competition was keen; the plants vied in producing colors and scents that would attract the winged carriers of pollen.

There would always be frontiers, Scott thought. But they might remain unconquered for a long time, here on Venus. The Keeps were enough for the undersea folk; they were self-sustaining. And the Free Companions had no need to carve out empires on the continents. They were fighters, not agrarians. Land hunger was no longer a part of the race. It might come again, but not in the time of the Keeps.

The jungles of Venus held secrets he would never know.

Men can conquer lands from the air, but they cannot hold them by that method. It would take a long, slow period of encroachment, during which the forest and all it represented would be driven back, step by painful step—and that belonged to a day to come, a time Scott would not know. The savage world would be tamed. But not now—not yet.

At the moment it was untamed and very dangerous.

Scott stripped off his tunic and wrung water from it. His clothing would not dry in this saturated air, despite the winds. His trousers clung to him stickily, clammy coldness in their folds.

"Ready, Kane?"

"Yes, sir."

"Then let's go."

They went southwest, along the beach, at a steady, easy lope that devoured miles. Speed and alertness were necessary in equal proportion. From time to time Scott scanned the sea with his telescope, hoping to sight a vessel. He saw nothing. The ships would be in harbor, readying for the battle; and planes would be grounded for installation of the new telaudio device Cinc Rhys had mentioned.

Signal Rock loomed ahead, an outthrust crag with eroded, unscalable sides towering two hundred feet and more. The black strip of sand ended there. From the rock there was a straight drop into deep water, cut up by a turmoil of currents. It was impossible to take the sea detour; there was nothing else for it but to swerve inland, a dangerous but inevitable course. Scott postponed the plunge as long as possible, till the scarp of Signal Rock, jet black with leprous silvery patches on its surface, barred the way. With a quizzical look at Kane he turned sharply to his right and headed for the jungle.

"Half a mile of forest equals a hundred miles of beach hiking," he remarked.

"That bad, sir? I've never tackled it."

"Nobody does, unless they have to. Keep your eyes open and your gun ready. Don't wade through water, even when you can see bottom. There are some little devils that are pretty nearly transparent—vampire fish. If a few of those fasten on you, you'll need a transfusion in less than a minute. I wish the volcanoes would kick up a racket. The beasties generally lie low when that happens." Under a tree Scott stopped, seeking a straight, long limb. It took a while to find a suitable one, in that tangle of coiling lianas, but finally he succeeded, using his smatchet blade to hack himself a light five-foot pole. Kane at his heels, he moved on into the gathering gloom.

"We may be stalked," he told the boy. "Don't forget to guard the rear."

The sand had given place to sticky whitish mud that plastered the men to their calves before a few moments had passed. A patina of slickness seemed to overlay the ground. The grass was colored so much like the mud itself that it was practically invisible, except by its added slipperiness. Scott slowly advanced keeping close to the wall of rock on his left where the tangle was not so thick. Nevertheless he had to use the smatchet more than once to cut a passage through vines.

He stopped, raising his hand, and the squelch of Kane's feet in the mud paused. Silently Scott pointed. Ahead of them in the cliff base, was the mouth of a burrow.

The captain bent down, found a small stone, and threw it toward the den. He waited, one hand lightly on his gun, ready to see something flash out of that burrow and race toward them. In the utter silence a new sound made itself heard—tiny goblin drums, erratic and resonant in a faraway fashion. Water, dropping from leaf to leaf, in the soaked jungle ceiling above them. *Tink, tink, tink-tink, tink, tink-tink—*

"O.K." Scott said quietly. "Watch it, though." He went on, gun drawn, till they were level with the mouth of the burrow. "Turn, Kane. Keep your eye on it till I tell you to stop." He gripped the boy's arm and guided him, holstering his own weapon. The pole, till now held between biceps and body, slipped into his hand. He used it to probe the slick surface of the mud ahead. Sinkholes and quicksands were frequent, and so were traps, camouflaged pits built by mud-wolves— which, of course, were not wolves, and belonged to no known genus. On Venus, the fauna had more subdivisions than on old Earth, and lines of demarcation were more subtle.

"All right now."

Kane, sighing with relief, turned his face forward again. "What was it?"

"You never know what may come out of those holes," Scott told him. "They come fast, and they're usually poisonous. So you can't take chances with the critters. Slow down here. I don't like the looks of that patch ahead." Clearings were unusual in the forest. There was one here, twenty feet wide, slightly saucer-shaped. Scott gingerly extended the pole and probed. A faint ripple shook the white mud, and almost before it had appeared the captain had unholstered his pistol and was blasting shot after shot at the movement.

"Shoot, Kane!" he snapped. "Quick! Shoot at it!"

Kane obeyed, though he had to guess at his target. Mud geysered up, suddenly crimson-stained. Scott, still firing, gripped the boy's arm and ran him back at a breakneck pace.

The echoes died. Once more the distant elfin drums whispered through the green gloom.

"We got it," Scott said, after a pause.

"We did?" the other asked blankly. "What—"

"Mud-wolf, I think. The only way to kill those things is to get 'em before they get out of the mud. They're fast and they die hard. However—" He warily went forward. There was nothing to see. The mud had collapsed into a deeper saucer, but the holes blasted by the high-x bullets had filled in. Here and there were traces of thready crimson.

"Never a dull moment," Scott remarked. His crooked grin eased the tension. Kane chuckled and followed the captain's example in replacing his half-used clip with a full one.

The narrow spine of Signal Rock extended inland for a quarter mile before it became scalable. They reached that point finally, helping each other climb, and finding themselves, at the summit, still well below the leafy ceiling of the trees. The black surface of the rock was painfully hot, stinging their palms as they climbed, and even striking through their shoe soles.

"Halfway point, Captain?"

"Yeah. But don't let that cheer you. It doesn't get any better till we hit the beach again. We'll probably need some fever shots when we reach the fort, just in case. Oh-oh. Mask, Kane, quick." Scott lifted his arm. On his wrist the band of litmus had turned blue.

With trained accuracy they donned the respirators.

Scott felt a faint stinging on his exposed skin, but that wasn't serious. Still, it would be painful later. He beckoned to Kane, slid down the face of the rock, used the pole to test the mud below, and jumped lightly. He dropped in the sticky whiteness and rolled over hastily, plastering himself from head to foot. Kane did the same. Mud wouldn't neutralize the poison flowers' gas, but it would absorb most of it before it reached the skin.

Scott headed toward the beach, a grotesque figure. Mud dripped on the eye plate, and he scrubbed it away with a handful of white grass. He used the pole constantly to test the footing ahead.

Nevertheless the mud betrayed him. The pole broke through suddenly, and as Scott automatically threw his weight back, the ground fell away under his feet. He had time for a crazy feeling of relief that this was quicksand, not a mud-wolf's den, and then the clinging, treacherous stuff had sucked him down knee-deep. He fell back, keeping his grip on the pole and swinging the other end in an arc toward Kane.

The boy seized it in both hands and threw himself flat.

His foot hooked over an exposed root. Scott, craning his neck at a painfully awkward angle and trying to see through the mud-smeared vision plate, kept a rattrap grip on his end of the pole, hoping its slickness would not slip through his fingers.

He was drawn down farther, and then Kane's anchorage began to help. The boy tried to pull the pole toward him, hand over hand. Scott shook his head. He was a good deal stronger than Kane, and the latter would need all his strength to keep a tight grip on the pole.

Something stirred in the shadows behind Kane. Scott instinctively let go with one hand, and, with the other, got out his gun. It had a sealed mechanism, so the mud hadn't harmed the firing, and the muzzle had a one-way trap. He fired at the movement behind Kane, heard a muffled tumult, and waited till it had died. The boy, after a startled look behind him, had not stirred.

After that, rescue was comparatively easy. Scott simply climbed along the pole, spreading his weight over the surface of the quicksand. The really tough part was pulling his legs free of that deadly grip. Scott had to rest for five minutes after that.

But he got out. That was the important thing.

Kane pointed inquiringly into the bushes where the creature had been shot, but Scott shook his head. The nature of the beast wasn't a question worth deciding, as long as it was apparently hors de combat. Readjusting his mask, Scott turned toward the beach, circling the quicksand, and Kane kept at his heels.

Their luck had changed. They reached the shore with no further difficulty and collapsed on the black sand to rest.

Presently Scott used a litmus, saw that the gas had dissipated, and removed his mask. He took a deep breath.

"Thanks, Kane," he said. "You can take a dip now if you want to wash off that mud. But stay close inshore. No, don't strip. There's no time."

The mud clung like glue and the black sand scratched like pumice. Still, Scott felt a good deal cleaner after a few minutes in the surf, while Kane stayed on guard. Slightly refreshed, they resumed the march.

An hour later a convoy plane, testing, sighted them, telaudioed the fort, and a flitterboat came racing out to pick them up. What Scott appreciated most of all was the stiff shot of uisqueplus the pilot gave him.

Yeah. It was a dog's life, all right!

He passed the flask to Kane.

Presently the fort loomed ahead, guarding Doone Harbor. Large as the landlocked bay was, it could scarcely accommodate the fleet. Scott watched the activity visible with an approving eye. The flitterboat rounded the sea wall, built for protection against tidal waves, and shot toward a jetty. Its almost inaudible motor died; the shell swung back.

Scott got out, beckoning to an orderly.

"Yes, sir?"

"See that this soldier gets what he needs. We've been in the jungle."

The man didn't whistle sympathetically, but his mouth pursed. He saluted and helped Kane climb out of the flitterboat. As Scott hurried along the quay, he could hear an outburst of friendly profanity from the men on the dock, gathering around Kane.

He nodded imperceptibly. The boy would make a good Free Companion—always granted that he could stand the gaff under fire. That was the acid test. Discipline was tightened then to the snapping point. If it snapped—well, the human factor always remained a variable, in spite of all the psychologists could do.

He went directly to his quarters, switching on the telaudio to call Cinc Rhys. The cinc's seamed, leathery face resolved itself on the screen.

"Captain Scott reporting for duty, sir."

Rhys looked at him sharply. "What happened?"

"Flitterboat crack-up. Had to make it in here on foot."

The cinc called on his God in a mild voice. "Glad you made it. Any accident?"

"No, sir. The pilot's unharmed, too. I'm ready to take over, after I've cleaned up."

"Better take a rejuvenation—you probably need it. Everything's going like clockwork. You did a good job with Mendez—a better bargain than I'd hoped for. I've been talking with him on the telaudio, integrating our forces. We'll go into that later, though. Clean up and then make general inspection."

"Check, sir."

Rhys clicked off. Scott turned to face his orderly.

"Hello, Briggs. Help me off with these duds. You'll probably have to cut 'em off."

"Glad to see you back, sir. I don't think it'll be necessary to cut—" Blunt fingers flew deftly over zippers and clasps. "You were in the jungle?"

Scott grinned wryly. "Do I look as if I'd been gliding?"

"Not all the way, sir—no."

Briggs was like an old bulldog—one of those men who proved the truth of the saying: "Old soldiers never die; they only fade away." Briggs could have been pensioned off ten years ago, but he hadn't wanted that. There was always a place for old soldiers in the Free Companies, even those who were unskilled. Some became technicians; others, military instructors; the rest, orderlies. The forts were their homes. Had they retired to one of the Keeps, they would have died for lack of interests.

Briggs, now—he had never risen above the ranks, and knew nothing of military strategy, ordnance, or anything except plain fighting. But he had been a Dooneman for forty years, twenty-five of them on active service. He was sixty-odd now, his squat figure slightly stooped like an elderly bear, his ugly face masked with scar tissue.

"All right. Start the shower, will you?"

Briggs stumped off, and Scott, stripped of his filthy, sodden garments, followed. He luxuriated under the stinging spray, first hot soapy water, then alcomix, and after that plain water, first hot, then cold. That was the last task he had to do himself. Briggs took over, as Scott relaxed on the slab, dropping lotion into the captain's burning eyes, giving him a deft but murderous rubdown, combining osteopathic and chiropractic treatment, adjusting revitalizing lamps, and measuring a hypo shot to nullify fatigue toxins. When the orderly was finished, Scott was ready to resume his duties with a clear brain and a refreshed body.

Briggs appeared with fresh clothing. "I'll have the old uniform cleaned, sir. No use throwing it away."

"You can't clean that," Scott remarked, slipping into a singlet. "Not after I rolled in mud. But suit yourself. I won't be needing it for long." The orderly's fingers, buttoning Scott's tunic, stopped briefly and then resumed their motion. "Is that so, sir?"

"Yeah. I'm taking out discharge papers."

"Another Company, sir?"

"Don't get on your high horse," Scott told the orderly. "It's not that. What would you do if it were? Court-martial me yourself and shoot me at sunrise?"

"No, sir. Begging your pardon, sir, I'd just think you were crazy."

"Why I stand you only the Lord knows," Scott remarked. "You're too damn independent. There's no room for new ideas in that plastic skull of yours. You're the quintessence of dogmatism."

Briggs nodded. "Probably, sir. When a man's lived by one set of rules for as long as I have, and those rules work out, I suppose he might get dogmatic."

"Forty years for you—about twelve for me."

"You came up fast, Captain. You'll be cinc here yet."

"That's what you think."

"You're next in line after Cinc Rhys."

"But I'll be out of the Doones," Scott pointed out. "Keep that under your belt, Briggs."

The orderly grunted. "Can't see it, sir. If you don't join another Company, where'll you go?"

"Ever heard of the Keeps?"

Briggs permitted himself a respectful snort. "Sure. They're fine for a binge, but—"

"I'm going to live in one. Montana Keep."

"The Keeps were built with men and machines. I helped at the building of Doone fort. Blood's mixed with the plastic here. We had to hold back the jungle while the technicians were working. Eight months, sir, and never a day passed without some sort of attack. And attacks always meant casualties then. We had only breastworks. The ships laid down a barrage, but barrages aren't impassable. That was a fight, Captain."

Scott thrust out a leg so that Briggs could lace his boots. "And a damn good one. I know." He looked down at the orderly's baldish, brown head where white hairs straggled.

"You know, but you weren't there, Captain. I was. First we dynamited. We cleared a half circle where we could dig in behind breastworks. Behind us were the techs, throwing up a plastic wall as fast as they could. The guns were brought in on barges. Lying offshore were the battlewagons. We could hear the shells go whistling over our heads—it sounded pretty good, because we knew things were O.K. as long as the barrage kept up. But it couldn't be kept up day and night. The jungle broke through. For months the smell of blood hung here, and that drew the enemy."

"But you held them off."

"Sure, we did. Addison Doone was cinc then—he'd formed the Company years before, but we hadn't a fort. Doone fought with us. Saved my life once, in fact. Anyhow—we got the fort built, or rather the techs did. I won't forget the kick I got out of it when the first big gun blasted off from the wall behind us. There was a lot to do after that, but when that shell was fired, we knew we'd done the job."

Scott nodded. "You feel a proprietary interest in the fort, I guess."

Briggs looked puzzled. "The fort? Why, that doesn't mean much, Captain. There are lots of forts. It's something more than that; I don't quite know what it is. It's seeing the fleet out there—breaking in the rookies—giving the old toasts at mess—knowing that—" He stopped, at a loss.

Scott's lips twisted wryly. "You don't really know, do you, Briggs?"

"Know what, sir?"

"Why you stay here. Why you can't believe I'd quit."

Briggs gave a little shrug. "Well—it's the Doones," he said. "That's all, Captain. It's just that."

"And what the devil will it matter, in a few hundred years?"

"I suppose it won't. No, sir. But it isn't our business to think about that. We're Doonemen, that's all."

Scott didn't answer. He could easily have pointed out the fallacy of Briggs's argument, but what was the use? He stood up, the orderly whisking invisible dust off his tunic.

"All set, sir. Shipshape."

"Check, Briggs. Well, I've one more scrap, anyhow. I'll bring you back a souvenir, eh?"

The orderly saluted, grinning. Scott went out, feeling good. Inwardly he was chuckling rather sardonically at the false values he was supposed to take seriously. Of course many men had died when Doone fort had been built. But did that, in itself, make a tradition? What good was the fort? In a few centuries it would have outlived its usefulness. Then it would be a relic of the past. Civilization moved on, and, these days, civilization merely tolerated the military.

So—what was the use? Sentiment needed a valid reason for its existence. The Free Companions fought, bitterly, doggedly, with insane valor, in order to destroy themselves.

The ancient motives for war had vanished.

What was the use? All over Venus the lights of the great forts were going out—and, this time, they would never be lit again—not in a thousand lifetimes!

5

And we are here as on a darkling plain
Swept with confused alarms of struggle and flight,
where ignorant armies clash by night.
                                                    —Arnold, circa 1870

The fort was a completely self-contained unit, military rather than social. There was no need for any agrarian development, since a state of complete siege never existed.

Food could be brought in from the Keeps by water and air.

But military production was important, and, in the life of the fort, the techs played an important part, from the experimental physicist to the spot welder. There were always replacements to be made, for, in battle, there were always casualties. And it was necessary to keep the weapons up-to-date, continually striving to perfect new ones. But strategy and armament were of equal importance. An outnumbered fleet had been known to conquer a stronger one by the use of practical psychology.

Scott found Commander Bienne at the docks, watching the launching of a new sub. Apparently Bienne hadn't yet got over his anger, for he turned a scowling, somber face to the captain as he saluted.

"Hello, Commander," Scott said. "I'm making inspection. Are you free?"

Bienne nodded. "There's not much to do."

"Well—routine. We got that sub finished just in time, eh?"

"Yes." Bienne couldn't repress his pleasure at sight of the trim, sleek vessel beginning to slide down the ways.

Scott, too, felt his pulses heighten as the sub slipped into the water, raising a mighty splash, and then settling down to a smooth, steady riding on the waves. He looked out to where the great battlewagons stood at anchor, twelve of them, gray-green monsters of plated metal. Each of them carried launching equipment for gliders, but the collapsible aircraft were stowed away out of sight as yet. Smaller destroyers lay like lean-flanked wolves among the battleships.

There were two fast carriers, loaded with gliders and flitterboats. There were torpedo boats and one low-riding monitor, impregnable, powerfully armed, but slow. Only a direct hit could disable a monitor, but the behemoths had their disadvantages. The battle was usually over before they lumbered into sight. Like all monitors, this one—the *Armageddon*—was constructed on the principle of a razorback hog, covered, except for the firing ports, by a tureen-shaped shield, strongly braced from within. The *Armageddon* was divided into groups of compartments and had several auxiliary engines, so that, unlike the legendary *Rover*, when a monitor died, it did not die all over. It was, in effect, a dinosaur. You could blow off the monster's head, and it would continue to fight with talons and lashing tail. Its heavy guns made up in mobility for the giant's unwieldiness—but the trouble was to get the monitor into battle. It was painfully slow.

Scott scowled. "We're fighting over Venus Deep, eh?"

"Yes," Bienne nodded. "That still goes. The Helldivers are already heading toward Montana Keep, and we'll intercept them over the Deep."

"When's zero hour?"

"Midnight tonight."

Scott closed his eyes, visualizing their course on a mental chart. Not so good. When battle was joined near island groups, it was sometimes possible for a monitor to slip up under cover of the islets, but that trick wouldn't work now.

Too bad—for the Helldivers were a strong outfit, more so since their recent merger with O'Brien's Legion. Even with the Mob to help, the outcome of the scrap would be anyone's guess. The *Armageddon* might be the decisive factor.

"I wonder—" Scott said. "No. It'd be impossible."

"What?"

"Camouflaging the *Armageddon*. If the Helldivers see the monitor coming, they'll lead the fight away from it, faster than that tub can follow. I was thinking we might get her into the battle without the enemy realizing it."

"She's camouflaged now."

"Paint, that's all. She can be spotted. I had some screwy idea about disguising her as an island or a dead whale."

"She's too big for a whale and floating islands look a bit suspicious."

"Yeah. But if we could slip the *Armageddon* in without scaring off the enemy—Hm-m-m. Monitors have a habit of turning turtle, don't they?"

"Right. They're top-heavy. But a monitor can't fight upside down. It's not such a bright idea, Captain." Briefly Bienne's sunken eyes gleamed with sneering mockery.

Scott grunted and turned away.

"All right. Let's take a look around."

The fleet was shipshape. Scott went to the shops. He learned that several new hulls were under way, but would not be completed by zero hour. With Bienne, he continued to the laboratory offices. Nothing new. No slipups; no surprises. The machine was running smoothly.

By the time inspection was completed, Scott had an idea. He told Bienne to carry on and went to find Cinc Rhys. The cinc was in his office, just clicking off the telaudio as Scott appeared.

"That was Mendez," Rhys said. "The Mob's meeting our fleet a hundred miles off the coast. They'll be under our orders, of course. A good man, Mendez, but I don't entirely trust him."

"You're not thinking of a double cross, sir?"

Cinc Rhys made disparaging noises. "Brutus is an honorable man. No, he'll stick to his bargain. But I wouldn't cut cards with Mendez. As a Free Companion, he's trustworthy. Personally—Well, how do things look?"

"Very good, sir. I've an idea about the *Armageddon.*"

"I wish I had," Rhys said frankly. "We can't get that damned scow into the battle in any way I can figure out. The Helldivers will see it coming, and lead the fight away."

"I'm thinking of camouflage."

"A monitor's a monitor. It's unmistakable. You can't make it look like anything else."

"With one exception, sir. You can make it look like a disabled monitor."

Rhys sat back, giving Scott a startled glance. "That's interesting. Go on."

"Look here, sir." The captain used a stylo to sketch the outline of a monitor on a convenient pad. "Above the surface, the *Armageddon*'s dome-shaped. Below, it's a bit different, chiefly because of the keel. Why can't we put a fake superstructure on the monitor—build a false keel on it, so it'll seem capsized?"

"It's possible."

"Everybody knows a monitor's weak spot—that it turns turtle under fire sometimes. If the Helldiver saw an apparently capsized *Armageddon* drifting toward them, they'd naturally figure the tub was disabled."

"It's crazy," Rhys said. "One of those crazy ideas that might work." He used the local telaudio to issue crisp orders. "Got it? Good. Get the *Armageddon* under way as soon as the equipment's aboard. Alterations will be made at sea. We can't waste time. If we had them made in the yards, she'd never catch up with the fleet." The cinc broke the connection, his seamed, leathery face twisting into a grin. "I hope it works. We'll see." He snapped his fingers. "Almost forgot. President Crosby's nephew—Kane?—he was with you when you cracked up, wasn't he? I've been wondering whether I should have waived training for him. How did he show up in the jungle?"

"Quite well," Scott said. "I had my eye on him. He'll make a good soldier."

Rhys looked keenly at the captain. "What about discipline? I felt that was his weak spot."

"I've no complaint to make."

"So. Well, maybe. Starling's outfit is bad training for anyone—especially a raw kid. Speaking of Starling, did Cinc Mendez know anything about his using atomic power?"

"No, sir. If Starling's doing that, he's keeping it plenty quiet."

"We'll investigate after the battle. Can't afford that sort of thing—we don't want another holocaust. It was bad enough to lose Earth. It decimated the race. If it happened again, it'd wipe the race out."

"I don't think there's much danger of that. On Earth, it was the big atomic-power stations that got out of control. At worst, Starling can't have more than hand weapons."

"True. You can't blow up a world with those. But you know the law—no atomic power on Venus."

Scott nodded.

"Well, that's all." Rhys waved him away. "Clear weather."

Which, on this perpetually clouded world, had a tinge of irony.

After mess Scott returned to his quarters, for a smoke and a brief rest. He waved away Briggs's suggestion of a rubdown and sent the orderly to the commissary for fresh tobacco. "Be sure to get Twenty Star," he cautioned. "I don't want that green hydroponic cabbage."

"I know the brand, sir." Briggs looked hurt and departed. Scott settled back in his relaxer, sighing.

Zero hour at twelve. The last zero hour he'd ever know.

All through the day he had been conscious that he was fulfilling his duties for the last time.

His mind went back to Montana Keep. He was living again those otherworldly moments in the cloud-wrapped Olympus with Ilene. Curiously, he found it difficult to visualize the girl's features. Perhaps she was a symbol—her appearance did not matter. Yet she was very lovely.

In a different way from Jeana. Scott glanced at Jeana's picture on the desk, three-dimensional and tinted after life.

By pressing a button on the frame, he could have given it sound and motion. He leaned forward and touched the tiny stud. In the depths of the picture the figure of Jeana stirred, smiling. The red lips parted.

Her voice, though soft, was quite natural.

"Hello, Brian," the recording said. "Wish I were with you now. Here's a present, darling." The image blew him a kiss, and then faded back to immobility.

Scott sighed again. Jeana was a comfortable sort of person. But— Oh, hell! She wasn't willing to change. Very likely she couldn't. Ilene perhaps was equally dogmatic, but she represented the life of the Keeps—and that was what Scott wanted now.

It was an artificial life Ilene lived, but she was honest about it. She knew its values were false. At least she didn't pretend, like the Free Companions, that there were ideals worth dying for. Scott remembered Briggs. The fact that men had been killed during the building of Doone fort meant a lot to the old orderly. He never asked himself—why? Why had they died? Why was Doone fort built in the first place? For war. And war was doomed.

One had to believe in an ideal before devoting one's life to it. One had to feel he was helping the ideal to survive watering the plant with his blood so eventually it would come to flower. The red flower of Mars had long since blown. How did that old poem go?

One thing is certain, and the rest is lies;
The flower that once has blown forever dies.

It was true. But the Free Companions blindly pretended that the flower was still in blazing scarlet bloom, refusing to admit that even the roots were withered and useless, scarcely able now to suck up the blood sacrificed to its hopeless thirst.

New flowers bloomed; new buds opened. But in the Keeps, not in the great doomed forts. It was the winter cycle, and, as the last season's blossoms faded, the buds of the next stirred into life. Life questing and intolerant. Life that fed on the rotting petals of the rose of war.

But the pretense went on, in the coastal forts that guarded the Keeps. Scott made a grimace of distaste.

Blind, stupid folly! He was a man first, not a soldier. And man is essentially a hedonist, whether he identifies himself with the race or not.

Scott could not. He was not part of the undersea culture, and he could never be. But he could lose himself in the hedonistic backwash of the Keeps, the froth that always overlies any social unit. With Ilene, he could, at least, seek happiness, without the bitter self-mockery he had known for so long. Mockery at his own emotional weaknesses in which he did not believe.

Ilene was honest. She knew she was damned, because unluckily she had intelligence.

So—Scott thought—they would make a good pair.

Scott looked up as Commander Bienne came into the room. Bienne's sour, mahogany face was flushed deep red under the bronze. His lids were heavy over angry eyes. He swung the door-curtain shut after him and stood rocking on his heels, glowering at Scott.

He called Scott something unprintable.

The captain rose, an icy knot of fury in his stomach.

Very softly he said, "You're drunk, Bienne. Get out. Get back to your quarters."

"Sure—you little tinhorn soldier. You like to give orders, don't you? You like to chisel, too. The way you chiseled me out of that left-wing command today. I'm pretty sick of it, Captain Brian Scott."

"Don't be a damned fool! I don't like you personally any more than you like me, but that's got nothing to do with the Company. I recommended you for that command."

"You lie," Bienne said, swaying. "And I hate your guts." Scott went pale, the scar on his cheek flaming red.

Bienne came forward. He wasn't too drunk to coordinate.

His fist lashed out suddenly and connected agonizingly with Scott's molar.

The captain's reach was less than Bienne's. He ducked inside of the next swing and carefully smashed a blow home on the point of the other's jaw. Bienne was driven back, crashing against the wall and sliding down in a limp heap, his head lolling forward.

Scott, rubbing his knuckles, looked down, considering.

Presently he knelt and made a quick examination. A knock-out, that was all.

Oh, well.

Briggs appeared, showing no surprise at sight of Bienne's motionless body. The perfect orderly walked across to the table and began to refill the humidor with the tobacco he had brought.

Scott almost chuckled.

"Briggs."

"Yes, sir?"

"Commander Bienne's had a slight accident. He—slipped. Hit his chin on something. He's a bit tight, too. Fix him up, will you?"

"With pleasure, sir." Briggs hoisted Bienne's body across his brawny shoulders.

"Zero hour's at twelve. The commander must be aboard the *Flintlock* by then. And sober. Can do?"

"Certainly, sir," Briggs said, and went out.

Scott returned to his chair, filling his pipe. He should have confined Bienne to his quarters, of course. But—well, this was a personal matter.

One could afford to stretch a point, especially since Bienne was a valuable man to have aboard during action. Scott vaguely hoped the commander would get his thick head blown off.

After a time he tapped the dottle from his pipe and went off for a final inspection.

At midnight the fleet hoisted anchor.

By dawn the Doones were nearing the Venus Deep.

The ships of the Mob had already joined them, seven battleships and assorted cruisers, destroyers, and one carrier. No monitor. The Mob didn't own one—it had capsized two months before, and was still undergoing repairs.

The combined fleets sailed in crescent formation, the left wing, commanded by Scott, composed of his own ship, the *Flintlock*, and the *Arquebus*, the *Arrow*, and the *Misericordia*, all Doone battlewagons. There were two Mob ships with him, the *Navaho* and the *Zuni*, the latter commanded by Cinc Mendez. Scott had one carrier with him, the other being at right wing. Besides these, there were the lighter craft.

In the center were the battleships *Arbalest*, *Lance*, *Gatling*, and *Mace*, as well as three of Mendez's. Cinc Rhys was aboard the *Lance*, controlling operations. The camouflaged monitor *Armageddon* was puffing away valiantly far behind, well out of sight in the mists.

Scott was in his control room, surrounded by telaudio screens and switchboards. Six operators were perched on stools before the controls, ready to jump to action when orders came through their earphones. In the din of battle spoken commands often went unheard, which was why Scott wore a hush-mike strapped to his chest.

His eyes roved over the semicircle of screens before him.

"Any report from the gliders yet?"

"No, sir."

"Get me air-spotting command."

One of the screens flamed to life; a face snapped into view on it.

"Report."

"Nothing yet, Captain. Wait." There was a distant thunder. "Detectors clamped on a telaudio tight-beam directly overhead."

"Enemy glider in the clouds?"

"Apparently. It's out of the focus now."

"Try to relocate it."

A lot of good that would do. Motored planes could easily be detected overhead, but a glider was another matter. The only way to spot one was by clamping a detector focus directly on the glider's telaudio beam—worse than a needle in a haystack. Luckily the crates didn't carry bombs.

"Report coming in, sir. One of our gliders." Another screen showed a face. "Pilot reporting, sir. Located enemy."

"Good. Switch in the telaudio, infra. What sector?"

"V. D. eight hundred seven northwest twenty-one."

Scott said into his hush-mike, "Get Cinc Rhys and Commander Geer on tight-beam. And Cinc Mendez."

Three more screens lit up, showing the faces of the three officers.

"Cut in the pilot."

Somewhere over Venus Deep the glider pilot was arcing his plane through the cloud-layer, the automatic telaudio-camera, lensed to infrared, penetrating the murk and revealing the ocean below. On the screen ships showed, driving forward in battle formation.

Scott recognized and enumerated them mentally. The *Orion*, the *Sirius*, the *Vega*, the *Polaris*—uh-huh. Lighter ships. Plenty of them. The scanner swept on.

Cinc Rhys said, "We're outnumbered badly. Cinc Mendez, are your sub-detectors in operation?"

"They are. Nothing yet."

"We'll join battle in half an hour, I judge. We've located them, and they've no doubt located us."

"Check."

The screens blanked out. Scott settled back, alertly at ease. Nothing to do now but wait, keeping ready for the unexpected. The *Orion* and the *Vega* were the Helldivers's biggest battleships, larger than anything in the line of the Doones—or the Mob. Cinc Flynn was no doubt aboard the *Orion*. The Helldivers owned a monitor, but it had not showed on the infrared aerial scanner. Probably the behemoth wouldn't even show up in time for the battle.

But even without the monitor, the Helldivers had an overwhelming surface display. Moreover, their undersea fleet was an important factor. The sub-detectors of Cinc Mendez might—probably would—cut down the odds. But possibly not enough.

The *Armageddon*, Scott thought, might be the point of decision, the ultimate argument. And, as yet, the camouflaged monitor was lumbering through the waves far in the wake of the Doones.

Commander Bienne appeared on a screen. He had frozen into a disciplined, trained robot, personal animosities forgotten for the time. Active duty did that to a man.

Scott expected nothing different, however, and his voice was completely impersonal as he acknowledged Bienne's call.

"The flitterboats are ready to go, Captain."

"Send them out in fifteen minutes. Relay to left wing, all ships carrying flitters."

"Check."

For a while there was silence. A booming explosion brought Scott to instant alertness. He glanced up at the screens.

A new face appeared. "Helldivers opening up. Testing for range. They must have gliders overhead. We can't spot 'em."

"Get the men under cover. Send up a test barrage. Prepare to return here. Contact our pilots over the Helldivers."

It was beginning now—the incessant, racking thunder that would continue till the last shot was fired. Scott cut in to Cinc Rhys as the latter signaled.

"Reporting, sir."

"Harry the enemy. We can't do much yet. Change to R-8 formation."

Cinc Mendez said, "We've got three enemy subs. Our detectors are tuned up to high pitch."

"Limit the range so our subs will be outside the sphere of influence."

"Already did that. The enemy's using magnetic depth charges, laying an undersea barrage as they advance."

"I'll talk to the sub command." Rhys cut off. Scott listened to the increasing fury of explosions. He could not yet hear the distinctive clap-clap of heat rays, but the quarters were not yet close enough for those undependable, though powerful, weapons. It took time for a heat ray to warm up, and during that period a well-aimed bullet could smash the projector lens.

"Casualty, sir. Direct hit aboard destroyer *Bayonet*."

"Extent of damage?"

"Not disabled. Complete report later."

After a while a glider pilot came in on the beam.

"Shell landed on the *Polaris*, sir."

"Use the scanner."

It showed the Helldivers's battlewagon, part of the superstructure carried away, but obviously still in fighting trim. Scott nodded. Both sides were getting the range now.

The hazy clouds still hid each fleet from the other, but they were nearing.

The sound of artillery increased. Problems of trajectory were increased by the violent winds of Venus, but accurate aiming was possible. Scott nodded grimly as a crash shook the *Flintlock*.

They were getting it now. Here, in the brain of the ship, he was as close to the battle as any member of a firing crew. The screens were his eyes.

They had the advantage of being able to use infrared, so that Scott, buried here, could see more than he could have on deck, with his naked eye. Something loomed out of the murk and Scott's breath stopped before he recognized the lines of the Doone battlewagon *Misericordia*.

She was off course. The captain used his hush-mike to snap a quick reprimand.

Flitterboats were going out now, speedy hornets that would harry the enemy feet. In one of them, Scott remembered, was Norman Kane. He thought of Ilene and thrust the thought back, out of his mind. No time for that now.

Battle stations allowed no time for woolgathering.

The distant vanguard of the Helldivers came into sight on the screens. Cinc Mendez called.

"Eleven more subs. One got through. Seems to be near the *Flintlock*. Drop depth bombs."

Scott nodded and obeyed. Shuddering concussions shook the ship. Presently a report came in: fuel slick to starboard.

Good. A few well-placed torpedoes could do a lot of damage.

The *Flintlock* heeled incessantly under the action of the heavy guns. Heat rays were lancing out. The big ships could not easily avoid the searing blasts that could melt solid metal, but the flitterboats, dancing around like angry insects, sent a rain of bullets at the projectors. But even that took integration. The rays themselves were invisible, and could only be traced from their targets. The camera crews were working overtime, snapping shots of the enemy ships, tracing the rays' points of origin, and telaudioing the information to the flitterboats.

"Helldivers's *Rigel* out of action."

On the screen the big destroyer swung around, bow pointing forward. She was going to ram. Scott snapped orders. The *Flintlock* went hard over, guns pouring death into the doomed *Rigel.*

The ships passed, so close that men on the *Flintlock*'s decks could see the destroyer lurching through the haze.

Scott judged her course and tried desperately to get Mendez. There was a delay.

"QM—QM—emergency! Get the *Zuni*!"

"Here she answers, sir."

Scott snapped, "Change course. QM. Destroyer *Rigel* bearing down on you."

"Check." The screen blanked. Scott used a scanner. He groaned at the sight. The *Zuni* was swinging fast, but the *Rigel* was too close—too damned close.

She rammed.

Scott said, "Hell." That put the *Zuni* out of action. He reported to Cinc Rhys.

"All right, Captain. Continue R-8 formation."

Mendez appeared on a screen. "Captain Scott. We're disabled. I'm coming aboard. Have to direct sub-strafing operations. Can you give me a control board?"

"Yes, sir. Land at Port Sector 7."

Hidden in the mist, the fleets swept on in parallel courses, the big battlewagons keeping steady formation, pouring heat rays and shells across the gap. The lighter ships strayed out of line at times, but the flitterboats swarmed like midges, dogfighting when they were not harrying the larger craft. Gliders were useless now, at such close quarters.

The thunder crashed and boomed. Shudders rocked the *Flintlock*.

"Hit on Helldivers's *Orion.* Hit on *Sirius*."

"Hit on Mob ship *Apache*."

"Four more enemy subs destroyed."

"Doone sub *X-16* fails to report."

"Helldivers's *Polaris* seems disabled."

"Send out auxiliary flitterboats, units nine and twenty." Cinc

Mendez came in, breathing hard. Scott waved him to an auxiliary control unit seat.

"Hit on *Lance*. Wait a minute. Cinc Rhys a casualty, sir."

Scott froze. "Details."

"One moment—Dead, sir."

"Very well," Scott said after a moment. "I'm assuming command. Pass it along."

He caught a sidelong glance from Mendez. When a Company's cinc was killed, one of two things happened—promotion of a new cinc, or a merger with another Company. In this case Scott was required, by his rank, to assume temporarily the fleet's command. Later, at the Doone fort, there would be a meeting and a final decision.

He scarcely thought of that now. Rhys dead! Tough, unemotional old Rhys, killed in action. Rhys had a free-wife in some Keep, Scott remembered. The Company would pension her. Scott had never seen the woman.

Oddly, he wondered what she was like. The question had never occurred to him before.

The screens were flashing. Double duty now—or triple.

Scott forgot everything else in directing the battle.

It was like first-stage anaesthesia—it was difficult to judge time. It might have been an hour or six since the battle had started. Or less than an hour, for that matter.

"Destroyer disabled. Cruiser disabled. Three enemy subs out of action—"

It went on, endlessly. At the auxiliaries Mendez was directing sub-strafing operations. Where in hell's the *Armageddon*? Scott thought. The fight would be over before that overgrown tortoise arrived.

Abruptly a screen flashed QM. The lean, beak-nosed face of Cinc Flynn of the Helldivers showed.

"Calling Doone command."

"Acknowledging," Scott said. "Captain Scott, emergency command."

Why was Flynn calling? Enemy fleets in action never communicated, except to surrender.

Flynn said curtly, "You're using atomic power. Explanation, please."

Mendez jerked around. Scott felt a tight band around his stomach.

"Done without my knowledge or approval, of course, Cinc Flynn. My apologies. Details?"

"One of your flitterboats fired an atomic-powered pistol at the *Orion*."

"Damage?"

"One seven-unit gun disabled."

"One of ours, of the same caliber, will be taken out of action immediately. Further details, sir?"

"Use your scanner, Captain, on Sector Mobile 18 south *Orion*. Your apology is accepted. The incident will be erased from our records."

Flynn clicked off. Scott used the scanner, catching a Doone flitterboat in its focus. He used the enlarger.

The little boat was fleeing from enemy fire, racing back toward the Doone fleet, heading directly toward the *Flintlock*, Scott saw. Through the transparent shell he saw the bombardier slumped motionless, his head blown half off.

The pilot, still gripping an atomic-fire pistol in one hand, was Norman Kane. Blood streaked his boyish, strained face.

So Starling's outfit did have atomic power, then. Kane must have smuggled the weapon out with him when he left. And, in the excitement of battle, he had used it against the enemy.

Scott said coldly, "Gun crews starboard. Flitterboat *Z-19-4*. Blast it."

Almost immediately a shell burst near the little craft.

On the screen Kane looked up, startled by his own side firing upon him. Comprehension showed on his face. He swung the flitterboat off course, zigzagging, trying desperately to dodge the barrage.

Scott watched, his lips grimly tight. The flitterboat exploded in a rain of spray and debris.

Automatic court-martial.

After the battle, the Companies would band together and smash Starling's outfit.

Meantime, this was action. Scott returned to his screens, erasing the incident from his mind.

Very gradually, the balance of power was increasing with the Helldivers. Both sides were losing ships, put out of action rather than sunk, and Scott thought more and more often of the monitor *Armageddon*. She could turn the battle now. But she was still far astern.

Scott never felt the explosion that wrecked the control room. His senses blacked out without warning.

He could not have been unconscious for long. When he opened his eyes, he stared up at a shambles. He seemed to be the only man left alive. But it could not have been a direct hit, or he would not have survived either.

He was lying on his back, pinned down by a heavy crossbeam. But no bones were broken. Blind, incredible luck had helped him there. The brunt of the damage had been borne by the operators. They were dead, Scott saw at a glance.

He tried to crawl out from under the beam, but that was impossible. In the thunder of battle his voice could not be heard.

There was a movement across the room, halfway to the door. Cinc Mendez stumbled up and stared around, blinking. Red smeared his plump cheeks.

He saw Scott and stood, rocking back and forth, staring.

Then he put his hand on the butt of his pistol.

Scott could very easily read the other's mind. If the Doone captain died now, the chances were that Mendez could merge with the Doones and assume control. The politico-military balance lay that way.

If Scott lived, it was probable that he would be elected cinc.

It was, therefore, decidedly to Mendez's advantage to kill the imprisoned man.

A shadow crossed the doorway. Mendez, his back to the newcomer, did not see Commander Bienne halt on the threshold, scowling at the tableau. Scott knew that Bienne understood the situation as well as he himself did. The commander realized that in a very few moments Mendez would draw his gun and fire.

Scott waited. The cinc's fingers tightened on his gun butt.

Bienne, grinning crookedly, said, "I thought that shell had finished you, sir. Guess it's hard to kill a Dooneman."

Mendez took his hand off the gun, instantly regaining his poise. He turned to Bienne.

"I'm glad you're here, Commander. It'll probably take both of us to move that beam."

"Shall we try, sir?"

Between the two of them, they managed to shift the weight off Scott's torso. Briefly the latter's eyes met Bienne's. There was still no friendliness in them, but there was a look of wry self-mockery.

Bienne hadn't saved Scott's life, exactly. It was, rather, a question of being a Dooneman. For Bienne was, first of all, a soldier, and a member of the Free Company.

Scott tested his limbs; they worked.

"How long was I out, Commander?"

"Ten minutes, sir. The *Armageddon*'s in sight."

"Good. Are the Helldivers veering off?"

Bienne shook his head. "So far they're not suspicious."

Scott grunted and made his way to the door, the others at his heels. Mendez said, "We'll need another control ship."

"All right. The *Arquebus*. Commander, take over here. Cinc Mendez—"

A flitterboat took them to the *Arquebus*, which was still in good fighting trim. The monitor *Armageddon*, Scott saw, was rolling helplessly in the trough of the waves. In accordance with the battle plan, the Doone ships were leading the Helldivers toward the apparently capsized giant. The technicians had done a good job; the false keel looked shockingly convincing.

Aboard the *Arquebus*, Scott took over, giving Mendez the auxiliary control for his sub-strafers. The cinc beamed at Scott over his shoulder.

"Wait till that monitor opens up, Captain."

"Yeah . . . we're in bad shape, though."

Neither man mentioned the incident that was in both their minds. It was tacitly forgotten—the only thing to do now.

Guns were still bellowing. The Helldivers were pouring their fire into the Doone formation, and they were winning. Scott scowled at the screens. If he waited too long, it would be just too bad.

Presently he put a beam on the *Armageddon*. She was in a beautiful position now, midway between two of the Helldivers's largest battleships.

"Unmask. Open fire."

Firing ports opened on the monitor. The sea titan's huge guns snouted into view. Almost simultaneously they blasted, the thunder drowning out the noise of the lighter guns.

"All Doone ships attack," Scott said. "Plan R-7."

This was it. *This was it!*

The Doones raced in to the kill. Blasting, bellowing, shouting, the guns tried to make themselves heard above the roaring of the monitor.

They could not succeed, but that savage, invincible onslaught won the battle.

It was nearly impossible to maneuver a monitor into battle formation, but, once that was accomplished, the only thing that could stop the monster was atomic power.

But the Helldivers fought on, trying strategic formation.

They could not succeed. The big battlewagons could not get out of range of the *Armageddon*'s guns. And that meant—

Cinc Flynn's face showed on the screen.

"Capitulation, sir. Cease firing."

Scott gave orders. The roar of the guns died into humming, incredible silence.

"You gave us a great battle, cinc."

"Thanks. So did you. Your strategy with the monitor was excellent."

So—that was that. Scott felt something go limp inside of him. Flynn's routine words were meaningless; Scott was drained of the vital excitement that had kept him going till now.

The rest was pure formula.

Token depth charges would be dropped over Virginia Keep. They would not harm the Dome, but they were the rule. There would be the ransom, paid always by the Keep which backed the losing side. A supply of korium, or its negotiable equivalent. The Doone treasury would be swelled. Part of the money would go into replacements and new keels. The life of the forts would go on.

Alone at the rail of the *Arquebus*, heading for Virginia Keep, Scott watched slow darkness change the clouds from pearl to gray, and then to invisibility. He was alone in the night. The wash of waves came up to him softly as the *Arquebus* rushed to her destination, three hundred miles away.

Warm yellow lights gleamed from ports behind him, but he did not turn. This, he thought, was like the cloud-wrapped Olympus in Montana Keep, where he had promised Ilene—many things.

Yet there was a difference. In an Olympus a man was like a god, shut away completely from the living world.

Here, in the unbroken dark, there was no sense of alienage. Nothing could be seen—Venus has no moon, and the clouds hid the stars. And the seas are not phosphorescent.

Beneath these waters stand the Keeps, Scott thought.

They hold the future. Such battles as were fought today are fought so that the Keeps may not be destroyed.

And men will sacrifice. Men have always sacrificed, for a social organization or a military unit. Man must create his own ideal. "If there had been no God, man would have created Him."

Bienne had sacrificed today, in a queer, twisted way of loyalty to his fetish. Yet Bienne still hated him, Scott knew.

The Doones meant nothing. Their idea was a false one.

Yet, because men were faithful to that ideal, civilization would rise again from the guarded Keeps. A civilization that would forget its doomed guardians, the watchers of the seas of Venus, the Free Companions yelling their mad, futile battle cry as they drove on—as this ship was driving—into a night that would have no dawn.

Ilene.

Jeana.

It was no such simple choice. It was, in fact, no real choice at all. For Scott knew, very definitely, that he could never, as long as he lived, believe wholeheartedly in the Free Companions. Always a sardonic devil deep within him would be laughing in bitter self-mockery.

The whisper of the waves drifted up.

It wasn't sensible. It was sentimental, crazy, stupid, sloppy thinking.

But Scott knew, now, that he wasn't going back to Ilene.

He was a fool.

But he was a soldier.

AFTERWORD

Working on *Depth Charge* was my first real glimpse behind the scenes, and it introduced me to how Baen brings these stories—stories written thirty, fifty, eighty years ago, and have stood the test of time—back in front of new readers' eyes.

One of the things that struck me, as I read over the multitude of proposed sea stories was how much *knowledge* has changed over the years. I'm a Xennial—when I was a child, Pluto was still considered a planet, the only place one saw a flip phone was in Captain Kirk's hands, and Geordi La Forge's touch-screen iPad in engineering was firmly in the fiction category. But scientists, researchers, and engineers are out there, every day, researching, testing, creating new devices and new tests, new revisions and new updates to the body of human knowledge and understanding.

Could humanity create microscopic life in more-or-less its own image?

Could we colonize the ocean floor, if aliens abruptly shut off the sun?

How would intelligent life civilize, when the underwater environment is so hostile to that essential tool of civilization—fire?

Hank mentioned in his introduction our unfortunate, incorrect assumptions about Venus's environment and how technology revised those beliefs. Today, as I write this, when I google "Oceans on Venus," the top two responses include "Venus never had oceans, it's always been far too hot" and "Venus could have been habitable, eons ago." Clearly they can't both be true, and thus do the research and hypotheses continue.

These fundamental changes in human "knowledge" remind me of a particular quote from Tommy Lee Jones in *Men in Black*: "A thousand years ago, everybody knew the Earth was the center of the universe. Five hundred years ago, they knew the Earth was flat. Fifteen minutes ago, you knew we humans were alone on it. Imagine what you'll know tomorrow." And that, I think, is the wonderful thing about science fiction, especially older, harder forms of sf where a particular theory or principle becomes an essential part of the plot. It asks the big "What if?" questions and, sometimes, the real world responds as if to say "Let's find out!" (I'm also reminded of the saying, "The difference between screwing around and scientific method is writing it down.")

Many thanks to Hank Davis, for working with the new guy and teaching him the ropes, explaining his reasonings for decisions made and stories selected or cut. Hank's personal knowledge of many decades of short stories across all manner of magazines, anthologies, and other publications is astounding (ahem) and invaluable. Thanks also to Jason, David, Joy, Leah, and the rest of the folks at Baen who patiently answered my questions. Lastly, special thanks to Toni for giving me this opportunity.

—Jamie Ibson, north of the ice wall

ABOUT THE AUTHORS

James Blish (1921–1975) may be best known for his *Star Trek* novel adaptations, but his enduring reputation in sf rests on his classic Cities in Flight series, comprising four novels: *They Shall Have Stars*, *A Life for the Stars*, *Earthman, Come Home*, and *The Triumph of Time* (also published as *A Clash of Cymbals*), in which the invention of the "spindizzy" and anti-gravity/faster-than-light drive/force field leads to whole cities leaving the Earth and wandering the stars. Another series of note is his "pantropy" series, which has humans colonizing the stars by being genetically altered to survive in vastly different conditions rather than living in domes or terraforming the colony worlds. ("Surface Tension," included in this anthology, is part of that series.) A third series, less orthodoxly linked, is his "After Such Knowledge" series, comprising his Hugo-winning novel, *A Case of Conscience*, a historical novel, *Dr. Mirabilis*, based on the life of Roger Bacon, and the novel *Black Easter* and its sequel, *The Day After Judgment*, which share a theme, but are set in very different time periods and different universes. His novel, *A Case of Conscience*, was a continuation of a novella with the same title, which itself won a Retro-Hugo in 2001. Writing critical reviews of sf stories under the pseudonym "William Atheling, Jr.," he became known as one of the field's premiere critics. He was a noted authority on the works of James Branch Cabell, Ezra Pound, and James Joyce. He was the Guest of Honor at the 1960 World Science Fiction Convention and was one of the field's true polymaths.

Fredric Brown (1906–1972) was a legend in the fields of science fiction and mystery, filling the pages of sf and mystery pulps in the 1940s with sharp, witty stories, and winning an Edgar Award from the Mystery Writers of America for his first mystery novel, *The Fabulous*

Clipjoint. More mystery novels followed, soon joined by such memorable sf novels as *Martians Go Home* (much later made into a pretty good, but not as good, movie), *The Lights in the Sky are Stars*, (which foresaw that when spaceflight arrived, it would be a government project, and short-sighted politicians would try to stop it, claiming it was a waste of money, years before anyone had heard of Senator Proxmire), and the nearly indescribable *What Mad Universe*. And anyone in need of a good horror novel should check out *The Mind Thing*. Brown was also known for writing short-short stories, taking only three to four pages to set up an intriguing situation, then hitting the reader with a completely unexpected ending, and "Fish Story," included in this anthology, is a sterling example of that fictional form, and of Brown's virtuosity. Renowned sf editor H.L. Gold once described Brown's short-shorts as "short and sharp—like a hypodermic." Nailed it, Mr. Gold.

James L. Cambias writes science fiction and designs games. His latest novel, *The Scarab Mission*, was published in 2023 by Baen Books. Originally from New Orleans, he was educated at the University of Chicago and lives in western Massachusetts. His first novel, *A Darkling Sea*, was published in 2014, followed by *Corsair* in 2015. Baen Books released his third novel, *Arkad's World*, in 2019; followed by a fantasy, *The Initiate*; and *The Godel Operation*, which introduced readers to the "Billion Worlds" universe. His stories have appeared in *The Magazine of Fantasy & Science Fiction*, *Shimmer*, *Nature*, and several original anthologies. As a game designer, Mr. Cambias has written for Steve Jackson Games, Hero Games, and other roleplaying publishers, and he cofounded Zygote Games. Since 2015, he has been a member of the XPrize Foundation's Science Fiction Advisory Board. Check out his blog at www.jamescambias.com.

Sir Arthur C. Clarke (1917–2008) was known as one of the "Big Three" writers of science fiction, along with Robert A. Heinlein and Isaac Asimov, and became a household name after the release in 1968 of *2001: A Space Odyssey*, coscripted by Clarke and director Stanley Kubrick, but he had been known to sf fans for two decades previously during which his numerous stories and novels received praise even from mundane critics, one of whom compared him to the young H. G.

Wells. After the Hugo Award was inaugurated, his short story, "The Star," won one of the earliest, for year's best short story, and that was followed by many more awards. His novels are more numerous than I have space to list, though I'll cite three of my favorites: *The City and the Stars*, *Childhood's End*, and *Earthlight*. When not roaming throughout the galaxy in his stories, Clarke also wrote down-to-Earth hard science stories, and his short story, "The Deep Range," included in these pages, is an example both of that and his fascination with the sea and what lies beneath its surface. He was an enthusiastic scuba diver, and put his personal experience into a realistic picture of an undersea future. In addition to "The Deep Range" (which he later expanded into a novel with the same title), he further got his literary feet wet in such short stories as "Big Game Hunt," "The Man Who Ploughed the Sea," "The Shining Ones" (included in my Baen anthology, *The Baen Big Book of Monsters*), as well as such novels as *Dolphin Island*, *The Ghost of the Grand Banks* and, moving the focus to an inhabited ocean on an alien planet, *The Songs of Distant Earth*. I also recommend his nonfiction book, *The Coast of Coral*, and will close by firmly stating that rumors that Sir Arthur wore special shoes to hide his webbed feet are wholly untrue.

Henry Kuttner (1914–1958) and **Catherine L. Moore** (1911–1987) each attracted attention with a striking first story, Kuttner with a powerful horror story, "The Graveyard Rats," and Moore with "Shambleau," in which a space-roving vagabond encounters the psychic vampire of the title. That story also introduced Northwest Smith, a quick man with a ray blaster, who was usually on the wrong side of the law, whom many readers suspect may be the model for the better-known Han Solo, but only George Lucas knows for sure. Both stories appeared in *Weird Tales*, the leading publication in the thirties of fantasy and horror stories. Moore wrote other stories of Northwest Smith, and also wrote a second series starring Jirel of Joiry, one of the earliest sword-and-sorcery heroines. Kuttner wrote a fan letter to Moore, under the impression that she was a man, and one thing led to another until in 1940 they married, and began collaborating on a string of stories, often under various pseudonyms, most frequently as Lewis Padgett and Lawrence O'Donnell, under which name the novella *Clash by Night* was published in *Astounding Science-Fiction*. It was followed later by a novel, *Fury*, set on the same watery Venus, though many years later, so not quite a sequel. The couple were extremely prolific in the sf magazines of the 1940s, then began writing mystery novels in the next decade, mysteries being a better paying field. Then in 1958, Henry Kuttner suffered a fatal heart attack. Catherine Moore continued to write for a few years, mostly doing scripts for TV Westerns, then retired from writing in 1963. Some have lately speculated that Moore was the real star of the collaboration, but L. Sprague de Camp and Ray Bradbury have told of visiting the Kuttners and watching as one of the couple worked at the typewriter, then would take a break, while the other would take over, skimming what had been written, then rattling the keys. Later the Kuttners had difficulty remembering who had written which part. Their collaboration was a magical meeting of minds, which is why I've done one biographical sketch for the two of them, rather than separate bios.

Fritz Leiber (1910–1992) seemed inclined to follow his parents' footsteps into theatre and drama as a youth, but published his first short stories in 1934 and 1935 and continued to write for most of the rest of his life. After seeing early success with his short stories, he contacted, and was encouraged, by H.P. Lovecraft, a year before Lovecraft's death. The next year he released *Two Sought Adventure*, the first story concerning the well-known and much beloved swords-and-sorcery duo, Fafhrd and the Gray Mouser, though Leiber wrote Cthulhu-esque horror during the '30s and '40s in addition to his fantasy and science fiction works.

He continued to write and publish during WWII while working as a quality assurance inspector for Douglas Aircraft. After the war, he became associate editor of *Science Digest* and kept writing, producing what Poul Anderson would later call "a lot of the best science fiction and fantasy in the business." Leiber published novels, short stories, and collections regularly over the next many decades. *The Big Time* won the 1958 Hugo for Best Novel, as did *The Wanderer* in 1964, followed by more Hugos for short stories and novelettes in the 1970s, as well as being named the second Gandalf Grand Master of Fantasy at WorldCon 1975, and he was named a SFWA Grand Master in 1981.

Gray Rinehart writes science fiction and fantasy stories, songs, and... other things. He is the only person to have commanded an Air

Force satellite tracking station, written speeches for presidential appointees, devised a poetic form, and had music on *The Dr. Demento Show*. He is currently a contributing editor (the "Slushmaster General") for Baen Books.

Gray is the author of the lunar colonization novel *Walking on the Sea of Clouds* (WordFire Press), and his short fiction has appeared in *Analog Science Fiction & Fact*, *Asimov's Science Fiction*, *Orson Scott Card's Intergalactic Medicine Show*, and multiple anthologies. As a singer/songwriter, he has three albums of mostly science-fiction-and-fantasy-inspired music. During his unusual USAF career, Gray fought rocket propellant fires, refurbished space launch facilities, "flew" Milstar satellites, drove trucks, encrypted nuclear command and control orders, commanded the largest remote tracking station in the Air Force Satellite Control Network, and did other interesting things. His alter ego is the Gray Man, one of several famed ghosts of South Carolina's Grand Strand, and his web site is graymanwrites.com.

Mary Rosenblum (1952–2018) wrote both science fiction stories and novels and mystery novels, the latter under her birth name of Mary Freeman. She was also an expert cheesemaker, teaching the art in workshops, and an aviator, earning her airman's certificate at the age of fifty-seven. Her first novel, *The Drylands*, won the 1994 Compton Crook Award for best first novel. Her story "Sacrifice" won the 2009 Sidewise Award for best alternate history, short form. Her story "Selkies," included in these pages, was followed by another story about the aquatic people of the title, "The Mermaid's Comb." One might wish that more stories set in that aquatic universe had followed, but tragically, the author died when a single engine plane she was piloting crashed in Washington state. Her other novels are *Chimera*, *The Stone Garden*, *Water Rights*, and *Horizons*, plus a short story collection, *Synthesis & Other Virtual Realities*. Her mystery novels, written under the name Mary Freeman, are *Devil's Trumpet*, *Deadly Nightshade*, *Bleeding Heart*, and *Garden View*.

Robert Silverberg, prolific author not just of sf, but of authoritative nonfiction books, columnist for *Asimov's SF Magazine*, winner of a constellation of awards, and renowned bon vivant surely needs no introduction—but that's never stopped me before. Born in 1935,

Robert Silverberg sold his first sf story, "Gorgon Planet," before he was out of his teens, to the British magazine *Nebula*. Two years later, his first sf novel, a juvenile, *Revolt on Alpha C* followed. Decades later, his total sf titles, according to his semi-official website, stands at 82 sf novels and 457 short stories. (This may be a conservative count.) Early on, he won a Hugo Award for most promising new writer—rarely have the Hugo voters been so perceptive.

Toward the end of the 1960s and continuing into the 1970s, he wrote a string of novels much darker in tone and deeper in characterization than his work of the 1950s, such as the novels *Nightwings*, *Dying Inside*, *The Book of Skulls*, and many other novels. He took occasional sabbaticals from writing to later return with new works, such as the Majipoor series. His most recent novels include *The Alien Years*, *The Longest Way Home*, and a new trilogy of Majipoor novels. In addition, the Science Fiction and Fantasy Hall of Fame inducted him in 1999. In 2004, the Science Fiction Writers of America presented him with the Damon Knight Memorial Grand Master Award. For more information see his "quasi-official" website at www.majipoor.com, heroically maintained by Jon Davis (no relation).

Brad R. Torgersen is a multi-award-winning science fiction and fantasy writer whose book *A Star-Wheeled Sky* won the 2019 Dragon Award for Best Science Fiction Novel at the 33rd annual DragonCon fan convention in Atlanta, Georgia. A prolific short fiction author, Torgersen has published stories in numerous anthologies and magazines, to include several Best of Year editions. Brad is named in *Analog* magazine's who's who of top *Analog* authors, alongside venerable writers like Larry Niven, Lois McMaster Bujold, Orson Scott Card, and Robert A. Heinlein. Married for over thirty years, Brad is also a United States Army Reserve Chief Warrant Officer—currently on long-term active duty orders, and with multiple deployments to his credit—who currently lives with his wife in the Mountain West. They have two dogs, one cat, and way too much pet hair all over the house.

Jack Vance (1916–2013) was renowned for his exotic science fiction stories, often told in a poetry-tinged voice, which frequently verged on fantasy. His episodic novel, *The Dying Earth* from the early 1950s, is an early example of this Vancean mode, set in a time when the sun